AWAKENING

Also by Janet V Forster

Odyssey; Book 2, The Last Anakim Trilogy

Ascension; Book 3, The Last Anakim Trilogy

AWAKENING

Book 1
The Last Anakim Trilogy

JANET V FORSTER
www.janetvforster.com

ONE DOG PUBS

First published in 2015 by One Dog Pubs

1

A CiP catalogue record for this book is available from the
National Library of Australia.

ISBN: 97809944088-3-9

Cover image by: © IDreamstime.com
www.janetvforster.com

For my husband, Rick,
whose support and encouragement knows no bounds.
And for my children, Tash and Callum, whose imaginative
ways have opened my heart and mind to dreams of a world
beyond this one … and to endless possibilities.

Prologue

The meadow was enchanted. Spring flowers in pinks and purples softened the gently sloping ground, their spice and citrus fragrances intermingled with pollen which drifted in sticky clouds on sunbeam-rivers, over the wild grass, through the trees and onto the young boy who bounced through the whispering tendrils.

I forced a smile, but it was small and quickly frozen. Like too-dry clay it threatened to crack and display the truth, the rancid bitter mud which simmered beneath, oozing and gurgling as it spluttered and crawled and so slowly suffocated.

A flick of raven hair and a flash of soft, unblemished skin. He darted from his hiding place behind an ancient tree, the limbs quivering and beckoning as the souls which hid within it cried out their disappointment. Their lives had been lived. Now they were no more than recordings in the blistered bark, their voices indecipherable pleas trapped in the groans and creaks of the trunk and limbs.

His chuckle made my face collapse and my throat ache, but he didn't notice. He was moving again. His legs first and then his body followed, like a kite lifting off the ground, arms slightly out to the side as though half boy, half bird. A little wobble could not stop his unrestrained momentum, and the ground rose to bite his cheek. His wail summoned me.

I swallowed hard and then scooped him up and swung

him high and ran with him. And for a moment we were completely in the present. He was a bird and I was the wind. His mouth fell open and then widened and so did his eyes and for that instant we were free together.

Afterward we rested, although even then he was not still. When I could wait no longer I stood up and held out my large hand to his tiny one. It was warm and slightly sweaty. His tiny fingers curled around mine, claiming me. He looked up, his emerald eyes wide and doting, dimples in his cherub cheeks. Around us the wings of the darkest angels clamoured and the shadows lengthened, but he was still too young to truly see and for that, at least, I was thankful.

'Come,' I said. 'Come with Mama.'

We walked and we walked, trying to escape the darkness which clawed out at him. Out of the meadow and through the rough bush, burrs catching on our legs as we stumbled across the uneven land. Boulders threw themselves across our path, but we clambered over them, tucking our heads to our chests as branches whipped our faces on the other side.

He became tired but did not complain, only slowing a little and dragging sorry feet. I picked him up and carried him, barely noticing his weight. And then, too soon, we were there. Miraculously the scrub disappeared and over a sandy rise, heaven waited. A sloping white beach lay in front of thundering cerulean water, which sparkled with millions of tiny silver stars under the low-burning sun. The waves hurled clouds of salty mist towards us and we were instantly damp.

He looked up at me, his miniature hand thrusting towards the waves and my throat constricted. I tasted bile.

'Big water, Mama.'

'Yes Erik.'

He wriggled to get down, his fatigue forgotten. I released

my grip and he slipped to the ground. His small feet mashed the damp sand as he leapt around in childish delight. The imprints would remain, slowly filling with water until the next tide rose to take them away.

Overhead the sky was slowly transforming itself. Toward the hills, the place from where we had come, the air was writhing like a snake in the beak of an eagle. Twisted layers of purple and black consumed the light, smothering the brightness and colour and slowly, inevitably, sucking us in. Change was coming, borne of the darkness, fallen spirits who would stop at nothing to take my son and consume him completely.

There was so little time.

Stooping down I gathered him up into my arms again, crushing him tightly to me. And finally he was still.

The boom and roar of the waves was now only a few metres away. I would not let them have him ... I would not let them snuff out the light that I could still see burning inside him. It was dimmer today, but it *was* still there.

Somehow I stumbled forward. Frigid water rushed over my feet like an angry army and the sand gave way. Surely my legs would not support me.

I tried to swallow, but choked. My breathing came in ragged gasps.

'Mama?' A little voice. A long way away.

Such heaviness in my arms.

'Mama?' In the distance, the horizon was brilliant. *That* was where he belonged. In the light. For all eternity. *My* little angel. Let him live in the light.

1

KATE

'Some things are best forgotten,' Mum said, her body and face becoming a mass of hard lines when I tried to ask about her family. I'd never met them. Photos, if there were any, were well hidden. I'd never seen one. It was like she'd been spat out by a tornado which had taken everything material with it, leaving only memories, which she frantically threw back.

'You are loved and wanted, Kit. You will never know what it feels like to be forgotten.'

'I know, Mum.' I stepped back slightly. She sighed and her body slumped. I tried not to ask because the impact of my questions was obvious. But every now and again curiosity overcame me. This was her way of dealing with the past; her advice to me was the same. What came before does not matter. Only she was wrong. It did. You cannot forget what cannot be forgotten and what continues to eat away at the present.

I grew to hate the faceless individuals who had stolen so much from her. I saw it every day, how she hurt, doubling over and weeping for no reason, the self-loathing as she struggled to cope, clinging to Dad and I in sheer desperation, terrified that we might one day turn on her, or leave her.

Dad had also been slapped around by life and was mostly

silent about his childhood. Outside of his mother, who I called 'Nanny' (a hangover from toddler years), who shared more than he would have liked with me about his background, we saw no-one from his family. He remained, in so many ways, the injured child, thanks to life with a violent, alcoholic father. Although he let me visit my grandmother and accepted my close relationship with her, he chose to remain distanced, unable to forgive her for his past, long after his father had died. I couldn't blame him. I hadn't been there.

I loved piano-teacher 'Nanny' in the simple compartmentalised way of a child. When I stayed at her quaint seaside cottage she taught me; encouraging and inspiring me to persevere when I might otherwise have given up. We played duets and sang songs from musicals together. Her home was old-fashioned, but immaculate. The silver always sparkled and even the highest shelves were dust-free.

When rain fell on the green tin roof of her house it sounded like buffalo stampeding. The floor of the large, red painted veranda was always cool underfoot, no matter how hot the day. Fragrant jasmine creepers crawled prettily across the burnt-orange bricks and framed windows were misty with humidity and salt. A winding path, leading up from the squeaky wooden gate to the front door was lined with brightly coloured kangaroo paw and daisies. That close to the sea everything rusted.

I could see the water from her front veranda, a patch of deep blue over the tops of the other houses and trees. In the afternoons small waves leapt like white rabbits across the cobalt as the wind picked up. At night as we lay in bed I was lulled by the gentle, hypnotic sound of the waves in the distance.

Nanny was a proud woman who did things the 'proper way'. But underlying her quiet determination was sadness.

Deep inside festered a wound that would never heal. Her childhood dreams had not been fulfilled. Instead, violence had found her and those she loved, and now guilt gnawed at her, constantly reminding her of her failures.

I loved her so much. Memories of times alone with her were among my most cherished.

'Okay if I go down to the beach, Nanny?'

'Of course, I'll drop you, Kit.' Her answer was always immediate. She'd drive me down at ten under the speed limit and drop me in the parking lot with a list of cautions, but in truth they were all for show. She was more relaxed than my parents ever were.

'Fish for lunch?' She would ask when she collected me. I'd run into *Fins* on the way home with sandy feet, clammy and sun-burnt with goose-bump prickles from the sea breeze. The battery smell of frying fish and chips would make my mouth water.

'Want one?' I'd ask, popping sloppy vinegary chips in my mouth and the odd one in Nanny's as we drove back.

'Look in the back, Kit darling.' Nanny's eyes sparkled like diamonds in the sunshine.

'Nanny!'

'I dashed in to get them while you were getting the fish, they're still hot.' Jam donuts for after lunch. Hot and sweet and sticky, filled with molten ecstasy and a sand-paper sugar coating.

'We're going to be rolling down to the beach tomorrow. I'll have to wear a sheet instead of my bikini!' I half-joked.

'It's for the hours of practising we're going to do later. You'll need the energy.'

And we *would* spend hours at the piano, flicking on lamps when the daylight dimmed and we could no longer see the music. The brandy and water Nanny sipped swayed in a small crystal glass on top of the old, but perfectly tuned, up-right piano and cast meandering trails of dappled honey-gold onto the wall. I remember learning Für Elise and the smell of lavender as she reached across me to turn the pages. I remember the softness of her skin.

One day at boarding school I was called away from class and into the Principal's office. An unsettling premonition gnawed at me as I wondered why. It was the first time I'd set foot in there.

'A call from your Mum, Katherine.' Mrs Halifax's smile wavered.

I became suddenly sluggish, each step an eternity as an alarm shrilled in my mind. *Don't go forward; go back … back into the safety of the past.* What would happen if I said, *no thank you*, if I made it hard for her? Instead I reached out, my hand trembling just a little and took the handset from her.

'Mum?'

'I'm sorry Kit-Kat. It's your Nanny.'

I waited and she waited and then I heard her sigh.

'She's gone. She just slipped quietly away in the night. No-one expected anything, she seemed fine. I'm so sorry. You two were so close.' Strange thoughts travelled through my mind on their way to someplace else. I wondered what Dad was doing, what he was thinking, what he was feeling. I wondered whether he was glad that the last connection with his past was gone.

And then I felt the ache of loss. I had never really felt it before. The ache which comes before tears, the ache which says *yes it's true*, when your mind refuses to.

Over time the sweet memories slowly returned and I held on to them, to my music which was hers as well. Sometimes she sat beside me as I played one part of a duet, pressing the keys with a slightly shaky hand as she performed her part, and as long as I didn't look at her square-on she was there. I kept a little lavender-scented cushion under my pillow for a while and in my sleep she lived in vivid dreams which left me confused for a moment on waking, grateful, but then saddened as she slipped from me again.

2

KATE

Thirteen long years of school ended in a blur as we galloped towards the finish, exhausted, but wild-eyed and desperate. Five years at boarding school did that to you. Five years of restriction and claustrophobia, of living in an artificially regulated world with incessant bells and rules and regulations. Five years of nothing sacred.

But now, finally, it was all over. Ten weeks of scorching summer sun stretched blissfully ahead of me before the start of the university term. While Mum and Dad were at work the house was *mine*. The easy space and solitude after the constantly crowded environment of school was like balm to a burn.

Our home was old, but if you didn't mind the doors which jammed or the scary wiring, you might have found it otherwise charming and well-maintained. Ten years ago it was typical of the neighbourhood, quaint red-brick, bigger inside than it seemed on the outside with rooms branching off a long high-ceilinged passage with bell arches and ornate architraves. A bright modern meals and living area had been tacked onto the back at some point in the past and upstairs my parents had added a new bedroom extension in recent years. It was a patchwork house, the layers of dreams adding magic rather than robbing it of its character.

The back yard was a good size and made private by a tall pittosporum hedge. To one side, perfectly positioned for a little afternoon shade, was a dark-blue rectangular swimming pool. In the afternoons Noodle, the Labradoodle, would lie on a sun lounge next to me, her body never quite fully extended and with one eye open lest I tempt fate and actually get wet. Any more than one big toe in the water and she would rush up and down the edge wailing like a banshee until I got out.

Weeks of sunshine and chlorine lightened my usually auburn corkscrews and made them even more unmanageable. Along with the hair problem, freckles multiplied across my nose and cheeks rebelling against the vast quantities of sunscreen I applied.

Noodle and I took regular walks along the leafy bay-side streets, the gate clattering shut behind us and making the picket fence wobble a little as we left. So much had changed in the years I had been away. Houses like ours were rare now. Instead, larger, more angular modern homes, with striking clean lines, dominated the landscape, erasing the many tiers of history, annulling stories of transitions, of aspirations, of love and loss. Patchwork was out. We passed a site in transition and Noodle lingered to sniff at a dusty pile of rubble which was all that remained of a story that was. She squatted, visiting on it one last indignity.

On pleasant days we strolled all the way down to the beach, to where the restless water carried bright-sailed yachts across the bay. Young boys ran after flapping kites which nose-dived into the sand and umbrellas did cartwheels. More confident dogs dashed into the shallows, scattering water with a shake as they returned with balls and sticks to be thrown again. Noodle kept her distance from them. Her anxiety made her seem aloof, but I knew better. If another dog ventured anywhere near us she tucked her tail so tightly between her legs that she could have chewed on the end of it if she'd chosen to.

And so the weeks passed like the gentle rolling waves in a warm current, the rip building and then lulling and then building again, but not so badly that it swept me from complacency, until finally the monotony of what had been so good the day before, brought about a new season and I began to yearn for something more. I began to think about things I usually tried to avoid thinking about. Maybe there was a trigger. A dead fish on the sea shore; neighbours moving on after so long, who knows, but the illusion of time standing still was broken. Fractured, just like that. In one moment I was drifting through never-ending space and in the next I was consumed by a search for self-awareness, identity and meaning and my vigorous morning walks became longer and longer as I considered biology.

What would it be like to meet my biological parents? What if they didn't want to meet me? What if they were completely awful? What if my dad was Daniel Craig? Oooh … weird thought. What if he was a famous politician? Enough said. What if they weren't even alive? Maybe they were no longer traceable. A lot could happen in eighteen years.

How would Mum cope? She'd been desperate to have a child, but my father was sterile after contracting bilharzia on a military trip to Africa many years before. The adoption process meant bitter years waiting and mounds of unnavigable red tape, but eventually, when they had almost given up, I had arrived with only a few days' notice and turned their world upside down.

Mum hated the idea that one day I might trace my birth mother. I worried about the upheaval such a development would bring to the delicate harmony which existed between

Mum and Dad at home.

Given her background, Mum's devastation at my desire to discover my origins was understandable. My father and I were her purpose, her security, her everything. We proved that she was okay. Seeking my birth parents was like piercing her heart with a knife, mutilating her sense of self. It reinforced her feeling that she was deserving of abandonment and unkindness, feelings she tried to bury every day.

'I can't cope with it Kate, not with that. Anything else …' she said, throwing the dough forcefully onto the floured counter, before wadding it back up into a ball and leaning firmly down on it. Home-made pizza from scratch. Who did that anymore? Not that it wasn't delicious. Pizza infused with love *and* suffering.

It was my turn to look away.

'Tell me you need me to stand on my head for three days to ensure a perfect performance, I'll do it.' The dough was starting to look a little sorry. Sorry for existing.

'I know Mum, but I want to talk to you about this. It's important. Something I need to do and I don't want to leave you in the dark.'

'I can't cope, Kit,' Mum almost shouted, her voice breaking in desperation. She turned her back to me, flinging cupboards open and reaching for ingredients which arrived too loudly on the counter.

'I'm sorry Mum.'

'Don't do it, Kit,' she pleaded, coming to me and gripping my arms with floury fingers, beseeching me with such intensity that I didn't know what to say. She was suddenly quieter. 'I don't want to lose you, Baby. Blood, suddenly you'll have brothers, sisters … you'll want to be with them.'

'They'd be strangers, Mum,' I said, taking her hand in mine.

'That's what you say now.' She looked into my eyes, searching for a depth of reassurance which did not exist, and then turned back to the pizza bases, spreading the blood which pumped from her wounds across the surface.

I looked down at the white fingerprints she'd left on my arms. 'I love you Mum. I could never love them as much.'

My curiosity was like a plague. It would not be denied. Damn inquisitiveness. Fantasy preoccupied me. I struggled with ambivalence. I wanted answers, but guilt loaded my shoulders thanks to Sam, the twisted serpent who personified my negativity and gave voice to my every insecurity. He would not be refused. He reminded me that every step I took towards discovery was a blow to them as real as any sledgehammer could deliver. He reminded me that I was selfish and I reminded myself that he was not real, but he would not be denied.

He'd been around for too long. In the midst of the greatest turbulence at home, as my parents had separated, reunited and then separated again, I had become sad and they had thought it wise to spend large sums of money on a therapist. I had only gone to a few appointments. Sam was the lasting legacy, slithering through my mind and onto my shoulder.

'Sometimes kids find it helpful to imagine a protector, someone or something you can carry within you that will help you feel safe, a voice which is positive and strong.' The counsellor had been male, with curly brown hair and glasses. Call me Ted, not Mr Brown, he had said. His face was friendly, but I really wasn't interested. Music was my therapy.

After an awkward silence I had nodded and he had continued. 'What do you think that voice might say right now, about what's going on and about you, the way you are handling things, how you're feeling?'

That this is bloody stupid! The thought was so loud it startled me. Quite unlike me too, I wasn't one for swearing or belligerence. I shrugged, but my face betrayed me.

'And there's the other voice, the negative one.' I nodded eagerly.

'And maybe it's been there for a long time. Maybe it's not just about what's going on with Mum and Dad right now?'

'Maybe not,' I agreed, remembering the time I'd had a memory lapse in a concert at primary school and Mum had cried and I'd felt like such a loser. She'd cried because of Dad, he'd been cruel just before, but at the time I had thought it was me. I'd tossed and turned for weeks.

'Maybe you believe that voice. Maybe instead of a belief that voice is more like a fact that sits inside you, like a reflection of reality.'

'Maybe,' I answered, knowing he was right but not wanting to make it too easy.

'Think of something, an image you can connect with this negative self-talk, something you can pour the beliefs or thoughts into so that you can stand back and see them more for what they are … which is not always the truth, but rather deep-seated unhelpful beliefs. Sometimes that helps to make them more debatable.'

And out of the blue, as the most ridiculous image took form and substance in my mind, I'd expelled Sam. He was like Kaa from the Jungle Book, all swirly eyes and slimy grin with just a flick of suave in the curl of his tail. The 'protector' never happened in the same way. I lied about the image of a horse, but I could never connect with it and it was always silent and disempowered. And now years later I still wasn't quite sure how I felt about Sam. After all, he was rather pessimistic, but he was also a constant companion. We journeyed together, my externalised negativity and I.

The thought that I might wait too long to find out about my biological parents haunted me, even as I too faced fears of abandonment, like Mum. Opening the door to reach out to the past didn't mean that it wouldn't slam shut in my face, or that monsters wouldn't emerge from the shadows behind it. Finally, after much rumination, I made a decision. Swallowing hard I punched my details into an online contact form for FIND (Family Information Networks and Discovery), a service which helped adopted persons find relatives. After providing them with my mobile number I waited for a call. It came just as I was tip-toeing along the edge of the pool hoping to sneak in, and woke Noodle who leapt from her lounge and rushed at me like a rocket, howling until I stepped away from the water.

'We can find out about past adoptions that are connected to Victoria and provide you with access to records and documents if they are available,' the woman said, as I consoled my furry friend. 'It's best to come in and talk through whatever we find.'

I travelled in to Bourke Street ten days later to meet with a counsellor who had retrieved some basic information. A few facts typed on a couple of A4 pages.

She delivered it carefully, glasses on the end of her nose as she read the information to me, her eyes flicking up too often as she gauged my reaction. I was unmoved, disappointed at the scant, cold, two dimensional facts. Typed black words on flat white paper, removed from the warmth which might have made them real. I don't know what I had expected.

My birth mother was eighteen when I was born, my father twenty. She was fair-haired and blue-eyed. He had brown hair and green eyes. Her name was Deborah Brayshaw and her parents were Julia and David. He was Nicholas Edwards and his parents were Catherine (with a 'C' which was different to mine) and Albert. Under occupation, he was listed as a trainee pilot, she a student. I was born at a rural Victorian hospital and was ten days old when I was placed with my adoptive family. That was it.

'It's not a good idea to try and contact your biological parents alone,' the counsellor warned, her chair scraping across the floor as she stood up. 'Your mother was happy to have these details released if you ever asked for them, but she consented a long time ago. Rejection at a time like this can be difficult; the pain can be unexpected, even if you prepare for it. Counselling can provide support.' I nodded and left, returning to the piano, my sanctuary.

3

KATE

Christmas came and went and time seemed to loop back on itself as I found myself once again fretting about whether or not to find out more. I didn't want to hurt Mum. I didn't want to count myself among those who had let her down, but I was worried about leaving my search for too long and having the avenues, however meagre, available to me now become windswept and barren in the future.

The Google screen flickered flirtatiously and I felt its call. I whipped back fingers which had already typed in Deborah B, gnawing on them for a few seconds before abandoning my better judgement and going the whole hog. Deborah Brayshaw. Enter. There was lots of photos and information, but nothing readily identifying any one specifically as the one who might be my birth mother, if she was even there. More than likely she had married and changed her name and my search was pointless.

Widening my search I tracked down eight phone numbers Australia-wide for 'Julia Brayshaw' (Deborah's mother's name). I made a note of them and then moved on to my next search.

Nicholas Edwards. Enter. There were loads, but one owned NE International Aeronautical Services, and I knew that my biological father had been a trainee pilot at the time of my birth. Surely it was him? His company was on social media. There were lots of photos of planes but only one of him. It looked dated and was strangely grainy, but he was big and handsome. My heart pounded hard in my chest. Could this be him?

I did nothing further for days, afraid of doing something irreversible that I might regret. But eventually, after coming up with a weak cover story, I took a deep breath and began to call the numbers I had found for Julia Brayshaw. I was lucky. I got her on the second try and I needn't have worried, she was totally at ease giving Deborah's details out to a complete stranger.

'I'm trying to track down Deborah for the school reunion, Mrs Brayshaw,' I lied. 'We don't have any current details on file for her.'

'Ah Deb,' she said, and I kicked myself at the shortened use of her name. Of course, who was ever referred to as Deborah! Not unless you were six and Mum had just seen you step in a cowpat in your ballet shoes. Dead give-away, super-sleuth! 'Surprised you found me,' she continued, 'I've been out of the area for so long now.'

'Yes, well …' I scrabbled for a good reason as to why I'd gone to this much effort to track her down, but she didn't notice my discomfort.

'Of course she's married now. Traitor went off and married a Kiwi!' Her laugh came from far back in her throat.

'Oh … err that's nice.'

'You don't need to be polite,' she replied, 'but he is a lovely bloke, the sheep-shagger.'

'Excuse me?' I clarified.

'They live over there … in New Zealand. He's a farmer, sheep. Not that they farm much else in cuckoo, sorry Kiwi, land. Anyway, they do pretty well. It's a beautiful farm, green and lush, bountiful. You don't see green like that over here. When it rains it sounds like thunder on the roof.'

Nanny's old house with the tin roof flashed into my mind and I felt a flicker of grief.

'Any kids?'

'Three. All boys. Big, strapping lads. They're great on the farm. Riding horses before they could walk. Deb does the books, all of the administration. She's made a good farmer's wife. Surprised me at first.'

'Oh?'

'I didn't know how she'd go with the isolation. But then sometimes you make more friends in farming communities than you do in the suburbs.' Her voice became wistful and I wondered whether an ocean of loneliness surrounded her. A quick impossible wish flitted in and then out of my mind as I cast it aside. I would never really know her. 'We're more than twenty a floor here,' she continued, 'but you wouldn't know it. They rely on each other out there in the bush.' A gentle miaow sounded through the phone and then the light thump of paws hitting the floor in the background. 'Off you go Bernie, I'll be there soon,' she said, explaining, 'It's his feeding time. He's my constant companion. Don't know what I'd do without him … especially now that he no longer pees under the bed.' She chuckled lightly, but I wasn't sure whether that was just for my benefit.

'Is she happy, Mrs Brayshaw?'

She took a moment to reply, and I wondered at her hesitation. 'Oh, I think so … yes, yes she is.'

'Would you mind giving me a contact number for her, or an e-mail address?' I asked hopefully, wondering whether I would need to provide some sort of proof that I was who I said I was.

I needn't have worried. 'Let me get my book,' she said immediately. 'I've got all of that in there.'

She returned, settling herself. 'Ah here it is.' I imagined her reaching for glasses and popping them onto the end of her nose.

'E-mail will be easier for you, I suppose.' She rattled off the address and I jotted it down, repeating it back to her.

'Many thanks ... and for filling me in on Deb's news.'

'Well I'm sure she'd like to hear from you, although she probably won't be over for the reunion!'

'No? Well, maybe I can do a paragraph on her for the newsletter.' I swallowed hard and a wave of heat engulfed me. This was my maternal grandmother. I was speaking to her for the first time in my life, but the foundation of our conversation was all lies, and everything built on it was tainted by that, like a crack running through cement. I felt like a worm. Hopefully she would understand when the time came.

We said our farewells and I locked away imaginings of a relationship with another grandmother.

The suspense was hard to bear, but I felt too nervous to ring Deb up out of the blue. Would she tell me to get lost? Did her family even know that I existed? E-mail was definitely the alternative for cowards. I composed and deleted a few hundred before going for simple:

Hi Deb,

I've recently been in touch with your mum who provided me with your e-mail address. I'm organising a school reunion and just want to confirm that this would be an appropriate address to use to make contact with you. Kate.

I paced, anxiously nibbling my nails and checking my e-mails every minute. Sam and I debated whether or not I *was* in fact a coward. Eventually I went for a walk, minus technology. I forced myself to make it a long one. Whether or not a tornado whipped beachgoers up into the clouds as I passed I cannot tell you. I was rewarded on my return with a response.

Hi Kate,

Sounds good. Keep me posted please. Deb

I took a breath and typed.

Deb,

I've been wondering whether you can help me out.

Do you know a girl with DOB 5/5/1989? I want to get in touch with someone who knew her. Kate.

Maybe the date would jog her memory. At least if her husband read it, he wouldn't get the significance. A confused e-mail arrived, but it was quickly followed by a second as she made the connection.

Kate,

I'm not sure if I'm on the right track here, but I recognise the date you mention. Can you provide me with more details? I'm very interested to learn more. Deb.

Hi Deb,

I confess. The girl is actually me. I was born on 5/5/1989 and placed for adoption. My biological father's name is Nicholas Edwards according to information I obtained. Does this mean anything to you? Sorry to be so cryptic before, but I wasn't sure how to approach this. Kate.

I waited for her response. Suddenly realising that I was munching on my thumb like it was a chicken and bacon sub and I had last eaten sometime last month, I stopped. It gazed back at me reproachfully. I wondered whether Deb had any bad habits, whether she smoked, or whether she'd leapt out of bed this morning with every intention to quit. Hopefully if that was the case then the last of them was buried under fermenting fruit and mouldy bread at the bottom of the bin, and one remaining sad and rumpled packet wasn't making faces at her from behind the tins of cat food.

Kate,

I am your biological mother. I cannot tell you what it means to me to hear from you! It's like I can breathe at last. I am over the moon! I've wondered and wondered, especially on your birthday every year, what you're doing, whether you're happy, who you're with. My prayers were that you were with a family who loved you and could give you the things I couldn't. I've felt so guilty. Please send me a photo and your phone number. I can't wait to talk to you. Love, Deb.

I almost knelt and prayed, but my initial insecurities were quickly replaced by others in a strange cocktail-mix which would never hit a bar. Apprehension, check; excitement, check; fear, check; guilt, double-check; crazy hyperactive fidgeting; check. I waited for her call, no more nails left to nibble, flicking my lucky red yo-yo instead.

Believe it or not, at nine I was runner-up in a local yo-yo contest. The winner won a golden-coloured steel yo-yo and I won five cheaper plastic versions, which I handed out to my friends. Unfortunately the next-door neighbour's son, Cameron, destroyed his mother's inherited Limoges collection while executing a rather unsuccessful 'around the world' with a yo-yo I had provided him with and I wasn't invited over again.

One last flick and then I tossed it onto the desk and flopped onto my bed. The ornate ceiling rose regarded me. So much to say, but where to start? Definitely not, *'I guess I didn't keep you up much?'*

At last the phone rang. I couldn't breathe. Barely managed to squeak a greeting. Deb, on the other hand, sounded warm and friendly; a lot like her mum but with a dash of Kiwi accent flattening her words.

'Thank you for making contact with me, Kate,' she said, her voice deep and slightly husky. 'I can't tell you how much it means. To know that you're okay, to put an end to the questions. Questions which I could never answer.'

I felt awkward, uncomfortable with her gratitude. To know that I had released her to some extent with so little meant that her suffering had been prolonged, because of me. Ridiculous of course. *I* was the one who had been abandoned.

'I'm sorry you've had to wait so long, Deb.'

My bedroom door creaked open and I froze. The phone felt like a gun in my hand. There was nowhere to hide.

'Please, don't apologise!' she continued, oblivious to my distress. 'You don't owe me anything. I'm just so happy that we're talking now!'

A furry maw appeared and nudged the door open further. *'Noodle. What the ...'* I scolded, covering the phone with my hand. She halted in her tracks and her tail crept between her legs. Slowly she turned to leave, her head mopping the ground.

'It's okay girl,' I called, hating the thought of her spending the night in the shed and refusing to come in because of me. Even the dog and I were co-dependent.

Closing the door quietly I returned to sit on my bed. Noodle hopped up and placed her shaggy head in my lap and I stroked her absent-mindedly as Deb and I spoke. Over the weeks, she provided me with photos and reams of information about my biological origins on her side, clarifying anything I asked her to. I realised that she was trying to replace what had been stolen, to provide me with a sense of origin, of identity and belonging.

I looked nothing like her. My hair defined me. At school I was referred to as 'the girl with *the hair.*' It was auburn and unruly, a heavy mass of thick tight curls tumbling down my back, and threatening to eliminate my face altogether. The only way to manage it somewhat was with litres of de-tangler, and a long-toothed comb used to scrape it back into a tight pony tail. If the eighties' Sinead O Conner look was in vogue I might have considered something like it. By contrast Deb had long wispy blonde hair and big eyes, more blue than my green, in an oval face. Her skin was a light bronze, not like my pale, freckled complexion.

And I wasn't built like her either. She was small, almost fragile. I was a little on the hour-glass side and tall enough to no longer worry that not eating carrots or spinach or whatever it was would stunt my growth. Her sons were also not much like her. I assumed that they took after their father. All three were the 'strapping lads' their grandmother had spoken of, handsome in that rugged, farmer kind of way.

'You look a lot like my mother,' she said. 'Your dark hair and your face, so serene, calm. Just like her.'

'Really?' I marvelled, unable to see it, although I *could* see the resemblance between Deb and her mother who was also delicately built, and her brother, while a touch darker, carried the same elfin features.

'But you've got Nick's eyes, there's no mistaking that,' she added. 'Piercing.'

I had received a lot of compliments about my eyes. They were unusual. Probably my best feature, when you got to see them through the hair. Mum said that the colour was always changing, depending on the light and what I wore, and my mood. She said that sometimes the green was almost turquoise, but that at other times it darkened to khaki, and the gold surrounding the pupil flared like fire. Eyes like a cat, she told me, hence my nickname, Kit-Kat.

At age eighteen, pregnant, and with her relationship to my biological father in shreds, Deb had plummeted into an emotional wasteland. She never doubted that giving birth to me was the right thing to do, but hadn't felt mature enough to raise a child. Her relationship with Nick had imploded even before she could tell him that she was pregnant and her self-confidence hung in tatters.

'It must have been so difficult for you,' I said on another night, tucked up in bed with Noodle as we spoke on the phone.

'We went to Monaco,' she said, reflecting on her time in seclusion at a farm in rural Victoria, hours spent creaking to and fro on an old rocking chair on a sunny veranda while swatting flies, 'Spain and Portugal. We saw Greece, virtually the whole of the Mediterranean. You should have seen my tan.' I hadn't seen her tan, but I could hear the sadness in her voice. She tried to hide it, to make a joke, but it only made it clearer.

Suddenly her voice changed, became lighter. 'I met Jim there.'

'In Monaco?'

'Yes.' And now it wasn't all about regret and that was a relief. 'He was managing the farm we stayed on.'

'Oh. I guess you got something good out of it, at least,' I replied.

Her voice changed again. 'You were the most beautiful baby. You didn't ask for any of this.' She wavered slightly but then continued. '*Please* remember that. It was a moment in time. You weren't there and then you were. *You* were the most beautiful thing to come out of it … and I am so sorry I wasn't there for you.' She swallowed hard. 'Don't forget that, Kate. You were meant to be. You were truly meant to be.'

I gathered myself. Reassurance seemed the best response. 'I know, Deb.'

But she wasn't satisfied. 'No, no ... You wouldn't understand, no-one would.'

'Understand what?' I asked, confused, but curious.

She sounded thoughtful. 'It was such a strange time and of course it was quite a while back now, and so I wonder about my recollections, about just how accurate they are.'

'Uh huh?' I prompted.

'I had some bizarre experiences in the lead up to your birth.' She spat it out suddenly, like it was some kind of a confession and then came to an abrupt stop.

I waited, asking when she didn't continue. 'What sort of experiences?'

'It's hard to put my finger on. It was so long ago.'

If I'd known her better, I would have called her on her cop-out, but instead I took to grazing on my nails. Across the sea she sensed my dissatisfaction. 'I think maybe I went just a little bit crazy at the time,' she admitted.

'Crazy how?'

She took time to respond. 'I felt ... kind of haunted when I was pregnant with you. There was something *other*, for want of a better word, with me. A presence.' She hesitated, but I wasn't sure what to say. 'A lot of the time it was just a sensation,' she said, 'but I heard it sometimes ... and I saw things too. I had the strangest dreams, so incredibly vivid.' She coughed. 'Mind you, although I didn't have them with the other three, I've heard that vivid dreams are common in pregnancy. It's all the hormones.' The clock ticked and Noodle twitched as she dealt with her own sleep demons. 'At first it scared me,' Deb continued. 'But later I realised that I wasn't going to come to any harm and I kind of accepted it. It seemed to be all about protecting you Kate, watching over you for some reason. I was just the vessel carrying you. When you went, it went with you. Vanished immediately.'

'Wow ...' I said, relieved when she continued without waiting.

'When I went back to the farm after you were gone, everything was very different. It was like the magic of the place had left with you.' Her voice became distant. 'I used to imagine that *otherness* following you and watching over you, because you were so special. I could see that at once. You must think I'm crazy.'

On the surface it did sound a little crazy, but who was I to judge. Who knew what the thought of having to give your baby up could do to a mother. And I had my own weird sleep issues which made the bizarre seem possible sometimes.

'I don't think you're crazy, Deb, but I think you were going through a lot at the time. Maybe it was all just too much.'

'I'm sure you're right,' she agreed quickly. 'And the mind plays tricks with your memory as the years pass.' Her laugh was short and hollow and I realised that it had been more than tough.

None of her friends from Three Kings had known about my arrival. My adoption had been arranged by her mother just prior to my birth. Over two days she had vacillated before I was taken away by a nurse, her heart and post-baby body pining for long months as she robotically returned to life. In the months after she had wept over the photos she kept secreted close to her. Eventually my black hair, green eyes and plump mewling warmth remained forever imprinted on her mind, frozen in time and space.

My desire to make contact with Nick concerned her.

'I wish I could be enthusiastic about you contacting him,'

she said, 'but I can't. I'm afraid. I know it's irrational … because you're right, I last saw him so long ago.' Finally she sighed, defeated.

'But in some ways, it feels like yesterday.'

'Oh?'

'His brother, Daniel, committed suicide. The last time we spoke was not long after he died. I think Nick had some sort of nervous breakdown. He was seriously unwell. It wasn't pleasant to witness, I promise you.'

I considered the tragedy of suicide, the impact on those left behind. 'That sounds awful, Deb, but I don't think it's a reason not to contact him now.'

'I know,' she acknowledged, 'and he came right. I mean Mum spoke to him later and said he seemed fine, so he must have recovered. It's just my memory. It was a bad time.'

'I'm sorry to bring that all back.'

'Don't be sorry. You deserve your answers. I just don't want you to get hurt.'

'I'm tough, Deb,' I lied, knowing my vulnerability and wishing I had more defences available to me.

'When I think back it's more than just that last interaction with Nick that makes me wary. It was his whole family. They were seriously strange. The feel inside that house …' I could almost sense her shudder. 'I can't tell you what to do, Kate, just prepare yourself.'

'I will.'

'I mean, I can probably answer a lot of your questions about them,' she cut in hopefully. 'I wasn't in his family's best books, but I don't think many were.' All these years later and I could still hear the fearful edge in her voice as she referred to them. She was a reluctant passenger on this voyage back in time. Back to a dark haunted place, to wreckage, pain and turmoil, love and loss, so entwined, the scars buried deep down. It had hurt her.

'Just prepare yourself,' she repeated, her tone strained. 'It's going to be a massive shock to him. I don't have a clue how he'll react. Be ready for anything. Then it won't be as hard if it doesn't go well.'

'I will,' I answered and then added, 'Deb … he's not your responsibility. I'll cope, please don't worry about me.'

'I know you will Kate, it's just that I brought you into this world, and I looked into your eyes when I said goodbye all those years ago. I knew that I had failed you then. I don't want to fail you now.'

She was afraid. For herself and for me. I was the child she'd let go of too early. I was the child she could not forbid, even if that was the right thing to do.

'You won't say too much about me to him, will you? Don't give him my phone number. I just don't know how I feel about it. There are difficulties for me – family stuff, you know.' I wondered about this man, about the contributor of fifty per cent of my DNA, about the second stranger I was potentially inviting into my life, about whether or not it was all better off left alone.

'Of course, Deb.'

'Three Kings wasn't a good place for us.' Her words came out as a sudden addendum. 'We shouldn't have gone back. My folks split up the day we arrived.' She laughed, but there was a bitterness to the sound. 'Mum was miserable for ages, we scraped by. It was so gloomy at home.'

Taking a breath she slowed herself. 'The magical moments I spent with Nick in the beginning offered me hope. Sometimes you wish things could remain frozen in time. But time passes and everything changes. Nothing stays the same. That was the way it was with us.'

4

DEB AND NICK

It should have been a paradise. Instead it was a place of loss, of suffering even. When we first drove over the hill and saw the shimmering ocean, the electric blue like sapphires on fire against the fine, dazzling sand, and the three huge silver-grey rocks wearing their charcoal crowns, standing to the right of the wide bay, we still believed. In paradise, in second chances, in love.

But within the day my parents had gone their separate ways; my father to his lover, my mother, George and I remaining in the small house we had rented, and that was only the beginning.

Three Kings, a small, cliquey community of a few thousand on the east coast of Australia, where sunshine, surfers, sunscreen and a good pair of thongs were never in short supply and the temperature rarely dropped below twenty-five degrees, even in winter. On rare occasions when the sun was diluted by the dark billowing clouds which swept rudely across the sky and the rain fell in big heavy drops, it remained warm, steam rising from the roads and the musty smell of damp earth in the air.

It had been around for a while. The three rock kings had been eager for company, tired of their solemn vigil and of the endless blue horizon and the consort of the gulls whose white spatter robbed them of their dignity. They had beckoned silently from their lofty frozen perches to the earliest visitors, ignoring the birds who circled noisily with shrieking caws. *'Beware, Beware!'*

It had begun as a tiny community which sprang up around a leaning jetty for the timber industry in the 1860s. The nearby stands of magnificent red cedar, bunya, kauri pines, beech, tallow-wood and bloodwood cowered as the echoing hammer of the axe resounded. Thick sawdust covered everything and the smell of cedar hung in the air. Sap leaked like blood, sticking underfoot in clumps of gum, and staining the ground. And the possums and parrots, owls and bats and nightjars fled the violent men whose mammoth shadows made day night and who robbed them of the shelter which had been theirs for hundreds of years, the trees which had been worlds within worlds, a near eternal presence, but which were no more.

But eventually the persistent clunk had stopped and the men and their horses and carts departed with whinnies and shouting and everything was silent again. Vast tracts of open fields lay where once there had been forest. Slowly vegetation regenerated and the maniacal shriek of the Kookaburra haunted the landscape once more.

Gold was discovered nearby and infrastructure improved, including rail. Around 1900 a small centre had developed to support the fruit industry, mostly sugar cane and pineapples, which had replaced the timber industry of earlier.

As the years passed the place defied outside influence, remaining small and old-fashioned even as the rest of the east coast mushroomed and prospered. Bigger towns shrivelled and died, lacking the sustenance to charge the life-blood which was their community, but Three Kings managed, money coming from a mysterious source somewhere other than the tourism so many of the coastal towns depended on. There was little expansion and few approvals for building permits but the population, a fiercely protective bunch, seemed gladdened rather than disheartened by this. New families arrived, but only to replace those who drifted away.

Even the main roads seemed to direct traffic away from Three Kings with dull ambiguous signage which was easily ignored. Most tourists headed to the next stop, not bothering to turn their heads at the dilapidated signboard and the fly-off which seemed more like a slump in the ground than a formal road. But those who travelled along the winding pot-holed roads and over the rise into the town were well re-warded.

Abruptly the road improved, like you had driven through a looking glass and were suddenly riding the back of a dark slippery eel as you crested the final rise and slipped down towards the ocean. A real surprise. A strangely beautiful place, with bays and beaches and bluffs and the houses nes-tled together in strips down the hill to the beach while out to sea the three formidable rock monoliths cast long shadows across the water. Inland across the wide expanse of the bluff lay a vast plateau surrounded by rugged ranges of volcanic peaks, which towered like the walls of a fortress over euca-lypt forests and fruit farms and open fields.

After Victoria, place of wintery charm, even in the middle of summer, when the famous south wind blew straight from the South Pole bringing iciness to even the sunniest day, it was appealing. Small and old-fashioned, yes, but the weather was warm and the beach made up for a lot.

We barely noticed the curiosity of the residents as we drove into the village and up to our house. George and I, eyes gleaming, noses to the window, gazed right through them, transfixed by the ocean. We escaped as soon as we could that afternoon. We had to. Usually it was the kids getting under parents' feet, but in our case it was the other way round. Mum and Dad had been arguing incessantly and we were so tired. Tired of trying not to say anything, of trying to keep calm, to breathe and let it go, of wanting to scream, *'Let me out, I'd rather walk.'* I think it was worse than usual, but maybe it was just a long trip and we were all together for a long time.

'We're going down to the beach,' George called out. I was surprised they heard him at all. There was a moment of silence before the arguing started up again. George raised his eyebrows and sighed, kicking the door shut as we left.

The house was a cramped three-bedroomed, white-painted weatherboard with a green tiled roof. An uninteresting rectangle, but someone had loved it once. Carefully laid brick pavers peeked out from under a jumble of untrimmed colour and an old concrete bird-bath lay on its side, a lizard on the sideways rim spellbound by the sun. A neglected fig tree too big for the garden shook and rustled as we passed, the group of brightly coloured Lorikeets who fed voraciously on its fruit squawking raucously after us.

'I hope they bloody shut up when the sun goes down Deb,' George quipped, lobbing a rotten fig in their direction and only further inflaming the commotion. A sweet, slightly rancid, odour stained the air but was overcome by saltiness as we reached the gate.

The road to the beach was abnormally straight and sloped gently downwards. A ten-pin bowling ace could potentially roll his ball all the way into the ocean, taking out the seagulls who loitered outside the fish and chip shop on the way. Pretty weatherboard houses, many with corrugated roofs and wide verandas, some fronted by picket fences, almost all better tended than ours, stood perpendicular to the road, their faces to the water, most of the way down to the elongated gravel car-park at the end.

'Ow, ow, ow, ow, ow,' I yelled to George as we reached the beach. I hopped awkwardly across the sand, surprised at how hot it was.

'Stop being such a girl,' he replied unsympathetically, not even glancing back at me as he dropped his things unceremoniously and rushed out towards the water, surfboard tucked under his arm.

'I won't be too long,' he shouted into the wind, dwindling as he bounced across the beach, striking straight out as he launched himself into the water. Soon he was just another dot, indistinguishable from the other surfers.

George was almost eighteen, just over a year older than I was. He'd become increasingly long and lanky over the past year, meaning that I now had to yell even louder to get his attention because I was short, only a whisper over the height of a four-drawer filing cabinet without any goodies on top. There was almost no-one over the age of ten that I could look down on and even my mother, who I had thought I'd easily top, was still at least an inch taller than me.

I climbed up onto a small outcrop of rocks noticing the wide crescent-shape of the beach. In the distance I could see the three Kings the township was named after. A dozen surfers were still out on the waves, tiny black blobs bobbing about as they waited for the best break. Bathers enjoying their last swim of the day were splashing and shrieking and lifesavers patrolled the beach, gesturing to those in the water to swim between the flags.

A gentle breeze picked up, blowing thick air into my face; I could taste the salt in it, so different to the frail, thin air I was used to. A burst of movement to my left caught my attention as a lifesaver dashed into the water, diving and striking out confidently towards a swimmer in trouble as he flailed in the water. I stood, hand to mouth, holding my breath as his rescuer reached him and ducked beneath the water, pulling him to the surface and then towing him back to shore in the crook of his arm with a powerful stroke, working with the sea as it propelled him back to the beach.

Following others I ran down to the water's edge, stopping some distance away as I watched the lifesaver commence CPR. His teammates helped with quiet efficiency, fetching various medical supplies and equipment, holding the pale, lifeless form in position. Along with the rest of the gathered spectators, I stood tense and absorbed in the moment. As an ambulance siren sounded in the distance, the man on the beach began to cough and splutter. A cumulative sigh of relief rivalled the sound of the waves as the lifesaver stood up and let others take over. Someone handed him a bottle of water and as he twisted the cap off he noticed me.

My heart stopped and then started pounding so hard it felt like my ribs might snap. His eyes belonged to the deepest parts of the ocean, where emerald swirled with sapphire and alluring golden treasure lay half-hidden in the depths. His hair, still wet from the sea, was deep mocha with gold-plating and curled haphazardly. He was tall and broad-shouldered and tanned with just the right amount of muscle. He was beautiful.

Something new and molten came alive inside me. Burning with such intensity that I felt instantly parched. Instinctively I licked my lips. His gaze dropped to my mouth and I flushed, breaking his gaze and marching rigidly back to my spot on the rocks.

Afraid to even peek in his direction lest I further embarrass myself, I was relieved when I glanced up to see George emerging from the water and heading up the beach. Involuntarily I looked to the side. He was standing quite still gazing in my direction, the medical fuss and commotion continuing around him. I didn't realise it at the time, but in a small community like Three Kings, newcomers were noticed.

I looked away swiftly. 'How was the water?' I asked, throwing George his towel. 'Did you see the drama?'

'I did.' He hopped around on one foot as he dried himself. 'Did you notice what a strong swimmer that lifesaver was? The conditions out there are pretty rough today, such a powerful current, you have to fight it constantly.'

We headed home, the low, rapidly sinking sun still blinding, both more relaxed but wondering what awaited us. The door swung open to eerie stillness. There were no cooking sounds or smells, no arguing.

'Maybe they've gone to get take-away,' George stated hopefully, dropping his wet towel onto the sofa. But as we neared my parents' bedroom muted sounds emerged. Mum was crying. We'd heard it before, just somewhere else. George signalled to me and retreated to his room. I took a breath and knocked on the door quietly.

'Mum, are you okay?'

'I'm so sorry to do this to you kids,' she choked, wiping red, puffy eyes and swallowing another sob. 'I know it's not easy for you, and at your age, Deb, you need to feel safe and secure. I'm failing you, your brother ...'

'That's okay Mum,' I said, hugging her as we sat together on the edge of her bed. Her face was hot and wet against my cheek. Her arms felt sinewy and I wondered when she had got so thin, why I hadn't noticed sooner. 'We're not kids anymore. You and Dad both try hard, we know that.'

'He's gone.' Her voice was flat, dead, old.

'Where?' I asked, without as much curiosity as you might expect. He had left before but he always returned. This time was different though. *She* was different, defeated. It was over. The final battle had been fought and she had surrendered.

'He's gone to that, that ...' She was unable to continue for a moment, but then she gathered herself. Her voice was subdued.

'I don't think he's coming back this time. It's different. He wants a divorce. There's someone else.' She sat up straight and looked at me, her expression pleading for understanding.

I shook my head. 'We've just moved here!' Today. We had just arrived. It didn't seem possible, not now, not after all of this. Surely he wouldn't have done something so cruel.

'How many times has he done this Mum? He'll come back, just like always!' Words of reassurance, hollow, even to my ears.

She touched my cheek gently. 'Oh Deb, I've known about this for a while. I'm just a coward.'

'Nonsense, Mum.'

'I just didn't want to acknowledge the inevitable ... what it would mean.' She sighed deeply, her hands scrunched in a ball in her lap. 'It's probably why things have been a bit more pleasant recently, until today anyway. We stopped trying ... we stopped arguing as much, there was no passion left. We were just treading water.'

'I'm so sorry, Mum.' I leaned forward like a safety net, arms outstretched in case she fell. For a moment she remained stiff before slumping against me.

'They met through work. He's been seeing her each time he's come out here. She only lives around the corner!' Her shoulders collapsed, but she raised her head, which I took as a positive sign.

'You're joking!' My head continued to swivel side to side long after it should have stopped.

'I don't know what he thought was going to happen when we moved here.'

'He could have let you know before we came,' I said, stroking her hair and noticing how the grey she usually coloured had crept between the fine light brown strands which fell to her shoulders.

'It's too late to go back now,' she continued, her normally gentle face, blotchy and tear-streaked. 'The old house is gone, my job ...' She sighed like a ten-ton lorry had parked itself on her shoulders, and it had, I guess. 'We'll have to get on here somehow.'

'Oh, Mum,' I said, feeling completely useless and secretly labelling my father a coward and then wanting to shout it, but biting my tongue. It would help no-one. 'I'm sorry, Mum.' The words stuck like fish bones in my throat before they spluttered out. I wanted to punch him about the head, but what else could I say.

Why on earth had he chosen to bring us to this place? It was beautiful, yes, but small. Too small to have a mistress and a wife and kids a street over. We could have rented somewhere near his work, saved him an hour's travel to and fro. I'm sure he could have continued to invent excuses which would have allowed him some time away. The great charade could have played out for a while longer. Or maybe today he'd finally just had enough.

He had been the whole reason why we'd come. Obviously we hadn't been opposed to the beach and the sun, but the location - this beautiful, tiny, hard-to-find place where newcomers were so noticed - had been his choosing. He'd requested a transfer, travelling backwards and forwards, spending only a night or two at home a week until we were ready to move. Allegedly he had been hard at work building up his portfolio (he was a real estate agent) and networking, but the extended absences made sense now. Things had been better with him away. Better for him too obviously.

I assume, because he never discussed it with us, that he had decided there was nothing left to salvage in his relationship with my mother. It had been bad for so long that in many ways George and I felt a sense of relief at their separation. Mum's life would improve. If we could just help her through the pain of betrayal, hopefully she would realise that there was more than unhappiness waiting on the other side.

I don't know where my father stayed that night, although I can guess, but he never returned to the family home to live. A few days later he appeared, his face drawn, self-consciously filling a couple of suitcases before making a hurried exit. Explanations were left to my mother who tried to be fair to him. In the early days of their separation I don't think he knew what to say to us.

He moved in with 'Dotty Dorothy' as we called her, a plump homely woman who always looked rumpled. We saw him occasionally, but the atmosphere between us was tense and uncomfortable, filled with simmering resentment on our side and too many unanswered questions. He threw himself into frenetic industry, building things in his shed, mowing the lawn and pruning trees, anything to avoid spending time with us, while Dotty made milky tea and floppy sponge cake. His skin became tanned and leathery from so much time outside and he grew thin. But I don't remember ever hearing a cross word shared between Dotty and my father. It must have been a relief for him after his fiery relationship with my mother.

My father was hopelessly irregular with his maintenance payments and in the initial months after their separation I regularly heard my mother pleading with him on the phone. To her credit, she realised that begging for money was demeaning and ineffective and managed to find a job as a bookkeeper in our tiny town.

5

KATE

NE International Aeronautical Services was owned and operated by Nicholas Edwards, a pilot who had started his flying career in the early nineties operating a range of aircraft. He had licences from around the world, both agricultural and commercial. Founded in Western Australia in the mid-nineties, the company had rapidly expanded to service the whole state as well as fulfilling a multitude of functions across the country and overseas. In fifteen years he had accumulated a total of twenty planes suited to various purposes.

I closed my laptop as the phone rang hollowly on the other side of the country.

Finally a woman answered with detached efficiency. 'NE International Aeronautical Services, good morning,'

'Nicholas Edwards please.' I tried for casual, but fell somewhat short, my voice tight like Sam was throttling me instead of sitting on my shoulder as usual.

'Not in the office today, can I take a message?'

'Oh,' I said, relief washing over me like water in a warm bath.

'Would you like to leave a message?' She prompted.

'Uh … it's personal,' I stuttered. I hadn't thought about leaving a message, but was suddenly certain that I wouldn't want him calling me up unexpectedly.

'I can give you his mobile number,' she said, as a phone started ringing in the background.

'Err, yes – thanks,' I replied, surprised that it was provided so easily and then remembering that I might have seen it on the website.

'One moment, please.' She placed me on hold to answer the other call.

I flipped open the lid of my laptop, the page was still up. There it was.

'Still there?' she said returning.

'Yep,' I answered, confirming that the number she gave me was the same as the one on the website.

'Thank you.'

'Have a nice day,' she ended.

You can answer a mobile anywhere, in the middle of a board meeting, in the bathroom. There are no limits to how far some people will go to remain accessible.

What would I say to him? How would I say it? I called before I could chicken out. A confident, deep male voice answered abruptly.

'Nick.'

'Um hi, just checking ...' I felt like an idiot, where to now? 'Are you able to talk right now? I'm not on a speaker am I?' I babbled, imagining how inappropriate it would be for his family to find out about me over speakerphone.

'Nope.' He said the word slowly, my floundering disconcerting him.

'It's just it's a personal call so ...'

'What's going on? Who is this?' He was suddenly terse, someone who received a lot of irritating calls, waiting to be suckered into some sort of sale.

I took a breath. 'My name is Kate. I'm not quite sure how

to put this without it being a shock. You're not driving are you, or flying a plane or doing anything dangerous?'

'No. What's this about?' More irritation, impatience. He was a busy man and becoming annoyed.

'It's about something that happened a long time ago,' I added quickly, fearing he might hang up. 'Do you remember Deb Brayshaw?'

I thought the phone had dropped out, the silence was so complete, but eventually he answered.

'Yes … of course, a long time ago.'

'Three Kings,' I prompted.

'Three Kings …' he repeated, suddenly contemplative.

The silence was full this time as he sorted through his thoughts. '… Deb. It's been so long since I last saw her. She left. Is this about her?'

'Sort of I guess. It's about me really, but I'm linked to her.'

I squirmed. How to say what I had to say? Again the silence stretched on, seconds like minutes, and I panicked, my heartbeat suddenly irregular, my hands sweaty. He waited, interested now. No impatience, just a void on the other end of the mobile.

'I know it's a lot to confront you with over the phone, but I'm not sure how else to go about it, so sorry in advance,' I finally gushed, eager to get it over with now. 'When Deb left all those years ago it was because she was pregnant … with me. She didn't tell you at the time … I guess she had her reasons.' I took a deep breath, wishing I could tell what he was thinking. 'She placed me for adoption, but she put her details and yours on my original birth record. Maybe so that I could find you one day … I don't know.' I felt breathless. Too many words tumbling out, too fast, but they were out now, whatever the outcome.

Nothing.

'Nick?'

After a moment he replied quietly, deliberately, like he had to reassure himself. 'I'm here.'

'It's too much, I know. Bombarding you with this ... like this.' What other way was there? I didn't have a clue. What conclusions was he jumping to? I wasn't out to make a claim on his hard-earned empire, but he didn't know that.

'You can call me back, my mobile number will be on your phone,' I said gently, adding, 'if you like.'

He was exhaling audibly, and I imagined his furrowed brow. 'Take some time, Nick. I'm not looking for a dad.' It was too late for that, wasn't it? 'I just wanted to find out about my background.'

He cut in unexpectedly, 'I'll take you up on that Kate and get back to you.' His voice was unreadable, almost professional, and distant. Maybe he was going to consult a lawyer first.

'Okay,' I agreed, realising that he was probably well practised at projecting a veneer when the occasion demanded it. I guess we all were and he was no different. Who wanted to bare their underbelly when they weren't yet sure whether it was a razor blade or a gentle pat that would come down on it?

'Just give me a little time to get my head around this,' he said, 'and I'll get back to you.'

This time the silence was because he'd terminated the call. I fell back onto the bed. I felt relieved. I'd pushed through my anxiety and made contact with him. But I also felt sad, like I had a sob stuck somewhere inside me and couldn't release it. His reaction had been different to Deb's. In fairness to him my message *was* a little bewildering, like he'd woken up someplace and was wondering how he'd got there. Only instead of a pretty blonde in the bed next to him, he discovered an eighteen year old daughter he'd never met, hopefully not in the bed but standing beside it. That had to be pretty freaky, enough to cause him to leap out of bed hoping he had jocks and socks on. The shock would take a while to wear off and when it did he'd either call me or his lawyer would send me a neat letter requiring signatures and witnesses. Maybe I'd get a down payment on a car, but I'd never hear from him again.

A week later, just as I was beginning to think the lawyer was the more likely scenario, he called. I'd almost given up, accepting that it was too confronting for him. Maybe he didn't believe it was true, or he had convinced himself of that. It would be easy enough to do. I was a stranger. He had not seen me born and he had not watched me grow from a child into a woman. He hadn't been there when I had fallen off my bike, or suffered through chickenpox. We hadn't laughed together and we hadn't cried together. We had never fought. We were two alien beings brought together by biology.

I wasn't the first to be rebuffed. Plenty of others had experienced unsuccessful meetings with their biological parents or been rejected. Deb was lovely and I was grateful that we had connected so easily. From what she had told me about Nick and his family, I knew it would be a different experience where he was concerned. Still, I couldn't completely escape the rejection which gnawed unpleasantly in my gut, awakening old insecurities and forcing them to surface. My sleep had taken a weird turn reflecting my subconscious state in vivid, unpleasant dreams and Noodle was on constant alert mode, yapping and running in circles when I got out of bed at night, even if it was only for a trip to the loo. She instantly relaxed when I shooshed her. If I spoke then I wasn't the crazy girl she knew from my night terrors and that was okay.

My mobile rang as I combed my hair after a morning shower, the thick tangles unmanageable as always.

'You're not doing anything inappropriate are you?' Nick mimicked as I answered, referring to the awkwardness at the start of our last conversation, teasing me.

I dropped the comb and did a sharp inhale and exhale before gathering myself enough to answer. 'Just flushing the chain now,' I said, surprised at my ability to joke in return and then embarrassed as my brain caught up and started doing cartwheels over the casualness of our interaction. We shared a brief, slightly strained laugh which ended too abruptly.

'Not really' I said, 'although you were close. I've just got out of the shower. I'm in my towel, dripping ...' I stamped my legs trying to shoo Noodle away as she licked them dry.

'I'm sorry I didn't call earlier.' He was suddenly serious, his tone softer, his words slower.

'I wondered whether you would call at all,' I said, nudging Noodle out of the door and then closing it quietly behind her and moving to sit on the edge of the bed.

'I wasn't sure at first.' His voice was dispassionate and I wished that I could see his face.

'It must have been a bit of a shock. I'm sorry you had to hear like that.'

'That's okay,' he said. 'You're a long way away. It would have been hard to pop over for a beer and a chat.'

'Yes, I guess so.' I nodded even though he couldn't possibly see.

My hair was making the sheets wet. I tried to wrap a towel around it one-handed finally managing to look like a lopsided Sikh.

'I was waiting to hear about a plane,' he continued, 'instead I got you.'

'Yes well … I could see how that would have been confusing.' My turban came undone and flopped over my eyes. 'I mean, I eat pickles at midnight and can do an infinite number of yo-yo tricks, but I've never managed to master taking off.'

He laughed.

'I was the last thing you would have expected,' I said.

'The past has come knocking at my door.'

'I guess so.'

'Strange, how things work out,' he said. 'There was a lot of stuff going on back then. Mostly in my crazy family, nothing to do with Deb. She was lovely …' He seemed to drift off into his own contemplations. Earth to Nick, Earth to Nick.

'Nick?' I said, holding the phone away from me for a second to check the display and confirm that the call hadn't dropped.

His voice cut in abruptly and I put the phone back to my ear. 'To be honest it was a pretty fucked-up time.'

I wasn't sure how to respond.

'Excuse the language,' he apologised, 'but that probably sums it up best. It was a difficult time for my family.' Certainly wasn't that great a time for Deb either once she realised that I was on my way, I thought.

'It's a long time ago now. We all need to move on.' His words made me wonder whether he had. 'So how long has it been? I could work it out I suppose, but you tell me. How old are you?'

'Eighteen.'

'Wow – eighteen. To be eighteen again.' He sounded thoughtful. 'I feel so old. I didn't even know that you existed, didn't even sense it.'

'Well you couldn't have.' *Weren't you even a little suspicious?*

'No?' He seemed to sense my mental reproach. 'I suppose not. Suddenly I have an adult daughter. It's beyond strange!'

'Must be weird.'

'Deb's kid! My kid. Life's surprises find you … You wake up one day, about to buy a plane and instead you get a daughter, an eighteen year-old daughter! It feels surreal. I guess I missed out on the nappies – that's good. Right?' He sounded sad.

'Sure.'

He remained silent.

'Does it fit that I would be your child, Nick?'

'If Deb said that I'm your father, then I wouldn't doubt it,' he said. 'She wouldn't lie.'

'She seems lovely,' I answered, without hesitation.

'She is.' He thought for a moment. 'What's she up to now?'

The inevitable question. I carefully considered my response.

'Farming overseas. She has three sons.'

'Oh …'

'She's happy,' I added, as an afterthought.

'Well, that's good,' he said, when I offered no further insights. He seemed to sense my reluctance and didn't object when I steered the conversation in another direction.

'Do you have any kids … other than me?'

'Other than you …' he repeated. 'No, it didn't work out for me. I've done okay business-wise, but the relationship thing, well I just wasn't much good at it.' He was silent for a beat. 'What about you Kate?' he asked, 'Have you been well looked after?'

'My parents loved me; they were desperate for a child.'

'They couldn't have one naturally?'

'No.' He remained silent, and I wondered whether he got what that meant and what that then meant about him … his life. Loneliness.

His response was insightful. 'You completed them.'

'I guess so,' I agreed.

'I wish I could have been there for you, Kate. Wish I'd known.' The tone of his voice brought home the fact that he had never known the completeness he had spoken of earlier, that he was plagued by regrets.

He sighed. 'But things happen for a reason. I mean … well … I'm not good at those sorts of things. Relationship things.'

'You're not being fair to yourself, Nick. You and Deb were so young.'

'True,' he said, 'but eighteen years have passed and it's still just me.'

'But …'

'Stop, stop,' he cried, belatedly realising the path our conversation was taking us down and not ready to go there yet. 'Why wallow today? Today I'm the lucky one. Blessed to be talking to you. We should meet … if you like.'

'That would be great, although you're so far away.'

I considered my bank balance, imagined my parents lighting a funeral pyre, mine, when I told them I was packing my bags and heading to the other side of the country to meet him. Not possible.

'I'm all over the place with my work.'

'Where are you right now?' I asked.

'Queensland. You?'

'Melbourne. I'm always here.'

'You're used to the cold. I need the heat, the sunshine … water you can actually swim in. I can't stand being stuck inside all of the time.'

'It's great right now, really warm. I've been in the pool

most days.' I looked through the window to the heavy sky, the wind whined.

'I don't like ice on top of the water when I swim,' he said, 'it plays havoc with my breaststroke.'

'Oh come on, it's invigorating.' I laughed, relaxing a little and he joined in.

'I'm used to Melbourne weather but there's a reason so many of us escape to Queensland when we get the chance.'

'I have a plane,' Nick said. 'I can come to you.'

'Wow, the final frontier, you'd do it?'

'I'd do it for you, Kate. Besides, I've just bought an arctic fleece. I need to try it out.'

'You'll look good in it,' I replied. 'Just remove the hood before you land, or you might get shot down.' We shared another chuckle.

'It's what I do, planes,' he said.

'I know, that's how I found you.'

'Oh?' He was only mildly curious, someone who had ways and means of accessing information about others should he so desire.

'On the internet, your website.'

'Well, I can fly to Melbourne in my plane.'

'O...kay.'

'It's just a small plane,' he quickly clarified. 'I'll fly into Essendon Airport and then catch a cab into the city to meet you.'

6

DEB AND NICK

For a while the beach became a place of blissful amnesia, smothering unhappiness quickly in a balmy blanket of sand and sun. We joined the others, often straight after school. Toes touching the sand, flicking the switch, on to off, letting the endless blue thunder carry our burdens for a while.

And at night, still feeling the gentle rocking of ocean songs, I dreamt about the surf lifesaver I'd seen on the beach. He became *my* rescuer, his strong muscular arms easily carrying me over the scorching sand, his startling green eyes clouded with concern and moving from my eyes to my lips as they drew nearer and nearer.

One mid-day my dream became real as George and I ambled through the car-park towards the beach.

'Hey, Nick,' George called, waving to someone.

The boy he greeted turned to look at us and my world immediately turned upside down. Glancing momentarily at me and then back to George he strolled over to us.

'This is Deb, my sister,' George explained as he neared.

'Hi Deb,' he said offhandedly, the depth of his vivid eyes taking my breath away. This close I realised just how big he was. My gaze was about level with his nipples, but thankfully he had a t-shirt on. I flushed with shame at the thought, anyway. He had all of George's height, but with none of the lankiness. Instead he was well filled-out, more man than boy with the broad shoulders and narrow waist of a swimmer.

'Hey,' I answered shyly, squinting up at him for a moment before looking away towards the beach. He turned to George, 'What are you up to?'

'Surfing.' George pointed to the sand where a couple of his friends were leaning on boards and chatting.

'Ankle snappers today,' Nick remarked.

'Ankle snappers?' I wondered anxiously. Surely not crocs?

'Tiny waves … barely worth it if you're surfing,' he clarified with a wink which made me blush and hate myself. He caught a stray ball heading directly for my head before I'd even realised that I was about to be knocked out, and threw it back effortlessly, his aim straight and powerful. I noticed sweat on his biceps and the smoothness of his golden skin, before drawing my gaze away guiltily and hoping the way it had stuck for a moment hadn't been noticed.

'We saw you, a few weeks ago, rescuing that guy who nearly drowned!' George remarked. I tried to breathe evenly.

He shrugged indifferently. 'I come from an amphibious family, swimming before I could walk. The only swimming lessons I ever had consisted of Dad tossing me into the pool when I was a baby.' I frowned at what seemed like a cruelty, but he laughed. 'Luckily it's in the genes. We all float, and so I bobbed straight up to the top.'

Nick gestured towards the lifesaving tower. The flag was fluttering in the breeze. 'You should try out if you're interested.'

'Maybe.' George was non-committal.

I noticed how the slight breeze made the curls at the base of Nick's neck move. Some of the strands of hair looked damp. I swallowed.

'I'll see how things go, get a bit fitter first,' George continued, 'and used to those rips.'

'Do *you* like the water Deb?' Nick asked suddenly, turning to me and catching me off guard.

'Oops,' I said, tripping over a rock the size of a small island in the sand. He grasped my arm to help me up.

'Sure, um, just as long as it's not too cold!' I answered, cursing my clumsiness.

'You *look* athletic,' he stated evenly, as I squirmed under his appraisal, wondering whether he had just passed me a compliment or implied that I lacked contours.

He stopped. 'Anyway, I've got to go, but it was nice meeting you, Deb.' I caught my lower lip between my teeth nervously. 'I'll see you guys around,' he said moving away.

I made an effort not to look back. I didn't believe I could pull it off without making a complete fool of myself and falling flat on my face again, cracking my skull open this time.

No sooner had we dropped our bags onto the sand than George had set off into the loud white surf. It didn't look at all small to me. Pulling off the shorts and top I had on over my bikini, momentarily disappointed at my lack of bustiness, I flopped back onto my towel with a sigh and covered my face with my hat. The day was pleasantly warm. A hint of freshness lingered in the breeze. Before long I was drowsing contentedly, my book set aside for later, and enjoying planet Deb, where I was a stunningly beautiful princess, served by an adoring knight, who looked very much like Nick.

'You look comfy.' My eyes flew open under my hat. God, it was my Knight. Grabbing my hat from my face I pushed myself up onto an elbow so that I didn't have to squint unappealingly into the sun.

'You startled me,' I said, a little abruptly. His eyes danced.

'Sorry,' he answered, lowering himself onto the sand un-invited and flipping Ray-Bans from the top of his head onto his nose. He looked out across the ocean, a smirk playing with his lips.

'You don't look sorry,' I said, because I didn't know what else to say. Somehow it came out harsher than I had intended.

'Should I go?' he asked, shifting awkwardly on the sand, suddenly uncertain of his welcome. This must be a new experience for him, I thought.

'Don't go.' I searched desperately for something to say. 'How do you know George?'

'School.'

He was at a Catholic boys' school one town over, and I was at the equivalent 'sister' school. There were no senior schools in Three Kings.

'What about a walk?' he asked unexpectedly.

'Sure, sounds good.' I stood and wrapped my towel around my waist quickly. The last thing I wanted were any further comments about my athleticism.

We walked along the edge of the sea in the shallow tepid water, foam clinging to our ankles until the bubbles popped. Tiny white clouds had appeared, drifting leisurely across the pale sky and the wind had picked up, flinging bits of sand which stung at the backs of our legs. But the sun was still hot on our shoulders and not in the least intimidated. He asked questions about my family, my brother and me. Where we'd come from, why we'd moved, whether we liked it, how we were settling in. I was flattered and slightly confused by his interrogation, but when I tried to turn the enquiry to him he gave little away, cleverly deflecting the conversation back to me.

'Have you been to MacArthur's Lake yet?' he asked, as we

returned.

'MacArthur's Lake?'

'It's a fresh-water lake, about half an hour away. The water is unbelievable, translucent around the edges, and turquoise in the middle where it's deepest. It's so clear and pure you can drink it.'

'Sounds amazing.'

'I'll take you one day,' he promised, as we sat down on the sand and waited for George who was just coming out of the water.

Girls passed us like a merry-go-round, too often and a little too close, the nicest glances in my direction openly envious, the worst, positively resentful. A couple almost kicked sand in my face. Nick seemed oblivious to the attention, occasionally waving offhandedly to someone, but reserving the intensity of his unsettling deep green eyes and lopsided smile, for me. Today, someone somewhere had picked my name out of a hat and it wasn't for mowing the lawn or washing the dishes.

'Come back to our place for fish and chips,' George invited, shaking the water off himself like a wet dog, his boardshorts flapping against his legs and then clinging to them with determination. I threw him a towel.

'Uh, sure,' Nick replied, caught by surprise for a moment and sounding unsure. I wondered what that meant.

'Let's go,' George beckoned, water still running in rivulets down his legs, the towel thrown carelessly around his neck and his light brown hair standing up in tufts, like he'd stuck a finger in a power socket.

We followed, stopping on the way to buy fish and chips from the sweaty little shop on the hill, and then continuing our upward climb with the afternoon glare in our faces. The breeze seemed to have lulled and perspiration trickled down my neck. I gathered my hair up high into a swinging pony-tail which brushed my shoulders.

'You look hot,' Nick said. His fingers touched the nape of my neck for an instant as we reached the gate. I shivered de-spite the heat and drew a ragged breath.

'Don't call my sister hot, unless you can handle a fat smack,' George half joked as he held the gate open for us. I cringed and Nick laughed.

'Okay then, she's not hot she's just sweating like a pig.' He yanked on my ponytail and I had to look up at him. Great Goliath he was tall. And yes, my eyes were definitely level with his chest which was awkward anyway, although maybe it was better than continually looking into his eyes. His smile dazzled me and my tongue became an obstacle which couldn't be overcome for a moment. It was so unfair. Even-tually I managed a weak, 'thanks a lot,' which was meant to be sarcastic, but was too long after the comment he'd made to really make any sense at all.

I could feel George's eyes burning a hole in the back of my head as we neared the house and turned to face him. He looked concerned, although he immediately tried to shrug it off by plastering a reassuring smile on his mug. It wasn't convincing.

Mum wasn't at home. Allegedly she was doing *more* over-time, but either her boss was a ghoul who forced his employ-ees into slavery, or she was seeing aforementioned boss, which seemed more likely. Especially since he had allegedly dropped off some invisible work for Mum a week ago, and only been able to stay for a total of twenty seconds, eighteen of which involved looking for a shoe, when George and I ar-rived home earlier than expected due to cancelled afternoon sports.

'So, how are you settling in?' Nick enquired politely, as

we sat outside the kitchen at an old wooden table in the garden, thongs discarded and feet bare, digging hungrily into enormous portions of fish with warm lemon wedges, and fat soggy chips leeching oil into the paper which flapped as the breeze picked up again. I picked up a can and placed it on the corner to keep it down.

'Pretty well,' George answered, 'although it's been a bit of a shock to the system after Victoria.'

'What, all the sunshine?'

'Well that, and the community. It's a bit different to what we're used to.' He flipped a chip into his mouth and I rolled my eyes. 'We felt like pond-scum for the first few weeks, but I think we must be cool now if you're talking to us!'

Nick laughed heartily. I popped a cola and glugged some down thirstily. It burnt my throat and I almost choked, mortified as his attention swung around to me.

'Have *you* felt like pond-scum too, Deb?'

My eyes were watering as I tried to clear my throat. I looked at the table. 'Aah, it's not been so bad …'

'Deb's been more focussed on Mum,' George intervened, rescuing me. The Lorikeets had started their cheerful afternoon bickering.

'Bloody birds,' he added.

'They're beautiful though,' I said.

Nick's eyes returned to me. I managed to hold his gaze for a moment before the intensity became overwhelming. The breeze caught his hair making the curls flicker like fiery embers across his face. My mouth fell open, but I couldn't speak as his gaze dropped to the nape of my neck and lingered there. I was no longer perspiring, I realised. Instead my skin felt dry and salty. The air, which carried the tiniest breath of coolness, felt like light fingertips on my skin. I closed my eyes, but when they opened I became aware of George shifting uncomfortably and forced them back to him. He slapped at a mosquito that was humming a little too enthusiastically around his legs and I heard the birds again.

'They'd make a nice head piece,' George said, nodding towards the birds and breaking the moment.

I laughed. 'George the milliner.' He grinned looking mightily relieved at the change in atmosphere.

Our streaky overhead palette was slowly becoming more varied with splashes of carrot and plum, even a little charcoal, against the pale backdrop. It was one of those charmed spontaneous evenings. Unrepeatable.

'I should get going,' Nick said as day finally lost its battle with night and the wind turned the garden into a bush disco.

'How are you getting home?' I asked, holding my hair away from my face. I didn't have a clue where he lived, but it wouldn't be far, surely, would he walk?

'If I could use your phone I'll call someone to pick me up.' Time and the weather had broken the spell, had stolen the moment. I wondered whether there would be others.

'No problem, it's just next to the front door,' George replied, leading him inside. I let the stirring darkness buffet me until they returned.

'I'll wait out the front,' Nick said.

'Oh? Already?' I felt unprepared for his departure.

He smiled, but it seemed polite, like he was already distancing himself, or maybe that was only my projection. 'They won't be long.'

I nodded. 'Thanks,' he added, taking my hand and giving it a brief squeeze before turning away.

'No worries,' George said. I stood mute.

He waved and walked down our short uneven path, past the upended bird-bath and through the gate. I stood on the porch watching, noticing the distant white horses tripping across the ocean under the moonlight and hoping that he would glance back at me. He didn't. Soon a dark sedan pulled up and he opened the door and slid in quickly. The car didn't fit. It was too stiff, too formal. With a polite drone it glided away.

'He's a nice guy?' George said, after he had left and we were sitting on the sofa, watching television and drinking hot chocolate before bed.

'Is that a question or a statement?' I asked, confused. 'Don't *you* think so?'

'I think so.' He fidgeted and then stopped and turned to me. 'Just be careful though.'

'What does that mean?' I asked, jumping up and following him into the kitchen where he had taken our empty mugs. I blocked his path, forcing him to face me.

He shrugged. 'I saw the way you were looking at each other.' I sighed loudly. 'It was hard to miss,' he added.

'Oh come on George!' I felt embarrassed. This was a new game.

'I'm just doing my big-brother duty, Deb, so don't be mad. This is new territory for me too! You're my baby sister and I haven't seen you like this before. I can see stars in your eyes when you look at him. I just don't want you to get hurt, that's all.'

'George, you're sweet, but I'm not a complete idiot.' I retreated with a sigh and flopped back down onto the sofa. Not that I was completely confident on that point, given my inexperience, but I didn't think he needed to know that. He collapsed next to me.

'I know you're not, but he's older, more experienced … more sophisticated than you are. I want to give him the benefit of the doubt. I just want you to take it easy, is that possible?'

I sighed loudly again. 'Give me a break, I've only just met the guy. He's okay …' I couldn't hide my irritation, but I was also mortified about the obviousness of my affliction. I hoped that if Nick had picked up on anything it had been that I was alluring and not desperate.

'Yeah right, absolutely,' he said sarcastically. 'He's okay!' he mimicked in a high pitched whine, breaking the tension. I thumped him playfully with a cushion.

'Apparently his family are a pretty weird bunch, *very* stuck up. There are lots of rumours at school.'

'What sort of rumours?' I asked, intrigued.

'Well, they're rich … *and* weird!'

'Mmm, and the rest of us are just plain weird,' I replied, disappointed at the predictability of the information. 'I guess no-one's envious of their success?'

'Yeah, there is that, of course. I guess everyone's pretty jealous.'

I laughed. 'Rumours. To be fair we should give him the benefit of the doubt. Even if it's true it's not his fault he comes from a *weird* family. I mean is there any other kind?'

He ruffled my hair in an annoying way as he pushed himself off the sofa and stood. 'You're right. I just don't want you to get hurt that's all. Get to know him first, Deb!' I could see the genuine concern in his eyes and had learned enough about life not to take it for granted.

I smiled and shook my head. 'I doubt he's interested in me anyway!'

He shook his head back at me but with a much more exaggerated motion, like I truly *was* an idiot. 'Deb, do you really think it was my company he was after this evening?'

I raised my eyebrows, afraid to hope.

'I don't think so!' George said with what seemed almost like despair as he turned in for the night.

Butterflies took flight in my stomach. Nick was nearly a man. One definitely worthy of cracking your head on a rock for. He might even be interested in me. Maybe secret wishes had hidden power.

'Night George,' I cried, leaping off the sofa with vigour and pecking him on the cheek as I passed him in the passage. Now was a time to retreat to night-time fantasies and forget the threat of reality.

7

KATE

I organised to catch up with Nick in the city at Southbank, along the edge of the Yarra. I caught the train to Flinders Street station and then walked over the bridge and down onto the sidewalk alongside the lethargic river, merging with the hustle and bustle of tourists, trendy students, well-groomed business people and lively street performers.

People queued for river cruises on flat-bottomed boats, and a red and white helicopter ferried passengers off for scenic flights from a helipad on the opposite side of the river. The activity distracted me from the knot in my stomach and helped me leave my nails alone. They were only just starting to grow.

A cool south wind blew making tiny waves leap in snowy flickers across the dark water. I shivered into my jacket, pulling it tightly around me and abandoning the rebellious wisps of hair which escaped from my pony-tail.

As I neared the pedestrian bridge, I recognised him immediately. He was leaning against the rails at the end, still big and powerfully built, wisps of grey flourishing at his temples giving way to a medley of mocha tones which might have been lighter years ago. He seemed to sense my scrutiny and looked up, his jaw dropping open for a moment as he noticed me. I knew why. My own reaction had been similar.

There was no mistaking our likeness, even though it was down to a single feature.

The one and only image Deb had sent me of him was black and white, and so it was his eyes which most surprised me. Even though she had said I had his eyes, I hadn't realised that she meant exactly that. Our eye colour and the strange swirls and striations were identical. It seemed strange then to admire his, but they sat with such exquisiteness in his face, the emerald, vivid, like a light shone beneath, against the tan of his skin. So striking, that whatever his age, he would always draw second glances.

Furrows across his brow logged the hardships of his life but he was still ruggedly handsome. He'd chosen casual beige chinos and a blue and red checked shirt for our first meeting, but his posture was tense.

'There's no mistaking it, is there,' he said, by way of greeting. Until he'd seen me in the flesh he hadn't completely believed, he'd needed the proof, which was certainly his now.

'I guess not,' I replied cautiously, our startling similarity making me feel strangely vulnerable.

'Kate.' His eyes, too much like mine, appraised me, noticing every aspect of my appearance and I felt almost unbearably awkward. I hoped he wasn't disappointed, that it wasn't, '*I guess she has my eyes, so I can't really deny her, but if I could ...*'

Before any more hideous thoughts could disregard the no-entry sign into my mind, he reached out tentatively and touched my arm, distracting me. Suddenly he pulled me close in a suffocating bear hug which, although surprising, felt warm and reassuring. Even better it gave Sam, the evil snake, source of aforementioned thoughts, the finger.

Just as I was about to expire, he released his grip and held me out at arm's length. His face was a jumble, eyes sparkling with what looked like regret, but happiness in the creases around them, pride too. His mouth was assembled in a grim smile, but only managed to turn up on one side, and the muscle in his cheek quivered. It was an intense experience. For a moment I had no words; I was newly-born, a baby looking up into the face of her proud new father.

Eventually I managed to speak, but my voice was slightly unsteady.

'This must seem so strange to you. You didn't even know I existed a few weeks ago.'

'Why now?' he asked, his voice a little gruff, his expression still intense, judging me by my response.

'It's been a while coming, Nick. Eighteen is one of those big moments in life I guess. Finally you can lock the toilet door.'

He nodded, still holding onto my fingers. His hands were like the paws of a bear, large and tanned and strong. He could break my fingers with a gentle squeeze.

'I've always wanted answers. I've wanted to fill in the void … but I didn't want to hurt Mum. This is hard for her.' I chewed on my cheek and then shrugged. 'As you get older you realise that a time will come when answers will no longer be available. I don't want to live with that sort of regret.'

He squeezed my hand and finally let it drop, severing our physical connection.

'No, of course you don't.' His words were at odds with his expression which had darkened. He turned away to the dense, sluggish water. Tossing a little emotional garbage in that direction would not slow it further. For an instant I wondered what it was that had caused the shadow to cross his features. Had it been my reference to my mother, not contacting him until now because of her, or was it something I knew nothing about? But then a helicopter lifted from the opposite bank, the whir and movement distracting us and when I glanced back at him his moment of gloomy reverie had passed.

'These things are a bit easier at my age,' he said, 'I have no parents left to disapprove, or give me grief!'

'I'm sorry it's taken me so long though.'

He shook his head. 'Don't be sorry. This happened to you,' he said. 'If anything Deb could have let me know a long time ago, but she didn't.' His irritation was unmistakeable, but then it was gone again, hidden under some semblance of neutral and another quick flash of regret. He'd said more than he wanted to, shown too much of himself.

'It wasn't easy for her,' I said, immediately claiming the defensive. He looked at me and sighed.

'I know you're right, Kate.' I became aware of the people around us as we walked in silence. 'Please don't judge me too harshly,' he said, 'I've lost my whole family over the years and never managed to establish one of my own. I guess I've turned into a bitter old man ...'

I relented. 'Of course, it's understandable.'

'It still seems unreal, I mean even now that you're right in front of me. I never saw Deb noticeably pregnant.' He frowned. 'Although she must have been the last time I saw her, I just didn't realise it.' Self-loathing settled on his features. He tried to dispel it, but it sat there stubbornly. 'I was distracted at the time ... self-absorbed.' I nodded.

'It must have been so hard for her,' he continued, 'she would have been so young.'

'My age.'

He looked out at the unfathomable murkiness of the water. It was impossible to read his expression. Then his eyes returned to me and they had changed again.

'Are you hungry?' he asked suddenly, and I nodded.

'Let's get something to eat.'

We walked past a number of restaurants and cafés. He made sarcastic comments about the Melbourne weather, which *was* rather diabolical for January when one shouldn't get hypothermia walking five minutes to a restaurant.

'It's just the wind,' I said, pulling my jacket around myself tightly and looking up at the sun which had chosen to come out from behind a cloud and shine brightly, but without heat. As if happy to be mentioned, the wind gusted a little more forcefully filling my mouth with hair from my pony-tail.

'God help us, we'll be frozen before we find shelter … and my will is not even up to date.' Nick winked at me as he grabbed my arm and pulled me into a small, bustling, Italian bistro. The aroma of garlic, basil and oregano wafted pleas-antly above the eager chinks and clinks of cutlery as patrons devoured plates piled high with pasta and seafood. We set-tled into a booth at the back where it was a little more private and I thawed slowly.

'I can't really see Deb in you,' Nick commented, after our lips had softened enough to speak.

'I can't either,' I agreed, a little more comfortable with his scrutiny now, and even managing a small smile as he contin-ued to examine me.

'You remind me a lot of my brother,' he said, angling his head to the side. After a moment he reached out and touched my cheek. 'It's the way you smile … and also your hair, it's darker than the rest of ours, and definitely darker than Deb's family. Daniel was a lot like you …' He seemed contempla-tive, his eyes on me but his gaze drifting inwards and the light behind his irises dimming.

I smiled uncertainly. 'And his eyes? Were they like mine

too?'

'The eyes,' he said, considering his answer, 'are a bit of a genetic peculiarity in our family. You wouldn't see the same on someone who wasn't an Edwards.'

'No,' I agreed, 'but I assume that not *every* Edwards has exactly the same eyes.'

'No, well of course not, but they run in our family the way red hair runs in others.'

'And your brother,' I prompted, like a dog with a not nearly well enough chewed bone.

He nodded. 'My brother had the same eyes. All three of us did.'

I regarded him for some moments before I spoke. 'It's a bit like that freaky old movie, isn't it, what was it called?' I tried to remember the name, so that my comment wouldn't be so ambiguous.

'The Village of the Damned,' he supplied helpfully, surprising me. I wondered whether he was a movie buff or whether he was like me and had seen it a long time ago, but been haunted by the creepiness of it.

'That's the one,' I nodded. 'The pathological kids with the shiny eyes.' I'd watched it on my own with only Noodle for company and she'd deserted me halfway through due to the eardrum torture every time the kids' eyes lit up, which was a lot by the end.

'It was based on a book, *The Midwich Cuckoos* by John Wyndham,' he added.

'I've felt like a cuckoo sometimes,' I observed, and then bit my lip wishing I hadn't. 'Silly though,' I babbled, to cover my discomfort, 'my folks wanted me in their nest, which by definition means that I couldn't really have been a cuckoo … and there were no other chicks to kill.'

He raised an eyebrow and passed me a menu. After opening it he spoke. 'My father's eyes were different, green but...' He paused and I found myself finishing his sentence.

'Not as weird.'

He regarded me carefully, a little surprised. 'I couldn't have put it better,' he said. 'They were nice eyes, but they were more of an ordinary green.'

Ordinary green compared to what? Something strange, something NQR. Looking into his eyes I felt disconcerted. They were like portholes and outside lay the sea and the sky, another place where light and shadow were reflections of a different reality, one which regarded you back with added intensity and curiosity. Were those my eyes? Was that why my brain fought so hard against what was there? Or was my discomfort related more to the revelling of a jolly serpent who couldn't resist an opportunity to snipe, to reduce what was extraordinary to a peculiarity unsuited to one so ordinary?

When I applied eye-shadow or mascara I focussed on my eyelids or lashes. I avoided the depths, they made me uncomfortable. Photos weren't too bad because a photo couldn't capture the sense of the passengers, or movement within. My brain didn't have to twist and turn to try and understand photos.

'You've got my curls too, you know,' he said, as though reading my thoughts and wanting to distract me. It worked.

'Yes, thanks for that!' I answered, relieved to abandon my complicated, madly imaginative speculations. 'I spend my life trying to control them, they're so wild.'

'You're beautiful, Kate,' he interrupted and I didn't know where to look.

'And you blush, just like Deb!' He banged the table lightly with his hand, his laughter a deep rumble. 'You should be used to compliments,' he admonished, shaking a finger at me in a mock reprimand.

I shook my head. 'Not really.' My parents never commented on my physical appearance, except when making a recommendation regarding what I was wearing. *'Beige is not your colour, Kit …'* Mum's heart was in the right place, but her comment inappropriately timed as I returned to the stage to perform with a little less confidence. They regularly complimented me on my performances or compositions, but not my looks.

'Well it's charming, anyway,' he said kindly. Our food arrived swiftly, although that might just have been a reflection of how caught up in each other we were. Scallops for him and a marinara for me.

'Bon Appétit,' he said. 'Hopefully the first meal of many together.' We chinked our glasses and focussed on our meals - which were delicious - before continuing to get to know each other.

His business interests were scattered around the world. He lived a nomadic existence. Setting down roots in any one place for long seemed to be a challenge for him. Bachelorhood suited him and his globe-wandering lifestyle.

Of three green-eyed brothers he was the only surviving. His eldest brother, Brendan, had been killed a couple of years before in a diving accident. He was one of a team repairing pipes on an oil rig and had never resurfaced. His body had never been found and sharks were surmised to have taken it. His younger brother by a year, Daniel, had committed suicide many years ago, prior to my birth.

Although his tone was matter of fact, lingering grief resided in the heaviness which tugged at his face as he spoke. Eighteen years had passed, my whole life, and his family were gone. One by one they had died. Only he remained. I wasn't sure whether that meant he was the lucky one.

'I'm the sole survivor,' he said with a bitter laugh, shaking his head and then grabbing his glass and swigging back the last of his whisky as though it was some sort of antidote for misery. It seemed to have the opposite effect as he struggled harder to let go of the dark expression which settled across his features.

We finished our meal, our dessert and our coffees, but he continued to order and consume one whisky after another, becoming increasingly disillusioned, a shadow of the man who had greeted me. I began to feel a little concerned, chewing on my cheek and then irritating a nail as I wondered how to deal with the situation. It wasn't one I had prepared for.

'You come from a long line of cursed human beings, Kate,' he stated morosely, shaking his head. His knuckles had turned blue-white around his tumbler and I leant forward to reassure him. I wanted to remind him that he was a good swimmer, Deb had told me, and that he would not drown in this sea of dark circumstance. He had made it so far. But suddenly it seemed too presumptuous and I wasn't convinced that my interpretation would fit with his and so I leant back and bit my tongue. 'I'm sorry that I've passed that on to you,' he mumbled.

I smiled nervously. 'I don't feel cursed Nick, although I understand that *you* feel that way after everything you've been through.' My heart felt inexplicably heavy, like I was absorbing some of his pain. 'This must be difficult for you. Seeing me and having to rehash the past.'

Did that explain the drinking? I gazed into the depths of my empty coffee cup and then back up to him. 'I don't want to add to your hurt. I don't want you to feel guilty about me when you didn't even know that I existed. I've been raised by wonderful parents who loved me. They were desperate to have a child.' It was the truth, but in the moment it sounded like propaganda. I shrugged, trying to dispel the tension which held my shoulders in its fist. 'If there was a curse, then I've escaped it!'

He regarded me for a long moment. 'The circumstances of your birth and the way Deb hid your arrival have allowed you to be raised differently … very differently to how you would have been otherwise.'

I shrugged, 'Fate has been kind to me in that way.'

'Fate?' he spat, immediately recognising his inappropriate response and softening his tone. 'In the end, these things have a way of finding you, Kate.'

I nodded, not completely understanding the depths of his despair, guessing and then adding the alcohol to that. 'You've lost a lot.'

'Don't pity me, please!' He waved his hand dismissively. 'I handled the whole Deb thing badly. God!' He dropped his head into his hands for an instant, almost immediately sitting up straight again.

The past. What would life be like if we could go back and change our mistakes? We'd change the future, maybe cancel ourselves out. I certainly wouldn't be here. 'Fate, Nick. You're a successful businessman and Deb's happy where she is.'

He grabbed my arms across the table suddenly, startling me and drawing me into the confusing depths of his eyes. There was too much going on to begin to interpret, but I could feel some sort of transfer of emotion. 'I was so drawn to her.' His stare was penetrating. I felt him willing me to understand, to forgive. 'Even at the end when I had no other choice, it was so hard to stay away. I did things to drive her away from me. I had to. I was a coward. I knew that if she came back to me I couldn't let her go and I had to.' Equally suddenly the strength left his voice and he released my arms, looking downcast.

'Why?'

'Smoke and mirrors ...' he answered mysteriously, explaining nothing. His glass was empty. He clinked the ice in it as though wondering what had happened to the liquid.

I looked at him expectantly and he sighed.

'Poor Deb. It was my family, Kate. Put simply, at the end of the day they just didn't want us together. You've heard it before. Rich bastards who don't want any but their own kind around.' His glass clunked down on the table and he held up his hands. 'I'm sorry,' he said. 'I shouldn't speak that way around you.'

'It's okay,' I said, fiddling with the serviette. I folded it and smoothed it out while I thought about what he had said. 'So her family wasn't acceptable to them?' I asked, remembering how sweet her mum had sounded on the phone.

He seemed unsure exactly how to respond. His lips parted as though to speak, but then pressed together into a tight line. Finally he nodded. 'In the beginning it seemed that simple, an 'us and them' thing. What I'd always known. But ... if only, it was much worse than that.' He regarded our surrounds, and I worried that he would order another whisky, but maybe he was just looking for the exit. Finally he spoke again. 'If I'd known in the beginning the extent of 'screwed-upness' that existed in my family I never would have dragged her into it.' He exhaled deeply. 'It must have been so hard for her to deal with her pregnancy on her own.'

'She was lucky, her mother supported her,' I said. 'I get the impression they were very close.'

He nodded. 'They were.'

Nick seemed less formidable now than when I had first met him. His posture had changed and he had become stooped. The more he drank, the more his shoulders slumped. It was the place the alcohol was taking him to, the place where he couldn't escape the sadness and regret.

'She's still around,' I added, trying to sound upbeat. 'Deb named me after her when I was first born. Julia. My adoptive parents called me Kate.'

'Julia,' he said, his voice reflective. 'I remember her clearly. She didn't have an easy life either.'

'She gave up a lot to help Deb, resigned from her job to go away with her and left her boyfriend behind. Seems like an old-fashioned way of doing things … the adoption and keeping everything secret. But that's what Deb wanted.'

'She probably didn't want my family finding out, or me I guess.' He brought his hands to his face again, but this time used them to push his hair off his forehead. I noticed a faint sheen of perspiration across his temples. 'If only she'd known …'

'Known what?'

He hesitated before speaking. 'My family are fiercely protective of their own. If they had known about your existence, no matter the circumstances, you would have had a home. Deb would not have been able to leave, to put you up for adoption.'

'She might still have chosen to,' I said, not exactly sure what to make of this new bit of information, but relatively sure that the type of protectiveness he mentioned would not be something Deb would have appreciated.

He chuckled, but it was a hard sound and a chill ran down my spine.

A fingernail had made its way into my mouth. I bit down on it and then released it. 'It seems strange to me that in such a small place, no-one ever suspected.'

He nodded. 'She did a good job of covering things up, or

maybe we just weren't paying enough attention. The family was preoccupied. Daniel had just died …'

'I'm sorry, Nick.'

He shrugged. 'It was a long time ago. We were all a bit messed up.'

'I'm not surprised.'

'And so, I guess she had to go through it alone. Thank God for her mother.'

'Absolutely,' I agreed. 'Somehow she made it through and met Jim and … well, she seems content now.'

'Content. I envy her.' He reflected for a moment and added with a grim smile. 'Not possible for everyone.'

A fresh whisky and soda arrived and my stomach lurched. He took a deep drink. This was definitely his last, although I wondered how I would go insisting on that if I needed to. He sensed my anxiety and reached out to pat my hand reassuringly. 'I'm really happy for her,' he said. 'She deserves it.' He turned away for a moment and I glimpsed a tiny tear at the corner of his eye.

It was gone when he turned back, but a look of deep regret had settled on his face. His eyes darkened as old ghosts consumed the colour. 'I wish I could tell you that we were your average family, that Mum used to make us packed lunches for school and Dad used to take us fishing and that we'd argue but we'd make up and in the end we all loved each other and that was the main thing.'

I couldn't help a grim smile, reflecting on Mum and Dad and their arguments, the tension which would linger for days at home sometimes. My fear. 'I'm not sure where you researched your facts on the average family, Nick.'

'No? Well, maybe you're right,' he agreed. 'My family background is not a happy one. In fact, it's hard to remember anything overly positive about it. Our family seemed more like a dictatorship. My mother was the ruler of the regime, even dominating my father, although he was the second in command of course.' He shook his head slightly. 'They're gone now,' he said, as though reminding himself of this truth.

I was unsure how to react. His body and face were a jumble of emotional cues. Celebration or sympathy? I remained quiet.

'It's easy to say. They're gone, dead and buried.' He frowned, and shadows eddied through his eyes. 'But sometimes I hear them, whispering, doubting, and I wonder.'

I searched for words and came up a bit short. 'Obviously they have had a huge impact on you ...' His laugh was bitter, cutting me off. I ploughed on. 'But *you* can let the past go now. Like you said, they're not around anymore.'

He raised his eyebrows and looked directly at me. The ghosts of the very people we were speaking of flitted within him. 'You are so very right, Kate. They are not, but you are.'

I swallowed. Yes, of course. I was a powerful link to the past he'd probably been trying to escape.

He waved my unspoken apology away. 'It's a fact that's all. Your origins are in my past and so unavoidably a lot has been coming back to me over these last weeks, but ... I'm not alone anymore am I?' He looked to me for confirmation and I nodded. 'I'm still processing that, because in a way it seems like a miracle and I'm not sure I deserve one.'

We sat in silence for a while as the restaurant started emptying around us.

'Deb and I were pretty irresponsible together,' he acknowledged. 'It was my fault. I was a crazy, hormone-fuelled kid, desperate to live in the moment.' He shrugged and then sat up a little straighter. 'I know I'm making excuses but our attraction was powerful. It blinded us to reality.' He gestured to me. 'That's why you're sitting across from me today.'

'I'm the consequence.'

He nodded. 'It's unfair to reduce you to that, I know.' He shook his head and ran his fingers through his messy curls. Guilt continued to nag at his forehead and he brought his hand up to rub his brow.

'When we get to know each other better I'll tell you more, I promise. I just don't want you to run ten miles right now.' He picked up my wrist and turned it over, lightly touching the blue of my veins. A slow shiver inched up my neck.

'You will probably curse me for the Edwards' blood in your veins, Kate.'

He dropped my wrist and gave me a lopsided grin. For a moment I glimpsed the boy inside as the darkness moved away.

'You've got me interested anyway,' I said with a shrug, trying for nonchalance, which was a very far removed state from my currently piqued curiosity. He beckoned for the bill.

'I have to give you a reason to see me again, you see,' he said.

'Of course we're going to meet again … if you can risk the Melbourne weather, that is.' He glanced outside with dread.

'Next time I'll bring the thermals,' he said, and I smiled.

The bill arrived and he paid and afterwards as he sat looking at me, I noticed that the quality of his smile had changed. It was less determined, a little more confused, only half of his mouth turned up, just like when we had first met. It was sadder. 'You're so forgiving. I wish I could be,' he said.

We stood and moved through the now semi-deserted restaurant. 'I might have felt differently if Mum and Dad had been awful. I don't know,' I said.

'I'm glad you can love, Kate. Don't ever let that go. Not even when life takes something so sweet and tries to throttle you with it. Don't get bitter and twisted …' I felt a flutter of anxiety. The realisation that life was harsher than I knew sometimes and, no doubt, some of that would head my way.

'I'll try,' I said quietly.

'Never stop trying, Katie.' His diminutive use of my name felt familiar. I liked it.

The waiters looked relieved as we headed outside. It was still blustery and the clouds weren't sure whether they were coming or going. I wrapped my arms around myself to stop bits of me from flying away, although my bag still tried and my hair was a lost cause. 'You can't drive,' I stated matter of factly, ready to restrain him if need be. The whites of his eyes were really quite bloodshot, although he was still amazingly coherent.

'No,' he acknowledged, touched by my concern, 'I'll get a cab.'

'You're not going to fly either, are you?' I asked, my hand on his arm, suddenly realising that he didn't have a jacket. Maybe the brisk air would help to clear his head.

'No, I'll fly back tomorrow. I've got some business to sort out tonight anyway.' I looked at him dubiously, but he was obviously a seasoned drinker. If I had consumed a quarter of the quantity of whiskey he had I would have long since given the tourists a display of sour-smelling abstract art on the pavement.

'Okay, well it's been great to meet you in person.' I looked up at him through the many wisps of hair which whipped across my face, and noticed that his hair was just as wild.

'What?' he said.

'Your hair is crazy.'

He chuckled, trying to smooth it with his fingers and giving up. 'Yours too.'

Suddenly his expression became complex again and I felt an irrational desire to be a child for him, to rewind time. An unexpected bead of moisture tangled with my eyelashes and I blinked rapidly to dispel it. 'I hope that we can do this again sometime soon, Nick.'

He grasped me unexpectedly in another tight hug, lifting my feet off the ground and making my head spin. For a moment I felt his possessiveness, his heart reached out to mine and his mind tried to push the world away. It was as though he wanted the moment to last forever, or maybe that was my desire, but it could not and he released me, whispering in my ear, almost regretfully as he did so.

'Do you dream, Kate?'

The abrupt transition was confusing. A question without sufficient context. He set me on the ground and held me at arm's length, his expression earnest, his eyes suddenly sober, a furrow across his brow deepening over one eye as he examined me.

What had I missed?

'Of course I dream,' I said, trying to shrug away my disquiet. The look of fear which crossed his face, like he was treading on ground which might suddenly open up and swallow him, didn't help.

'Good dreams?' he asked, drawing his arms away. My heart sank although I wasn't sure why. Maybe because I had a sense of it then. A sense that all wasn't right, that he already knew my answer. Although, that was ludicrous, of course.

'Sometimes ...' I answered, feeling disoriented, sensing the clock tick, but time standing still. 'Sometimes, not so great. Just like everyone.'

'No,' he said, and I looked into the depths of his emerald

eyes. For a moment there was something else reflected in them like an infusion of colour in the space between every-thing, before my mind shut it out and it was gone.

'Not like everyone.' His voice was slow and heavy, bur-dened by secrets and my heart pumped something cold and slithery through my veins as I realised that one day those se-crets would surely be mine as well. I too might be saddled by weights too heavy to bear. It was only him and me now, after all. A feeling of doubt sidled up from my stomach but I swallowed it down heavily. I had needed to make contact with him and now that I had, I couldn't go back.

Still I spoke cautiously. 'What do you mean, not like eve-ryone?'

'You're an Edwards. You are not like everyone else. I think you know that already.'

And then he was gone, turning away and slipping through the crowd, leaving me surprised, muddled and all alone.

8

DEB AND NICK

The unexpected shades of the lake took my breath away. Clear around the edges, but God had been playful, turning the centre into a kaleidoscope with turquoise swirls which turned to azure, and then indigo in the darkest water.

I had been perched on the back of Nick's sleek black and chrome motorbike for a little over thirty minutes, when we broke through a cover of almost tropical vegetation at the crest of a hill and in front of us lay this surprise. An expanse so wide it seemed almost like an inland sea, a bay, surrounded by dazzling white beaches and rocky outcrops, and further back by the bush and hills.

My morning began uneventfully. Another lazy Saturday on the beach, with George trying his luck with Michelle, petite and blonde with freckles and an easy smile. My novel was uninteresting, but I buried my head in it anyway, trying not to eavesdrop.

'Hey Beautiful,' I heard in my ear. My cheeks flamed, the heat spreading to my neck and throat in what I imagined were vivid blotches, annoyingly conspicuous.

'Nick,' I said, my heart completing three full cartwheels and threatening to convulse as I gazed up into his wide grin. I tried not to notice the smooth golden skin which covered the muscles on his arms, or the tautness of his chest or the bead of perspiration which inched down his neck. Instead I turned my attention to the sand.

'Come out to the lake with me,' he said, kneeling down beside me.

'Um,' I stumbled, not able to think clearly about whether or not that was actually a good idea.

'It's a beautiful day. We can go now and spend the day there. What do you think?' His smile was very persuasive.

'Well ...'

'I know it's late notice, but we can't let this perfect day pass us by.'

The sun shone in a completely blue sky. There wasn't a cloud in sight and the wind hadn't picked up yet.

'No, of course not,' I said, shaking my head. 'It's not like we have many.'

'Well this is even more perfect than most.' He laughed playfully. 'Plus, you're here, and I'm here ...'

'I don't think there's anything too urgent I have to do to-day,' I said, pretending to actually consider.

'Excellent.'

I stood up and started dusting sand off myself. 'I haven't got anything though. What do I need?'

'Just bring yourself.'

'Oh ... well that's easy enough,' I replied, shrugging shyly and then feeling slightly insecure about heading into the un-known with him and without any *stuff*. After a moment's thought I picked up my bag and shoved my towel inside it. I had to take something.

'I'll let George know we're going so that he doesn't think you've been abducted by aliens.' He walked off to where George sat before I could stop him. I wondered what George would say, given his concerns, but he shook off the fleeting look of uncertainty which crossed his face and replaced it with a somewhat tentative smile and nod. I waved to him and grabbed my bag.

Nick returned and took my hand in his, easily, like it was the most natural thing to do. George wouldn't like it, but I wasn't going to look at him now to make sure. The air was fresh in my face, the sun warm on my back as Nick pulled me across the sand. I felt a little confused, unsure what to make of his hand in mine, whether it was a sign of friendship, or something more. A flutter of anxiety unsettled me for a moment. What had he made of my easy acquiescence to this time alone with him? Suddenly I felt very aware of my vulnerability. He was the most handsome guy I had ever met. He made parts of my body turn to liquid and burn with desire. Desire for something I had never had, only imagined. I couldn't think clearly around him which was probably not a good sign. George was right. He was more experienced than me, worldlier. He was used to getting what he wanted.

As I stumbled after him I wondered just how far I was getting in over my head.

We reached the carpark and he dropped my hand and walked straight over to a dazzling motorbike. The sun bounced off the silver body but my sunglasses softened the glare. I hung back, confident of my mother's disapproval.

'Come on,' he said impatiently, dismissing my dubious expression, but going for reassurance when he realised that it wasn't going away. 'I'm a safe rider, I promise. I'll obey the road rules and make sure I stay under the speed limit.' His eyes were earnest, but the way he said it made me wonder just how often he did just the opposite. 'You can trust me, Deb. Look, I brought a helmet just for you.' He held out a shiny red one.

'At least it will hide the blood!' After a last moment of hesitation I succumbed to the sense of excitement pulsating through my body and hoisted myself onto the low-slung seat behind him, pulling the helmet on. As he started the engine and the thunderous retort became a low throb it felt like my body had become a conducting rod. Anticipation was like lightning crackling through me. It settled down low as I realised that I would be wrapped around him for some time. Tentatively, as the vibration of the bike radiated outwards from my torso in a regular, pulsating thump, like the sound of my heart amplified, I shifted closer and reached around him. He felt good, solid and hot. In a wave of sound and heat and petrol fumes we departed.

And now we were here, at the top of a hill, admiring the indescribable view. I felt alive, invigorated by the journey, by the wind in my face and on my body, and my physical connection to Nick. I loved the bike. Riding it was active, not passive like when you were in a car. We three moved together leaning into the bends and communing with nature, the elements whispering around us and merging with the heat and throb of the beast beneath us. Speaking wasn't practical, but it would have ruined the experience anyway, the otherworldly togetherness we shared.

As we neared the lake I noticed that it was quite busy. People were swimming, playing volleyball and jogging or cycling. Barbeques were starting to sizzle, attracting throngs of mostly men to worship at their fiery plates.

We continued past the main carpark along the narrow road which meandered around the lake, until Nick stopped in a quiet bend, pushing the bike into the forest a little way so that it was obscured from the road.

'That was awesome,' I said. He smiled broadly back at me, his eyes illuminated with dancing sprites, or so it seemed.

'I knew you'd like it.'

'I've never even been near a motorbike,' I said, handing

him my helmet and examining the bike for a moment. I noticed its deep silence, the sleek dark beauty of the black and chrome machine.

'Harley Davidson,' he said, gesturing to a badge which meant little to me.

'Right.' I was nodding with what I hoped was just the right amount of respect when a memory unexpectedly popped up. 'Aah, the Bikies.'

He laughed and I realised that I'd just put my foot in it. 'Not that I'm implying anything.'

His grin was cheeky and made my heart pound. 'They're not the only ones who enjoy a good ride,' he said.

I didn't know what to say. I felt like an idiot.

'Err ...' I tried, and he laughed again.

'Come on, I'll show you my special place.'

He took my hand and led me through the undergrowth. There were a few things I belatedly realised about his bike, and him by association. It was the brand most preferred by the notorious bikies, it was a great ride ... and it must have cost a fortune. His world and my world were very far removed. He hadn't even finished school and he had a bike like that. I felt suddenly uncomfortable in my bargain-bin top and shorts which had come in at under ten dollars. Thankfully, the gold flickering through the verdant canopy overhead, casting curiously capering shadows onto the ground, caught my attention. We crossed over a shallow, translucent stream running over what looked like beach sand, and walked for about ten minutes before we emerged at a small rocky cove. There we clambered over rocks and down onto the soft white sunny beach. Nearby the clear water of the lake lapped gently at the shore.

'It's enchanted,' I said, in awe of my surrounds. He remained silent, trapped in the moment. This was Planet Nick, his special place, an unexpected jewel, private in the midst of all the people-noise and activity somewhere around us.

'Nick?' His eyes were distant. His grip on my hand tightened.

Suddenly he returned.

'We used to come and swim here, when we were little,' he said, dropping my hand and wandering along the shore. Simple pleasures in simple times. Lost now?

His mood rippled like an estuary at the turn of the tide and he laughed mischievously. Suddenly he disappeared, emerging on top of an enormous grey rock, positioned like a sentinel and jutting quite far out into the lake, with his bathers on. He ran along it discarding his t-shirt and shoes onto the sand below.

'What are you doing?' I yelled as he clambered onto another rock which jutted even further in.

'Come in!' he shouted as he leapt off the rock recklessly, his knees tucked under him, the glee of his inner child evident in his innocent abandon. The water echoed its indignant cry as his body shattered the glassy surface, waves rocking erratically to the edge.

Dropping my top and shorts to the ground I dashed into the inviting water, just a little self-conscious in my bikini. It hit me like a cricket bat to the head. Ice cold. I gasped.

'You must be joking!'

'Come on!' he called impatiently.

I forced myself to hurry into the glacial liquid, knowing it would be nothing but slow torture any other way.

'The water ... IS ... F...R ... EEZING!' I shivered uncontrollably, wishing I owned a wet suit as I swam with jagged strokes out to where he waited on a small pontoon floating in the tinfoil glare of the lake. Kicking my legs I hoisted myself up onto the sunny platform and lay down next to him, dreading the swim back.

His gaze trapped mine as I turned my head to the side. His irises had taken on some of the azure of the lake and danced at my discomfort.

'That's mean.'

He laughed, but turned away and presumably tried to arrange his features so that they were more sympathetic. I lifted my arms above my head, trying to expose as much of my body as possible to the warmth of the sun. Slowly my blood began to flow again.

'It's really lovely.' The rocking motion soothed. I dozed. A shower of chilly droplets stung my skin and I opened my eyes to see his face hovering over mine.

Everything stopped, even the pontoon seemed to still. Oh God, please help me, I prayed. I'd never been this close to him, besides on the back of his motorbike, but his back, nice as it was, could never compete. For a moment I forgot how to breathe. I seemed to need to inhale air, and swallow at the same time which is impossible. You have to do one or the other.

His irises had deepened and evolved into a medley of blues which moved like the liquid lake in front of the green which had retreated into the background for now. The difference in the colour was quite startling.

'Your eyes ...' I said as I contemplated them. He shook his head and more icy droplets rained down on me. His lips curled into a naughty grin and I became aware of the heaviness of his body on mine. I was trapped by him.

'Move, Nick,' I said, a range of complicated feelings squirming around inside me. He didn't. Instead his mouth fell onto mine. His lips were cool and hard, softening and warming as they ignited a response within me. Reaching up I clasped my hands around his neck and pulled him closer.

The moment became fiercer. Heat seeped down into my stomach and then to my groin where it became an aching need. I think it was the same for him for just a moment, before he groaned, reluctantly wrenching himself away and diving off the pontoon.

Disappointment. A bucket emptied too suddenly. It was a long moment before the more rational aspect of my brain kicked in. I sat up slowly. A part of me still ached, but I was relieved that he had been the one to pull away. I'm not sure that I could have been that strong.

'Stop it,' I yelled, lifting my hands in mock surrender as polar water splashed onto me. 'Don't be cruel!'

'You've got to get used to the water unless you're going to stay out there permanently,' he shouted back.

'I just might,' I replied sulkily.

'You've got to swim back,' he chuckled, moving towards the shore with confident strokes.

'Don't leave me out here, Nick!' I cried anxiously. He didn't answer. 'Well that's very nice,' I said to myself.

Taking a deep breath I jumped in. The shock of the water was like a cold slap, startling me, but helping to quell the still-smouldering remnants of desire. I guess it did the same for him. When I arrived at the shore he was pulling on his shorts and t-shirt. Shivering again, my teeth chattering, I dried myself, trying not to focus on the way his t-shirt clung to his damp chest muscles, the outline of his nipples against the material. He was annoyingly playful, tousling my hair and commenting on the ungainliness of my flamingo hop as I stood on one leg and dragged on my shorts.

'I'll get you warm soon enough,' he said, beckoning for me to follow him.

'Oh?' I was curious and a little disappointed as he

marched ahead of me through the forest and up a steep incline. My footwear was hardly suitable, but I followed anyway. From the top of the hill we looked down on the lake and then past it all the way to the ocean. The panorama was breathtaking, everything baking under the wide sky, quiet aside from the birdcalls and strangely still. I listened for the breeze through the trees, but it was absent. Even the air felt dryer up here. Words would break the moment and so we discarded them, watching the tiny speckles moving like ants across the distant white sand below us as we sat like Gods upon our pedestal.

9

KATE

I was seventeen when I first experienced a night terror, although they were not then what they are now.

The first one found me on a hot summer night when I woke suddenly believing that I had just seen a large snake slithering under my bed. It wasn't Sam who was lazy and preferred lounging on my shoulder with swirling eyes. Terrified, my heart pounding like a jack-hammer, I rushed through to my parents' room and started shouting loudly and probably incoherently, about a snake in my room. My father, woken from a deep sleep and flustered by my panic, grabbed a golf club and staggered bleary-eyed into my room.

Confusion descended. The room was cloaked in darkness until we turned on the light. How could I have seen a snake in such absence of light?

'It was just a dream Dad,' I said, feeling silly as realisation sunk in.

'You seemed so sure, Kate,' Dad answered, moving the curtain aside carefully with the club as I hid behind him.

'I know, but I'm not anymore.'

We dismissed the incident and returned to bed, relieved that there wasn't actually a serpent hiding under a bed in the house.

At first it seemed like an isolated experience, a crazy sort of dream which had continued for a while whilst I was waking. I fell back to sleep easily and peacefully and in the morning it seemed even more unreal. I could barely remember what had happened, although my parents reminded me and Dad kept his club out.

But over the months and especially since finishing school and contacting Deb and Nick I had begun to experience them more frequently.

'What's going on Kit?' Mum asked one afternoon, as she hung water colour paintings of Australian flora on the pale peach wall in the dining room, and I stood back gesturing so that she could get them straight.

I shrugged unconvincingly, half wishing that I could tell her the truth, but not yet ready to go down that path. 'I don't know, Mum,' I lied, and Sam hissed. But in dreams, my guilt could not be repressed and it found expression in the darkest hours of night, in wild panic and bizarre sleep-dances. Nick's parting words hadn't helped.

'Maybe it's Uni,' Mum guessed, tapping the hook into a different spot. 'All the excitement of finishing school and starting something new.' Night terrors in adults are usually associated with trauma but excitement was a much nicer explanation.

'I'm sorry if they scare you, Mum.' Last night I'd leapt out of bed screaming in panic, at what I could no longer remember, but as I came to I'd hated myself at the sight of her drawn face, and tried to get her out of my room before she noticed just how badly I was shaking. I'd lain in bed afraid to sleep, overwhelmed by frustration and for several minutes I had trembled uncontrollably.

'It's not so bad now, Kit,' she said, stepping down off the small ladder and interrupting my reverie. 'In the beginning it was frightening. I just want you to be happy.' She was no stranger to nightmares, had hoped that world would not find me.

We admired the paintings. 'Beautiful, aren't they?' she asked.

But not all of the experiences I had *were* terrifying. Some were simply strange. Sometimes I thought I was awake when I was actually asleep. Wispy tendrils stretched down to me from the ceiling. Their presence made no sense. Where there should be only air I observed long grey shapes. They weren't static, although they didn't move very fast, just slowly radiating and then beckoning, like delicate wings. Eventually I realised that their presence was an indication that I was asleep. Sometimes I felt like I left my body behind, escaping with the essence of me, whatever that was, becoming lighter and lighter until slowly I became absorbed by the wisps and they became invisible to me because I was a part of them. And everything seemed simple and pure, glowing, bending and waving, slowly spiralling movement and swirling colours, the meaning unimportant.

But more often than not I went to a darker place and my mind held onto a sense of violence which seemed to pervade the encounter – the barrel of a gun, cold steel pressed against my forehead, about to go off. Ominously quick snakes or spiders slipping down towards me from the ceiling. A sense of terror, and of evil which left me nauseous on waking.

I felt haunted by this peculiar twilight world even though recalling my experiences with any degree of accuracy was almost impossible. Within moments of waking the memory faded. Usually only the red sense of persecution, of blood and death, of peril lingered.

One day I called Deb and asked her about them.

'I don't know,' she said. 'I had some really vivid, unsettling dreams while I was pregnant, but that's it and nothing like you've described. Could they be stress-related?'

'Nick mentioned something about weird dreams in his family,' I replied, noticing the change in the quality of the silence as I mentioned him.

She huffed. 'If that's the case, it's only one of *many* peculiarities in his family!' Her voice softened as she spoke again. 'His brother Daniel had problems, Kate. Depression … and drugs. He was only young, but obviously his issues were serious … I mean, to kill himself …'

'Must have been,' I agreed, wondering what it was that had been bad enough to push him to that point.

'They used to lock him in his room.'

'Seriously?' I asked, shocked. 'That doesn't sound good.'

'I think it was like a suicide-watch thing, so don't think too badly of them. I did, but now that I'm a mother I understand it a little more. You'll do crazy things to try and keep your kids safe.'

'I'll take your word for it, because it does sound a little extreme to me. I mean, surely there were other options?'

She hesitated. 'His family was very private. I don't think they would have turned to an outsider for help.'

'It's a pity they didn't, I guess.'

'Maybe,' she agreed. 'They were very influential, but they were seriously strange. There were *always* lots of rumours about them. Some said that it was thanks to the Edwards family that Three Kings had even made it into the twentieth century. That they were the main benefactors of the place. I think that's definitely possible. I mean the place just didn't make any sense.'

'Oh?'

She laughed. 'You'd have to go there to know what I mean, Kate. It sort of just existed but with very few actual businesses, and most people rented homes through a real estate agency. There was hardly ever any property for sale. It doesn't make any sense that it would have been viable, by any stretch of the imagination. Some of the rumours were just plain crazy. Who knows, maybe they even started some of them, sometimes it's the best way to hide the truth.'

'In plain sight, you mean?'

'Who knows? I mean, there were some which definitely had no foundation. At school, some of the kids said they were aliens and responsible for the red tide we experienced.'

'Red tide?'

'It was just the result of algal blooms, unpleasant freaky red water, like blood, but a natural phenomenon, nothing more. It only happened once in the time I lived there. Someone said they'd heard his mum chanting in a strange language as they passed their house, but that would have been impossible. Their house was like a fortress and it was miles away from where the rest of us lived. No, it was just the usual teenage garbage, kids feeding off each other. The Edwards family were really well respected on the one hand, but on the other hand people recognised that something wasn't quite right about them and feared them. I did too.'

I had recognised the same about Nick already, the not quite definable difference. We feared what we didn't understand. 'Respect and fear go hand in hand,' I said.

She thought for a moment, 'Nick was a closed book in a lot of ways. I knew there wasn't a lot of love lost between him and his parents, but he never really told me much about the issues Daniel was experiencing in the lead up to his death.' She seemed to reflect. 'Maybe he wasn't at liberty to discuss it. Anyway, he never mentioned strange dreams.'

We ended the conversation and I reflected on the history of my own sleep issues. When I was a child I used to sleepwalk on occasion. Mum would find me sitting fully clothed on the toilet mumbling to myself, or eating pickled cucumbers from the fridge, something I still enjoyed, and gently urge me back to bed. I'd wake with the taste of vinegar in my mouth but would rarely remember any of it. Maybe it was a precursor, but the terror and panic my unconscious now embraced had not been part of it.

Sometimes when night terrors recurred night after night for a period of time I was filled with unease as I drifted off to sleep. But in the mornings as sunshine filled my room and the sheer drapes billowed in the breeze the feeling usually evaporated.

Occasionally the feeling of being haunted would linger. The sense that life was a little off-kilter, just not quite as it seemed, that maybe what I had always taken for granted was actually not quite so.

10

DEB AND NICK

After a time we reluctantly headed down the hill. I was the first to speak. 'Whereabouts do you live, Nick?'

'Three Kings, but not in the village, like you,' he replied, moving through the foliage ahead of me. 'A little further on, along the top of the bluff. There are quite a few houses out there.'

'Oh?'

'It's just residential,' he added.

'Maybe I'll get out there one day.' He said nothing.

After a while I prompted him. 'What about siblings?'

'Two brothers. One younger, one older.'

'And they still live here?'

'Yes. Daniel, the younger, is here most of the time. He's musical, kind of a prodigy. He's tutored at home. Brendan is here sometimes. He works with my father.'

'Oh … and you all get along?'

He stopped suddenly and turned. 'Surely you don't want to hear about my family, Deb.' His voice had grown cold.

I flushed, uncomfortable at his tone, but refused to be shut down. 'Why not? You asked me about mine.'

He shook his head and marched off again. I struggled to keep up with him. 'They're up themselves.'

'We're not exactly the Brady bunch!'

He beat a path through the bush vigorously. We walked for a while in silence, but finally he relented, slowing down and letting me catch up. 'My folks are difficult Deb, and I don't like to talk about them.' He shrugged. 'They both come from privileged, extremely protective backgrounds and they've never known any differently. I guess neither have I, but the difference is that I want to live in the real world, discover it at least, and know that there is a difference.' I considered his Harley Davidson and wondered whether he realised the potential sacrifices the *real world* might demand of him.

'So they don't understand the appeal?'

'No. They don't understand why I would want anything different. I need depth in my life. I want to know what rough feels like, even if it is so that I can appreciate the smooth.' He stopped, realising I needed to rest. I leaned against a tree.

'We're all unique,' I panted, thankful for the respite and noticing that he was also perspiring. His face was slightly flushed under the tan and tiny beads of sweat trickled down his forehead.

He snorted. 'We've always revolved around them, marched to their drum, no questions permitted. It's so ingrained in them. I think they're genuinely taken aback that I want to do my own thing.'

'Parents have set ideas about how they want their kids to turn out. At least they care enough to want something good for you, maybe they don't want you to get hurt.'

His laugh was short and hollow this time, but he came to my side and leaned against the broad trunk next to me.

'What my parents want has very little to do with me, believe me. It's always about a bigger picture … or more accurately, their picture. That's the way it's always been.' He thought for a while. 'I was tutored until I was twelve, just like Brendan, cut off from the world. But my grandfather insisted they send me to a 'normal school' when I got to secondary level. It wasn't an option for Daniel, wouldn't have met his needs, but he threatened to change the conditions of the family trust unless they sent me. My folks gave in grudgingly, but they hate outside influences and my grandfather isn't around anymore.'

'They can't keep you protected from life forever,' I said, noticing the way his posture had changed. The tension in his muscular frame made him look a little menacing.

'No, maybe not, but they would like to try. They've got my life all laid out.'

I peeled bark off a tree and wondered what it would be like to fall into a niche, rather than have to search for one. Would it be a luxury or an affliction I would have to bear? I had to admit I wouldn't mind the opportunity to find out.

He stretched and exhaled, suddenly conscious of the stiffness across his shoulders and forcing himself to relax. His face lightened and then immediately darkened. 'I want to fly, but they won't hear of it.'

'They won't be able to stop you Nick. You'll be eighteen soon.'

His sigh was deep. 'They have ways and means. You would be surprised at the lengths they would go to.' He snapped a twig, picked up another. 'Unfortunately I'm used to a certain way of life and they know that. It's given them power over me in the past. I've got to accept that I can't have everything my way, that's all.' His eyes were green again, hypnotic spirals sinking into me, and his voice was slow and deep, the words carefully pronounced. 'I want everything, Deb.'

My chest tightened. He was speaking about more than what related to his parents. I tore my eyes away from his.

'Maybe that's the first lesson for me,' he said. 'It doesn't work that way!'

'No, maybe not.' I stared doggedly at the entangled, twisted forest, chaotic but beautiful.

'You see. I knew this would happen. I'm going on and on about them and I didn't want that.' I turned to face him, noticing his frustration giving way to tenderness.

'Are *you* okay, Deb?'

'I was just thinking about my father. Your parents show too much interest. My father shows none. I don't know which is worse. I'm sure he loves us, but it would be nice if he showed it once in a while.'

His hand found my shoulder, a reassuring squeeze, nothing romantic. 'He's crazy. You're beautiful and sweet and very special and he's an idiot for not telling you that!'

I smiled up at him.

'I mean it,' he said, looking at me earnestly. 'Anyway, let's forget them, all of them. For now at least. Surely we have something better to talk about than the failings of our parents!' He began to move again and I followed.

'Food ...' he said suddenly.

'Food?'

'Are you hungry?'

'Actually, I'm completely famished!' My stomach growled loudly, awakened and eager to make its presence known.

'Good.'

We exited the trees near to the more populated area of the lake. Appetising aromas came to us from a rustic café where we ordered sandwiches and chocolate milkshakes, hungrily filling the void created by swimming and our earlier exertions. The sadness of family was forgotten for the moment.

Afterwards we headed back to the beach, unburdened

and close for a short while. George was still there, but alone.

'You've been gone a while,' he said, suspicious as he noticed my bright eyes and flushed cheeks. Nick wandered off.

'We grabbed some lunch after we swam at the lake. It's beautiful up there.' I felt awkward, like I was hiding something, although I wasn't, not really.

George eyed me up and down. 'Great, well I'm glad you had fun.' He seemed resentful.

'Where's Michelle?' I asked.

'She had to go, something she had to get to.' He averted his gaze and I felt a wave of pity for him.

'Anyway, I was just about to leave,' he said. He threw the last of his things into a beach bag.

'Okay, me too.' We waved to Nick who seemed absorbed in conversation with someone down on the beach and only raised a hand absentmindedly in return. After a moment he wandered further away with his companion.

'That's his older brother,' George volunteered.

'Oh?' I answered. It was hard to make out details, but his brother was as broad and tall as him.

They continued to walk away from us, the world around them forgotten, and I felt a sinking sensation. Our kiss was definitely a bigger deal to me than to him.

George knew me well. In the face of my self-doubt he seemed to release some of his own. He flung his arm around my shoulders, pulling me to him roughly so that we did a sort of lop-sided walk up the beach.

'You like him a lot, don't you?'

'I do,' I conceded, realising that if I wasn't going to let on to George about how I felt, that there really wasn't anyone else I could tell. 'He's special, so strong and confident, but sort of vulnerable too ...'

'I guess his looks have nothing to do with it?' he laughed.

'Course not,' I lied with a smirk.

'Vulnerable, how?'

'He's like a little boy when he talks about his family. Brave, but still searching for their acceptance.'

'Yeah – it's weird seeing him the way we do, because I think his reality is mostly lived in a very different world. That's what I've heard anyway. We only see him in this setting. The life he has here, down on the beach, maybe that's his escape for a time from the continual expectations at home. He can fantasize when he's away from there, pretend, but at the end of the day he goes back.'

He looked across to where Nick now stood with his brother in the distance.

'Why do you think he didn't introduce us to his brother?' he asked.

I shrugged. 'He likes to keep family stuff separate, because he's unhappy at home. He doesn't want that to ruin ... taint how he feels here with us.'

'Or maybe,' he added tantalisingly, 'he doesn't want you to freak out when you see him and his brother together!'

'What does that mean?'

'There's a striking genetic similarity. Definitely no mistaking they're brothers. It's the eyes. I'm sure you noticed his.'

'Well, yes, of course.' They were rather startling.

'They're exactly the same,' he said. 'Unlikely as that may seem.' It did seem unlikely, although if they were just plain blue or brown, we wouldn't be having this conversation.

'Well, they *are* related. Like you said, it just comes down to genetics.'

'You should watch yourself with him, you could get hurt.' Worry crossed his forehead as he verbalised my own fears. He screwed up his mouth indecisively. Short of locking me in my bedroom, I was growing up and there was nothing he could do about it.

'Maybe,' I allowed.

'What does all this mean if you start seeing him?'

'You're thinking too far ahead, George. You don't *have to* introduce your family before you've even had a date!' I tried to sound light-hearted, noncommittal, but he was right. Maybe I was jumping in too fast, forgetting that it was gravity that kept my feet on the ground.

'Love is meant to be spontaneous, led by your heart, not your head!' Of course, that's probably also why there were so many hurt people in the world. I kicked the sand as I walked.

'... and your eyes,' he returned curtly.

'Yes, well I'm not going to say that I wasn't struck by his hot body when I first saw him.'

'A bit shallow don't you think? Just like all the others out there struck by the very same thing.' He sounded resentful. 'The rest of us are somewhat dismal in comparison!'

'Give it a rest George.' I nudged him in the ribs. 'You're fishing for compliments!'

'I'm not joking.' And he wasn't. 'Those three have a 'following' in this place. Three brothers all so attractive to the opposite sex, like nectar to bees! It's unnatural.' He was truly jealous. 'I'm sure it'll get them into trouble,' he added, sulkily.

I pushed him away, a little irritated. 'Probably,' I said.

He noticed my despondency. 'Sorry.'

'You sure know how to dampen a girl's spirits, George!'

'I'm just worried that he's the wrong guy for you. It's too easy for him, that's all.'

I rolled my eyes. 'Not everything is easy for him.'

'But women are.'

'... and of course nothing is coloured for you today by

your failure with Michelle,' I said, my voice taking on a bitchy tone I immediately regretted.

'Not that you've asked.' He spoke quietly.

'Sorry George. Really, I am.' We'd looked out for each other since our folks had divorced, providing comfort when we needed it. He was still looking out for me.

'I love you. I know you want the best for me.' I gave him a tight hug and he didn't resist me. 'And maybe you're right.'

11

KATE

A scorching February arrived. Hot dry winds blew relentless desert heat across the cracked ground and trees wilted in the parched parks.

'Only three days to go, Kit-Kat,' Mum said. Her sewing machine buzzed as she fed strips of floral material under its vigorous feet. Summer holidays were over. I looked down at my hands. The nails were unattractive, like well-chewed mango pips. I hid them in a fist. I was excited, but nervous too. Still, I had to stop biting my nails. Adults didn't bite their nails, did they?

'Are you counting down, Mum? Can't wait to get rid of me?' I passed her a piece of material from the pile of similarly-patterned fabric at her elbow.

'Course not, but it's so exciting. You are *so* lucky. I would have given my eye-teeth to do what you're doing.' Her eyes sparkled.

'What, to tread in the footsteps of Luca Salvatore?' My tone was a little on the sarcastic side.

'Don't be cheeky, Kit!' Mum had every one of his many CDs in a neat stack next to her sewing machine and reminded now, she reached over and popped one into her CD player. Soon his satin voice eased itself over the top of too many violins and a light percussion. Luca Salvatore had attended the Conservatoire for a year or two before becoming one of the most commercially successful opera singers ever. Mums everywhere drooled over his bronzed body and slick image as he wandered golden beaches, singing love songs in his rich, and very smooth, tenor. Mum sewed and hummed, a small dreamy smile on her face. After a while she turned it up and I drifted away.

My father's spin on Uni was rather less optimistic.

'They'll fill your head with nonsense, Kate. Never had to face the reality of life outside their artificial academic environment.' He said it with a gruff voice, but I knew a little pride hid beneath.

Melbourne Conservatoire. I'd certainly have to work on my posture, no more hanging my head like I was afraid it would get lopped off if I straightened it. And I'd have to learn to show my teeth when I smiled, and my nails! I'd have to start snapping elastic bands around my wrist or something to stop biting them.

University was a colourful, noisy place inhabited by a wide range of interesting people. Hopefully it would be less restrictive than school with more encouragement to express creativity without inhibition, with artistic abandon. The main part of the Conservatoire was situated in what had once been a grand old house on the periphery of the university. It had been extensively renovated to suit the purposes of the music department.

Most of the practice rooms were located ten minutes' brisk walk from the main Conservatoire buildings, next to the open-air drama theatre. I often stopped on my way there for a few minutes to watch a rehearsal or a production. The kids were as funny as the performers. They responded with such honesty, leaping from their seats and pointing and shouting with unreserved glee, or indignation. *'He's behind you! No, not there! On the other side!'* Déjà vu. Sweet unambiguous childhood memories, chuckling from the back of your throat and living in the moment.

The practice block was made up of a number of small sound-proof rooms for piano or single instrument practice and four larger rooms for ensembles. Pass-cards were used to access the building.

There was also a theatre complex which stood in the centre of the campus, mainly for music performances and productions. The larger classical ensembles practiced there and master classes, in which experts in the field would guide and critique musicians in their performance in a relatively public forum, were often held there too.

The Jazz department was exiled to an ugly, flat modern building and had its own rooms which vibrated to a cacophony of sounds. Saxophones and trumpets, trombones and bass guitars played alongside thumping piano in wild, vibrant improvisations and walking past without nodding or tapping along to something was impossible.

I was enrolled in a Bachelor of Music. Piano performance was my major and saxophone my second instrument. I wasn't used to the crowds and the jostling after my quiet holiday. Everything seemed so loud and busy. Thousands of students roamed the campus. Postgrads sat with heads together engaged in deep and meaningful discussions while lovers engaged in slow sensual embraces in the midst of the hastening throng. People were everywhere, on the lawns, in the canteen, on corridors. Toilets flushed and doors banged, someone shouted and a boy in a Rasta-hat played guitar, oblivious.

I felt anonymous, melting into the background noise, observing my surroundings with little returned scrutiny. There were others like me, but mostly people hung out in groups. Many were tethered to technological devices, multitasking, fingers moving in a blur. Laughter drifted across quads, intermingled with the sounds of frenetic conversation, friends catching up after long holidays. No-one asked me my business, and at lunch time I sat alone and lonely, in one of the few secluded spots, self-consciously eating my sandwich, messaging school friends who had scattered far and wide, and regularly shrugging off Sam who was burrowing down so low I was sure that he would slither out of my shoe, a happy camper. As soon as I had my schedule for the next day and knew where I needed to be, I beat a hasty retreat home. Sam 1, Kate 0.

As the weeks passed my self-consciousness lessened. Sam backed off a bit. I became acquainted with a couple of the other first year music students. We came from a variety of backgrounds. Nishlyn was an international student, a talented jazz pianist from India. He had the longest fingers I had ever seen and the whitest smile and his hair was short and black and gelled to within an inch of its life. Lara was a classical clarinettist on a scholarship and we were all in awe of her talent, although she was unassuming, neat and a little mousy-looking.

We were deep in discussion one afternoon as we departed from the practice block, when a voice called out to me.

'Kate.' I jumped in surprise. A face from the past. Madison Andrews, tall and lithe with the face of a model, oval and pale with hazel eyes and pouty lips. I knew her from school, a fellow musician a couple of years ahead of me. 'Mads … wow, hi, how are you?'

'I should ask how *you* are, how you're settling in.' She smiled broadly and then spontaneously grabbed me in a bear

hug and swung me around, her brilliant tie-dyed scarf flapping in my face as she did so. Laughing, she dumped me unceremoniously on the ground.

Lara looked nervous. She rushed off to a tutorial with a
wave.

'This is Mitchell.' They had hair to match, a shaggy but-
tery blond, hers just a bit longer.

'Hi,' I said, greeting him shyly.

'Mitch is doing his masters, he's almost finished,' Mads
stated. She didn't need to tell me that it was a masters in music. He fit the stereotyped image of a certain type of muso
exactly. Lean build, a little too skinny, with a jagged dirty-
blond haircut, ripped black top, tight jeans and lots of tattoos
and piercings. Not the type Mum would want you to bring
home, but the sort who drew eyes, with his easy swagger
and flippant smile.

'How come I haven't seen you around, Mads?' I asked,
trying to ignore the way Mitchell was sizing me up, but cursing the fact that I'd chosen today to wear my nice new jeans
and trainers which were still so white they hurt the eyes. I
stepped on one shoe and then the other, but dirt refused to
stick.

'Mitch's band was on tour, we've just got back,' she explained. Suddenly the groups of girls loitering nearby, hands
covering mouths, whispering and giggling like schoolgirls
made sense. I'd thought it was my shoes. This was Mitchell
Eli, local Rock God, lead singer and keyboard player in a
jazz-rock-fusion band called *Hot*. The name said a lot about
the egos of those in the band. There were posters all over
campus, good-looking guys in tight clothes.

Mads linked arms with him possessively like I was some
sort of threat. I looked around.

'Err, well I'd better go,' I said, suddenly feeling even more awkward, 'another class.' I gestured in the vague direction of the auditorium and stepped back.

'It was good to see you, Kate, we should catch up sometime.' Mitchell's attention was wandering and she looked anxious as he noticed the girls.

'That would be good Mads. Nice to meet you, Mitchell.' He winked at me and I blushed involuntarily. I had already decided that he was a creep.

Kristina, my piano teacher, was waiting for me. She checked her watch as I walked in.

'I'm so sorry, am I late?'

'Almost. I'm used to *you* waiting, I suppose.' Her smile was gentle as I sat down at the piano.

I was a little fish at the conservatoire. Maybe not even a fish, more like two-millimetre plankton in a very large pond. And there were plenty of tuna around and even the odd whale. At school music had made me special, but here everyone was talented, some especially so. I tried to shrug off my insecurity, to use every opportunity to learn and grow, to understand what I was up against and address that constructively. It mattered more on some days than others that I couldn't play the opening of a Rachmaninoff concerto without music after listening to it once, or that my improvisations on the sax were more like a strangled rooster than Charlie Parker.

Life was a competition and I was going to have to get used to it.

12

DEB AND NICK

'No-one knows where they are Deb … overseas somewhere probably. They do this regularly. Their parents take them along when their father goes away on business.' George was exasperated with me, but still trying to be patient. At least he didn't say, 'I told you so.'

Nick was gone, without so much as a backwards glance, a 'thanks for the kiss, but you don't do it for me.'

In the months since my parents' separation and subsequent divorce, George and I had clung to each other like near-drowning swimmers, taking it in turns to breathe. He hated seeing me sad.

I was such a basket case. An empty disillusioned space had clawed its way into my heart in the wake of my father leaving. His easy forgetfulness had turned my sense of validity and self-worth to slush.

Grieving at the loss of the father I had never really had, but wanted, I was searching for someone to fill the void, someone extraordinary. I wanted love. I wanted to love. I wanted to feel an unspeakable connection, to know safety. I wanted a bond that would never be broken. But deep down I knew that the fairy tale I dreamed of was so far removed from reality that my search could only ever reinforce what could not be. George was right, I *was* unsophisticated.

July came with unsettling winds and I turned seventeen. We celebrated quietly at home with a couple of my school friends. Anna was pretty in a homely way, but her personality made her beautiful. She smiled easily with deep dimples in rosy cheeks and she couldn't be unkind if she tried. Elizabeth was tall and quiet, with straight black hair and a long face. She wore rectangular glasses and looked as studious as she was.

'The table looks lovely,' Anna said to Mum, after she'd handed me a small gift wrapped in bright paper.

'Oh, it was all George,' Mum replied and George nearly collapsed from embarrassment. We all turned to him in surprise.

'Err, well, Mum got the stuff, I just laid it out.' He fiddled with a napkin.

'And who taught you to turn the serviettes into birds?' Elizabeth giggled.

'Read about it somewhere,' he mumbled. Anna lifted one and started to examine it and suddenly he seemed reassured. 'You do it like this,' he said unfolding and refolding, suddenly proud of himself. I winked at Elizabeth.

'George, can you take out the prawns?' Mum called as she turned the tap on with her elbow like a surgeon. An alien had possessed the body of my brother this evening. He was not one to assist in the kitchen. His repertoire was usually limited to warming food in the microwave, or take-out. On very odd occasions he had been known to boil an egg.

He grabbed an oven mitt and I noticed him quickly snatch a glance at Anna to make sure she was watching. That explained the current state of affairs anyway.

We ate grilled prawns followed by baked salmon and finally a completely decadent chocolate cheesecake which Mum had ordered for the occasion.

George gazed at Anna who giggled every time he said anything while Elizabeth and I rolled our eyes and pretended our napkins were love-birds and made kissing sounds. Mum ignored our childish antics and escaped to her room as soon as dinner was over. We moved to the lounge and watched a movie. Anna and George sat side by side with their legs touching while Elizabeth and I shared a sofa and blanket, munching our way through enough chocolate to ensure we would never again be described as athletic. When he thought no-one would notice George awkwardly slipped his arm around Anna's shoulders. A bubble of maniacal laughter threatened, but I bit my tongue and forced myself to focus on the screen.

Eventually George took the girls home and I headed off to bed, wondering whether he would get lucky.

Sitting on my pillow was a tiny black box. I wondered whether Mum had placed it there, although that seemed unlikely. She'd already presented me with expensive perfume I knew she couldn't afford. Picking it up I examined it. A small note was folded inside.

'Deb, I've missed your smile. Happy birthday, Nick.'

A silly, silly grin lit up my face. 'You're a complete imbecile Deb,' I whispered to myself, relieved, happy even.

'A slow learner,' I added to no-one.

Throwing caution to the fairies, I rushed to the window and looked out. The night was still and black, except for the distant crash of the ocean.

'This is crazy!' I thought.

'You're too smooth, Nicholas Edwards,' I called into the darkness.

'Where are you Nick?' I murmured. There was no answer and I closed the window.

Nestled inside the box on soft white tissue paper was a

small platinum angel on a delicate chain. Tiny diamonds glittered across its lustrous surface. It was expensive. It would require explaining. I slipped it on. The cold heavy presence of the metal felt solid and reassuring around my neck and I fell asleep with it nestled against my skin, a small smile on my face. Somewhere, even if for only a moment, he had thought of me.

13

KATE

In breaks between lectures and other classes, the air-conditioned practice block was a welcome escape. I knew the route to the practice rooms well. Along the main campus lane and then left down a narrow, shady road where the trees reached inwards and knit together like a leafy jumper creating a tunnel, past the amphitheatre to the long rectangular block on the right.

Almost as predictable as my route was the presence of the boy leaning against one of the beautiful old gnarled trees. He looked about twenty, with interesting hair, short on the sides and longer on top with a cow-lick that made it stand up straight where it probably should have fallen forward. I empathised. He dressed casually in the nondescript manner of many students, but there was something about the way his jeans hung on his hips and his t-shirt pulled across his chest that drew your attention. Tanned leather straps wound around his left wrist instead of a watch, and the edge of a tattoo showed where his sleeve ended.

He seemed pensive, focussed on the hillside park area which ran down the other side of the small road and which was populated by hundreds of students. Some ate, others lay on the grass, dozing after a late night, some couples kissed and still others sat in circles talking and laughing. A few read alone.

Despite his relaxed stance, his body seemed tense and vigilant. I wondered what he was observing or seeking, whether anyone else noticed his regular appearance there, or cared. Imitating James Dean for long periods of time was not illegal after all. Maybe if I moved closer I would see a hat on the ground nearby, half filled with coins, or maybe he was a stalker and keeping my distance was wise.

The constancy of his presence seemed strange, suspicious even. I wondered how many hours a day he stood there, how many of his lectures he was actually getting to and what on earth could be so interesting. Perhaps he was a philosophy major. It was none of my business.

As I turned down the hill on this particular day, the knobbly roots which grew through the road conspired against me and grabbed an ankle. I fell, hitting the ground hard. My teeth rattled and for a moment I felt nothing. Then my elbow started to sting and my wrist began to throb.

Intense violet irises gazed down at me as I struggled to make sense of a jumble of features. I closed my eyes and opened them and he moved around to face me.

'Are you okay?' He'd come to my assistance. I felt a silly rush of excitement.

'Err ...' Confident hands grasped me and helped me up, so that I was standing within inches of him. For a moment I forgot my injuries. Up close he did not disappoint, although his face seemed too solemn for someone still so young. A worry line indented his forehead in a way that seemed permanent. I wondered why. A few strands of hair had managed to fall forward, partially obscuring one eye. He brushed them away roughly.

'Thank you ... I'm fine,' I said, trying to salvage a little dignity, 'it just stings a little, but I don't think it's too bad.' My eyes watered, but I swallowed resolutely as he collected my books and picked up my bag for me.

'I'm such a klutz!' Why did I have to meet men like this in ways like this? It seemed so unfair. Now I could look forward to going home and reliving this at least a thousand times, with Sam my trusty companion, of course.

He didn't agree which was something at least. 'They need to fix up the road before someone sues them!' he stated, very seriously. I wanted to tell him that it was okay, that things really weren't that bad, were they? I would definitely recover. I kept my thoughts to myself.

'There you go.' He handed me my things and retreated before I could say anything more.

'Thanks again,' I called after him.

Continuing more tentatively down the road I noticed for the first time just how many roots broke the surface. I wouldn't be able to practice, but shutting myself in for a while would be a relief. Maybe I would recover my dignity, or maybe I could just crack my head on the piano a few times. It might help. When could I look forward to a little grace and elegance? I imagined, thanks to Sam, tripping as I walked onto stage, or slamming my fingers in the lid of a concert grand. A lifetime of humiliation waited.

As I neared the rooms I thought I saw him again, but further down in the actual park area, which made no sense. He had headed away from me in the opposite direction. Unless he could teleport, or I had a concussion, it was not him.

'You're an idiot,' I said to myself, and Sam quickly agreed. If I could only see the boy's face it would explain the mystery. Stopping I turned to look more carefully but as if sensing my scrutiny he wandered further away, leaving my curiosity unsatisfied.

I remained in the practice block for half an hour recovering my composure before walking towards the tram stop.

'Kate, stop!'

I did and turned around as Mads caught up to me.

'I've been calling and calling you,' she admonished hand on hip, but dropping it as I turned.

'What on earth happened to you?'

'I fell outside the practice rooms, hurt my wrist and elbow! Luckily some lovely man came to my rescue!'

'Poor girl. You're a bloody mess!' she laughed.

'Thanks a lot!'

'Really, there are easier ways to find a man!' Oh? I envied her knowledge.

'Seriously though,' she continued, examining my arm, 'they need to fix up the road, it's ridiculous. How many potholes and bumps are there? It's like Swiss cheese! They'll get sued soon!'

'That's what he said.'

'Anyway, I think you'll live.' She dropped my arm. 'I was looking for you. It's a good thing I spotted you. Mind you, I would have messaged you anyway. There's a room in the house if you want it, David's moved out.' Mads shared a large, old house with three others. 'I know you said you want to move out. It's so convenient, just a stroll to Uni, forget trams and trains and all that.'

'Sounds good.'

'Come over tomorrow afternoon and I'll show you around. You can meet everyone and decide what you want to do.'

'Okay.'

'I'll send you the address. We need another girl,' she said, already heading back in the direction she had come from.

'I'll be there Mads.' I waved to her as she headed off. 'See ya.'

My wounds weren't that bad, although you wouldn't have known it from the way Mum drowned me in disinfectant.

'Surely that's enough Mum,' I complained through gritted teeth, as we sat on the edge of the bath in her ensuite and she liberally poured the stuff over me.

'Well, you wouldn't want to get an infection,' she tutted.

'I don't think I'm going to get an infection, but I would like a little skin left on my arm,' I retorted, my discomfort making me ungrateful.

'Would you rather I didn't take an interest?' she asked defensively. We were heading into dangerous territory. I rolled my eyes, but not so that she could see.

After a few moments of silence, she started to pack everything away into the medicine cabinet.

'You need to look where you're going, Kit.'

'I know, Mum.' I didn't explain why I had been distracted.

I headed over to Mads' place the next afternoon after classes. The house was elevated from the pavement and loomed imposingly over me as I looked up at it. It was two-storied and old, in need of a bit of a touch-up and a lot of tender loving care, but that was the way with most of the homes rented out to students by landlords who often lived overseas.

I had no doubt that it was worth a fair bit. It was in a prime position near the university and the house itself was large and charming. The metal gate, set into the middle of a red brick retaining wall, squeaked and opened onto meandering stairs which led up through a reasonably well-tended garden to a plain white front door with a rectangle of stained glass in the top. A small, seventies-style, concrete swimming pool in a roughly oval shape, in need of resurfacing and with a rusty slide on the far side, was set into a wedge of flat land to the left of the stairs. Although it needed some attention, the pale blue water looked inviting.

I rang the doorbell and waited as a series of seemingly endless chimes sounded.

'Allo,' came a soft French voice as the door opened. A slightly built man in his mid to late twenties, no taller than me, with a tan complexion and a placid face framed by prematurely thinning dark hair, looked out expectantly.

'This is Pierre,' Mads sang exuberantly, clattering down the stairs before I could say a word, 'he's a French lecturer … from Mauritius though, not France.' She clapped him on the back, nearly sending him out of the door.

'Hi, Kate,' I said, introducing myself as I wondered whether he needed assistance. Recovering quickly he extended a cool hand.

'Welcome to our 'umble abode.' His voice was lilting and silky. 'I'm sure Mads weel show you ah-round. We are three boys 'ere but don't wohrree we know 'ow to look after owselves!'

'Actually, it's the guys who have to hassle me to do my chores! They do most of the work around here!' Mads laughed. I could believe it. 'They know what's good for them, don't you Pierre?'

He nodded passively, 'Of course.' I liked him instantly, and not just because he did the chores. I didn't know him, but I recognised an old soul.

The house was old, but appealing in its own way. There were stairs which led down underneath the house to a spa, and doors which opened out onto the slightly dilapidated, but still useable pool area. The available bedroom was on the ground floor. The carpet was a little musty and featured a

floral pattern Nanny would have loved, but it was a gener-
ous size with large windows letting in the light, and looked
out onto the overgrown garden.

'I'll take it Mads,' I decided impulsively, enjoying the
view of the scruffy plants outside the window. The rental
was almost affordable, I'd just have to make sure I got a job,
and I yearned for the independence.

'Excellent. I can't wait for you to move in.' She hugged me
briskly before dashing out of the door. The bronze in her kaf-
tan caught the light from the window and made her magical
for a moment.

'Anyway, I'm late. Late, late, late, but I'm very excited that
you're moving in. Love you. Bye,' she called, dashing off and
taking her magic with her.

'Bye then,' I said to the draft, closing the window and
looking around at the now still and empty room. For a short
while I felt excited and then I felt guilty. How would Mum
and Dad react?

I told them after dinner, tentatively, the steak I'd just eaten
sticking like an echidna in my throat. Mum's face fell immediately. Her chin quivered and I felt horrible.

'So soon, Kit?' I knew she was already blaming herself,
wondering what she had done wrong. *Nothing Mum, the
cuckoo has grown, and soon will be flown.*

I'd been at home for less than six months. Life was calmer
now that there was less tension between my parents, but it
was still difficult. Less tension didn't mean no tension, and
sometimes the most innocent remark, in an otherwise peaceful moment, triggered unexpected volatility. The threat of
disaster was always simmering, and I tread carefully, trying
to maintain the fragile harmony but it wasn't my place, not
anymore. They needed to work things out.

'It's not far, Mum,' I reassured her. 'I'll come and visit you often. You can come and see me too.'

Her attempt at a smile meant a lot. I had expected defensiveness to mask her pain. After all the years I'd been away at school, after all of the pain, Mum and Dad cursing each other, things were a fraction easier now and maybe they had been hoping that I would stick around for a while.

'It's not you Mum, or Dad,' I explained, looking across at him and squeezing his hand. He sat very straight in his chair, his face indecipherable, everything just where it should be. I didn't need their approval, of course, but I'd feel better if I had it.

'We know Kit, honestly,' Mum answered, astonishing me with her quiet acceptance.

'It makes sense Mum. The travel and ...'

'It will be good for you ... I know.' She blinked and one tear slipped silently down her cheek. Swallowing hard she managed to hold back the others. I felt wretched, my hands moved to my mouth.

'I'm sorry Mum.'

We sat in silence for a while until Dad started tapping complex rhythms on the table absentmindedly. It became so annoying that neither Mum nor I could dwell on sadness. Maybe that was the point.

'Dad ...' I began, about to tell him to quit it in the nicest way possible. I didn't swear, couldn't even imagine it in my parents' vicinity. There were certainly instances when the air around Sam was pretty blue, but well, that was between him and me.

'Of course we'll still give you your allowance,' my father said slyly, effectively deflecting my irritation with a knowing grin.

I considered the rental. 'Err, thanks Dad that *would* be helpful. I want to look for a job as soon as I can so that you don't have to worry though.'

'Let us do this one thing for you, Kate.' I got it then, the unspoken message behind his words. *Don't take everything, not this soon.* An allowance tethered me to them somewhat and they needed that right now. They were afraid.

I nodded. 'Yes, of course. I appreciate it.'

'When will you go?' he asked.

'I can move in this weekend. The room is vacant already.' My father gave my mother a grim smile. They'd survived before, they would do it again. This time even I thought things might be better. Now there was a breath of fragile hope, enough to believe in maybe. My mother sighed and stood. She walked around to me and kissed my forehead.

'You're our life, Kit-Kat. We'll miss you,' she whispered.

'I know Mum. I love you.' I turned and held her tightly, her cheek warm and damp against mine.

Dad and I remained at the table, examining the intricacies of the mahogany wood grain. It was beautiful and drew your hands to stroke its smooth sensual surface. It was okay that he didn't say anything. After a while I offered him a coffee.

14

DEB AND NICK

Days passed and I heard nothing more from Nick. October arrived and with it heat, flies and the last term of school. The days were long and dull. Minutes ticked by slowly in the hot, stuffy classrooms; the air-conditioners strained and wheezed inefficiently in the muggy air. Momentum built through interminable lessons as we waited impatiently for the bell to ring so that we could finally hurtle out into the heavy air, onto the sand and finally into the cool water.

And then after days of endless pale blue sky, melting sidewalks and wilting plants, Nick reappeared on the beach. At first he was nothing more than a mirage, a shimmering image on the sand bathed in bright sunlight. I had forgotten his size and his vitality, the vividness of his eyes, but my breath caught only for a moment, before I composed myself, feigning a level of indifference and forcing myself to remain rooted. He didn't come over and I tried not to look at him but my hand drifted automatically to the necklace I wore under my uniform.

Anna nudged my arm, distracting me. We were sitting in the thin shade of a spindly tree.

'Isn't that Nicholas Edwards?' she asked innocently, forcing me to look over to where he stood.

'Looks like it,' I said, pretending disinterest and keeping

my eyes focussed on my book.

'I wonder where they've been this time. He looks good, doesn't he?' I wished she would move her hand from her brow, make her stare less obvious.

'Mmm ...' I didn't look up. She eyed me curiously and then snapped my book shut.

'What's up, Deb?'

'What do you mean?' I couldn't help the defensiveness as I ruffled pages trying to find my place again.

'You used to be friends. I would have thought you might have gone over to say hello, or something?'

I took a breath and tried to speak calmly, but I couldn't shake the wariness in my voice. 'We were just acquaintances and he's been away for ages.'

'Okay then, whatever you say,' she said, hurt by my clipped tone. I felt guilty.

'I've got to go Deb.' She stood abruptly. 'It's getting late. I'll see you tomorrow.'

Throwing my book into my bag I stood. 'I didn't mean to be short with you Anna, sorry.'

'Has it got anything to do with this?' she asked, pointing towards the necklace I wore. I took the angel in my fingers and tucked it back into my top.

Did it? She hadn't been fooled by my lie. It was very definitely not a market trinket.

'It's okay Deb. Just remember, we're meant to be friends and what are friends for?'

'I know,' I answered, unsure how to explain that since my parents' split, except for George, my buffer against the world, I struggled to share my burdens with others.

'Tell George bye, I'll see him tomorrow.' She pulled me into a quick hug before leaving with the others and I finished packing up my things, suddenly feeling very exposed.

George was still somewhere out there on the slow swells but there were few bathers. It was time to go.

As I dusted sand from my legs, Nick looked across at me. We stared at each other for a long moment before he came over. As he neared I smiled tentatively.

'Deb,' he called.

'You've been doing some breaking and entering,' I said as he reached me, referring to the black box I'd found on my pillow. A small smile touched his lips, but didn't reach his eyes.

'Thanks for the birthday present,' I said, trying not to read anything into his reaction. 'It's beautiful … of course.'

'It looks good on you,' he answered, barely glancing at it, looking out at the waves instead.

'Would have been nice if you'd delivered it in person.' I hefted my bag onto my shoulder.

'Yes … but it wasn't possible, unfortunately.' I looked at him and then to the Three Kings who seemed to lean forward as if to hear our exchange.

'Oh?'

'Sorry, it's lame I know.' He looked ill at ease, shifting from one foot to the other and making minimal eye contact.

'So where have you been?' I asked, a little annoyed that I had to work so hard for information.

'Family crap, travelling with my father.'

'You've missed a lot of school.' It sounded petty, but I had to say something. I could see it meant nothing to him. He'd probably had a tutor.

'You look great.' He appraised me for a moment before drifting back to the sea. What mysteries floated out there?

'You too. You obviously didn't go anywhere cold,' I said, referring to his tan.

'Not for long, anyway.'

We both remained silent for an awkward moment before I started to turn, to walk away.

'I missed you Deb,' he blurted unexpectedly. My heart raced at his words, but at the same time I was afraid. Shut up, I wanted to shout but I didn't.

Instead, I let my bag drop to the sand again. 'Would have been nice if you'd called to let me know you were going away.'

His shrug was infuriating. 'It was all so sudden.'

'Surely you could have called from somewhere. Surely you could have found a moment to pick up a phone.' I cursed myself for letting go, for showing him that he had the power to injure me.

'I'm so sorry Deb. It's hard to explain.'

'Whatever … you're not obliged to explain to me anyway.' Bending down I picked up my bag more resolutely.

'I should have just stayed away from you in the first place.'

'Well, why didn't you then?'

He couldn't answer. 'We're going away for a while,' he said, running his hands through his hair and leaving it wild. He fidgeted, unsure of my reaction, a small rock suddenly in his hand. Luckily it wasn't in mine.

'Oh … what's the problem then?' I asked sarcastically.

He threw the rock and it landed with a thunk in the damp sand near the water.

'I have no choice.'

I shook my head. We always have choices, just not necessarily the ones we want. 'You've just got back …'

'We're going away for longer this time, six months, maybe a year. A different sort of trip. My folks have a catamaran. They want to sail around the world, a holiday. Pah!' He tried to smile, but it was more of a grimace. 'We're going to leave at the end of the year, immediately after my graduation.'

'Oh.' I wasn't sure what sort of answer he was expecting, what I could manage. A tangle of emotion gnawed away inside me, irritation, anger, frustration, but I also realised it wasn't only because of him. *I* needed to let him go.

'So, a family holiday. That's nice, I guess.' I remembered what he'd said about his relationship with his parents.

He remained silent, but staring at me with an intensity I did not understand. Not in the current context. This time I was the one to turn away to the ocean.

'How will you go, stuck with your folks in a confined space for that long?'

'It's going to be hard, hopefully we'll make it back alive.' His smile was crooked, maybe only half joking. 'It's something my folks have always wanted to do, and with me graduating, I guess they think we'll never do it as a family if we don't do it now. It's a while to go before we leave, but I wanted to tell you.'

'You wanted to prepare me.' I laughed wickedly, shaking my head. He was letting me down the nice way, or so he thought. But why the mixed messages, why send me the necklace after all of this time? It just wasn't fair.

I gazed back at the vastness of the ocean, tumultuous blue stretching out to touch the endless white horizon. The three grey men tutted to me. *'Let him go, girl.'*

'You should go.'

'Yes,' he said, reaching out to touch me for the first time, to stop me for a moment.

'Friends?' I looked down at his tanned fingers on my arm, my own clutching my bag straps rigidly. What was he asking of me?

'Will that make you feel better?' I asked, moving my arm, so that his fingers fell away. He froze.

It was only one kiss, I thought. One kiss. *Stop being so dramatic, Deb!*

'Thanks for telling me anyway, Nick.' Now my voice was deceptively cool, calm.

'But friends?' I said. 'I don't know.'

He looked at me sadly, but didn't speak.

'Friends would be a struggle for me right now to be honest.'

'I'm sorry Deb.' He looked down for a moment and then back at me

'Mum's home early tonight, I've got to go.' I flashed a brave smile before I turned and headed quickly across the sand. I didn't look back.

'I'll see you around Deb,' he called, but I did not reply.

As I walked up the road, I yanked off the necklace, almost throwing it to the ground. I wanted to scream and stamp my feet like a spoilt child. Why send it to me? Why raise my hopes? That was cruel. Just like going away and not bothering to call and then saying he'd missed me. Rejection stung, self-pity irritated my eyes, but I swallowed it down in a lump and continued to move.

'That you, Deb?' Mum called from the shower when I got home, slamming the door so hard the walls vibrated. I was so preoccupied I'd forgotten she would be there.

'Oops, yes Mum,' I answered. Marching to my room I closed the door more quietly. I returned the necklace to its box and placed it at the bottom of my jewellery case, determined that if I wasn't going to chuck it, I would at least avoid looking at it.

There was a soft knock on my door. 'You okay?' Mum poked her head into my room. She was still flushed and wrapped in her towel.

'Just one of those days, Mum. You know?' I folded my

arms behind my head and stared up at the ceiling.

'I know, Deb.' She stepped into the room and sat on the edge of the bed, her hands resting on my legs. 'Would a manicure help? I've got a great new colour, really bright, Fuchsia. You'll love it. And you got all the buffers and lotions from Elizabeth for your birthday. Let's have some girl time tonight.'

I sighed and tried to let Nick go. Girl stuff. That's definitely what I needed. Nice and safe, the greatest danger was getting a little polish on the bedspread. I could cope with that.

Days and then weeks passed, exams arrived and I forced myself to focus, committing myself to study groups with others so that I couldn't get out of it. I saw him occasionally down at the beach which was quiet at this time of year, a fleeting greeting and nothing more. Sometimes I saw him with other girls. I recognised the way they looked at him, the unveiled attraction, the adoration no different to my own and it made me sick.

In the quiet darkness of night when distractions were few I continued to irritate myself by thinking about him. Tortured memories of one sweet kiss, imagining what might have been, agonising before casting out what was futile.

One night at the end of term I woke with a start. My room was still and dark, only shadows made moving monsters on the walls as the trees outside swayed in a light breeze. Moving to the window I let in some fresh air. Someone was out there. A dark shape on the road. Nick. His face turned to me in the dim light. He made no move to beckon to me, just remained locked on my face, his eyes slightly radiant. A tiny shock of ecstasy radiated through me as I rushed recklessly to open the window further, to climb out, to run to him. But as I did he leaped onto his motorbike and with a thunder which broke up the night he roared away.

I stumbled back, the hyperactive air intruding on my turmoil, ruffling my hair, flipping and flapping papers, upsetting ornaments as the curtain caught them. I flopped back onto my bed. Black and white phantoms capered in wild chaos across my ceiling. I reached under my pillow to the tiny box I now kept there.

'Goodbye Nick,' I whispered.

15

KATE

Mum and Dad helped me pack, supplementing my meagre possessions with a toaster and kettle for my room. 'It's a house-warming gift, Kit,' Mum said, as I admired the matching pink set. She couldn't buy me rompers and booties anymore, but she was meeting her needs in other ways. In less than an hour we had carted my furniture, digital piano, computer and clothes into my new room. Soon I was unpacked and organised, my groceries stored away in the kitchen on shelves labelled with my name. Someone was organised, I suspected Pierre.

Four of us lived in the house. Mads and I were studying music, Pierre was a French lecturer and Francois (who was not French, despite the name) was studying a Bachelor of Science.

Francois and Pierre quickly became the siblings I had never had. The feeling was mutual. Pierre missed his family, and I reminded him of his sister who had moved to Spain to be closer to her Spanish husband's family. Francois was an only child like me.

'Play that sad one,' Francois said one night as he, Pierre and I sat sipping green tea from Pierre's dainty china mugs in my room. It had become a ritual, one which required the right tea, the right mugs and the right time.

'No, no, not sad tonight. Play Chopin, the waltz,' Pierre argued. The two of them had propped my pillows against the wall and were leaning back as though in a Turkish lounge. I played both, first the waltz so that Pierre would have the fortitude to listen to *Lost*, the one Francois loved, the one about a child facing darkness.

They were silent when I finished and then Francois spoke.

'You're going to be a superstar Kate, with the right management of course.' He wiggled his eyebrows and I laughed. 'We've got to get you on YouTube.'

I shrugged noncommittally, a little dubious about his judgement, although it was a nice compliment. We sat in companionable silence, the house dark and quiet around us, sipping. The only other sound in the room was the loud ticking of Francois' watch.

'Doesn't that irritate you?' Pierre asked eventually.

'It doesn't,' Francois replied unperturbed, and I giggled. They were lovers. Their names had started a conversation which had become increasingly guarded on the surface, increasingly tender and private underneath. They fit, like two pieces of the same jigsaw, and I saw that. But there were complications they did not speak of, and I didn't pry. I saw the expectation in the eyes of Francois' parents when they visited, understood the pressures placed on the shoulders of an only son.

'M n M' (which was how we referred to Mads and Mitchell) were out most evenings, often returning only as dawn slowly farewelled night. Sometimes they didn't return at all, choosing to head straight to university. Although Mitchell wasn't officially a member of our household and had an apartment of his own a few blocks away, he kept a toothbrush and clean underwear on the only neatish shelf in Mads' room.

Because of her insecurity about Mitchell's fidelity, Mads followed him to his performances, chewing her lower lip in frustration until it was almost shredded as she watched the exchanges between the girls who ogled him seductively and his reply, a suggestive grin, which made words unnecessary.

He performed five nights a week, surviving quite successfully on little sleep, but the impact on Mads was significant. She was slipping.

'Morning Mads.' I greeted her cheerfully, but she sat in a daze at the kitchen table, a pot of coffee in front of her. Her lips didn't seem to move as she mumbled an indecipherable reply.

'Have you even been to bed?' She had a recital at lunch time and should have been well rested this morning. Instead she looked like one of the living dead.

She shook her head and then seemed to regret it, touching it tenderly with her hand. 'No, but I'll be okay, just need to get some caffeine into me.'

'You need to eat and sleep. Here.' I shoved my bowl of cornflakes at her. 'Eat!'

Mads' father had abandoned both her and her mother when she was young. He had avoided all contact with her while remarrying and fathering several other children. Mads seemed intent on punishing herself for his disinterest, his lack of heart and cruelty.

She picked up the spoon reluctantly and began to eat. 'Will you have a chance to get a few hours' sleep?' I asked, serving myself more cornflakes.

'Nah, but I've done it before,' she said. 'I'll have a shower and I'll be fine. Stop fussing, Kate.' She was right. I was mothering her and she didn't want to be mothered. It wasn't my place to give her advice.

Mitchell was the centre of her universe, her sun. Sometimes he gave her life and sometimes he took it, but either way she revolved around him, continually abdicating her own interests for the sake of his. It was romantic, just not sensible.

He was talented and very ambitious, determined to pursue fame and fortune. I didn't think that Mads would remain a fixture in his rise to glory, but that was only my opinion. She was fun to have around, a good laugh, and a distraction when he needed it, but his commitment was to his art and his career. He enjoyed women indiscriminately, even flirting with me on occasion. My disinterest only further inflamed his pursuit. I still thought that he was a creep.

'Kit!' Mum had arrived, her voice shrill from the front door. She didn't bother to knock, just walked straight in.

'You're early, Mum,' I cried, rushing out into the entrance hall. Giving her a smacking kiss I ensured that she ventured no closer to the kitchen by steering her in the direction of my room. My mother would not appreciate the sight of Mads right now and I would be the one, not Mads, to receive endless unwarranted advice from her as a result.

'Here,' she said, thrusting a scruffy old bear at me.

'What's this?'

'Fritzy, of course,' she replied, as though that explained it.

'I know it's Fritzy, Mum, but what is he doing here?' He was *my* bear after all, left at home for good reason.

'I thought he'd bring you good luck.'

'Oh?' I examined him, but he remained unchanged and without a horse-shoe necklace or anything added. I'd had him since I was tiny and he'd been through a series of misadventures. He had been chewed up by the dog, who swallowed his lederhosen and expelled them in an interesting assortment of red and blue patchy poo, and he'd fallen into the toilet at Nanny's, after which Mum had washed him in disinfectant and knitted him a little red and green jumper and shorts which made him look a lot more cheerful than he should have been. Nothing could be done about the fur and he remained mangy.

'I don't know about luck, Mum.' Fritzy had really been rather unlucky.

'Well he's still around isn't he?'

'I guess so.'

'That's kind of a miracle isn't it?' We both looked at him with new-found respect.

'Sure is.'

'And you had him at the hospital when you were little and you pulled through pretty well.' Anxiety crossed her face, like she was suddenly worried I wouldn't realise his value, that he might be discarded on a Salvos pile or worse.

'He *is* a very precious bear Mum.' I squeezed her arm and then tucked Fritzy into my bag which was thankfully large. Still his head refused to stay inside and kept popping up as though insisting on a seat with a view.

'You ready?'

'I guess so.' I took a deep breath. 'Let's go.'

'You drive,' Mum said, 'it'll help you relax.' But looking at Mum I could not relax.

'I can't believe you're going to get your licence Kit.' Her eyes were an intense ball of emotion. Pride, nerves and sadness, the inevitable loss.

'Only if I pass, Mum,' I reminded her.

'Kit, Kit, don't have a fit!' Mum cheered as we arrived at the squat licensing office. It was just the two of us in the car, but I blushed all the same and my anxiety sky-rocketed.

As the examiner, a big, stern-looking man with small eyes behind rectangular glasses, and a mouth set in an unyielding line, beckoned to me, Mum grasped my hand and gave it a crushing squeeze between her cold ones.

'You'll be fine Kit-Kat, just remember the brake is the middle pedal.'

'I'll try Mum.' I smiled nervously, nursing my hand.

The examiner's severe demeanour and clipped instructions ensured that my grip on the wheel remained white-knuckled and stiff throughout the test. Sam nudged me to the point where I actually considered planting the car in a tree, but somehow I managed to force my attention back to the road and pass.

'Well done!' Mum exclaimed, rushing to clasp me in a tight hug.

'Thanks Mum,' I gasped.

'Ooh, you're so sweaty!' she said indelicately, releasing me quickly. I avoided a quick sniff under my arms.

'Well. It's all yours,' she sighed, handing me the keys to the little yellow hatchback, my belated eighteenth birthday present. She was getting a new car.

Contained excitement. I tried not to show too much of it outwardly, in case she feared it would result in carelessness. My smile only stretched halfway across my face, but I couldn't help my eyes. She was suddenly tentative, obvious reluctance marring her earlier exuberance.

For a moment she too struggled to assemble an appropriate expression, failing to hide the truth. Relief and pride crossed her face, a tiny unavoidable tear lurking at the corner of one eye. She tried not to blink. Mum was really trying. *I* felt like crying now.

'Drop me off at Dad's and you're on your own.' She had been preparing that statement for a while and she pulled it off well.

'Just be careful Kit,' she added nervously, as she opened

the door to get out.

'Of course Mum,' I replied, somewhat impatiently.

'I have to tell you that, I'm your mother.' She was suddenly terse. 'It's my job to worry.'

I felt bad. No-one worried about you like your mother. To see me driving off into the unknown inside a little tin can with wheels was tough for her. Her baby, racing off to join thousands of others on the roads, hurtling around at impossible speeds, all in different states of distraction.

I planted a big kiss on her lips and returned her earlier hug. 'I *will* be careful, Mum. You know that.'

'I know Kit. We're so proud of you.'

But as I carefully backed away my confidence evaporated. I looked around. Where did it go? I'd only just passed my driving test, first time! But suddenly I didn't know where to look or which levers were for the windscreen wipers or which for indicators. Anxiety churned bitterly and I forgot to check my blind-spot, nearly colliding with a truck. The driver flashed his lights and hooted at me angrily before finally thundering past. I crawled along timidly in the left lane, sitting as low as possible in my seat, hands so sweaty I feared they might slip from the wheel. Heads turned. *No, it's not the Queen everyone, it's Kate Richardson.* I avoided a royal wave to the curious. Even Sam was silent for a while.

16

DEB AND NICK

It was July and I had just turned eighteen when I saw him again. The timing wasn't great. I'd put a lot of hard work into my final year, redirected my energy. I still wasn't sure exactly what I wanted to do, but I wanted options. Now the final culmination of my effort was nearing.

Other things had changed. Mum was working long hours, but openly dating Mario, her boss. He was friendly and laid-back and didn't interfere with us, which earned him bonus points from me. Sometimes Mum invited him home for dinner and we'd eat well and drink a little wine. Happiness made her younger, more care-free. Her eyes sparkled in a way I had never seen and there were flowers in the house now, music sometimes and bottles of wine in the pantry cupboard for special occasions. She was having fun and being spoilt and adored and we loved Mario for that.

George wasn't around much. He was now a Commerce student, commuting over an hour each way to Uni, hoping to move into shared accommodation when he could afford it. He worried too much about Mum and me, about leaving us on our own. Reassurance that we would be fine meant nothing to him. He'd taken on Dad's role a long time ago.

I had dated a couple of guys, but nothing serious. They were nice enough, but seemed insubstantial, immature.

Their main focus was on getting drunk, or getting lucky, and I wasn't putting out, so they lost interest. To be honest I didn't really care. School was my priority.

Weekends I worked a shift on the checkout at our tiny local supermarket. It was tedious, but the money was okay and I was trying to save for a car. At the rate I was going I wasn't going to be buying it any time soon.

It was a busy Saturday morning when I looked up and saw him waiting one back in the queue, tanned and healthy. He looked more rugged than I remembered and his hair was lighter and longer than when I'd last seen him, but it was still unruly.

For a moment I froze, before letting my hair fall like a shroud around my face. It provided a convenient screen to hide behind. I wasn't sure what to say, given the awkwardness of our last exchange. Did I pretend he was forgotten? He moved a step closer as the customer in front of him moved forward to pay and I struggled to look up, to smile knowing that he could see my face. My neck felt rigor-mortis stiff as I tried to twist it in his direction. The dreaded flush of heat arrived, radiating through my body like steam was escaping from my pores. *'Piss off and die,'* I screamed angrily to myself, cursing the blush which made my emotions so easily readable by others as I fumbled with the groceries, my fingers like sausages as I scattered change.

'I'm so sorry,' I apologised, humiliated. At last the transaction was complete and the customer departed. My relief was short-lived.

Now I *had* to look up at the man I had ineffectively tried to banish from my dreams, the one who had continued to haunt my imagination.

He stood before me like some sort of apparition, like I'd stepped back into yesterday. For just a moment everything stopped. 'Hello,' seemed obvious, but didn't come to me. We took a moment to appraise each other, detecting changes, noticing the march of time. There were little lines at the sides of his mouth, like he'd grimaced once too often, and the stubble on his jaw looked darker and coarse. He was grown. A man. I wondered what he saw when he looked at me. Whether he noticed that my hair was longer, that my skin was paler, whether I was still athletic or rounder in places? I wondered what he was doing at my till.

Then we were back in the moment, the murmur and noises of the shop around us.

'What are you smiling at?' I asked.

'You,' he answered directly. 'I think you just made the supermarket a bit of extra profit!' I blushed at my incompetence.

'Sorry.' A troubled expression crossed his face. He placed the last of his items on the conveyer belt. 'I didn't mean to embarrass you. It's good to see you. You look great.'

'Yeah right, love the uniform!' Navy trousers and a turquoise top with three rocks on the pocket. Very original. I guess it could have been worse.

'Blue suits you!' Annoyingly I blushed again.

'You're looking good,' I said.

'Just need a haircut and I might start feeling semi-civilised again!' He ruffled his hair self-consciously and took another step closer. I could reach out and touch him if I wanted to. Of course I didn't, just breathed and focussed on the formation of something intelligible.

'It looks nice,' I managed.

'You think so?' I returned my gaze to the items he was purchasing. I could feel his eyes on me. Chocolate, one large bar of dairy-milk, two litre cola and multivitamins.

'You've got all of life's necessities here,' I said, packing them into a bag and trying not to drop anything.

'Yeah, well I've got to stock up on the basics.' His smile was casual, but his eyes weren't. I didn't know what they were, what the deepest shades of green hid, I was afraid to go there to the swirl and flickers within.

'Glad that you've got your priorities right,' I said, trying to keep things light, like I'd seen him yesterday and we were the friends we'd never been. 'How was your trip?' I faced the register.

'Hmm, let me see. Five of us who don't get on at the best of times, floating around in a sardine can in the middle of the ocean for almost ten months. I'll leave it to your imagination.'

'Sounds glorious.' I glanced at him for just a moment before I checked the total on the register. He hesitated, but unable to delay any longer, paid.

'I'll see you around, Deb.'

'Yep, see you,' I replied, my tone as casual as possible as I moved on to the next customer.

I sensed him retreat and risked a glance a few moments later, just catching a glimpse of him as he exited the shop. After so many months, the emotional turmoil which gripped me was truly sad. 'Pathetic creature!' I mumbled to myself, as I mentally dissected every aspect of our conversation. 'When will you just give it up?'

I'd fretted enough about him, what was the point? My exams were all that mattered at the moment. Get through them and then escape this place. I suddenly realised that the pendant he had given me was between my fingers and that the next customer was looking nonplussed.

'I'm so sorry,' I said, releasing it and moving fast to make up for my distraction.

'You looked like you were someplace else,' he said.

'I guess I was,' I admitted.

17

KATE

Summer drew to a mournfully early close. Withering winds swept freezing air across the city, ripping leaves from trees and depositing them in untidy brown and orange mounds which were magnets for toddlers and despairing mothers. Pedestrians walked carefully along wet pavements, heads down against the bitter wind. It was unusually damp, nothing seemed to dry out completely. Everything was wet and muddy. Intermittently the weak autumn sun demonstrated its feeble protest, but mostly it was grey and dull.

A gig playing piano and singing at a five star hotel bar-restaurant in the city became available. Mads knew the manager, Adrian, whom she had worked for before, but she had just signed a contract to play in a club for six months as part of a duo and so was unavailable.

'I've never done that sort of work before Mads,' I protested when she suggested I audition. Mind you I'd never worked before full stop.

'It's easy money, Kate. You could sight-read that sort of music with your training!'

'What about the singing?'

'Your singing is great,' she said, and then clarified, 'It's definitely good enough for a restaurant.'

With Mads at my side urging me on, I called Adrian and

organised an audition. I'd need to play a bit of jazz, light classical, slow pop and possibly even a little country. I prayed that no one from The Conservatoire came in to listen. They hadn't taken the Kenny Rogers appreciation class.

I arrived at my audition with a knot in my stomach, quivering cold hands and stiff fingers, wishing I'd had the shot of port Mads had recommended beforehand. At least I looked presentable. Mads had taken on the role of personal stylist and insisted on make-up, sheers and heels. Presentable, but quite unlike myself.

The hotel was Victorian, built in the late eighteen-hundreds and very grand. I felt immediately plain and inadequate against the stylish sophistication and charm evident in my luxurious surroundings. Chandeliers glittered magnificently as efficient, perfectly groomed staff in neat uniforms conducted their business in hushed tones on plush red carpet.

'Can I help you, Madam?' a male receptionist asked making me feel at least fifty years old.

'Err, I'm here to see Adrian Vale, it's Katherine Richardson.' He picked up a phone and dialled an extension. 'Have a seat,' he said, 'he won't be long.'

Just as I balanced on the edge of one of the plush armchairs he arrived, his legs first in long strides and the rest of his body playing catch-up.

'Katherine, Adrian,' he said brusquely, extending a warm hand to meet with my icy one as I stood.

'Kate's fine,' I answered shyly. He was tall and good-looking in an anonymous, managerial sort of way. His hair was fair and clipped short and he wore a dark formal suit.

'We'll go to the Amber Room,' he said, gesturing for me to follow and walking so briskly that I had to jog along next to him. Given that I could barely walk in my heels it was no easy feat. We entered an empty room which looked like an unused conference facility, but housed a baby grand in gleaming walnut in the corner.

'It's a beautiful piano,' I said as I pulled out my music. He sat back in one of the many chairs in the room.

'Would you like a tea or coffee or something?' he asked, as though suddenly remembering to be hospitable.

'I'm fine thanks.' Too many images of misadventures with the tea. Tea in the piano, tea on my clothes, tea on his clothes, choking on the tea …

I played and sang with a quavering voice, aware of every imperfection and ending hot and clammy with embarrassment.

'Excellent, excellent,' Adrian remarked, clearly tone-deaf. 'When can you start?'

'So you want to hire me?' I was certain of some misunderstanding. Maybe he'd just asked, *'when can you depart?'* and *'excellent,'* referred to the fact that I'd finally finished.

'Yes, yes,' he said, with a wave of the hand. 'No point wasting time with more auditions when you'll be fine.'

Such great praise. 'Okay. Great. Well, I can start whenever. You let me know and I'll be here.'

'You'll be in Mercatura, the restaurant downstairs, Thursday to Saturday, starting next week. That's three nights a week, seven to eleven, made up of four, forty-five minute sets and fifteen minute breaks. You can eat your dinner at the hotel buffet. Whatever you like.' A rumble of words and then silence.

'Perfect,' I said and then more meekly, '… and the pay?'

'Two thousand a month.' My mouth dropped open and I quickly closed it. That seemed easy. 'Just let us have your bank account details and a tax file number.' What on earth was that? Dad would help.

I bounced out of the hotel. Mercatura. I knew it only by reputation. An excellent restaurant. Very expensive.

I acquired the necessary tax file number, a suitable accompaniment to my driver's licence and was really starting to feel quite important. My first night arrived quickly. Huge rectangular windows framed by heavy cream and gold drapes looked out onto leafy gardens and an ornate fountain. Chandeliers hung from high ceilings above the burgundy-covered tables. I'd heard about the chef. Eccentric and talented. He had become infamous a few years previously, after a histrionic reaction to a patron's request for tomato sauce had seen him arrested for assaulting the guest with the tomato sauce container. No charges had been brought and he had returned to his position. No-one since had dared to ask for any sort of condiment, but the restaurant was always full and he had become a necessary part of the character of the place.

I fiddled with the microphone levels anxiously but finally, unable to procrastinate any longer, I started my first set. I started with instrumentals, but after a little positive reinforcement, which included a smattering of applause and encouraging smiles I took a deep breath and launched into my first song. I chose Vienna, it was low and easy and it went well. More applause.

'The table over by the window would like to know what you'd like to drink, Kate,' a waiter asked, startling me.

'Err, I'll have a port, please,' I said, a tentative smile my nervous thanks to the table at the window. When it arrived I sipped it slowly. The liquid made a warm puddle in my stomach.

Before I had finished my next song there was another glass of port lined up next to my first.

I caught the waiter the next time he ambled past.

'If I get any more offers of drinks, I'll just have a soft drink, thanks.'

He smiled and nodded his head in the direction of the table of businessmen in the corner. '*They* don't want to send you soft drinks.'

'Well at this rate, I'll end up having to call a cab to get home.' He laughed unsympathetically and moved away.

Although the restaurant was frequented by a number of different types, the bread and butter clientele of the hotel were businessmen who would often continue drinking at the bar or go out to clubs after their meal. They were away from home and lonely, or bored.

With Mads' help my image had changed dramatically, at least after dark. In the bright light of day I was almost unrecognisable. Jeans and t-shirt, no make-up, my hair caught up in a spiralling pony-tail. But at night I was transformed. Sometimes the contrast took even me by surprise, a tiny inner voice calling out, '*Who is that?*'

A false sense of familiarity developed after an evening of snatches of conversation with patrons and drinks sent to the piano. I *assumed* good intentions, but I learnt that the men who waited around for me to finish my last set were not as interested in my conversation as they were in sex, a simultaneously disappointing and thrilling notion, which caused me more than a few headaches.

My night terrors continued to worsen. To some extent my sleep was disturbed on most nights. Sometimes they were mild. I would sit up in bed with a vague memory of having shouted but sleep would overcome me quickly.

At other times I leapt out of bed, crazed, and ran to the door where I woke confused, my heart beating erratically, my breath short, with a sense that in slumber, my death had been imminent, that violence lurked near.

One night I gave up on sleep and called Nick in frustration while I sat in the darkness. My clocked blinked a red-eyed two a.m. at me. It was late, but he seemed to be a chronic insomniac.

'Why were you asking about dreams all those months ago, when we first met?' I asked him, 'Remember?'

'I remember a lot about when we first met, but not every word,' he lied and I heard the clink of ice in a glass.

I sighed. 'I know you remember Nick. It was a weird thing to say. You must have had a reason.'

'Must I?' He was drinking, which was usually the case when I called him late. He called himself a 'functional alco-holic', was almost proud of it.

'You asked me if I dreamed. It came out of nowhere. What did you mean?' I stroked the quilt on my bed, remembered Nanny making it, the care and love in the details.

'Why do you ask now, after all this time?'

'I'm not sleeping well. I'm having crazy experiences in my sleep, nearly every night and I'm getting sick of it.'

Time skipped a beat before he answered.

'My brother, Daniel, used to have problems with night-mares and sleep-walking. We had to start locking the door to his room not that long before he died. He wanted us to. It helped him feel safer. Us too, I guess. He was worried about what he might do while he was asleep. He started seeing a therapist who was trying to help him, but ... well you know how that all turned out.' The ice clinked again.

I wasn't sure how to console him, or whether he even needed consoling after so long. 'Suicide is so hard to under-stand.'

'Yes.' He sounded vague.

More silence. Spectres capered along my wall and somer-saulted across the ceiling as the trees and bushes moved in the wind and lights from the odd passing car played tricks in the night. I shivered and turned on the lamp.

'It sort of runs in the family,' he said suddenly.

'Nightmares?'

'Kind of.' I wondered about his reluctance to explain. Maybe it was just as well. He became increasingly morose as he drank and this was obviously an emotional topic. 'Don't talk to anyone else for now about any of this, Kate. People don't understand. They'll think you're crazy, dangerous ...'

Yep, it was definitely one of *those* nights. *He* was crazy. 'Well no, Nick,' I admonished, 'I think most people will think I'm having bad dreams!'

'People are quick to judge,' he insisted.

'Yes? Well maybe I'll talk to a professional.'

'We should meet soon. There's more to tell you, but I don't want to do it over the phone. It's complicated.'

I sighed heavily.

'Agree Kate? Don't tell anyone until we meet, after that it's up to you.'

'Okay. I'll call you tomorrow to organise something,' I agreed reluctantly.

'We can organise something now.'

'You're drinking. I can hear it in your voice.' I didn't mention the constant clinking which accompanied our conversation.

'When am I not drinking? I'm a very functional alcoholic.'

'Why do you drink when it just makes you sad?' I asked, memories of gloomy conversations with him playing in my mind. Alcohol took him to a world of regret and loss.

'When I'm drinking I can wallow.' He sounded choked up and I felt bad for prying. 'I'm allowed a bit of self-pity. I'm a drunk after all.' He laughed bitterly. 'Sometimes feeling the sadness, reliving it, remembering it is the only way I can really feel alive, that I can remember what was real. The rest of the time, I push it aside, to get on with life. Work, work, work. That's all there is now … well, until you came along anyway. I'm still getting used to that. I want to protect you Kate. You're special.'

'I don't need protecting Nick. I'm a big girl.' Yawning I flopped back onto the bed.

'You're still a child.'

'Give me a break! Look after yourself.' I switched off my lamp and tried to ignore the shadows.

'I'm not kidding. You've been sheltered. You're in the big bad world now.'

'It's not that bad. Actually, I'm enjoying it.'

'There's a lot of craziness out there … I know, I'm a little part of it.'

'Yeah, you're not kidding.' This much was, at least, true.

'Come on, let me do that much …' he begged. I pulled Nanny's quilt over myself. It offered warmth, but not always peace.

'Sure,' I said, placating him.

More empty promises. I filed them away in my mind with the others made during insensible conversations, and one of my own, to stop calling him in the middle of the night.

'I'm going to call you tomorrow to organise for us to catch up so that you can tell me all about this dream stuff when you're sober.'

'Night-night Katie,' he replied sweetly.

'Go to bed Nick. Please, don't drink any more tonight.' How easily I fell into co-dependence. I tried to shrug off the burden of responsibility weighing on my shoulders and rest, but I couldn't avoid fretting about his welfare.

18

DEB AND NICK

I expected to bump into Nick at the beach or the shops, but the days passed and I didn't. Slowly the tension which had started to gnaw away at me after seeing him eased, and I threw myself into my studies. I *would* do well. I would escape Three Kings and I would forge ahead, my destiny was my own.

Weeks passed and I joined my brother and his friends at MacArthur's Lake for an early mid-term break. A large crowd had already gathered by the time we arrived, some playing volleyball, others swimming or reclining on the sand. It wasn't yet noon but a few had already started drinking. Music and laughter, cars arriving and doors slamming, carried in the air.

No-one noticed as I left them behind, wandering along the winding path at the side of the lake, and then off it into the thick undergrowth, trying to find the spot Nick and I had walked to so long ago.

After some minutes of searching, my legs criss-crossed with thin scratches from branches and foliage, I chanced on what seemed to be an overgrown trail through the trees. Picking my way over branches and through more scratchy vegetation, hoping there were no snakes around, I belatedly wondered whether it might have been a good idea to let someone know that I was heading into the bush. I arrived at the stream, as translucent as I remembered, a liquid magnifying glass hovering over the sand. My toes squeaked in my thongs which were totally unsuitable for the terrain, and put me at imminent risk of slipping or tripping and spraining my ankle, but I had gone too far to turn back now and so I pushed forward.

Up ahead I could see the brightness of the white beach, its glow like a golden angel beckoning to me through the dark shade of the foliage, embracing me in light and warmth as I clambered over rocks and slid down onto the sand, relieved at my safe arrival. I kicked off my thongs, my feet sinking into the warm soft graininess of the beach, and surveyed the cold turquoise water, not tempted by its frigid embrace. In the distance the dull rumble of humanity continued, but here it was private, insulated. I wondered how many others were enjoying secluded, secret spots around the lake, how many were lovers, how many were hiding from love.

Under the trees it had been cool, but now cloaked in glorious warmth I basked in the sun. The water lapped nearby, gentle rhythmic whooshing. Birds fussed and called, busy wings flapped.

I drowsed. Behind me the leaves rustled as my mind roamed. His feet landed in the sand. Sleepily I imagined that he had come, that he too had journeyed to this place on the other side of everything. I languished in my delusion.

But then there was more. More than just imagining. Instinct's prickle.

I inhaled and he was there … the sweet toxic essence of him had touched the air. Fingers touched my face, stroking my temple, down my cheek bone, into the nape of my neck. Nick. How? It didn't matter.

'Deb?' I opened my eyes and found his brilliant ones. 'I

want you. I have always wanted you.'

'You have a strange way of showing it,' I said. He gazed down at me for a long while, a flurry of indecipherable emotions twisting his expression.

'God help me,' he cried, his voice hoarse with desire. His lips fell onto mine. I was instantly weak. So weak, like I was melting into the sand, like I was his to consume. I wanted to be consumed. I clasped his neck as his body pressed along the length of mine and we came together in a tight frantic crush.

Finally we broke apart.

'I don't want to let you go,' he said.

'Don't then,' I answered, my body yielding to something warm and molten.

He kissed me again, deeply. This time his tongue dipped into my mouth and I caressed it with mine as his fingers moved down to my tummy, to where my shirt had pulled out of my shorts. He touched my skin.

'Oooh.' I gasped and wriggled.

'Aha, a weakness,' he laughed, breaking the mood and tickling me mercilessly.

'Stop, please, stop!' I screeched, squirming and trying to push him away, unable to catch a breath, suffocating on my laugh until my gaze locked with his and the world spun.

And then he was everywhere. His mouth on my mouth, demanding, his body hot and heavy on mine, the hardness at his pelvis grinding into me, his hand on my breast, massaging. Closing my eyes I tried to focus on breathing normally. It was impossible. The sensation of him against me was like walking a tightrope without a safety wire and wanting to do cartwheels. I drew breath in ragged gasps as he lifted his mouth from mine. Flames flickered in his eyes.

I recognised his question. 'I want to Nick.'

I wanted the magic before it was too late, before the inevitability of life shattered our pleasure. My imagination had tormented me for long enough and right now I didn't care whether or not he would go away again, or what the future held.

The tension left his muscles as he gave in to himself and I writhed up against him.

'You're making me wild, Deb,' he groaned.

'Do it,' I ordered.

Around me the world blurred and spun. My body began to buzz, to thrum with a throbbing desire, so strong it possessed me. He pushed my shorts down and released himself. Then, a sudden sweet pain as he entered me, carefully at first, watching my reaction.

'It's okay ...' I whispered, my throat tight. I could feel him inside me, filling me. 'Don't stop.'

We started moving together. His face hovered over mine. He was so beautiful, so intense. His eyes were burning. I could see myself in them, an inferno raging all around me. Then his mouth found mine again. He groaned and we began to move more urgently, our bodies in unison, slowing only at the greatest depth as he touched the core of me and life around us ceased.

19

KATE

Winter had dug its frozen claws in deep and was set to continue for a couple of months more. I was tired thanks to work, Uni and a bit too much partying.

Mads and I were hanging out more, although Pierre and Francois were reluctant to include her in our tea sessions which were kind of sacred. Still, I spent a lot of time with her and sometimes when Mitchell wasn't around, which was rare, we lay on her unmade bed and talked about our lives, our hopes and dreams, and boys. Occasionally we fell asleep, our faces still stained by laughter, enveloped in childhood for a moment, innocent and close.

Part of the reason for our closeness was that she was working at a club only a few minutes' walk from Mercatura. When I had finished my last set I sometimes watched her until she was done at midnight, and then we'd go out. Mostly we ended up at the Spice House where the building throbbed to the sound of *Hot* until the early hours of the morning and the bouncers knew us.

'Didn't I see you here last night, little girl?' Steve, the burliest of the bouncers, wearing a t-shirt at least three sizes too small, asked. 'Shouldn't good little girls be at home in bed asleep?' He peered down at me. I wasn't intimidated. His partner, Brad, who was half his size, both width and height-wise, had told me that animated movies like The Lion King and Ice Age, made him cry uncontrollably.

'Shouldn't you be keeping an eye out for patrons with knives, like the guy two back, instead of badgering little girls, Steve?'

'Excuse me, Sir,' Steve said, his terrifying face and large bulk heading rapidly towards the person I'd just mentioned as he motioned for me to enter the club.

Mads was already surrounded and I headed to the bar to get a drink.

'She draws them to her like maggots to a carcass, doesn't she?' Luca, the young blonde bartender observed, glancing in her direction wistfully.

The crowd around Mads stood out from the rest of the patrons. There was an aura of dark fatalism that pervaded the space around them. As if all of the inconsistencies of life had been removed, leaving only a gloomy certainty which needed escaping.

I shrugged, but I knew that he was right.

'Just don't get tainted by them. They're using, the clubs full of it tonight,' he warned, drifting away to serve another customer.

They used drugs openly, which left me feeling both unsettled and tantalised. I tiptoed around the edge of their world, trying not to let the danger there touch me but I felt the pull, the fear of endless temptations, of succumbing and losing myself to that dark world.

Deep down Mads and I weren't so different. In many ways we were the same, both artists, the product of sheltered, but broken childhoods. Both of us had faced abandonment. We were searching for our place in the light.

'Baby, Baby, Baby.' Mads buzzed over to me, grabbing my

hands and spilling my drink as she pulled me into an embrace and tried to dance with me. Her face was flushed, her pupils like saucers. I wondered what she'd taken, guessed some kind of amphetamine, maybe ice. Dark rings under her eyes were starting to show through her make-up.

Placing my drink on the sticky bar counter I tried to shake the liquid off my arms as she laughed and vanished into the throng. She had been succumbing more and more easily to the mind-altering substances she had initially dismissed as nothing more than a dalliance. More and more the strength of her outer persona, her image, hid the Mads I had once known, the tender, funny girl, with a soft side. Her inner child was crying out, suffocating, slowly smothered as she became a shell filled with darkness, embracing more and more of the gloom around her. Mitchell's frenetic existence and her terror at losing him to it were robbing her of her soul.

The DJ was on again and soon Mitchell appeared next to me, too close, swigging my drink as he waited for his to arrive. Girls crushed in around us.

'Aah, that's disgusting,' he said, gesturing for the bartender to pour a drop of vodka into my lime and soda. I shook my head, but it was added anyway.

'Whatcha doin' Katie baby?'

'You know, this and that,' I said. 'Watching your girlfriend for one,' I added, hopefully reminding him that he had one.

'Oh?' he asked, not even mildly curious. His eyes darted greedily across the assembled hoard.

'She's on something.'

'Well I think you're the only one who's not. Maybe you should try something, it'll help you relax and have some fun.' He looked back at the girls in tight scanty clothing and I noticed him narrow his focus and settle on a tiny girl with long black hair. I shook my head in disgust, but he was already moving away. The sickening clash of too many fragrances followed him.

'I'll see you around,' he called over his shoulder. I didn't bother to reply. He wouldn't have heard me anyway, and probably wouldn't have appreciated what I might have had to say.

Few could manage a lifestyle like Mitchell's and still function at his level. Of course he used meth, but it didn't seem to impact on his performance. He bounced back like a jack-in-the-box.

I moved away to where I could watch the dancing, standing in a shadowy, slightly secluded corner just behind the band as they started up again.

The steadily moving mass fascinated me. Some gyrated, intent on the rhythm, others lusted, their hips pushing and searching greedily. Hips ground and bodies swayed and bent. Others seemed to have abandoned themselves to the night, their gazes vacant as the music moved their form, like a puppeteer manipulating a puppet. A haze of sweat, heat and movement under the pulsating lights. The hypnotic melody and rhythm of the band provided a delusional backdrop.

'Excuse me,' I said as a bulky silhouette blocked my outlook. I moved slightly to try and see around him but he moved closer, obscuring both my view and the view others had of me and I started to feel insecure.

'Hey babe,' he brayed, reaching out to touch my arm. I backed away. 'Don't go, not after all the effort I've made to cross that bloody crowded floor to get to you.' His breath was sour and involuntarily I took another step backwards.

'Somewhere I need to be,' I mumbled. His grasp tightened around my wrist and he tugged me closer.

'Don't give me that crap. I've seen you standing here for ages ...'

'Well I'm going now.' I tried to yank back my hand and step away from him but in a move quicker than I would have thought him capable of, he used his body to pin me against the wall and I felt his hand on my leg, pushing up under my short skirt. He was very strong. I couldn't get away.

'Get off me,' I tried to yell, but the pressure of his bulk against my chest crushed the air from my lungs and I couldn't get any volume out. Stuck in a dark deserted corner of the club had suited me previously, but it was really working against me now. We remained unnoticed, the noise of the band and the movement of the dancers continuing uninterrupted around us.

'Didn't you hear her mate? She said get off her!' Suddenly his suffocating weight lifted off me and I gasped with relief. In a blur strong arms spun him around and rammed him against the wall, an elbow to his throat. I stumbled back, caught by confident hands which gripped my shoulders.

'Thank you,' I whispered, as the room tilted and swayed around me. Spinning. Faster and faster. The boy's face, the one from the park. *There must be a God*, I thought as I gazed into his violet eyes. Then everything gave way to weightlessness and darkness.

20

DEB AND NICK

We lay on the beach side by side and silent, drying in the sun after the briefest of swims in the frigid water. Our hands were intertwined. My body glowed and tingled magically. Even the glistening lake looked enchanted, millions of tiny twinkling icicles dancing across its surface.

The sky was soft and endless above us. Only the lengthening shadows, creeping towards us from the trees at the edge of the forest, indicated that the day was moving on. I felt deeply connected, like the energy from our bodies was seeping into the sand, charging the tiny particles we were lying on, lighting brilliant diamonds to warm the sun. The trees sang soft lullabies and the birds were angels. For a moment we disappeared into nature's panorama, content.

Like all things amazing, it was temporary.

'I'm sorry I'm so hard to read sometimes,' Nick said, his words forcing the angels' regretful retreat. His brow furrowed and he looked away.

What could I say? He wasn't joking, that was for sure. In fact, it was definitely the understatement of the century. Trepidation rippled through me. Where was he going with this? I glanced over at him, lingering on his strong profile and watched him watch the drifting sky.

His chest rose and then fell abruptly. 'I want to be with

you, Deb.' He turned onto his side and raised himself up on an elbow, switching to holding my hand with his other hand. 'So fine, so delicate,' he said, toying with my fingers, 'like a sparrow.' I turned to face him and he lifted my fingers to his lips.

'I don't want today to end.' He smiled sadly, recognising the inevitable.

'Me neither,' I answered. A cloud trapped the sun for a moment and the sand became dull, like the diamonds had been nothing but an illusion.

'What are you thinking?' he asked.

'I'm thinking that clouds are coming.'

He looked back up. 'My father says that everything ends … bad things … and good things.' He extended a hand up to the sky to the cloud which hung stubbornly above us and it seemed as though he moved it with a gesture and we were bathed in glory again. 'Magic.'

'Yes. Magic.' I agreed. Today was all about magic.

He touched the pendant which dangled from the necklace around my neck and the tiny diamonds cast flickering speckles onto his chest. 'Whatever happens, we have this moment to hold on to … always. Some people live their whole lives and never experience anything like this.'

We observed the lake together, like it was the dawn of creation, as if we'd been before anyone else. 'I feel sorry for them,' I said.

He shrugged. 'I guess they don't know any differently.'

'This experience will change things, won't it? Nothing will ever be quite the same.'

And like that I reminded him of something which took him from me for a while, the uneasy silence indicating a spell broken. He stood and pulled on his t-shirt and then changed his mind and sat, but with his arms around his knees, distanced from me.

The moment was over and I wasn't sure why.

'Life is complicated isn't it?' he asked suddenly, breaking the silence. A cool breeze had picked up. I pulled on my top. It was getting late.

'Is that your way of telling me yours is, Nick? Mine is not too bad. School, work, eating, sleeping … you know, deciding what I want to do next year, the usual things.'

His mouth turned up on one side as he grimaced. 'I guess so. My life is complicated.' George's words of long ago rang out within me. 'I don't remember it ever being any different.' His face became haunted. 'Something always comes up and steals away what you thought you had.'

'What do you mean?' I asked, unclenching my teeth and forcing myself to relax my jaw.

He threw his hands to the sky and let them drop with a slap. 'There's always something creating a complication.'

'Oh?' It was impossible to stop the sinking feeling inside from stealing a part of my face.

He shook his head dismally, his eyes narrowing. 'My folks, they don't like your family.'

'What? We don't even know them. I think I saw a photo of your dad in the newspaper once, that's about it.' Gossip came to mind. 'Is this the whole snobbery thing? We're not good enough? Not rich enough anyway!'

He brought his hand to his chin, his mouth becoming crooked, like he wasn't sure how to explain what he wanted to say. 'There's always that, Deb, it goes without saying with them, but this is something else, something that goes way back. More like a feud.'

I almost laughed, but he was serious and my face fell. 'That sounds like something from the dark ages Nick! How can you have a feud going on when one party doesn't even know about it?'

He bent his head back and looked up at the sky and then back down to me. 'It's ridiculous, I know. Grudges … very old ones! Something happened before we were born. Do you know that our families, your father's and mine, have been in this region for generations? Yours moved away. There was a reason for that, something which isn't spoken of. You were never meant to come back.'

'This is the first I've heard of it,' I answered, confused, although something niggled at me. Why *had* my father chosen Three Kings? It made little sense when we could have been located in a bigger centre closer to his work, to school.

He picked up a dry stick and started to shred it with quick rough tugs. 'There was an arrangement, some sort of agreement. You and I … well, we were never meant to meet.'

I wanted to dismiss what he said as nonsense, to tell him that it was madness, but I couldn't rid myself of the niggle.

'I know it sounds crazy Deb.' His gaze softened and he dropped the last of the stick to the ground with a sigh.

'Why would my father have brought us back here then?' I asked, desperate to make sense of it.

He shrugged. 'I don't know.'

'Surely I'd know … at least something about this.' But that wasn't necessarily the case, not with the way my relationship with my father was.

He shook his head. 'You wouldn't necessarily Deb. I didn't until recently.'

I stood up and wandered down to the water. 'Maybe it's another family, they're confused.'

He followed, coming up behind me. 'No, they're adamant it's your family. That's why your dad moved away.'

I felt a flicker of shame and clasped my arms around myself.

'What is the big mystery anyway?' I wondered, looking out at the placid, slowly shifting water.

His arms encircled my waist and I leant back into him. I felt his breath against my hair. 'They won't tell me.'

'They're just trying to manipulate you.'

'You're probably right,' he sighed. 'It's such a big deal that I don't get involved with you, but they won't let me in on why exactly. I'm just expected to bow to their authority, even now! Crazy bastards they are anyway. Master manipulators.' He sounded angry.

'Anyway, it doesn't matter Deb. That's what I wanted to tell you.' His hug grew tighter. 'I've told them I'm going my own way. I've had enough. I'm *going* to be a pilot. I'd rather saw off my own foot than work for my father under any circumstances anyway.' He laughed bitterly.

'I'm not completely cut off, for now anyway. I think they're hoping I'll change my mind when I realise the financial sacrifices I'll have to make.'

I nodded. 'Life is short. You can make your own way.' He turned me around and took both of my hands in his.

'You make it sound so simple.'

'You should follow your dreams, Nick.'

His smile was bittersweet. 'You're so innocent and good. I don't want to freak you out with my family stuff – we're all a bit warped.' He pulled me into a tight embrace. Heat radiated off him. I felt it recharging my heart.

'You're not like them.'

'I've let you down Deb, made you sad. I don't always know how to handle things in the way I should but I'm going to try and make things right, if I can.' He twisted a stray strand of hair that had crossed my face around his finger.

The sun caught it. 'Spun gold,' he said, marvelling and then burying his hands deep in my hair.

'If only …' I whispered, as his face moved in closer to mine.

21

KATE

Brilliant rays of sunlight hit my pupils like bright burning needles as my eyelids fluttered open. I immediately brought my hands up to cover my eyes and turned back into the pillow for a little protection. Counting, one to five and back again, I slowly drew breath. Where the hell was I?

Peeping out from between my fingers I found myself alone and sat up. The room around me was unfamiliar, but not forbidding. Wide windows covered by white blinds let streaming golden light into a stark, very white room. Nothing adorned the walls. Shadows provided welcome relief. A white quilt camouflaged me but underneath I was fully clothed which was a relief. I felt stale and clammy, my head throbbing like it had been pulverised by a sledgehammer, as my brain threatened to break from its confinement at any moment. Somewhere outside the dull rumble of traffic provided a constant bass.

Disoriented and uncertain, with a touch of panic thrown in for good measure, I tried to remember what had happened and where I was, but it was a relatively pointless exercise. Only vague, fuzzy memories came to mind. I struggled to stand, but sat back down quickly, nursing my head as the floor threatened to smack my face, noticing as I did, my shoes placed neatly together at the base of the bed.

Soft white towels sat in a neat stack on the edge of the bed. Welcome to the Hotel California! A note in neat print sat on top of them. I squinted to focus. *'Will explain everything when you are ready.'* Would that be a good thing, or was ignorance bliss? I looked at the closed bedroom door, unsure who was on the other side of it, but knowing that if I walked out now without freshening up, fate would intervene and I would regret it.

I stood up slowly, closing my eyes until the dizziness passed and then headed unsteadily in the general direction of the small ensuite. A shower. Thank you for small mercies! The warm water washed away some of the grime and relieved the achiness, but it was like my mind was wrapped in a thick wet towel that would let nothing through.

After drying myself I wandered back to the bed to pull on my soiled clothes. Magically they had been replaced, hopefully by friendly goblins and not gremlins, with clean sweats. They were black, a little big and baggy, but fresh. I looked anxiously to the door again. 'Don't come in, don't come in, don't come in', I chanted hopping on one leg while I pulled up the bottoms awkwardly with one hand, simultaneously trying to grab the top and pull it over my head, but instead being blinded by it as I failed. Panic. I dropped the bottoms, pulled on the top and then yanked them up. The door had not moved.

'Thank you, thank you, thank you.' I towel-dried my hair and then dragged my fingers through the knotty mess, uncertain as to whether showering had improved my appearance which was now rather bedraggled, but at least sweeter-smelling. My mouth tasted like I'd been chugging battery acid and I rinsed it out with water but it made little difference. It was the best I could do right now.

Moving to the door, I felt uncertain about leaving the relative safety of the room. I placed my fingers on the handle, bracing myself for a moment before I opened it and stepped tentatively out into a wide passage. Now I could see more of where I was. A bland, but luxurious modern apartment with large, panoramic windows at the end of the passage letting the city in.

Delicious smoky aromas and sizzling sounds drifted down the passage. My stomach growled aggressively, forcing me forward. Standing at a wide stove, cooking like he did it a lot, was the boy who had come to my aid for the second time last night. He turned and a mug of coffee appeared magically in my slightly shaky hand. The bitter aroma pierced the foggy veil of my mind.

'Thank you,' I said, my voice as hoarse as a lawnmower. I noticed his startling indigo eyes, so dark they were almost purple this morning.

'Sit, I'll get you something to eat.' He gestured to a white leather seat at a contemporary glass table and I dropped into it.

'I'm James, by the way. I heard the shower and assumed you'd be hungry!' I looked down at the clothes I was wearing. He'd assumed a little more than that.

'Your clothes are over there,' he said, pointing to a plastic bag on the sofa.

'You didn't have to ...' I blushed, feeling embarrassed at what was either a liberty or amazingly considerate.

He placed an enormous plate of bacon and eggs in front of me, ignoring my polite decline. 'I made it for you,' he said, moving back into the kitchen.

I was starving. 'It smells fantastic,' I said, like a dog with a hollow stomach, up on hind legs with paws bent, saliva pooling.

'Don't wait,' he called. I didn't need a second invitation.

After a while I realised that I hadn't introduced myself. 'Kate,' I sang out around a mouthful of food, embarrassed by my gluttony.

From a distance he was watching me eat, but strangely it didn't bother me. Maybe I was just too hungry to be self-conscious.

'This is *so* good,' I said, tucking in like a pig at the trough, talking and eating, doing exactly what mum had said not to if you wanted to make a good impression. 'I was lucky you were around last night. I was a bit out of it.' I tried to slow down, to swallow before I spoke again. The truth of what had happened only increased my humiliation. Indistinct memories, juxtaposed, fought for viability and died quickly. Obviously I had consumed too much alcohol, although I couldn't remember exactly what I'd had.

He moved from behind the counter and neared the table, and I noticed the way his jeans were slung around his hips, and how the soft worn leather belt only just held them there. His t-shirt clung to his abs and chest like a drowning man and the muscles on his arms bunched as he toyed with a dishcloth. I swallowed and my eyes moved guiltily up to meet his. A smirk twisted his mouth as he noticed everything and I felt blood course across my cheeks. Humiliation. When would I get used to it?

Dropping my eyes to my food, I promised myself I'd keep them there … at least until the next mouthful.

'That guy at the club must have put something in your drink, you passed out cold!'

I didn't look up. 'I can barely remember him …' A bulky shadow blocking the lights. Fear.

'He was probably watching you from much earlier on,' he said, matter-of-factly, as he moved into the lounge area to open a window. I wondered whether I could risk a glance at his back, but it was too dangerous. Below a back was a ... butt and I didn't want him to catch my eyes there.

Instead I tried to focus on his words. 'Do you really think so?' I'd heard of it happening to others, just never thought it would happen to me.

'I've never passed out like that before. I still feel weird.' I looked up, but not at him, at the view of the city, the skyline and stadiums, the spires and the river, all under a crisp blue wintery sky. Another thought crossed my mind and I did turn to him. He was watching me. His gaze did unsettling things to the blood in my body. I steeled myself. 'What would have happened if you weren't there to rescue me ... again?'

'It wasn't just me,' he said.

'Oh?' Something knocked on the door to my brain. Clues to puzzles, but I didn't know which clues fit with which puzzles. It was very frustrating.

'Dark corners on your own in a place like that,' he continued, shaking his head, 'probably not such a great idea. That sort of thing happens all the time in clubs, you wouldn't believe it. It's not a good idea to go alone.'

I frowned. Bits and pieces were coming back. 'I wasn't alone. I was with friends, sort of. My friend's boyfriend plays in the band there. It's almost like a second home. I guess we've got a bit slack, we just come and go, don't take the precautions we might somewhere else.' I suddenly felt irresponsible, although I wasn't sure why. He wasn't my father. 'You'd think that with so many people around nothing could happen, right?'

He smiled, recognising my embarrassment. 'Well, you wouldn't be the first person to make that mistake.' His hair was fascinating. Crazy. Strands flopped in all directions, and some stood straight up. It moved like it had a life of its own. Our eyes met again and I bit my lip as my cheeks flushed.

'What happened to that guy anyway?' I asked.

His grin became mercenary and I glimpsed another side of him. 'Don't worry about him bothering you, or anyone else for a while. We sent him back to where he came from, but with a little less confidence.'

What had they done? 'Err, that's good I guess,' I mumbled uncertainly, bringing my fingers to my mouth and then quickly removing them. 'I really appreciate it … obviously.'

'We thought you might.'

'We?' I asked, determined to follow through this time.

Footsteps sounded opportunely on the wooden floor. 'Ethan …' James said and I turned to greet the new arrival. Instead my jaw fell open. Standing at the entrance to the kitchen was a replica of James. Identical, down to the violet eyes and the hair!

'I should have warned you,' James chuckled. 'But then, some things never grow old.'

Ethan smiled, but his smile was not quite the same. It was tighter and more restrained and accompanied by a curt nod of his head at me. His lopsided hair was a little more coherent than James' and still wet from the shower. He sauntered into the kitchen, slinging himself into a chair across from me and waiting expectantly. His demeanour was very different, super confident and slightly surly. He gazed unwaveringly at me.

'Err Kate,' I said, uncomfortable with such open scrutiny. I looked away, seeking James, but he had left the room. For a moment I felt abandoned.

'You're looking a bit better than you did last night,' Ethan said, diving into the mound of food James had placed in front of him. By comparison my meal seemed like a tiny snack.

'I guess that wouldn't take much,' I answered, acutely aware of how horrendous I must have looked passed out last night. Not that I was looking fantastic right now. My hair was doing a bizarre electrocuted-hedgehog impression and I felt like 'The Yeti' in the baggy sweats I was wearing. Self-consciousness made me want to pat down my hair, cake on make-up, tell him that I wasn't this ugly, usually. Somehow, I resisted, tolerating the awful awkwardness which slithered across the back of my neck. My gaze fell to my feet. At least they looked dainty in my shiny black strappy sandals.

He, of course, looked great. Superficial differences between the two of them were few. They both looked equally strong and lean, almost wiry. Ethan's hair was exactly the same caramel-brown shade, slightly neater maybe and just a fraction longer. But even if it wasn't I would have known, even after my very brief encounter with him, that this wasn't James sitting across from me. It was something in his eyes, beyond the colour, a harder flash, cynicism, a deeper knowledge borne of dominance, of protecting his brother. Ethan was the Alpha male. It radiated from every pore.

'Thanks for everything last night,' I said, unsure of the roles each had played, but knowing it had been a team effort.

'We were there,' he said with a dismissive wave, like it had been just another day at the office.

'Well thank you anyway.' He studied me for a moment and I felt like a deer in the headlights.

'No problem.' He finished his coffee in silence and then took out his phone.

Suddenly the pieces fell into place. 'You're the guy I've seen in the park ...'

He nodded as he scrolled across the screen. 'Yeah, that's me.'

I brought my thumb to my mouth unconsciously as I thought out loud, '… and James was there too … up at the top of the road.'

He nodded again, still preoccupied by his phone and not feeling the need to explain anything, or confirm that I was in fact a genius. I shook my head. This was too hard today.

After a while he chucked his phone onto the table and leaned back. His t-shirt rode up, exposing a sliver of firm tanned torso. I looked away quickly as my blood raced. This was too confusing.

A clock on the wall. 'Oh my gosh! Is that the time?' I exclaimed, leaping up from my chair. I'd forgotten all about meeting up with Nick.

'I've got to get home. I'm so sorry. I'm meant to be meeting someone for lunch. I forgot all about it …' Flustered, I babbled, wondering where my car was and how I was going to get back.

'I'll take you,' he said smoothly. 'Best not to drive just yet.' He pushed his plate aside.

'Oh, yes, right. Thank you.' He rose nimbly from his chair.

'We'll drop your car off later.' They had my car? 'Where do you live?'

I gave him the address.

'That's not far,' he said, grabbing a dark coat off the back of a chair and shrugging it on. 'It won't take long.'

The coat altered his appearance, making him mysterious and piquing my curiosity again. 'Are you guys studying at the uni?'

He walked to the door and I followed. 'Kind of.'

'Oh?'

'A research project.' So little information and no reciprocal questions, like sucking blood from a stone.

James appeared. 'I'm just dropping her off,' Ethan told

him. For a moment I felt disappointed that it wasn't James, and then I felt ungrateful.

'Don't worry Kate, he's a softie inside, really,' James whispered sarcastically, just loud enough for Ethan to hear. Ethan shrugged, noncommittally, like he didn't care either way, and reached for the keys which were sitting in a stone bowl on an antique hall table near the door.

'I'll drop your car off later, soon as I get a chance,' he said. I stepped into the elevator with Ethan giving James a small wave as the doors closed. I would see him again.

We descended into the parking garage where a sleek black SUV was parked. The apartment, the car – they must come from a wealthy family. As we exited the building I noticed that it was a small, modern block of apartments on a narrow leafy lane. We turned onto the main road and passed trendy shops, restaurants, cafes and nightclubs. Couples braved the winter air which was starting to warm just a little. Coats drawn they enjoyed the thin sun, with warm coffees and hot brunch sustaining them long enough to read the paper.

'Thanks for going to so much trouble,' I said awkwardly, trying to make conversation.

His hand gripped the steering wheel tighter. 'What sort of people would we be if we stood by and watched something bad happen?'

'You'd be like a few I could name, I guess,' I retorted. A quick, amused smile flitted across his face. 'Thanks for the clothes too,' I had to add. Just couldn't help it. Manners. School or parents, I didn't know who was more to blame.

He looked at the roof and then laughed, although it wasn't warm. 'You're not getting the message are you? Keep them, they're just old sweats. Give them to the Salvos when you're finished with them.'

On the way back I sent a somewhat frantic text to Nick

organising for him to meet me half an hour later than we had previously arranged.

'Leave me here,' I said, jumping out of the car as we arrived. 'I'll be fine.'

'Nope, I'm walking you to the door,' he argued, around at my side in a flash. 'We haven't got you this far, only to have something happen to you right outside your door.'

I should probably have felt insulted, but I was in too much of a rush, and in all honesty there was a fair likelihood that I could trip and fall on my face. It had happened before.

As I opened the front door we nearly collided with Mads.

'Where have you been?' she demanded, grabbing my arm and yanking me inside. I was surprised that she'd even noticed. She, Mitchell and her other friends were often so caught up in their own experiences that they didn't notice who was coming or going.

Mads' gaze moved to Ethan and her eyes narrowed as she noted my strange outfit. 'Mads, this is Ethan. And it is not like that,' I despaired. 'I was in a bad situation and he and his brother helped me. Someone put something in my drink. I was completely out of it.'

'What? Who?' She sounded genuinely concerned.

'Some guy who got a bit aggro, tried to grope me. They basically rescued me!' I stopped abruptly as I noticed Ethan edging away, looking very uncomfortable. I felt an unkind flicker of satisfaction.

'You're a hero Ethan,' Mads cried exuberantly, about to fling her arms around him and give him a big kiss. I held onto her arm tightly. I didn't think that would go down well. Ethan seemed to have turned to marble, but she didn't notice. 'You … and your brother of course.' She turned to me and I was touched by the worry in her eyes.

'That's terrible.' She pulled me to her in a clumsy hug,

kissing my forehead. 'We'd hate for anything bad to happen to you. We'd miss you.'

Yep, Ethan was definitely out of there. I wondered whether I would ever see him again. Maybe in the park at Uni pondering the reason why. Why in God's name did women cry? Maybe he should get together with my father.

'Ahem, see you around then,' he said, already halfway down the stairs.

'I promise to be more careful next time.'

'You're a human being, Kate. We all make mistakes, that's life. Don't be so hard on yourself,' Mads jumped in.

'Still …' but what was left to explain?

'Take care of yourself, Kate,' Ethan called. Then he was gone.

'Wow!' Mads cried. 'Quite a bit of man isn't he? Only eyes for you though.'

'And that's bad is it?' I could see that she was put out by the minimal notice he had taken of her. She was used to men falling over themselves around her.

'Course not,' she said, with a lightness her face belied.

I looked down at the baggy track-pants I wore, hitched up at the waist so that I didn't trip on them. The tangle of copper-wire masquerading as hair had evolved into a wild rats' nest, which even the rats shunned. 'He had a strong sense of moral obligation … and that's all.'

'Have a little faith in yourself. It's more than moral obligation. That much I can tell you.'

Maybe it was my feet, they didn't look too bad. A little cold and white, but the sandals were pretty!

'Well there was a lot going on and his brother is pretty nice too,' I added, twitching my nose mischievously.

She threw her hands into the air. 'No wonder you didn't notice, you had your eyes on his brother!'

I couldn't help myself. 'His twin.'

Her mouth fell open. 'You're joking! Identical?'

'Absolutely,' I nodded.

'No! No, it's not natural. I don't believe it.' It was like I'd won the lottery. Still, she was right, the whole scenario was peculiar. And since when did this sort of thing happen to me?

'Yes, well it is all a bit surreal. But they are definitely i-den-ti-cal,' I laughed, rubbing it in. 'Anyway, I'm a wreck Mads and I'm meeting Nick in ten minutes so I'd better run.'

She stopped me, reaching into her pocket and pulling out a small parcel. 'I almost forgot. This came for you … on Friday.' It was small and hard, a little box wrapped in brown paper. 'Sorry, I forgot.'

She passed it to me and I left her in the hallway still dwelling on Ethan and James as I rushed into my room to change. I despaired of getting my hair to do anything manageable, instead scraping it into a pony tail so tight it made me look feline. Wild curls spiralled out in all directions at the back. I grimaced at my reflection in the hall mirror. Not a cat, a Panda. My face was pale, with dark rings around my eyes. It was the best I could do right now.

22

DEB AND NICK

The elongated shadows were quickly devouring the light. 'We'd better get back,' I said, worried that my brother would be organising his friends into drunken mobs with flashlights and beacons to search for me.

We clambered over the rocks and into the gloomy mouth of the twilit forest.

'Let's just keep this between you and I,' Nick said over his shoulder, as he cleared a trail ahead of me. 'I don't want to ruin everything!'

My face twisted. 'That's hard, Nick.' I wanted to yell my feelings from every hill, from the tops of the tallest eucalypts, I wanted girls everywhere to know that he and I were in a relationship, if that's what this was, that he was no longer available. It was impossible to hide my disappointment.

Stopping, he turned to me and when I reached him he touched my cheek gently. 'This is important, Deb ... for now, we'll work something out.'

What choice did I have? I had to trust him. 'I guess we can try and unravel a bit more of this mystery in the meantime,' I said.

He resumed his walk, holding back the low-growing branches for me so that I wasn't stung in the face by one. As we neared civilisation, the bush grew less dense and we

merged with a more frequently trodden path which meandered along the waterline. Dusk was gathering. Insects
hummed and gnats swarmed silently in coal-dust patches,
the ending day an opportunity for moving on, the Kookaburra's call a warning as a Willy Wagtail took flight, his
wings scattering the sky above us.

Nick slung his arm over my shoulders casually, almost fa-
miliarly. The warmth and heaviness of it felt reassuring, but
as we got closer he withdrew slightly, noticing the rowdiness
of my brother and his friends who were still apparently
oblivious to my absence.

'I'll take you home,' he insisted protectively, concern fur-
rowing his brow as he noticed the state of my intended chap-
erone. 'Just tell your brother you've met a friend or something.'

I wandered over to George who was looking a little unsteady. 'Who's driving, George?'

'Ish no problem, Mandy'll drive us later,' he slurred. I noticed his bloodshot eyes. 'Sheez not drinking.'

I looked across at Mandy, relieved to see her in a respect-
able state, a bottle of water in her hand. She chatted to an
overweight boy who was oblivious to the sausages he was
charring on the barbeque. Great plumes of smoke and sparks
spiralled from the grill. He wielded the tongs in one hand
and a stubby in the other, unconcerned. I raised my eyebrows and shrugged involuntarily.

'You look like you've had enough!'

'Yesh, Mum,' he said with a mock salute, nearly taking his
eye out with his can.

'Well, whatever then ... I love you.' I hugged him briefly.

'You too Shish.' He patted me on the back like I was his
pet dog.

'I'm going home. I've met up with a couple of mates. I'll

see you tomorrow.' The lie came too easily and I swallowed down a globule of guilt. I could see Nick out of the corner of my eye, only because I knew he was there. He leant against his motorbike, his arms folded, but perfectly still.

'She you then,' George slurred.

'Try not to have too many more!' I scolded, exasperated.

'Thas my shishter, the good girl … Go on, go home. She you tomorrow.' He weaved unsteadily.

I kissed him on the cheek and walked away, ignoring the antics going on around me.

As I neared Nick I realised how much a part of the dusk he seemed; his stillness almost rendering him part of the scenery. Only his eyes flashed like a wild animal at night. Pushing himself off his bike as I neared he dropped his arms so that he appeared a little more relaxed. Behind me my brother was already cavorting around with his friends again, another long night which they might regret tomorrow.

'What can I say?' I said, as I neared Nick, unavoidably grinning at the carryings on of the crowd, 'he's an idiot sometimes!'

'Will he be okay?' he asked, slightly troubled.

I wasn't as worried. 'He'll be fine. This happens a little too frequently! Mandy will look after him, she never drinks.'

'Well, we've got the whole evening now,' he said. The thrum of the bike silenced the cicadas. 'You hungry?'

'Sure,' I answered, realising that I hadn't eaten anything the whole day. 'I'm absolutely ravenous.' The air began to move as he opened up the throttle, silky cool whispers on my sunburn.

We stopped and picked up Indian take-away, eating with our fingers at a wooden table in the growing gloom, shrouded in companionable silence and a sweet fragrant cloud. As our stomachs filled he told me about his months on the ocean with his family, the unusual places they had visited, what had happened when the toilet on board had blocked. He joked light-heartedly about the conflict, avoiding detail, telling it without drama, even chuckling on occasion. But his smile never quite reached the creases around his eyes. He hadn't wanted to go. Living in such close confines, with no chance of escape, with people so absorbed in their own interests, in their plans for his life, must have been hard.

'What are you going to do next year?' he asked, abruptly changing the subject.

I wiped my oily fingers on a paper serviette. Who knew? He had turned my world upside down. Again! Was it a good idea to let him know that? 'Good question,' I said, swatting at an invisible insect as I tried to arrange my features so that I wouldn't be immediately readable. 'I'm trying not to think about it too much at the moment. I get stressed out because I don't really know. I need to focus on doing as well as I can in my exams, and then I'll see after that.'

He emptied his cola and then scrunched up the can with one hand. 'There's so much pressure on you in the last year at school,' he reflected, tossing it into an open bin which stood at least four metres from us.

'Wow, that's amazing,' I said, impressed. His face flushed in the dim light.

'I'm an idiot.' He shook his head.

I shook mine back at him, but couldn't help the smile which seemed to stretch all the way across my face. 'You're a guy!'

'That explains it does it?' he raised an eyebrow and pretended to consider.

I nodded. 'Pretty much.' Inexplicably a strange memory

came to mind. 'At least you haven't run naked past my window like one of George's friends used to do when we were younger.'

Our eyes met.

'Don't give me any ideas,' he replied too seriously. We burst into insane laughter, like you do sometimes when everything falls into place and the chuckle that builds in your throat cannot be contained within your body, but must be released in great gusts and spasms. Eyes watering and snivelling we stopped just short of rolling around in the dirt and kicking our legs in the air. The lights of a car neared, the beams widening over our shaking forms as it slowed, but then it sped up and passed, the driver possibly a serial killer who wanted to be taken seriously.

Only when we stopped did we realise how hushed it had become. Even the forest creatures had been quietened by our insanity. I wiped my eyes and after a moment a cricket began to trill.

It was still hard to speak, giggles stuck in my throat. I took a breath and tried. 'I might even take a year off next year, maybe go on a working holiday overseas, see some of the sights you've been talking about. I've been saving for a car, but the money might be better used for something like that. I've got enough saved to buy a suitcase anyway.'

It was almost completely dark now. The moon was out full and bright, casting a blue-white glow like a night-light and making the large pockets of moving shadows under the trees pitch black and unfathomable. If he wasn't around I would have been spooked.

He crushed my drink can, making a loud cracking sound, and I wondered whether he would throw it, but he didn't. 'It might be the only opportunity you ever get to take that much time out. Once you finish studying there's always such a sense of urgency to get a job.'

'Yes, well some of us have to pay off our debt!' I meant it to be light-hearted, but it came out wrong, like a barb. I kicked myself.

'I *do* know that I'm privileged Deb,' he said, his eyes hardening. '*I'm such a moron*', I thought, '*and he is so moody!*'

'Sorry,' I answered, not sure exactly what to say. 'I didn't mean to rub it in.'

He remained silent, fiddling with the can and I rushed to fill the gap, babbling. 'Travel might not be a bad idea for me, a little time to decide what I really want to do. Maybe something creative, like graphic design, but I don't know if that's a sensible choice. I love it, but I need to go into a field where I can get a job quite easily. I don't want to study something for years and years and then end up as a shop assistant because I can't get my foot in the door! Maybe I'll do the whole pub thing for a year, see a bit of the world first.' At last I shut up.

After a moment he spoke quietly, his head lowered, his hands still on the can. 'I miss you already.'

Relief. I exhaled and my shoulders dropped. 'I know what you mean,' I said, thinking back to when he had told me that he was leaving on his trip. I wondered whether I would ever have the courage to leave *him*.

Another car passed, casting glaring high beams over us and into the woods, making the creatures of the night scurry and hide. As it departed I realised how accustomed I had become to the dark. Beside the moon, the only light was a small globe dimmed by the many insects which made it their home and grave, but which still attempted to reach out to us feebly from the distant toilet block.

'You should do it, Deb. If that's what you want, you should go. There's so much out there, just waiting, waiting for you to touch and taste, to open your eyes to new experiences. It will definitely change you.' I couldn't catch the subtlety of his expression in the dim light, just the radiant intensity of his eyes, but I sensed that the tables had turned.

'You could come with me,' I stated impulsively, suddenly excited at this new idea. 'We could experience it together.'

He shook his head. 'That would be great Deb, but it's not possible for me. Not right now.' He became wistful for a moment. 'You need to go, expand your horizons. Australia is not the world, and this place ...'

'Three Kings?'

'Yes, it's a strange little world here, shuttered. Before you know it, this is all there is.' For a strange moment I sensed rather than saw the shadows that flitted across his face. His mood had shifted again and I lost him for a while. But picking up on my confusion he suddenly smiled and I caught the flash of his teeth and the release of the dark angel from within him.

A strange trilling sound rang through the forest and then silence fell. An owl hooted and I shivered.

'I don't even know what I'm going to do, travel's a possibility, study a little more likely, maybe I'll get to do both,' I said.

'Right now it feels really good to be alive.' He raised his forearm from the table, his fingers spread. Instinctively I raised mine to meet his. Heat radiated between us as we gazed into each other's eyes, his glinting even in the darkness. For a charmed moment, everything else was forgotten and the magic lingered.

'Today has been really strange,' I said, my fingers still entwined with his, '... good strange,' I quickly clarified. 'Magical.' It was impossible to adequately express what I wanted to. 'It feels so incredibly unreal to be sitting here with you.

It's like a dream I hope never ends, but I'm afraid I might wake soon.'

He pulled me to my feet and suddenly I realised how alone we were. The road was silent and everything seemed still and dark, even the breeze slumbered and the clouds hid the moon, making his expression indiscernible.

Mum was still out when he dropped me at home. After a long shower I collapsed into bed. Although my body was exhausted, I lay awake for a long, long time, my mind refusing to slow. I was no longer a virgin and that was a big deal. My body ached gently, a needless reminder of my evolution. Every aspect of the day tormented and tantalised me. Light and shadow, grit and bliss. Tangled emotions, like the darkest chocolate, bitter and sweet. Our encounter at the lake turned my gut to jelly, and teased my body with the deepest desire. A twinge of sadness farewelled childhood. I was a woman now and I would have to embrace the complications of the adult world.

Completely drained, I finally fell asleep.

23

KATE

Nick was waiting outside in a sleek white rental car. He was reading the newspaper intently and I wondered which item caught his interest to such an extent.

'Sorry, have you been waiting long?' I rushed towards him, a little out of breath.

'No, not too long, just a few minutes.' He popped the passenger door for me with a wide smile of greeting.

'How are you?' he asked, a slight frown creasing his brow as he noticed my haggard appearance.

'Didn't have the best night last night,' I minimised.

'No?'

'It's a long story, a near miss. Anyway, everything turned out okay.' I clasped my bag on my lap, waiting for him to start the engine.

'All's well that ends well. Is that it?'

'Sort of.' I fiddled with the straps on my bag, uncomfortable with explaining the circumstances of my evening, impatient to leave.

'What happened?' His tone was out of character, a demand. He wasn't going to drop it.

I sighed. 'In a nutshell, someone put something in my drink and tried to take advantage of me. Luckily I had friends watching out for me.' Not too far from the truth.

'You look so pale.' His fingers touched my chin for a brief moment. He gently turned my face towards him so that he could examine me further. I felt embarrassed.

'Don't worry, I'm fine now,' I said.

'Really!' I reiterated firmly, noticing a doubtful look cross his face. 'No need to make a fuss.' I managed a crooked smile.

'Do your folks know?'

'Are you joking? No, and I won't be telling them. They don't need to know. What good would it do? They'll just freak out completely, get really worried. Sleepless nights and all that. They'll be here this afternoon with a removal van. It's not worth it. The problem has been sorted out and I'm going to be more careful next time.'

He looked at me for a long time. 'Well, if you're absolutely positive.'

'Please, Nick. Start the car. Let's go. I am completely sure.'

The car roared to life, its fierce engine and lowered suspension an unpleasant surprise.

'This obviously isn't one of those new hybrids!'

'No, I think the rental agency wants to take single-handed responsibility for raising the emission levels in Australia. They have a fleet of these.'

'Probably got them cheap.'

'They look good anyway,' he said, as I leaned across to hear him.

'Well that's okay then,' I shouted.

We thundered towards St Kilda.

'I haven't forgotten what we were talking about today by the way.'

'No, I didn't think you had,' he replied.

We grabbed a late lunch at an eclectic café, watching the interesting mix of passers-by. The menu was schizophrenic,

Asian alongside French and American-inspired dishes. The food didn't work, but a funky vibe provided by a colourful troupe of gifted musicians made up for it.

After our meal we ambled across to a park. The afternoon was surprisingly pleasant for mid-winter. A mild aberration brought about by the unlikely combination of clear skies and the absence of the icy south wind. Black swans slid across the mirrored surface of a glassy lake under the watch of the trees, which stood like sentinels. City buildings stood out starkly against the bright blue sky in the distance.

We walked side by side, arms touching, along the path which wound its way around the water.

'So, what was it that you couldn't tell me on the phone?' I asked abruptly, tired of the delaying, when I realised that he wasn't volunteering the information.

'Kate,' he said stopping, suddenly stern, 'you're impatient, but maybe you'll wish you weren't!'

'Well at this rate, we'll never know!' I felt exasperated, but refrained from stamping my foot.

He couldn't resist a grin at my almost-tantrum. 'Relax, I'm going to tell you, but you'll have to keep it in confidence!' I wasn't sure whether or not he was being serious, but his face had become earnest again.

'A secret? I'm intrigued. I'll do my best.' We recommenced our walk.

'You'll have to.'

I raised an eyebrow. 'Weirder and weirder. James Bond isn't going to jump out from behind the next bush, is he?'

'Who knows? It's quite possible.' His voice was not quite as light-hearted as I would have liked. 'You come from a strange background I'm afraid.'

I nodded. 'You said so, in fact the word you used was 'cursed', which seems slightly more ominous than strange!'

'Yes, it does feel that way sometimes.' He touched his chin as he considered. 'You would have been better off not finding me at all. I'm pretty confident about that.'

I shook my head adamantly. 'That's not for you to decide, Nick.'

'No, maybe not.' His eyes became distant. Long-buried memories were being conveyed to the surface and he was sorting out how to explain what he wanted to say. I didn't hurry him.

'You already know a little about my family. I come from a very controlling background, controlling *and* powerful.' This much I knew. So far, so good.

'When I was nineteen I found out that there were reasons things were the way they were, reasons why everything was so strange.' He shook his head sadly. 'It was hard to cope with ... I had to get away, escape the madness. I managed for a while anyway.' His smile was grim as he shook his head. 'But of course these things have a way of finding you wherever you are and you get sucked back in.'

'It's hard to escape family,' I said, thinking about the weirdness that went with family, and the number of people who clung so desperately to those who treated them so badly.

'Yes,' he agreed, 'and when you're born into a family like ours I don't think escape is a real option.' My circumstances enabled my escape for a time, but life was curious, because here I was - and through my own doing.

A couple collided with us, distracting me, as they were dragged along by an eager border collie with its eye on a swan near the bank. They waved apologetically, disappearing in a cloud of dust along the path, and as it settled Nick spoke again.

'There were reasons that I ended up on my own, Kate, reasons I've struggled, simply trying to live a normal life. As a child I never understood why my parents were so over-protective, why they imposed themselves and their will onto every aspect of our lives. It was suffocating.'

'It must have been hard,' I agreed, but he didn't seem to hear me, or even notice the commotion as the collie began barking at the swan, who turned to face it and raised wide wings. The collie dropped and the humiliated owners tugged it away.

'Of course, it was always obvious that there were secrets.' He shrugged his shoulders. 'I just never realised the enormity of them. I remained uninformed, until they had no other option.' He looked puzzled. 'I'm still not completely sure why they chose that path, but that was the way it was.'

'Maybe they were trying to protect you,' I guessed.

'Now, with the benefit of hindsight, I think that *was* what they were trying to do. To let us live a little of life innocent, without the burdens that would come later.' He became pensive. The breeze ruffled his hair, cajoling him to forget the loss and sadness of the past. It didn't work. 'They were afraid,' he said, carefully. 'I never realised that … but they were.'

'What were they afraid of?'

He turned to me, the depth of his emerald gaze disconcerting. 'Of what knowledge would do. What it had already done in the past. Too much information too early or too little, too late …' He grimaced, his face contorting like he was in pain.

'I was angry for so long. My brother had just died and we were going through so much. I didn't need this as well. Initially I refused to believe them … but ultimately I had no option. I was faced with everything that had been kept from me for all those years. In a matter of moments the world I knew ceased to exist. I felt betrayed, hated them for the freaks I thought they were. I ran ... but I *had to* believe. Eventually I went back. You see, much as I hadn't wanted to accept it, I was one of them, an Edwards. I would never feel the same sense of belonging anywhere else, not with my background.' His sigh was deep. 'I tried to live my own life as much as possible, maintained separate business interests. They accepted that, which was a surprise. I guess it was preferable to losing me altogether.' His voice had become increasingly heavy, burdened by the weight of the past, by what he could not change, what he had been forced to accept.

I touched his arm briefly, trying to comfort him and he noticed me this time. His smile was tight.

'I've accepted that it was difficult for them, Kate. I'm not angry anymore.' And in the moment he truly seemed resigned.

I stopped, and he halted next to me. He picked up a couple of pebbles and skimmed them across the water so that they skipped like firewalkers. It seemed like a completely ludicrous pastime at a moment like this, but it was somehow soothing, taking me back to beach holidays with Nanny. The gentle outward see-saw of ripples softened the surface of the lake, shattering our reflections into a million more accurate reflections of the chaotic truth.

'Poor Deb got caught up in the middle of it all,' he said, dusting dirt from the stones off his hands.

'It wasn't the best timing, I suppose.'

He nodded. 'We were always doomed. There were longstanding issues between my family and hers, which I found out about around that time too.'

'Her father and your aunt?'

'You know about it?' He sounded surprised.

'Just what you said that first day at the restaurant,' I reminded him.

'Oh, yes. Well, Deb's father and my aunt, Sofia, were involved romantically.' A war raged inside him. He struggled to continue. 'My father was very protective of Sofia. Their father wasn't around then … anyway, Sofia should never have become involved with him.'

'Why?'

'Because …' His face became a jumble of uncertainty, his mouth pulling off to one side as though about to leave the rest of his features behind.

'Because?' I prompted, at last.

'Because she should have known better.' His words came in a burst, but they made little sense to me. My eyebrow rose of its own accord. 'She *knew* that it would never be okay, but she let herself get involved with him and fall pregnant. Who knows, maybe she even planned it? I don't know, I didn't know her but I have heard since that she was the type to tempt fate, to push the boundaries.'

A girl who pushed the boundaries and tempted fate, who went after the guy her parents disapproved of. Wasn't that what was expected of teenagers? I could relate. I nodded sagely anyway.

'When my family found out what had happened they made life difficult for him.' He rubbed his jaw while considering. 'That's probably an understatement. They pretty much forced him out of the town.' I tried to think of the means they might have employed to achieve that and shivered at the thought. 'It's hard to understand if you don't know Three Kings, which most people don't, but they pretty much owned the place.'

It *was* hard to imagine, living in a city the size of Melbourne.

He gazed out at the lake. 'Your grandfather could never have had anything to do with the child,' he said, running his fingers through his hair restlessly. 'My family would never have permitted it.'

'What happened to Sofia?' I asked, the tension in my gut advising me in advance that the answer would not be pretty.

'She died ... some years later.' I stared at him, willing myself to understand the man who was bringing such great upheaval into my life, to truly understand his motivation, the level of his honesty.

'How?'

'She killed herself ... drowned.' His answer didn't help. Another one! He shook his head, as if reading my mind, and then started scuffing grit into the lake, waiting for my next question, dreading it.

I hesitated. His reluctance was obvious, but the question had to be asked. 'And the child?'

'She took her son with her,' he said, his look intense as I inhaled sharply. He was desperate for me to understand, to accept what was so unacceptable, but I could not hide my shock.

I couldn't get the image out of my mind. A mother killing her son and then herself. It happened, but nothing could be more unnatural. I couldn't ask for the gory details, wasn't sure whether that would be fair to him, or to me. Had she loved him? Maybe she'd done it *because* she had. But how *could she*? Before I could stop myself, my mouth formed the question.

'How old was he?'

'Nearly four,' he said, his voice little more than a whisper. Just a baby. A boy I had never known and yet my heart hurt for a life unlived. I felt nauseous.

'Was it because of what happened with Deb's father?'

His lips twisted, but it was a while before he spoke. Finally he shrugged. 'Sort of. I mean they created the child together. The child was the issue in the end.' *The child*. How could a child of three be *the issue?*

'I don't understand.'

'This is so hard. I never imagined having to explain it.' A faint sheen of perspiration had appeared above his lip, even though the temperature was dropping.

'Try, Nick,' I encouraged gently, thinking that at some point someone had had to explain this to him.

'His name was Erik.'

'Erik,' I repeated, the tiny corpse assigned a label.

'Our family line is not like others, Kate.' This was a point he'd been trying to get across for a while, I realised, and it was definitely beginning to sink in.

'We're different. Unique.'

'Uh-huh,' I said, thoughtfully and maybe just a little doubtfully, given how many crazy families there were in the world. This one had a penchant for killing themselves. 'You aren't going to tell me that on my twentieth birthday I'm going to get very hairy and start howling at the moon when I get my period are you? It won't help with dating,' I despaired, trying to lighten the mood a notch so that we didn't end up going down the path of so many others in our family.

'No, no, nothing like that.' His smile was small, but a light shone for a moment and I was glad. At least whatever it was wouldn't be stereotypical. 'It's equally perplexing though,' he added, making my heart sink.

'Not the whole vampire thing either, I hope?' He shook his head and lifted his hands to the heavens as if beseeching an answer from there. I guess a voice from a cloud might not be that unexpected at this point.

'Will you just let me finish?'

I could see the effort it was taking for him to explain this to me and so I shut up. The grooves in his brow had been progressively deepening all afternoon and were now like twisted canyons across his forehead. Whatever this was, he had locked it away a long time ago. He had used a steel safe, wrapped in a heavy security chain before placing it in a ship, which he had sent to the middle of the ocean. There he had blown it up and let it sink into a massive crater, down, down into bottomless depths, where the light never penetrates and the only observers are sightless.

He had hoped never to reveal it again. I recognised that much in his face, in his body, in the slope of his back, the loss in this moment, the submission. I had taken him back to that place of perpetual night. Swallowing hard I recognised how deep-seated his suffering was. He had no choice but to tell me. He owed me this effort and so I let him continue uninterrupted.

24

DEB AND NICK

Although the sun had already sipped the dew from the lawn and the breeze had started its gentle whine, the house was quiet when I woke up. My brother's door stood ajar. He lay where he had fallen on his bed, snoring loudly, his room a scene from a post-apocalyptic movie. Mum's door was closed. She must have returned home very late as I hadn't heard her come in before I fell asleep.

I poured orange juice and ate cereal before straightening up the living area and washing dishes noisily, but the tranquillity around me remained. Sunlight streamed through the windows, beckoning me.

I had to go. Not sure when either would surface, I left a note on the kitchen counter so that Mum wouldn't worry and exited the house, singing to myself. I should have been studying, of course, but sitting still long enough to focus on a single word was impossible today. The birds were scattering fruit from the tree and bits fell into the birdbath below, turning it into a potent punch in the sun.

The ground seemed to move and then the hearty rumble of his bike hit me as I was about to step onto the sand. He had an uncanny knack of finding me.

'Another coincidence?' I asked, an eyebrow raised, 'or were you waiting for me?'

He shrugged with a chuckle and tried to look innocent. 'Jump on. Come on, I dare you,' he teased. He was very cheerful this morning, brightly enthusiastic, the boy inside the man showing. 'I want to take you somewhere.'

'Oh, and where is that?' I asked. He ignored my question and without even completely stopping grabbed me, one-armed, and swung me onto the back, laughing at my surprise. 'There you go *Your* Royal Highness!'

His enthusiasm was contagious - like smiles, not measles - and I relaxed. 'Are you kidnapping me, Prince Valiant?'

He manoeuvred the bike so that we were facing the exit. 'Only if you want to be kidnapped!'

'This might just be your lucky day.'

He revved the engine, making speech pointless. An unexpected nodule of anxiety bit like an ulcer. Where were we going? Ignoring it I focussed on the firm feel of his waist, and the heat which radiated through his t-shirt. Strange creatures came alive inside me, waking to dance and writhe, to spin in my stomach and then sink into the most private part of me, heavy and wanting, impatient. I swallowed hard as a flush of heat broke across my forehead, and moved closer to him, my front pressed tightly against his back, my nose and mouth near to the hollow on the side of his neck, close enough to smell him, to taste him if I wanted to. That was better. I inhaled deeply and he turned his head to the side with just a flicker of knowing. And then a chuckle. 'Don't forget your helmet, Miss Brayshaw.' He passed one to me and pulled his own on, forcing me to give him a little more room. 'We wouldn't want to flaunt road safety laws, now would we?' I snapped my visor down noisily relieved to hide my flushed cheeks and he opened up the throttle.

We rode for about twenty minutes, leaving the areas I was familiar with behind. After a while we started a slow ascent until the road wound its way along the top of a bluff over-looking the ocean. Behind us, the small township of Three Kings crept up the side of the hill with the beach below and the large rocks out at sea. But here, away from everything, sat a strangely private suburb. Exclusive hideaways were set far back from the road, many perched higher up on the hill behind tall walls and gates. Magnificent homes were built in an eclectic range of styles. Some were contemporary with flat or strangely-angled roofs, jutting off the edge of the hill, or creeping up it in boxy modules of wood, stone and glass. Others had been here longer, imposing but traditional, old world.

'Looks like a high crime neighbourhood,' I shouted to him, the wind quickly whisking my words away.

'The more you have, the more paranoid you become,' he shouted back.

We arrived outside a large wrought-iron gate bordered on either side by a great white wall. A leafy green and purple creeper wove a living tapestry in and out of the curls of iron-work so that it was impossible to make out the view of what was on the other side.

Nick clicked a remote and the gates opened with a slight whine onto a long twisty driveway, which took us into the fortress and ended at a large turning circle in front of a sprawling white-painted mansion. A four-car garage and workshop was set to one side. On the other side the house stood, tall and imposing, with wide stone steps leading up to a broad shady veranda and a newer extension which looked like a sunny conservatory area on the right. Enormous dark teak double doors stood at the top of the stairs like formidable sentinels. He'd brought me to his home.

'What are we doing here?'

'Don't worry,' he reassured me. 'They left early this morning. Business beckons from afar.' He made a dramatic flourish with his hands and I giggled, mostly out of nervousness.

'Well at least they didn't take you with them this time. That's good!' I eased my grip on his waist as curiosity got the better of me and I looked around.

The bike came to a stop and he kicked out the stand. I got off. 'Come.' He took my helmet and then moved ahead of me towards the stairs. 'I thought I'd take the opportunity to show you where I live, where I come from … why I've turned out the way I have!'

'I guess this might give me a few clues,' I acknowledged, following more cautiously, but noticing everything. The perfectly pruned plants and manicured bushes, the absence of weeds in the grass and flowerbeds, barely any leaves on the drive even though there were trees all around, the way the windows sparkled and reflected the garden and sky perfectly without a hint of saltiness.

The most breathtaking fountain appeared in front of the conservatory. A female angel touched down in the middle of a pool, her wings spread out above her overshadowing her delicate form but creating a space in which she seemed to find some sort of refuge. They seemed to radiate the rays of the sun, blazing the bright whiteness of alabaster, while her body beneath was dappled under their shelter. She bent down slightly, her dainty arms reaching outwards, cautious, as though she feared the sun would reach past her wings, and touch her thin skin and she would be drawn to heaven and gone forever.

Water spouts cascaded from the pedestal beneath her into an upper basin where it was more turbulent and then into the surrounding pool where a young boy reached up towards her, his face filled with longing. For all of its glory, there was a sense of melancholy about the tableau, unful-filled yearning, because the boy so clearly desired her touch, her goodness and love. But in this frozen scene all he could do was long for it, he would never have it.

As I considered the boy something icy washed over me, like the Victorian south wind had somehow made its way east. I shivered, but then it was gone.

'Wow …' was all I could manage, disconcerted by the emotional connection I felt.

'It was a commission. A long time ago. I was a child. Some famous sculptor did it,' Nick explained.

'The boy is lost,' I said, 'and she's afraid …'

He placed his hand on my shoulder, gently drawing me away. 'It's art … open to interpretation.'

We continued to the stairs and then up them. He took my hand as I reached the top one, seeking to reassure me. I won-dered where the army of staff hid, whether they were cam-ouflaged so as to give the illusion of privacy. 'There's no-one here, Deb, it's Sunday.'

It felt good to have my hand in his. 'I'll have to take your word for it,' I answered, shifting from foot to foot, waiting for an ancestor to pop out of the woodwork and demand to know what I was doing here, or a haughty butler to remind me that riff-raff should use the back entrance.

Squeezing my hand he laughed. 'We should be quite safe, Deb. It's only me around. Not that that should reassure you.' He winked mischievously, sending my heart into free-fall. Blood roared in my ears.

Dropping my hand he held the door open for me and bowed as I walked in. It closed behind us with a deep thud. The interior wasn't what I had expected, whatever that was – maybe something flashy and over the top.

'It's lovely,' I mused, my fingers tracing the carvings

along the back of an antique bench-seat in the entrance area.

He watched me, amused. 'You look amazed.'

'Maybe,' I agreed, 'I wasn't sure what I was expecting, something modern maybe.' I was surprised by the tasteful, refined furnishings. The dark furniture looked heavy, antique. Rust and gold coloured Persian rugs warmed the glossy timber floors, family portraits and old oils in ornate frames hung on the walls. There was history here, it was almost tangible. The past embraced us like the walls had eyes, very old eyes which looked back into ours and measured everything. Or was it just me, measuring myself, failing as I doubted my own worth in this place where I was so uncertain of my welcome?

Although he had said we were alone, the house felt occupied, watchful. Maybe it was the spirits of the past and the stories which attached themselves to everything in this home. Nothing was mass produced, characterless. It was all old ... unique ... infused with something intangible.

'It's an old house, and it's old money,' Nick explained, gesturing to what surrounded us. 'Everything in here has been around for a while. The furniture, rugs, the paintings ... everything in the house is inherited. My parents hold onto things, they're very sentimental. The house has been in my father's family a while.'

I nodded, suddenly more curious about my own history, one I seemed to know so little about. 'You'd see why they would, every piece has a history.'

'Which is impossible to escape,' he replied cynically.

A strange longing came over me as I regarded the walls. 'The paintings, all the photos, it's very nice,' I said, walking up to framed photos of other places, other times, and examining them. Handsome men, many with the same startling eyes, their builds strong, their jaws determined, dashing into the ocean to save a floundering swimmer, playing cricket and golf, receiving philanthropic and business awards, riding in hot-air balloons with their lovers or wives, champagne glasses raised. Good-looking and successful, wealth and power, an intoxicating combination.

The women were a more varied group, but no less stunning. Some were fair-haired, others darker, but they were all remarkable. They gazed directly into the eye of the camera, with easy smiles and high foreheads and striking wide-set eyes.

'The eye thing is very unusual.'

He nodded. 'We're freaks, Deb. Haven't I been trying to tell you that?'

'Well, I wouldn't go *that* far,' I answered with a smile.

He shook his head. 'That's just because you don't know us, believe me.'

Turning to him I reached up to place my hands on his shoulders. 'Your eyes are amazing, Nick.'

His irises seemed to luminesce, the darker green becoming streaked with emerald and then merging with the gold which swirled around the pupil, becoming almost green-yellow in places for a moment, cat-like. And then streaks of olive appeared as the gold bled into the colour. As he turned slightly to the window, the colour changed to blue and green, and then only green when he looked back at me. Green with fire in the middle. And then the colours merged and marbled again, constantly picking up and reacting to each and every light variation around us. A branch moving against a window in the breeze, a cloud moving in front of the sun and dimming the light through the windows, minute shifts in my movement in front of him. The colour changed constantly. But strangely only if you stood this still and this close to examine them, was it that obvious.

'They're definitely not normal.'

'Well it's not just me so beware, we're coming for you.'

'They're like a kaleidoscope ... filled with life from other galaxies.'

He gestured back to the wall of photos. 'Whatever they are, they are not unique, as you can see.'

He was quite right, of course, a bizarre genetic anomaly which was probably best left to science to explain.

One photo stood out from the others. The quality was a little grainy and so it was quite hidden by the vibrancy of the others. Taking a step closer I peered at it. The family were assembled, but it was unlike the rest.

'Sofia,' Nick murmured, noticing my interest as I examined a face which hadn't appeared in the others, 'my father's sister.'

'Sofia,' I repeated. Something tugged at me. I reached out and touched her face. 'She looks sad.' The pain on her face was almost contagious. In fact the whole gathering looked formal and unhappy, the subjects dressed in dark clothes, with expressions to match. She was in the middle, an unusual beauty, even with her tortured green eyes and drawn mouth. I wondered how her face changed when she smiled and the pain left her eyes, whether that was even possible. The family leaned in slightly towards her, their sideways glances almost furtive. She seemed unaware of them. Her arms were slightly extended, her palms facing upwards, like she was imploring something higher, or God, something a photo could never capture. She seemed so fragile, like a touch might topple her, make her crumple or disintegrate in a puff of dust. It seemed strange that this photo had ever been taken and that other more appealing ones wouldn't have replaced it.

'She looks ... troubled.'

His brows met in a heavy line. 'I don't know why they keep it up.'

A wall of conceit and then this, hidden in plain sight, something painful, excruciating even, some sort of reminder … or warning. I shrugged. 'History, maybe. We want to forget the bad stuff, but it's a part of life too.'

He regarded me for a long while, and finally nodded.

'She's not like everyone else,' I remarked. Her hair was dark, almost black and worn long and straight, the style quite different to the others.

'No, she's not,' he agreed. There was something raw about the way he said it. Realising that I had noticed he tried to alter the tone of his voice, making it lighter. 'Daniel is probably the most like her, looks-wise.' Daniel's hair was almost as dark as Sofia's, but wavy like Nick's. His eyes were impossibly bright, made even more vivid by his dark hair.

'He's very striking.'

'Don't go getting any ideas.'

I raised my eyebrows and pretended to consider, finally stating boldly. 'He's a bit young for me. I prefer my men a little more mature.'

He smiled. 'I'm not mature.'

'You'll do,' I laughed. I gestured to the photos. 'I've never had this. My folks fell out with their families on both sides. It's always just been the four of us, and now the three of us! We didn't grow up knowing our cousins, didn't have the sort of family connections you have. I always missed that, envied friends going away on holiday with their relatives. It must be fun.'

He grimaced at my idealism. 'Like anything there are pros and cons. My family congregate in this area, and that's not just our immediate family, relatives too. No-one is ever too far away from here. Our lives revolve around this tiny place.

Sometimes you wonder why? Why, in all this time, we never moved away?'

I shrugged, not finding it at all hard to understand. 'Why would you? It's beautiful here, peaceful, plus your history is here. There are lots of reasons to stay before we even start with the weather and the ocean. People seek out places like this.'

'Places like this,' he mused, as though he knew a lot I didn't, 'places which remain perpetually small while the rest of the world is ever expanding, cluttered and crazy. That doesn't happen by chance, Deb.'

We moved away from the wall of photos to the stairs. I had noticed the security on our way, had even remarked on it. This was a strange community, a cluster, part of Three Kings, and yet, not really. Secluded, isolated by choice in this island suburb surrounded by hills and sea and bush.

He ran his fingers through his hair, which was tousled and messy already and I longed to feel it against my own fingers, the soft thickness on top, the shorter roughness around the nape of his neck. 'People here have secrets,' he said interrupting my thoughts. 'You can't take them at face value, not like your world.'

My snicker was louder than intended. 'My world? Where *do* you think I live, Nick? It has nothing to do with *my* world, or *your* world. It has to do with human nature! There are more than enough secrets sneaking around in *my* world, don't worry. One day the skeletons will burst out of closets all around the town, consume everyone, and take over and that's *all* there will be. Skeletons … in shorts and tees and thongs!'

'I guess so,' he chuckled, quickly serious again. 'But up on this hill, people are hiding something or hiding from something, it's that simple.'

'Well, yes, that seems obvious,' I allowed. 'Maybe the skeletons here are a little bigger.'

'This house has layers of skeletons, and on top of the layers there are skeleton sprinkles. Sometimes they rattle so loud, you can't hear yourself think!'

'Mmm, a skeleton layer-cake,' I said, following him up the stairs onto a wide landing.

I moved to tall arched windows which let in the sun and the sea. The sea air was fresh and salty. It blew into my face, taking the wisps of hair off my face and neck and blowing them back. The view was stunning. Below I could see the umbrella-top of the angel's wings, and the winding driveway meandering down the hill partly obscured by trees. Above it all was a wide blue ocean horizon, speckled with white horses. As I gazed at the view I sensed him behind me.

'It's stunning,' I said, my breathing hitching a little as his body pressed up against mine.

'It pales next to you, Deb,' he whispered in my ear. My heart thudded.

'Come.' He took my hand and tugged me into a large room on the opposite side. It overlooked a rectangular swimming pool and a large flat expanse of perfect lawn with a tennis court in the far corner and a small pavilion next to it.

'So, this is it, my *lair*.'

His room was uncluttered and masculine, everything in its rightful position. 'Your room looks skeleton free,' I advised, pretending to look around the back of the door for one, 'no cobwebs either, that's good.' After living with my brother I had come to the conclusion that males were slobs, but obviously this one wasn't. The room didn't seem lived in though. Unlike the common areas of the house, it was bland, clinical, without personality, disappointing.

'I can't really take the credit for the neatness,' he smirked.

'We have staff!'

'That's horrendous,' I laughed. 'So really you're a pig, just in disguise!'

'That's harsh,' he said, kicking the door shut and turning to me. The band of creatures in my belly started their wild cavorting again, the friction of their movements making parts of me very hot. Grabbing my hand he pulled me over to the large bed which sat in the middle of the room.

He patted the dark doona cover. 'I wanted to introduce you to my bed.'

'Hello bed, how do you do?' I answered cheekily, imitating his pat.

'Do you want to know what happens to naughty girls in this house?' he asked, with mock severity.

'Do they get sent to your father's study?' My giggles threatened to become uncontrollable. Nerves, excitement, fear, desire, cartwheeling around in my gut. Tingling everywhere. 'Do they get spanked?'

'Tsk, tsk,' he tutted, shaking his head. I tried to smack him playfully on the arm but in an instant I was pinned under him. His mouth consumed me with burning intensity.

'Sorry,' he grinned, as we fell apart. 'I just couldn't restrain myself.'

Tiny pulses throbbed everywhere.

'So soft,' he whispered, pressing his lips to the pulse which throbbed in the nape of my neck. It tickled and I tried to stifle a giggle, not to squirm. For an instant he looked indignant. I burst into inappropriate laughter, but at the same time I inhaled the sweet apple cinnamon smell of his shampoo and then his mouth fell onto mine again and I was silenced.

'Aah, Nick,' I groaned, as he pushed up my top and his lips touched my nipple. Pleasure made my head buzz. His attention moved to the curve of my waist, his hands searing my skin as they arrived at the top of my hips and slipped under my shorts. As he found the pulsing core of me every cell burst into life.

'Slowly Baby,' he said, pulling my top over my head. He threw it into the far corner of the room. Pressing his ear to my chest he listened to my heart.

'What are you doing to me?' I groaned.

Instead of replying he sat up and tugged off my shorts and then my panties, tossing them to a similar place of exile.

'You're exquisite, Deb.' I sought to cover myself with my hands as he gazed down at me.

'You shouldn't be shy, you're flawless, like a Botticelli Angel, only thinner.' I smiled and stretched my arms up over my head. His gaze roamed down my body, his hands following, touching the places his eyes went.

'Your skin is like silk,' he said, dropping his mouth to my navel and kissing me there. I felt his smirk as I tried not to wriggle and then he moved and his body was against the length of mine. The building heat inside me overwhelmed me. I tugged his shorts down and he kicked them off.

Flesh on flesh. My blood began to rush, like rapids building. As his mouth found mine again he thrust deep into me. And when he could go no deeper he withdrew slowly, only to thrust into me again. Slow and deep. And again … Until every nerve ending screamed for release. Suddenly the tempo changed. Faster and faster with feverish energy, our kiss broken, his head hovering over mine. Our eyes locked as tight as our bodies as I travelled to the magical land I'd only recently discovered. Gripping his back hard we rode along an impossibly thin edge until finally euphoria hit in spasms of ecstasy as we tumbled over it together.

25

KATE

I slumped onto a bench beside a picnic table and Nick sat more gracefully across from me. His breath drew the leaves from trees, but then he began.

'I don't know what you believe about these sorts of things, but there have been some in my family who have had very unusual capabilities.'

Here we go, I thought. 'Like Superman?'

'They don't don capes and prance around, but they do transition into something supernatural.'

I looked doubtful and then tried to rearrange my features so as to look as though I was genuinely considering this alternative, but it was a challenge. He noticed. 'I have been a witness to that change,' he stated emphatically, but I didn't know him well enough to truly trust his certainty, or his sanity. I remained silent. 'In our family they start off like any other human, born and raised like normal babies who grow into relatively normal children. It's impossible to tell early on, especially since not all transition.'

I couldn't help the way my eyes narrowed.

'It's the word,' he said. 'It doesn't help. It belongs to the realm of movies and make-believe. But this is not, believe me. Replace supernatural with something else, like 'peculiar' or 'bizarre' and that might help.'

I scratched my head hoping to find a flea. That would make more sense. 'Don't mind me for now, just keep going,' I urged, although with a flicker of reluctance.

'They have had many different abilities over the years,' he continued. I looked away so that he wouldn't read my expression so clearly. 'Some have been able to alter reality. Some have been super strong and agile. Others have been able to read minds or the true feelings of others. There have even been those who have been able to manipulate nature to suit their purposes. *Most* have enhanced senses.' He stopped suddenly. I felt the pull of his gaze and turned to him.

'It's been a source of constant preoccupation in my family for many generations, as you can imagine.'

'I can,' I said, imagining coming home to Mum and Dad hoisting the house onto their shoulders because we were going on holiday. It would be good in some ways, but there would always be the downside. '*Dad, where is Mum, and why is there a possum doing laps in the pool?*' '*You know your mother, dear, dinner was late again, and she knows what happens then …*'

'There are rules to be followed, of course,' he said.

'Of course,' I replied, my right eyebrow so high it was in danger of lifting off my face.

He hesitated, and then blurted it out. 'Regarding sexual relations with humans after the transition.'

'Right.' My eyebrow was now almost completely vertical.

'Rules which need to be followed to ensure …' He hesitated again, his earlier momentum lost.

'Y-es?' As I prompted him I wondered whether I truly wanted the details. Blood-lusting beasts with fangs did horrible things to fluffy critters in my mind.

'Well, to ensure that order is maintained and that truly bad things don't happen. We have a duty to be responsible and to ensure that those from our line are responsible. It's why my parents tried to ensure that we only closely associated with those from other families … like ours.'

'Responsible how?' I asked, guessing that he meant more than a phone call the day after.

He took a moment and then began to explain. 'Usually the transitioning process occurs sometime between the ages of thirteen and twenty-one. It can take a while, but it's usually obvious once it starts. Most find humans slightly aversive … in a physical way … as soon as they begin their transformation. Afterwards they are no longer attracted to them at all, so it's a non-issue. That's the way it's supposed to be.'

'O-kay,' I stammered when he came to a stop.

'Sofia was different. Of course, she wasn't the first, it had happened before. She chose to be with Deb's father sexually and to produce a child.'

'And what then?'

He huffed and puffed and then seemed to gather himself. 'I think the best way to say this is just to get it out.'

'I couldn't agree more.' Let it be a quick death, not slow and agonising. I gazed at him expectantly. Surely nothing could beat the now breakdancing blood suckers in my mind.

'Kate,' he said, his voice matter of fact, 'our family are descendants of angels.' I continued to gaze at him, although my lower lip had dropped slightly and the rest of my features had arranged themselves into a pattern louder than any words. *Yep, clearly insane, the poor bugger.*

He continued regardless. My fingers found reassurance in the solidity of the mobile in my coat pocket. If I had to call for an ambulance I could do so quickly. I tried not to imagine what I might say to the dispatcher.

'Do you know anything about the offspring of angels and human beings?' He was clearly not daunted by my expression which was gradually evolving into some approximation of the figure in the painting, *The Scream,* by Edvard Munch.

'You've got me there.' I shook my head too hard. Unruly curls whipped across my face and slashed streaks of lip-gloss across my cheeks. Pushing them away I tried to rub the sticky patches unobtrusively. 'I didn't even know there *was* any such thing ... outside of novels, anyway.'

'You can read about it in Genesis, about God's sons, angels who were attracted to human women, who procreated and created aberrations, called Nephilim.'

I stopped and turned to him. 'Nick, just to be clear are you saying, Sofia was some type of angel and so it wasn't okay for her to ... err ... have sex with my grandfather?'

'Yes,' he said quietly. We regarded each other for a weighty moment and I felt I was quite justified in a little nail-biting. Actually I was starting to feel like sticking my whole hand down my throat.

'I wish that I hadn't skipped all those RE classes to practice piano.'

'Sofia's child was fallen,' he continued. 'The offspring of an angel and human union is a hybrid, neither human nor angel but with supernatural abilities used to spread darkness. They are a part of the darkness and it is an immutable part of them.'

I shook my head as his words confounded me. 'Why would Sofia do that, Nick? I thought angels did good things.'

'Humans and angels have something called agency. It's the ability to make our own decisions and act on them. Free will, if you like.'

'Her choice doesn't make sense though, given the consequences.'

'We're not righteous anymore. We are *all* a bit fallen because of the choices made by those who lived in the past.' He shrugged. 'But as far as Sofia goes specifically, I don't know what she was thinking at the time, why she did that. I never knew her.'

The shadows were lengthening quickly now. The last warmth was draining away. 'The hybrids are not *a little* fallen though, Kate. They are like weapons of mass destruction. They have amazing abilities and little fear. They are capable of destroying life as we know it.'

I honestly just didn't know what to say at that point. It all seemed so completely unbelievable.

'Put simply,' he stated, his face increasingly earnest, 'the offspring of a union between an angel, even one who is not perfect, and a human is an aberration. Left unchecked, the world would become a place of suppurating evil.'

'So she killed the child,' I said, finally understanding. 'And then she killed herself.'

'She made the choice to procreate in that way and ultimately she realised the true consequences of her decision. There was nothing else she could do to change the outcome.'

He looked at me and I looked at him, and then I looked at my finger nails and chewed on them some more. They didn't deserve to be chewed, but it seemed inappropriate to make another joke to deflect my uneasiness.

'Of course what happened with Sofia certainly impacted on my family not wanting me to have anything to do with Deb. I'd only just been born when Sofia and Erik died. It wasn't spoken of as I grew up. My parents only told me about it when I was much older. They hadn't wanted questions … suspicion. Sofia told Deb's father that the baby had died at birth. He believed it because Erik arrived early, but that wasn't the truth. Erik and Sofia lived in Three Kings at our family home for a number of years, under close supervision before …'

'… she killed him,' I finished, my voice flat.

'Erik *was* an aberration.'

'How can you ask for my understanding?' My stomach churned. 'He was only three, and the truth is you *never* knew him.' My voice sounded thin, feeble like a breath of air might steal it away. I coughed to hide the choking sensation, the constriction in my throat.

When he spoke his voice was filled with despair. 'He was a beautiful boy. Looked just like her.'

'Murder,' I whispered.

His eyes flicked up to mine. 'I don't *expect* you to under-stand it all right now, Kate. It's a terrible shock. Maybe you will one day, but it will take time.' He fell silent. We watched the endless parade of mutts and in the distance a car squealed, as though alive. 'My parents kept a photo of him,' he finally said.

One photo, the only remaining proof of the short life of a child. He died before he could live, already damned in the womb. 'So like Sofia, only so much more … dangerous.'

My smile was without humour. 'He was only three, barely old enough to string a three word sentence together. The only way he was doing any damage was with a high pitched wail to the eardrum.'

'There were issues. I think that at first they hoped he would be different. There hadn't been a baby like Erik in so many generations … But at the end of the day, it was what it was, what it always had been. Sofia knew. She made the de-cision in the end.'

I shrugged my shoulders hard, surprising Sam and almost dislodging him. Could there ever be circumstances which would justify such an action? I couldn't imagine them. What I *could* imagine at this point, was a completely deluded fam-ily making irrational, superstitious decisions. 'That sounds crazy, like killing a child who hits another because he might grow up to be a psychopath,' I said passionately.

'There was no *might* about it, Kate. Sofia killed herself and her son, because of what was already occurring.' I listened to the lunacy of what he was saying. I wondered about the role of genetics in mental illness and in sleep disorders and felt sickened by what I had just heard.

Suddenly he sounded tired. 'There are so few of us remaining.' He looked to the heavens and I wondered who watched from there.

'Are *you* an angel, Nick?'

'I am not an angel in the way that Sofia was an angel but I am of that line, as are you, which means that I am also not fully human. I never transitioned but Daniel did shortly before he died.' His eyebrows formed a sharp V as he examined his hands. 'These days it doesn't always work out the way it should. A reflection maybe of the state we live in.'

The trees swayed, the leaves chattering unintelligibly like many very tiny and excited aliens had just arrived on planet earth. The sound died. 'Could *I* turn into some kind of monster?'

His haunted expression suddenly became emphatic. 'No, no, Kate. Erik was born that way.'

'But what about Daniel?'

'Daniel,' he repeated quietly. 'Well, it wasn't surprising that one of my brothers transitioned. Our parents were both of the same line. But I never transitioned, and Deb is human so it's extremely unlikely that you will transition.'

'So the issue is only with fully transitioned angels and humans then?'

He nodded.

'What about the sleep issues I'm having, the night terrors?'

'Runs in the family I'm afraid.' He sounded apologetic.

'Which is not to say there's not *something* a little different about you.'

'Like what?'

The golden light of the setting sun reflected in his eyes. 'Your presence is significant, Kate.'

I took a moment to consider whether clarifying his statement was a good idea, but couldn't help myself.

'Why?'

He took a deep breath and spoke with more force, as though saying it louder would bring home the importance to me. 'Because there have been no others. Not for a very long time. No new arrivals. You are the very last in our line.'

I stood and turned away from him. Suddenly I noticed that the afternoon was completely lost, that the creeping cold had sunk its teeth into the day … and into my life.

26

DEB AND NICK

I examined Nick as he lay with his eyes closed. A faint pulse beat on his forehead. Touching his skin lightly I felt the warm throb of it beneath my fingers. Moving down to his jaw I rubbed the tips of my fingers against the roughness there and then I touched his hair, running up from the back, from where it was recently short and spiky to the tousled part on top. Taking a handful I pulled on it gently.

'You're an angel, Deb,' he murmured sleepily as I nestled back into him. We remained that way for a long while, curled together, his arm thrown protectively over me. It felt so good. Too good. I thought about the questions he had raised about his family and my family.

He opened an eye. 'You look pensive.'

'I'm irritating myself, trying to stay in the moment but it's not working.' He took the pendant which hung around my neck between his fingers.

'It wasn't so hard earlier.' He grinned and my lips twitched in reply.

'Does this help?' His lips found the curve of my side.

'Ooh, that tickles.' I thrashed around like a flea after too much sugar.

'Stop, stop. I give up,' I cried. 'I'm only thinking cheerful thoughts from now on.'

He leapt out of the bed. 'Good.'

He led me to the shower, turning on the water with one hand while holding mine with the other. 'Are you okay?' He looked pointedly at me.

Suddenly I was shy. My cheeks warmed. 'What do you mean?'

'Does it hurt ... there I mean?' He touched me gently.

'A little.'

'Come,' he said, pulling me into the warm water with him. We kissed as it cascaded over our heads and into our mouths. Almost choking we broke apart laughing.

'Doesn't work as well as in the movies,' he remarked.

Afterwards he tossed me a thick white towel.

'You must be hungry. It's way past lunchtime.'

I hadn't thought about the time, but now that he had mentioned it there was no escaping the hunger which gnawed at me like a giant rat. Nodding enthusiastically I slipped into the white bathrobe he held out for me. 'How come I'm always famished when I'm with you?'

He chuckled wickedly. 'I know how to work up an appetite. That's why!' Grabbing the cord of my gown he tied it up for me. 'Hopefully I can also satisfy it!'

My heart was light as I followed him out of his room but as I stepped across the threshold a wave of uneasiness washed over me. It was as though inside his room we had been on another planet, separate and safe somehow, but now we'd returned to earth with a thud and something waited, something not altogether pleasant. The feeling was strange, irrational, but it also felt like the truth, and the truth was that we were no longer alone. Nick was unaffected. His expression was confused when he turned back to me.

'What is it?' He reached for my hand.

I stood cautiously, three or four steps in front of his doorway, like a deer heading out of the forest and down to the waterhole. Psychic intuition wasn't usually my thing, but right now something was creeping me out.

My eyes darted to corners in which shadows hid. 'I don't know, exactly. Something doesn't seem right.'

I never saw another presence as such, not with my eyes, but I could *feel* it. It was like there was someone in the passage behind us, someone … or something, skulking in the shadows and blending with the background, to the point that it was almost invisible.

'Is someone there?' I called tentatively.

Nick shook his head as though I were mad. 'It's just you and I. There's no-one else here.'

But the air had changed. It was as though it had suddenly gained mass and become something. I was certain that he noticed it just then too. His demeanour adjusted slightly and the fire in his eyes went out. He shifted, eager to get away, or that was my interpretation anyway.

'Come, Deb.' He sounded impatient.

'Whose room is that?' I asked, resisting his pull and pointing to the door at the end of the hallway. It was closed but the air seemed to be travelling listlessly in that direction.

'It's Daniel's.' He hesitated. 'But he's not here. *No-one is here*, it's just you and I.'

'It *feels* like something is here,' I said.

He shrugged, but his shoulders were tight. 'It's just the skeletons I was telling you about, Deb.'

A drape flapped wildly at the window and he looked relieved. Moving across to it he closed the window. The drapes settled. 'See. That's all it is. The weather is changing. You're imagining things. Maybe it's the lack of food. Come and eat.'

Maybe he was right. As he spoke, the air seemed to clear.

Had it been nothing more than the day letting go for a moment and then gathering itself? The sun began to shine again. Nothing more than a moment, a moment which had passed. A moment in which my imagination had added two to three and come up with, what?

Something cold and dark.

'Come.' He drew me towards the stairs more forcefully. This time I followed him down, pausing for only a moment to glance back. Something flickered, but maybe it was just the light ... or the cat. The hairs on my neck said otherwise.

'I'm definitely in need of that food you mentioned,' I agreed, vowing not to look back again.

By the time we had reached the bottom I was feeling quite myself again. His cooking skills surprised me. Delicious scrambled eggs on toast accompanied by crispy bacon. I poured large glasses of fresh orange juice. We gobbled everything down hungrily at the large country-style kitchen table, our feet touching as we ate in silence. My hair made puddles on the table and dripped down my back.

'I'm impressed,' I said, when my plate was almost empty.

'Don't get too excited,' he cautioned. 'I can do a couple of things and eggs are one of them.'

'And the other?'

He put his hand to his chin and pretended to consider. 'The other has nothing to do with food.'

We froze at the sound of footsteps. Shoes ringing out on the courtyard, each footstep echoing ominously. *Please don't let it be his parents, I prayed.* My heart hammered unpleasantly. His eyes narrowed as the kitchen door swung open and he focussed on someone behind me, his jaw tight. I was afraid to turn, but I had no choice.

It was Brendan, his brother. I felt relieved even though he was clearly displeased at finding me there. Surely his brother was preferable to his parents. He stood eerily still, a handsome, slightly older, softer version of Nick. His hair was a touch lighter and he looked a little less athletic, but the resemblance was clear in his features and the curl of his hair, his dazzling green eyes.

At last he moved and the spell was broken. 'Who is this?' he enquired, his voice deep and calm, but demanding nevertheless.

'This is Deb. Deb this is Brendan, my brother.' Nick's voice was a monotone. I wasn't sure whether he was angry at himself or at Brendan. He'd made the decision, after all, to bring me here. Glancing at me he tried to assess what I was thinking, but I was only waiting, my instinct shifting into survival mode as the raised tension in the room became increasingly palpable.

'Oh, right,' I fumbled, aware of the delay in my answer, the robe I was wearing, my wet hair and bare feet. 'Nice to meet you Brendan.' My heart hammered.

'Can I have a word Nicholas?' Brendan asked curtly. I thought him rude for not making any effort to reply to me. Nick glanced across at me apologetically. His answer to his brother was clipped.

'What is it?'

I gripped the edge of the table, fearing the conflict which might follow. Noticing, Nick lifted my hand and gave it a squeeze.

'Don't worry Deb, I'll sort this out,' he said, with a tight smile.

'In private please,' Brendan said walking away.

With a loud screech, which made a slinky black cat napping on a small kitchen stool tear from the room, Nick pushed back his chair.

'I'll be one minute,' he told me, squeezing my shoulder

briefly as he passed. 'One minute. Please … don't move.' Bending, he kissed me tenderly before following his brother.

I remained where I was, stunned for a moment, before I gathered myself together. So, this was it, the inevitable intrusion, and what would follow? Standing up I cleared the plates and glasses to the sink. My hands shook. From somewhere in the house I heard raised voices.

Of course it had something to do with me. I wasn't meant to be here with him, was I? I wondered at how my mother would react if she caught me sneaking around the house with a boy she'd never met, only semi-clothed. She wouldn't be happy, but I think she'd come around, eventually. She was a parent, but she was semi-reasonable.

Suddenly the walls closed in and my heart sank. Why had Nick brought me here? What could his family possibly have against me?

'I didn't know anyone would be here,' I heard Nick say. His voice sounded stony.

'Well, that doesn't make it okay,' Brendan replied.

Nick mumbled something inaudible, but Brendan's voice, which oozed resentment carried.

'I *had* to stay, Nicholas. For Daniel. He's your brother, too, and he's not well.'

Daniel *was* home and something was wrong. Very wrong. I'd disregarded my instinct, but I'd known all along. We had not been alone. And even more disappointing was that Nick might have even suspected and had lied to me. I felt sick.

'You're doing the wrong thing by her, Nicholas.' Brendan's voice had an edge to it that sounded dangerous. 'Life is not all about you. You need to consider others, the family, the consequences … Before it's too late.'

A door slammed loudly and footsteps resounded as Nick stormed back into the kitchen.

'Deb? Deb!' he called, but I was already up in his room, tugging on my shorts. He entered like a tornado, grabbing my arm to stop my frantic movements.

'I'm so sorry.' I wrenched my arm from him and pulled on my top. 'That was never meant to happen.'

'You lied to me, Nick.'

'No, no ...' He rubbed his hand fiercely across his jaw.

'You suspected Daniel was here, didn't you?'

'I didn't at first, I promise you that.'

'But you realised. You made me think that I was crazy. Why wouldn't you just have admitted it?'

He shook his head. 'Because ...'

'Why?'

'Because Daniel's not well. He needs privacy.'

'You shouldn't have brought me here.' I couldn't help the intensity which filled my voice.

'Our time together wasn't a mistake, Deb.'

Slumping onto his bed, I dropped my face into my hands. I felt disappointed and confused.

'I care about you, Deb ... so much.' He sat down next to me. 'I'm so sorry that this turned out the way it did. If Brendan hadn't come in then we would have left without Daniel even being an issue.'

'We would still have had your lie between us.'

'Sometimes a lie is not so bad,' he said, but I shook my head. Maybe we had grown up in different worlds, but it was not okay in mine.

'A lie is never okay,' I stated emphatically. 'Without trust we have nothing.'

'I'm an idiot, Deb. I don't know what I was thinking. I've never brought anyone here, into my room, my ... world. You're the first ... but maybe it was a mistake,' he admitted.

Everything settled. I was the first? That was a surprise. I

turned to him. His eyes were changed. Unfathomable. Deep and dark. 'I've never brought anyone here,' he whispered.

I exhaled and my perspective seemed a little clearer. Why was what his brother thought such a big deal anyway? 'I just wish I knew why he hated me so much.' He leant forward and kissed my forehead gently.

'It's not you personally, Deb,' he said, pulling on his clothes.

When he was dressed we headed out onto the landing. 'There's just one thing I want to do,' I said, heading off down the passage. He stared at me in surprise.

'What is that?' he called jogging after me. I ducked out of his reach.

'I want to meet your other brother.'

'Stop Deb,' he ordered, his hand locking tightly around my wrist just as I reached for the door handle. 'You can't just go in there.'

I tried to wrench my hand free, but he wouldn't release it. 'Why not?'

'Because he wouldn't want you to.'

I considered my options. 'It's disrespectful,' he added.

We regarded each other, both aware of the heaviness in the air here. There were shadows in too many places and I felt slightly disoriented. A sluggish current of cold air slithered around my ankles as it entered the room.

He released my arm, but his posture remained tense. 'Not now. If you want to meet him, we can do it another time.' His words made me pause in my single-minded pursuit of understanding.

'But what's wrong with him?'

'He's depressed.' He spoke reluctantly out of loyalty to his brother. 'He has these issues from time to time.'

'I'm sorry, Nick.'

'Obviously he doesn't want anyone to see him that way.' Shame washed over me. What had caused me to behave in this way? It was out of character. Something about this place unnerved me in a way I had never experienced before.

'You're right. Maybe some other time.'

We exited hastily through the back entrance, avoiding further confrontation with Brendan whose navy sedan was still parked in the driveway. Nick revved the motorbike aggressively and headed off, driving somewhat erratically. I clung to him and said my prayers, but wasn't unhappy as the house disappeared behind us. As we left it, the uneasiness I had felt slowly receded.

We rode on and on, up into the mountains, winding around bends at ludicrous speeds and crazy angles, the asphalt almost grazing our knees. Ridiculously I felt safe with him.

Eventually he stopped at a dingy road-side café and bought colas and we drank them at the side of the road, the trees crowding in around us.

His eyes were remote, hovering somewhere in the vegetation but without seeing.

'You're so far away.'

'I'm here Deb,' he said. The insects shrilled and cars whizzed by so close they ruffled my hair.

'Family,' he spat suddenly.

'Mmm, hmmm,' I agreed, downing the last of my drink.

He cracked his can and stood. 'Fuck them all!'

I glanced up at him. I couldn't remember hearing him swear before.

'I'm going to ask my mother about what you were saying the other day. Find out what it means, whether there is actually anything to this *feud*. I mean even if there is ...' I shook my head. It was kind of ridiculous. 'It will probably be hard to understand.'

'I wish you wouldn't. I can't imagine anything good coming out of it.'

'What do we have to lose? It's that or we may as well give up now, accept our fate. I mean, I know I'm going to die one day, but I'm not going to lie down in the middle of the road right now.'

Unexpectedly he laughed, a little of his baggage expelled into the wind. 'You're crazy,' he said.

I looked down at my watch. Anguish had stolen hours. Long arms of afternoon embraced the twilight.

'I'd better get back,' I said, standing. 'My mother is going to call the police any second!'

He took both of my hands in his. 'We could just keep going.'

His face was slightly obscured by the growing gloom, but his eyes shone like beacons, burying themselves in mine. He gestured towards the open road. 'We could ride on into the dusk, let the night consume us, leave only the mist behind.'

I gazed in the direction he pointed, to where the road disappeared between the trees, entranced for a moment by his fantasy.

For an instant I wanted to run, to run with him, away to where the wind was always fresh. But running would bring its own burdens, and it would curse our freedom. He dropped my hands and laughed grimly, breaking the spell.

'It's okay Deb, I'm not really going to abduct you. You're quite right. We need to get back, face our responsibilities, and fulfil our obligations ...' His voice bled with bitterness.

'You're not a mind-reader, Nick!' I cried. I dusted off my shorts.

'No?'

'That's not what I was thinking at all.' I tried to put my

arms around him, but he was rigid with tension and scuffed the dirt with a shoe. 'If we run we will never be free, we'll be looking back instead of forward.'

His eyes filled with resignation. I felt a pang of sadness.

'I'm sorry,' he said, looking down at the ground he had been kicking. 'You're so much more optimistic than me. So much less cynical.'

I shrugged. 'We haven't had the same experiences.'

Placing his hands on my shoulders he looked deep into my eyes for a moment before wrapping me up in his world. I wound my arms around his waist and he moulded to me. 'You've experienced hardship, and yet you still believe in redemption … hope.'

'Hope, yes,' I answered, nodding against his chest. 'What do we have without hope?'

'We'd be hoping for a miracle,' he whispered.

'The light is yours Deb,' he said, as we parted at the garden gate. 'Not everyone can hold onto it the way you can.'

He retreated to his bike. It roared to life and then he was gone, the thunder fading until the road was still again. I remained where I was for a while, watching the empty road and wondering whether he had ever been there at all. But my lips tingled, and the pendant around my neck was heavy, and so I knew that the passion and insanity, the foreboding had all been true.

27

KATE

Nick stood behind me as we gazed at the lonely glow along the west which marked the sun's farewell. 'Our kind cursed themselves a long time ago,' he said, 'but since Erik *nothing* has been the same for our family.' I didn't speak, just watched the sky bleed as the sun died. 'I don't know how any of it explains you …'

I shrugged. 'I don't know either, Nick, but have you ever considered basic biology?'

There was a moment of silence, in which the chill extended its fingers into our bones a little more.

Suddenly, as though clutching onto a moment of courage, he grabbed my arm and whipped me around so that I was facing him, forcing me to acknowledge him, to react. 'Daniel didn't commit suicide Kate. He was … destroyed.'

If a reaction *was* what he was looking for then he got one. I tore my arm away from him.

'How is this helpful?' I cried. 'Enough. I don't want to hear it. I don't want to know that the family I come from are a bunch of murderous psychotics.' I clasped my hands to my ears like a small child, but I figured it was a pretty valid reaction. Even Sam had vacated his usual spot and was nowhere to be seen, frightened away by the insanity which attached itself to the individual who stood before me.

'You have to,' he insisted, leaning in too close, his eyes unsettling me further with their intensity and the way the colours merged and marbled. Mine didn't do that, did they? Suddenly his voice softened and he straightened. 'You have to,' he repeated. 'You have to know what my ... *your* family is like, how intense they are.'

'But you are the only one left,' I cried, my voice steely and deliberate. 'And the only *things* I've inherited from you are my eyes, crazy hair and a tendency to experience night terrors. Can't we leave it at that?'

'I would,' he said, 'but there are others ... extended family, if you like. And the balance of our existence is very fragile right now.'

I felt his scrutiny on me like a microscope over a petri dish. Finally he sighed heavily. 'There *is* something about you. The others will realise that.'

I sighed.

'Not like Daniel. He was increasingly out of control. We had to lock his bedroom door, restrain him, but nothing worked. He was dangerous ... becoming more so ... and he had powers which were exceptional.'

A frosty surge of disgust washed over me as we stood in tense silence.

'It wasn't easy, Kate. But the world would have been a very different place right now, if it hadn't been done, I can promise you that.'

I glared at him. 'What, no greed or terrorism, no poverty or disease, no wars or major climate-related disasters?'

'You're cynical,' he said. 'There is a lot further we could all fall, believe me.'

I wondered why I should. 'I don't know why it went so wrong with him. It shouldn't have, although there are always negative influences. This fallen state we live in makes us more susceptible ...' His frown deepened, like he was still trying to make sense of it all these years later. 'With Erik we knew the door to evil was wide open. We expected problems and we got them. Bad things happened, but they shouldn't have with Daniel. All he wanted was to live a simple life without bothering anyone. He was musical, like you ... artistic, sensitive ...'

He sucked air in deeply as though trying to fortify himself before continuing. 'There was always a veil of secrecy in our family. No-one knew my parents' suspicions ... not even me, at first. All I knew was that he wasn't well and over time I realised that the situation was out of control, but I didn't *fully* understand. Not until he was gone.'

The wind bit into me and I rubbed my hands together. Nick's eyes were full of wishes, alternative endings, variations which were lighter, happier. Underneath all of that I sensed fear.

'You were conceived around that time,' he said, his voice almost a whisper, 'a time of such turmoil.' He reached out to touch my arm, but I pulled it away. A part of me wanted to run, but I remained rooted to the spot by that other part, the curious one, the one which asks what happens when match and igniter fluid come together.

'They explained everything then. I thought they were completely mad at first.'

At some point he must have felt the nausea I felt right now. His heart had raced and his world had disappeared from under him as his parents had told him what he was telling me. His experience had been even worse. His sibling had been murdered.

'There was no-one after you, Kate. No births ... not from our family or any family like ours. None. We're paying for mistakes. Newer ones and some very old ones, but we will never pay our debt, not until there are none of us left.'

I thought about everything he had said. 'Maybe that's not such a bad thing.'

'If only that were the case. I'd be the first to celebrate.' He scratched at an invisible speck of dirt on his trouser leg. 'We are *all* barren. It's nothing any doctor can pick up on … modern technology cannot explain it.'

I hadn't thought a lot about children, except to think that they would be a real nuisance in my life at this point, and so I didn't feel sudden grief at the potential loss.

'You're an anomaly, Kate.'

The darkness had deepened and I suddenly became aware of the rumble of traffic, like everyone was leaving us behind. Bright yellow cubes of light from faraway buildings shone in the gloom, enhancing the feeling of desolation. In the midst of it all, we were so alone.

Tendrils of icy air slipped under my collar. 'But there's *nothing* unknown, Nick. You're not an angel and Deb is a human, so … Don't tell the others about me.'

'You don't *need* to tell them as such.'

'What do you mean?' I asked, trying to keep the desperation out of my voice.

'We are not like other families. There are those amongst us with finely tuned senses ... and others who stay near to me. I'm afraid I may have already led them to you.'

'Thanks a lot,' I felt like saying as dread seized me. Who were these people I hadn't chosen to have in my life and why couldn't they just leave me alone? Yeah, I was the last in the Edwards line, but big deal, someone had to be.

'You may not be an angel, Kate,' he said, 'but you carry our genes and you are the last of our kind. You are extremely precious.'

Not that long ago I was a bastard and life was simple. Bitterness surged like an acid tide in my gut.

'You must think I'm delusional! I wouldn't blame you. I've been there, remember.' He moved towards me, but I wasn't ready to face him yet, and so I wandered further away, back along the route by which we had arrived, when life had seemed simpler.

After a while I relented and let him fall in beside me. 'Truth is, I don't know what to think.' My hands were all over the place, too busy. 'I can see how, if this is all true, that it must have been horrendous for you.' He waited.

I kept my head down. 'But … I feel angry at you for bringing this to me and if others have found me through you …' I swallowed, trying not to let the emotion which escaped into my voice betray me. I breathed until the thin quiver in my throat had died. 'I know I came to you, I wanted answers … and once I came, well I guess it was too late.' So many sighs. A quick glance at him. I had unintentionally started a ball rolling and the momentum was building. Where were these others now? Did they perch on the tops of buildings or blend in with the night? 'I guess at least I now know that I didn't suddenly pop out of the ether in a pink Bonds romper … or did I?'

He chuckled regretfully. 'I wasn't there at the exact moment, but I'd say it's pretty unlikely.'

'Like the rest of this you mean?'

'Yeah,' he agreed.

'I feel so vulnerable.'

'How could you not?'

'We don't even know each other that well. It's little more than half a year since we first met up and you're telling me that Sofia was an angel and that she killed herself and her tiny son who was some sort of aberration. That Daniel was changing into an angel, but it wasn't working out the way it should have and so he was murdered. You say that I'm the last in a line of cursed beings, but that I won't transition into a monster. The truth is you don't *really* know that, do you? Not with the way things have been since Erik.'

A long way off someone shouted and tyres screeched. There was a lull in the traffic before the rumble started up again. 'Regardless, I'm of interest to others like you who regard me as some kind of unknown, but rather interesting quantity simply because of my position on the totem pole.' I glanced sideways at him. 'I've always wanted to be special, maybe even a little different, but I'd probably rather *not be* the type of precious you're talking about.'

We reached the car.

'Kate?' I turned back to him and he took both of my hands in his, squeezing them tight. 'Whatever happens and whatever you think of me, your existence is a blessing to me. I can't emphasize that enough. It wasn't planned, I know, but you're here and you're beautiful and talented, and you have green eyes and my curls because you are meant to. I wish that came without all of the accompanying crap.'

My shoulders collapsed. 'It's not your fault Nick. It's just life. Fate.'

'I wish things could have been different, though. I wish I could have seen you grow up, been more to you, loved you and picked you up when you cried. I wish I'd known you were in the world earlier … but maybe that wouldn't have been so good for you.' He shook his head, his face crestfallen. Blinking hard he dispelled the moisture which had gathered in his eyes.

'Do what you can to establish good sleep habits. Try not to stay out too late, eat properly, get regular sleep, and don't drink too much. I know I can't talk, but I'm not having the

AWAKENING

same sleep issues, right now. Stay away from drugs, even caffeine. Cut it out if you can. Do whatever you can to help yourself by controlling your environment.'

I raised an eyebrow. Focussing on the practical, he tried to find a handle when there wasn't one. If this was about birth control, I might have been tempted to disregard his advice, but given the nature of our conversation I decided that there was no harm in following it.

Only the car expressed itself on our journey home, the vulgar roar unburdening us of the need for further explanation, clarification, and injury.

He kissed me lightly at the gate. 'At least now you understand why I drink,' he said with a wink, leaving me in a slump of exhausted disbelief and agitation. I sensed the weight of his burden shifting across onto my shoulders, the craziness of it bewildering my mind.

After a while I drew leaden feet up the seemingly gigantic, never-ending steps and went inside. The tiny parcel Mads had given me lay unopened on my bed where I had left it. A mystery. I wasn't sure that I could deal with another, however innocuous, today but I picked it up anyway and carefully opened it. A note slipped out. It was from Deb.

'This was very special to me once Kate. You should have it now. Love, Deb.'

Inside in a plain black box lay a shiny platinum angel, sparkling with tiny diamonds, on a delicate chain. Instinctively I knew that she was relieved to let this painfully beautiful piece of her history go at last. It was tied to sorrow and heartache, to great unfathomable depths. It was tied to what was mine now.

I curled up on the bed, exhausted and over-loaded. The clock blinked six p.m. The metal of the pendant warming in my hand was the last thing I remembered as my mind shut

233

off altogether and I drifted off to sleep, my inner turmoil overcome for the moment.

28

DEB AND NICK

School seemed interminable. I wandered through my lessons zombie-like. When I arrived home Mum continued to torture me with descriptions of the gruesome scenarios she had imagined, after I returned home late the night before.

'Mum?' I asked later, as we set our small kitchen table for dinner, 'Is there anything weird between our family and the Edwards family?'

'Like what?' she asked, her attention too focused on the steaks sizzling in the pan.

'Like something that goes back a while, something that maybe Dad was involved in?'

She was quiet for a moment. 'What did Nick say?'

'Not much, just that there's an issue between the families and his folks don't want him seeing me.' I returned to the counter to grab serviettes as she dished up the food, setting George's aside for when he returned from work later.

'He said that Dad wasn't meant to come back here, which is weird.'

'You should really talk to your father about this,' she said, not meeting my eyes.

'Oh come on!' I waved my hand rudely, exasperated by her stalling. 'We can't discuss the weather!'

She sighed and gave up. I was usually easy-going, but

when I chose to stand my ground I could be stubborn. Now was one of those times and she knew it. 'Let's eat and I'll tell you what I know when we're finished.'

She ate pensively while I gulped down my food impatiently. After washing and drying the dishes we moved to the sofa and she took my hands with a sad smile.

'Wow, is it that serious?' I asked tentatively, my stomach sinking like a lead balloon.

She shrugged. 'I don't know Deb. I'd hoped to escape telling you. Really, I didn't think it was necessary to burden you with something from so long ago … but they're obviously not going to let it go.'

'Unfortunately not,' I agreed.

'Fate works in such mysterious ways.' Her hands covered mine protectively.

'Such as?'

'You and Nick. With all the good-looking boys around here, it was Nick you fell for.' I nodded, waiting, realising that she was making assumptions about Nick and I that I couldn't deny.

'Your father's family came from around these parts – did you know that?'

'Not until Nick told me the other day.'

'Your dad never talked much about them, but they were here for generations, until about twenty years ago. They're scattered all over the place now. Don't even keep in touch. Anyway, they were here for a long time before that.' Anxiety flitted across her face like a ghost in a graveyard.

'He's not going to be happy about me telling you this, but given we're practically estranged I guess it's too bad.' I nodded, encouraging her to continue. 'He told it to me in confidence before we moved here. I guess he thought he had to.' Her voice faltered.

'Go on Mum, I have a right to know.'

'Why he wanted to come back here will always be a mystery to me.' She inhaled so deeply the rug seemed to move closer.

'When your dad was young, probably only a year or two older than you now, he fell in love with Nick's aunt. Her name was Sofia. Sofia Edwards. She was beautiful of course, but off limits. She was engaged to someone else, not that your father would ever have been considered a suitable match for her, but she was a bit of a rebel. They met up secretly and she fell pregnant. Her family found out then about their trysts and you can imagine what a shame that was to them, how she had let them down and tarnished the family name.' I nodded, captivated by her story, my mind reeling at the thought of my father involved in something so exciting *and* troubling.

'They forbade her from seeing him, although he said that she wanted to continue the relationship anyway.' She shook her head pensively. 'It didn't matter anyway, they were so powerful. They ordered him to stay away from her and to keep the pregnancy a secret. They intimidated him. Plied him with money and forced him to leave town. He had to. If he hadn't, they would have made life very difficult. Sofia disappeared. The family home was a fortress. He only heard from her once again.'

'And his child?'

'Died,' she finished, explaining. 'He came early.'

We sat in silence. My father had a history, a life, I knew nothing about. I remembered Sofia from the photo, her dark painful expression, the lean of the others towards her, their expressions possessive, almost predatory now that I thought of it. I shivered.

'That's terrible Mum. Do you think that's why he came

back here?'

She nodded. 'Maybe he wanted to show them that he could hold his head up high here, make them realise that they had never had a right to deprive him of his home.' She shrugged. 'I don't know.'

It still didn't make sense to me. 'But how did he manage to rent here, wouldn't they have known it was him?'

'He used my maiden name on the lease. Forged my signature. I only realised when we separated.'

'It's a sad story,' I said, unsurprised by his deception. I felt myself softening a little towards him. I knew little of the depths of defeat he had experienced in his past although my mother had certainly suffered for it.

'They made it impossible for him. He had to move away, get a new job, and start a new life. Even extended relatives, who knew nothing about what had happened, found themselves tormented by that family. They wanted them out, every last one of them and they got their wish. They were very influential. They are *still* very powerful. You shouldn't underestimate them, Deb.'

Shaking my head slowly I wondered just what kind of a nest I had stepped into.

'Your father went through a pretty tough time, but that's as much as I know. We met a couple of years later and he never spoke of it. I think he tried to put it behind him, to pretend his past had never existed, but it haunted him, turned his heart into a dark, cold place. He only told me when he decided to move back here, but it explained a lot. He said the work opportunity was just too good to pass up and maybe he was right, but we could have lived a long way from here and been closer to his office.' She thought for a moment. 'There was something that drew him back to this place, and I mean something other than Dorothy.'

'It's hard to understand why he'd ever want to come back here.'

'Maybe the Edwards would have let it rest if it wasn't for you and Nick getting together.'

'They sound awful.'

'Powerful people are used to getting what they want. They don't like it when things don't go their way, Deb.'

'No,' I agreed.

She leaned forward to straighten up a stack of books on the coffee table and knocked one off. Leaning down I picked it up for her. 'Maybe you should leave this place, Deb. Leave now before suffering really touches your life, damages you.'

'It seems so silly though, Mum.' I placed the book on top of her pile. 'I mean, I understand a little more now about why they don't want me around, what they have against Dad, but that's ancient history.'

'It *was* a long time ago,' she agreed, 'and it wasn't as though he committed a crime. It was immoral yes, but nothing more than that. When you and George became friendly with Nick, I started worrying a little, but still … after all this time I thought they might just let sleeping dogs lie. I haven't even heard mention of Sofia Edwards since we've been here. It's like she never existed.'

The hair on my neck prickled. What *had* happened to Sofia?

'I saw a photo of her at Nick's house,' I said, noticing her shocked expression too late.

'You've been to his house?' she demanded.

'Yes, well just once when his parents weren't there.'

We both sat pondering, surrounded by the sounds of silence, the creeks and moans of the wind, the humming fridge. Mum stood up and began switching on lamps, as we both suddenly became aware of how gloomy the house had become.

'You should be careful,' she warned, her face aged by concern in the lamplight. Moving to the kitchen she filled the kettle with water, turning it on before returning to the sofa.

She sat down slowly, a thought weighing on her mind. 'You've not done anything have you Deb? Anything ... you know?'

My face flushed and she brought her hand to her mouth.

'Please tell me you used protection!'

How could I answer? How could I explain the power of the connection which had brought us together, which seemed to override conscious thought? Loss clawed its way across her face. She swallowed.

'Deb!'

'I'm going to the chemist tomorrow, Mum. It won't happen again, I promise.' She exhaled, trying to calm herself, to reassure herself. Her lips twitched as she tried not to tell me how irresponsible I was.

'The more I think about it, the more I think that *any* connection with that family is ill-advised. I don't want to meddle, you're eighteen now, but won't you consider ending it? Now, before you're in too deep.' I could hear her desperation, but leaving him wasn't an option I was willing to consider.

'It's too late.' I placed my hand on her arm. 'Maybe it was always too late. Like you say, fate brought us together. I know you don't want me hurt and if I could choose differently I would, but I can't. Of course I wish his family weren't monsters and didn't hate us. I can't begin to understand how they could hold on to a grudge after what must be more than twenty-five years.'

She smiled sadly. 'Some people have the ability to hold onto bitterness forever Deb. No matter how hard you try to prove yourself to them your energy is wasted.' She spoke from experience.

'You've suffered in your life, Mum,' I said, as the kettle began to shriek. She jumped off the sofa, relieved to have somewhere to run to, some way to deflect the conversation.

She spoke from the kitchenette. 'I want you to have a different life. I've found peace so late. I want happiness for you, and love. I worry that if you do this, that won't be the case.' The teaspoon clinked against the side of a mug as she stirred. 'You're only a couple of months away from freedom. I don't want that stolen from you.'

She returned to the sofa with two steamy mugs of tea and a shot of brandy for herself on a tray. I guessed she needed it. Usually I made the tea, but tonight the roles were reversed. We sat companionably and she seemed to forgive me, knowing that I needed her. After a while I rested my head on her shoulder and she played with my hair, dragging the fine, almost white strands through her fingers. We both retreated to our thoughts for a while.

Finally she seemed to come up with a new perspective, one in which she blamed herself. 'I'm sorry I didn't tell you about this before now. Maybe I should have, but who can know the future?'

I stood up and stretched. 'You've told me now Mum, that's what matters.' My body was ready for bed, but my mind was buzzing. I was certain that sleep would elude me.

'I love you,' I said, leaning over and kissing her forehead.

'I know you do, and I love you Deb, so much.' She clasped me to her so tightly my breath rasped in my chest. 'Always, no matter what,' she stated, finally releasing me so that I could breathe more easily.

29

KATE

I opened my eyes to what seemed like midnight, momentarily disoriented in the complete darkness. The clock next to my bed blinked. It was only seven thirty. Unusually, the house was still quiet and the gap beneath my door did not glow. I yawned and stretched, immediately regretting it as my head started to throb. Two headaches in one day seemed unfair. Fumbling around for tablets in the drawer next to my bed, I decided that a nice soothing bath would be a good idea and so after I'd swallowed two painkillers, I stumbled bleary-eyed into the bathroom. Relaxing in warm water was an appealing fantasy but not possible after the events of my day, which insisted on breaking through every calm meditative thought I could muster. Eventually I gave up and hauled my lobster-pink body from the water with a heavy sigh.

I pulled on old but much-loved, once-pink, flannelette pyjamas, washed to paper thinness, but with no holes in obscene places, and thick socks with zebra stripes, leaving my hair in a shambolic bun on top of my head. I glanced in the mirror on my way out.

'You make a God-awful superhero,' Sam noticed happily.

'Get away pesky serpent,' I whispered tersely, 'anyway, it seems more like super-villain in the Edwards family.' I attempted a forbidding expression, one that would instil trembling terror into the coldest heart of the biggest barbarian, but suddenly noticed a piece of lettuce stuck between my front teeth. It somewhat detracted from the fierceness of my expression (a vegetarian monster is not that scary), and I shook my head at my stupidity, quickly rinsing out my mouth and hoping that Nick hadn't noticed earlier.

A gentle rain had started falling, soft static outside the window. I had just turned on the kettle and was rummaging in the breadbin trying to find a piece of bread which had been baked this side of the millennium and would not crack a tile if dropped on the floor, when I heard the endless multitonal chime of the doorbell.

I froze. And then I remembered. It came flooding back with all of the cruelty of a school bully who had just noticed a sticky toffee wrapper stuck to your bottom. With everything that had happened in between it seemed like years ago that I had been attacked in the club. James. My car. I looked down at my pyjamas, my socks.

The chimes started up again. Was there no mercy in the world?

I opened the door a crack, stuck my nose out, sighed, and opened it a little wider. He was dripping on the doorstep, his face shadowed by a hood covering his head to keep the rain off, my keys proffered in his outstretched hand. It was probably just as well I couldn't make out his expression.

'Are you okay?' he asked, moving forward into the light, quite unaware that I regularly dressed this way.

The weekend had taken its toll. I swallowed hard and tried to smile, but somehow I failed and my lip wobbled and my eyes watered. After a while I gathered myself enough to lie unconvincingly.

'Yes, fine. It's just been a *really* long weekend.' Had it really only been less than a full day since he'd rescued me?

He wasn't persuaded, but handed the keys across to me anyway. I'm sure his instinct was warning him away. The sooner, the better.

'You're parked on the road near your front gate.'

'Oh. Thanks so much.'

'No problem.' He hesitated, then turned to go.

'Would you like to come in for a moment? Cup of tea, or something?' Idiot. What does, 'or something' mean. I felt a hot rush and bit my lip.

He looked up at the quiet house and then across at my drawn, but red, face.

'Just for a short while, I've got to get some work done.' *And then please never bother me again.*

I took him through to the kitchen and tried not to pour boiling water on myself, or drop the sugar bowl on the floor, while he sat at our functional, but ugly, chipped wooden table looking self-assured and too gorgeous for eight o'clock on a Sunday evening.

'There you go,' I said, 'white, with two.'

'Err, okay. Thanks.'

How did he have it then, was it black with one? I scratched my head, but that failed to provide enlightenment. Had I even asked?

Realising my anxiety, he took a sip and smiled, brightening the room. 'It's good Kate, thanks.'

I moved to the table and sat across from him, staring into my cup. 'Why are you in the park up at Uni so often?' I asked bluntly.

He took his time, considering his answer, which made me realise that what had seemed simple, wasn't. When I looked up at him it was directly into his penetrating gaze.

'It's none of my business really.' I shrugged awkwardly, tapping the side of my cup as I looked into its murky depths again. 'It's just that I noticed you quite a while back …'

'I noticed you too.' I clunked my mug down too hard on the coffee table and gulped.

'You're joking!'

'Seriously,' he insisted.

'Oh.' I focussed on my pyjama leg, fiddling with a small hole, but stopping quickly fearing a gaping tear. I took a loud sip of tea, nearly choking as I swallowed, realising that his piercing gaze still hadn't moved.

'It's probably more of your business than you think.'

'What does that mean?' I asked, puzzled.

'Well, to you it might sound crazy.'

I laughed the laugh of an asylum inmate. If only he knew. 'Crazy! My life is all about crazy at the moment, so bring it on!' My sudden change in demeanour brought the point across a bit too emphatically. I could see in the way his body now leant away, rather than towards me, that he did not doubt me.

'Well …' He was unsure, his eyes settling on his hands for a moment before flicking back up to me. I waited. 'We're there for you,' he said, his voice calm, a measured foil to my hysterics.

'For me? When you say 'we' do you mean you *and* Ethan?'

'Yep, we're usually both around, somewhere.'

'When you say me, you mean …' I looked about the room, but it was still just the two of us, no ghost of Christmas Past lurked in the shadows.

He nodded, raised his eyebrows slightly. His eyes glinted.

'But I don't even know you.'

'Well … we know you a little more than you know us.'

'How?'

'Nick.' Of course, there had to be a connection. Probability. What was the chance of someone like James coming into my life, without something being screwed up about it? My stomach flipped nauseatingly and I started to feel clammy.

'Are you … family?' I stammered.

'No, no … not your family, Kate.' I exhaled. Of course, the eyes were all wrong.

But another realisation dawned and I shook my head, exasperated. 'You're from *another* family.' Did that whole world have to land on my doorstep today? 'You're *like them*, aren't you?' I cried indignantly, leaping to my feet and nearly upending the table.

'Careful. Don't hurt yourself,' he said, jumping up after me. How patronising. I waved him away, a range of obscenities I hoped Nanny couldn't hear from heaven, spinning around rudely in my mind.

'It's more complicated than that,' he tried to explain. I sank back onto my chair and he seemed relieved.

Chin on fingers I thought. 'I've seen you around at Uni since the beginning of the year!'

'Nick just wants to protect you,' he said, trying to placate me, 'to make sure nothing bad happens to you.'

'Other than a sprained ankle from falling over my own feet, or being licked to death by my dog, it was incredibly unlikely anything *was* going to happen to me before *he* came on the scene. He can't just step in and take over my life, infect mine with his madness,' I grumbled. 'I wanted this on my own terms.'

He was pragmatic. 'It doesn't always work like that.'

'I wanted to fill in a few blanks, that's all.' Tears of frustration filled my eyes so unexpectedly I was unable to stop them overflowing.

He sprang up and yanked a piece of kitchen towel from

the roll, handing it to me. On second thoughts, he leant across and brought the whole roll to the table.

'Too much has happened this weekend,' I snivelled, wanting to run and hide, to bury my head under my pillow and wake up to a brand new day, with sunshine and rain, but no crazy families potting each other off or strange abilities I didn't understand.

He seemed less assured than when he had first appeared, possibly because I was such a wreck and there was more to come. There was something appealing about his reaction, reassuring maybe because it made him seem human. I took a slow breath, trying to pull myself together. Finally I folded my hands demurely in my lap. I would stay. I would cope.

He seemed relieved. 'Everyone needs help sometimes Kate, and your situation, well, it's more complicated than most.'

'He didn't even know I existed until a few months ago!'

'But now he does. Others do too.'

'Like you?'

He shrugged, noncommittally. 'I guess so.' We sipped our drinks in silence for a while. When we were finished he stood up and took the cups to the sink. I remained frozen in my seat, thinking.

'He could have told me about you earlier.' It felt like a betrayal.

'His life is not easy.' His words made me realise how little I actually knew about Nick's daily life. He had drawn me into this barbed maze but I knew only the superficial things about him, the things he'd told me. And I knew that he drank too much, that was hard to hide. But he was mysterious, arriving in hire cars, flying in and out in his own aircraft, not seeming to stay in any one place for more than a few days. I didn't really have a clue what went on in his life on a day to day basis, how different it was to mine, how impacted he had been by this … this curse and the circumstances of his past.

'Maybe he didn't want to worry you before he had to, or maybe he just had other things on his mind,' he added, uncertain of my long silence. I looked up at him. He smiled reassuringly as our gaze met, moving his fingers through his mocha-and-gold hair, brushing it off his forehead for a moment before half of it flopped down again and the other half remained standing straight up. Suddenly I wanted to touch it, feel the thickness of it between my fingers. I stood up, transfixed for a moment. He was so close. His torso almost touched mine. A sweet spiciness lingered in the air. His fingers touched my face and I felt instantly feverish, my thoughts incoherent. I could barely hear him.

'You've been raised in a world removed from the one you were born into, the one he knows, Kate.'

My head cleared as he stepped away. 'I want to go back. Back to when I was certain of my dullness. It's not that long ago, honestly.'

He smiled slightly as he took in my get-up and hair. 'You were never dull,' he said, walking into the entrance hall. It wasn't necessarily a compliment.

'What about you James?'

'Me?' he asked, in mock innocence, rocking back on his feet.

'How are you involved in all of this?'

'That's a long story.' He deliberated, weighing up how much to share with me, deciding on the nuts and not the bolts, for now. 'We've been a part of this all of our lives. Born into it, just like Nick was.'

30

DEB AND NICK

The next afternoon I waited for Nick down at the beach, per-spiring in my school uniform. I'd been replaying my conver-sation with Mum for most of the night and through the in-terminable school day I'd been trying to make sense of it all. Not even Mr Warden's gut-heaving Biology dissection had managed to distract me for long.

But he did not appear. Nor did I see or hear from him the next day. He'd vanished, again, like a star in the morning. And wasn't I the idiot? Duh! Insecurity burnt charred holes through my self-confidence. Why had I had sex with him so soon? Why had he only told me that there were issues be-tween our families after we had had sex? My self-doubt was a powerful force, taking no prisoners. It tainted my memo-ries and made me regretful, nauseous.

I tossed and turned in bed, rewinding and replaying our last moments together over and over. Eventually his reac-tions were so distorted, so exaggerated that I no longer knew the truth. There was no point going on like this. Tomorrow I would have to find him and face him.

I got up as a key grated softly in the front door lock. Al-most one a.m.

'It's past your bedtime Deb,' George yawned as he dragged himself in, exhausted after a long shift on the back of Uni.

'Can't sleep,' I mumbled. 'Do you want a hot choc?'

He tossed his bag onto the sofa. 'Nope, I'm bushed, heading straight to bed.' He stopped suddenly and turned. 'Is it because of Daniel?'

'What?' I nearly fell off the chair I was half sitting on.

'How's Nick holding up?'

I regarded him, curious about the question, the words he had used.

'How would I know?'

'Mandy saw you leaving with him on Saturday. No secrets here, you should know that by now!'

'Well I wouldn't have a clue how he is. I haven't heard from him since Sunday.'

I saw a look of surprise cross his face and then regret. Regret that he'd said anything at all. Goose-bumps prickled on the back of my arms. 'What is going on, George? What *about* Daniel?' I demanded.

'Surely you know Deb?' I felt that sinking feeling I'd been feeling quite a bit lately return, a combination of tell me and don't.

I made my jaw move. The words sounded stiff. 'What *about* Daniel?'

He steeled himself for a full minute as I paced, nervously waiting for the axe to finally fall. Eventually he managed to spit it out, his voice flatter than the flounder we'd had for dinner. 'He committed suicide, Deb.'

I froze.

'No!'

'Gassed himself in one of their cars. His Mum found him.' All I could do was keep my hand on my mouth. My brain was full of the sound of rain, great sheets of it. His voice seemed to come from a long way off.

'He's dead, Deb. I'm so sorry.' My eyes prickled. How could he know *all of this*, when I knew nothing of it?

He was babbling and I suddenly realised that his arm was around me. I hadn't felt him put it there. 'I was just wondering how Nick was. I didn't realise you hadn't heard yet.'

'Oh no, no, no, no,' I gasped, imagining the suffering Nick would be experiencing. I turned away from him. Daniel was everyone's favourite. He was the different one, the one who looked more like Sofia, with darker hair and brooding eyes, beautiful in a poetic way. The youngest son, smaller, quieter, softer around the edges. Sensitive and artistic Nick had said once. Bile burnt the back of my throat. They'd been keeping watch over him as he struggled with depression. They had failed to keep him safe. What hell would they be living in now?

'How come you know this and I don't?' I managed, my voice as harsh as rocks in a food processor.

'Tiffany at work told me. She lives up on the hill with the rest of them … It's not common knowledge yet … I just assumed you knew. I'm so sorry. I'm such an oaf.' I reached out to touch his arm.

'It's not your fault,' I said. There hadn't even been a whisper at school.

Morning arrived after a long night and I carefully selected and sent flowers along with a note expressing my sympathy, asking for him to call me when he could, telling him I wanted to be there for him. But I heard nothing and so the next day I got George to drive me out to his house. The high white walls surrounding it seemed cold and forbidding, like a kind of prison and the impersonal, officious rejection at the gate was equally repellent.

'It's like another world out here,' George remarked as we drove away in his old white Toyota. It *was* another world, I thought, gazing back at the receding fortress.

The weather had changed suddenly and all around us trees thrashed and leaves blew across the road like crowds of drunkards in a whirl of fury. Rain splattered in bursts against the glass, like God was having a bit of fun with a hose-pipe. But in a moment's break in the rain I noticed the Edwards' house and garden sitting as still as a photograph, in an improbable shaft of sunlight which broke through the clouds directly above it. For a moment I thought I saw an angel hover in the brightness overhead.

And then the house disappeared from view and I turned back to George as the windscreen wipers whipped backwards and forwards.

'Where did this come from?' he said, hunching forward as we crawled along. The car rattled as the wind buffeted us, but as we rounded a bend we were bathed in eerie stillness and sunlight so bright we were instantly squinting. The windows fogged and we quickly opened them to let in the humid air.

He shook his head. 'Someone's having fun with us mere mortals today.'

The towering clouds were forbidding in the rear-view mirror, all the more so because they stood out in such strange and stark contrast to the flat cloudless turquoise all around them. They held a warning, but I wasn't sure what.

31

KATE

The door sprang open and Mads surprised us, bursting through with Mitchell a couple of paces behind.

'You can take your stuff and fuck off,' she shouted angrily at him as she swished past, unconcerned about whoever else might be exposed to their fall-out, 'for someone who thinks he has a big dick, you have no balls.'

'Err, Mads.' I tried a meek, but foolish, interruption.

'Yes, I know Kate,' she said condescendingly, hands on hips. '*You* don't swear,' she knew nothing of Sam, or my general mental state which I kept well hidden, 'and you're a virgin, but some of us are not so saintly. Some of us are unable to contain ourselves so successfully.' My face began to melt, and she stopped, belatedly realising that I was not alone. She turned to face James, and Mitchell nearly collided with her.

'Err, hello again,' she said, gratifyingly mortified at her mistake.

'This is James, *not* Ethan,' I stated, outwardly calm, inwardly consumed by violence as I marvelled at how I had not grabbed her by the hair and smashed her face into the wall.

'Oh, the brother,' she said. A quickly-hidden flicker of distaste shimmied across James' face as he flattened himself against the wall. A hush fell.

'I was just leaving,' he said, with a nod to Mitchell.

'See you Mate,' Mitchell responded, unfazed by Mads' commotion.

'Kate,' James farewelled, slipping through the door. I looked from Mitchell to Mads, shook my head and raised my eyes like a parent with a child who had just trodden dog poo through the house, and then dashed out after him. Better to give them a little space.

'James,' I called, treading carefully on the wet steps, my socks instantly soaked through. He stopped a few steps down and turned to me.

'You can't leave me like this. I have so many questions.'

He hesitated. 'They're not that bad, honestly,' I said gesturing to the house. I wrapped my arms around myself. 'They're just having an argument, probably had a few too many drinks, or something.'

He shrugged indifferently. 'They're not my housemates.' Of course, why would he care?

'You can't just leave,' I repeated more firmly, wondering how I would stop him. I took a tentative step closer to him and my socks squelched.

'No?' He remained where he was. I wanted to reach out to him, but I didn't. 'You should go back inside,' he said, looking down at my soggy stripy feet, 'it's cold out here.'

'I'll give them a few minutes,' I said, nodding my head towards the house as I shifted from one foot to the other and shivered.

'Well you can't stand there. Do you want to sit in the car?'

'Sure,' I said squelching after him.

The road was scattered with puddles which reflected the glow of the street lights. He ignored my car which sat in half of one, although who could blame him. The yellow seemed almost luminous in the night, enough to make possums nauseous. I couldn't begin to imagine him in it, driving here. Maybe it had been magically transported. His sleek midnight one was parked behind it.

'Who *are* you people?' I asked when we were sitting inside.

'We come from a rather unusual family,' he answered too seriously, making me suddenly wish I hadn't asked. 'Kind of like the one you come from … although with a few differences.'

'Bloody hell!' My exclamation came out louder than I had intended. 'I don't usually swear,' I added.

'I heard,' he answered, referring to Mads' earlier comment. I felt my face light up like the backend of a bus at night. I mentally struck her from my Christmas list. Outside small droplets of water clung to the window, nervously awaiting the morning sunshine, but the rain had stopped for now.

'Maybe I should start.'

'Maybe,' he agreed. Maybe I should do a lot of things. His fingers on my arm made me turn back to him. In the dimly lit car his eyes shone.

'It sounds so crazy!' I exclaimed, wringing my hands in my lap. His touch tingled on my skin for a moment before he moved his hand quickly away like it should never have been there. I felt a silly flicker of loss.

'I don't blame you for thinking so.'

'Educate me then,' I said, wondering whether that was wise. Surely I'd be better off running blathering into the night, foamy spittle flying from my chops, in my wet stripy socks and faded flannelettes.

'For your ears only, Kate.' His expression was intense. I stifled a silly snigger as I imagined how short the trip to the asylum would be was I to ever mention anything I had been told today. His stare endured and I nodded quickly.

'We are not exactly human.'

'Mmmhmmm, right,' I said, not over the moon at hearing, for the second time today, that there were aliens running amok on earth, some claiming to be family, some eager to wreak havoc and destruction on our civilisation.

'It's not easy to tell on the surface,' he continued.

My eyes narrowed, just as they had with Nick as I scrutinised him. He was ridiculously good looking. His hair looked soft in some places and spiky in others and fell untidily in the most appealing way. It cried out to be touched, to be grabbed in handfuls and ... My heart pounded and I swallowed, trying to let the thought go and moving on to his face. Not that that was any easier. His skin was smooth, almost pore-less, only his jaw seemed rough, like it would graze your skin if he brought his mouth to yours. Aagh ... His nose. It was slender and aquiline. And his eyes. Wide set and deep enough to lose yourself in. Mesmerising eyes. Blue striated marble and ringed with violet and black, softly radiant. But they changed, and so that was only how they were right now, a snapshot, in this moment. I caught myself, almost hypnotised by his physical presence and on the verge of slobbering great jugs of saliva, and swallowed loudly. 'Ahem,' I coughed.

But still, to think of him as something other than human. I chewed on my cheek.

And then to take that a step further, to consider the possibility that I might be ... what? Half an alien? I shook my head involuntarily. That just would not compute.

'You're going to tell me about angels, aren't you?' I despaired. He smiled.

'I can tell you about angels, but you wouldn't recognise one if it took you to Barbados in a hot air balloon.'

'Oh, I don't know,' I answered, 'don't they all have weird eyes?'

'What, like yours?'

'Mine aren't *that* weird.'

'Anyway, there are easy ways to cover them up if necessary.'

I exhaled heavily, but said nothing.

'For an outsider to really *know* an angel was an angel, they would actually have to see it vanish in front of them, or perform some sort of miracle.'

'Well that *would be* amazing, James,' I replied, nodding enthusiastically. 'That would definitely do it for me. If you could organise something like that I think I could believe all of this.'

His smile was indulgent, but then he shook his head. 'It doesn't work that way, although if you're ever in the right place at the right time, who knows?'

I knew it. Tricks reserved for Christmas. My suspicion immediately returned. 'Well it should. Otherwise, how will you ever convince anyone?'

He avoided my gaze. 'Convincing people that angels exist is not something I do much. Usually we stick to ourselves and lead quiet lives. If there's something we're involved in, we try not to be obvious about it.'

'So, *you're* an ... angel?' I asked, stumbling over the actual word. I couldn't see wings and he hadn't levitated or performed any other miracle, so how was I to tell, definitely? Then again, what *were* the odds of a pair like James and Ethan existing, and not only that, but existing in my world? Yep, there was a catch. It sure was a big one.

And I was right about the eye thing. His weren't green, but they were strangely coloured with interesting striations and they merged and marbled like Nick's. My heart sank as

I came closer to acknowledging the truth of what my mind was trying furiously to reject.

He smiled, but infuriatingly, did not answer my question. A *'Yes, and at Easter and Christmas time I glow in the dark,'* would have been nice, or alternatively, *'No, I was just checking your rating on my gullibility meter,'* would have been annoying, but even better!

'It's obvious that you *think so*, anyway,' I stated petulantly. He didn't reply and so I was forced to fill the silence. 'Where did you come from in the first place?'

He contemplated his response and then took the plunge, ignoring my increasingly incredulous expression. 'Our kind existed long before human beings.' I pressed my lips together in a stiff smile and nodded for him to continue.

'Not necessarily here on earth …' My head flopped back and my eyes rolled alarmingly in their sockets.

'… but ultimately,' he continued, as I forced my head forward and tried to be polite, which was hard because my eyebrows were packing their bags and migrating to the moon, 'we were sent here.' He looked at me meaningfully, like I might have some inkling as to what he was talking about - maybe from Nick - which I didn't really. I rubbed my forehead and shrugged apologetically. After a moment he spoke again.

'In the beginning, our role was to support and encourage the growth and development of humans by using our powers to intervene for their benefit. It was a symbiotic relationship. Two different vitalities meeting to form one loving stream, like a leaf dancing on the wind, a beautiful partnership, dedicated to growth and stemming from a place of love and purity.'

I nodded. Good so far.

'There were other angels that had fallen before us and

been expelled from heaven, and the world was fallen then. But we were still pure, still heavenly beings, not like those already cast down, or imprisoned.'

I placed my hand across my forehead and looked at him from under my fingers. He'd jammed his hands into his coat pockets and his leg had started jiggling. He gazed out of the windscreen. 'But it was only a matter of time before we too became corrupted and lost our sense of whom and what we were.' He shook his head. 'It shouldn't have happened. Not with the type of relationship we shared with our Creator. We lived in His presence unobstructed by the things that keep people from knowing Him fully. We had no excuse to rebel and turn away … but that's just what happened.'

A deep breath seemed to fortify him and he stilled his leg. 'We were made good but we were given free will, just like people. And just like people we chose to follow a path which set in motion a chain of events which separated us from God. Only it was so much worse because of the closeness of the relationship we had shared. Because of what we did our spirits were tainted forever.'

I dropped my hand from my forehead to my mouth and then rubbed it across my face while exhaling rather deeply.

'Let me help you, Kate with a quick summary of thousands of years,' he said. I wasn't convinced that would be a good idea. 'There are many groupings of fallen angels. Satan was the first and he waged war with his followers against God, in Heaven and through spirit possession and exerting negative influence on earth. Others followed at later stages, including heavenly beings, called Watchers, sent to watch over earth. They rejected God by interbreeding with humans and creating abominations called Nephilim, evil beings, human-angel hybrids. God banished them from heaven and cast them down to earth where they continued to conspire against him, interbreeding with and corrupting humans and spreading darkness across the world. Noah and his direct line were the only family on earth at that time whose genealogy was uncorrupted. He was purely human. God sent the great flood to cleanse the world of the evil that was consuming it. It succeeded in destroying most, but not all of the Nephilim. The Watchers who had caused the corruption and spread of evil were confined to a realm from which there was no physical escape. But they were still very powerful. They remained the rulers of the spiritual darkness of the world and they could still influence world events, especially through their progeny.'

'Progeny?'

'After the flood there was another wave of angels who were sent to watch over the earth. They also fell, but their fall was different in nature to the ones who had come before.'

'Different how?'

'The imprisoned Watchers tricked them into debauchery with human women using the remaining Nephilim who, being the Watchers' progeny, were under their influence. But this lot of angels *were* different to the Watchers who had come before. The Watchers and those they had spawned were never repentant. These were. When they came to their senses they refused to enter into a covenant with the Watchers who wanted to use them as their free agents on the earth to ensure that God's promises would never be fulfilled. Instead they came together. They agreed to bring a halt to interbreeding with humans and to return to assisting rather than corrupting and debasing. As far as possible anyway.' He looked at me meaningfully. 'They took the name Anakim, which had originally referred to their offspring who eventually all died out on earth. They tried to keep themselves separate from purely human souls. They made efforts to do penance and fight their fallen natures. But there was no way back into the light.'

I swallowed hard, confused by the strange tide of emotion which surged inside me as he spoke. Maybe it was his expression, the way his forehead furrowed and the darkness stole his eyes as he spoke of loss. Maybe it was the gritty edge to his voice, which made me realise that true or not, he believed this to be fact. This was his reality.

'Are you from this Anakim line?'

He nodded. His fingers swept thick hair off his forehead, grasped it in his fist for a moment and then let it go. It immediately fell chaotically. Whoever said family history was boring and took to needlecraft instead, didn't know what they were missing.

'We were marked for all time. A cross where our names had been. Once we were special to God, but we failed him, just like the others, and were exiled for ever.'

'Did all angels fall?' I asked, drawn in by his tale of despair.

He shook his head. 'No. There are those who still enjoy what we once had. Those who are so much stronger than we ever were. They will never fall.'

'But this happened so long ago. I don't understand how it affects you now. Why you are still marked when you weren't even there?'

'It's very hard to explain, Kate.'

He lapsed into a silence so deep it seemed bottomless. I turned to watch the reflections in the puddles. They flickered and became medleys of light and darkness when the wind blew across the surface. You could get stuck in the parts and lose your sense of the whole. Eventually he spoke.

'We were once purely spirit beings, but when we came to earth our spirits animated a physical body. When we fell our bodies became mortal, even though our lifespan was extended compared to humans. When our body eventually dies our spirit is bounced back to earth from a realm on the other side of the Watchers' prison. It lives on again and again in subsequent mortal lives on earth because there is no longer anywhere else for it to go. Because of our remorse, our prison is a step up from the place the Watchers inhabit, but it is a prison of separation, regardless. I know it's hard to understand, but the spirit which fell back then, lives on in me now. It is my nature, the very essence of my being.'

I pressed my fingertips to my eyelids. 'It seems cruel, James.'

'This wasn't done to us,' he said. 'We always knew the consequences. This is about personal responsibility. We cursed ourselves and we cursed those who came after us, kids like Erik who were infested with darkness.' A small dark-haired boy stacked blocks in my mind and I felt a wave of sadness. James frowned.

'There are fewer and fewer of us left.' He found my eyes and held them with his own unfaltering ones.

'Where do the spirits go now then?' I asked at last.

'They are consumed by an entity created by the Watchers,' he said, his expression hardening. 'An entity whose sole purpose is to gather darkness, like a building storm the likes of which has never been seen.'

I waited, the frown over my eyebrows making my head hurt, but he did not continue. 'Sounds terrifying.'

He nodded. 'It is. Just because we would not agree to a pact with the Watchers in the beginning, didn't mean they gave up.' His smile was twisted and grim. He shook his head. 'They never gave up. At every opportunity they sought out our vulnerabilities, holding up their temptations like a carrot to a donkey which hadn't been fed in weeks.

Sometimes it worked. Spirits corrupted in that way cannot return to this realm. Instead they grow the Watchers' power on the other side, their ability to influence here. It becomes a vicious cycle.'

He looked at me, his expression solemn, but strangely not hopeless. Suddenly his voice lifted. 'Some have seen an angel filled with light, the very antithesis of the darkness-gatherer, who walks on earth. This angel takes us home.'

'That sounds nice,' I said, not adding that it would also make a good ending to a children's movie. I worked to assemble my features into a more encouraging expression. 'So maybe there is some hope, after all.'

An increasing number of tendrils were escaping from my bun and I began twisting them back up into it and away from my face. His gaze fell to the nape of my neck, just behind my ear. It lingered there and made me wonder whether Sam had actually shown himself, for once. With a flush I brought my hand to my neck, but the coward was hiding. James looked away guiltily.

'What is it?' He opened his window a fraction. Cool air trickled into the car.

'There are others out there who watch you, Kate. Not just Ethan and I. They wait to see whether *you* are *The One*.'

'Me?' I almost laughed, but his expression stopped me.

'They wait to see whether you have potential. You are the last born of us … and an unknown.' I sighed, already tired of hearing it, and at the same time anxious about what awaited me because of it.

'The only thing I possess any potential for is making a toasted sandwich and maybe choking on it.' The words flew out of my mouth, courtesy of Sam, who regarded me impassively with languid eyes. All was quiet again. I counted to ten to stop myself from leaping in with something inappropriate.

'And there are still others out there who watch from deep, dark places.'

'I have it on very good authority that I am unlikely to transition.' The skin on the back of my neck was creeping up into my skull. 'I know for certain that my mother is not an angel, and I'm relatively certain that Nick isn't one either,' I continued, nearly choking on the 'a' word. 'So everyone can just relax, or alternatively get very depressed because I am not *The One* after all.'

A small crooked smile caught one corner of his mouth. 'You are not marked like the rest of us.'

'Whatever that means, James, remember I am *not* an angel, so obviously I wouldn't be.'

'It doesn't matter. Those from our families are all marked, angel or not.'

'Marked how?'

He reached over and touched the spot on my neck just behind and slightly below my right ear. My skin tingled.

'Your skin is clear,' he said, dropping his hand.

I placed my fingers to my neck protectively as he swivelled awkwardly in his seat, turning so that the right side of his face and neck were visible. 'Look carefully,' he said. I moved nearer, gazing hard at the spot just below his ear. The overhead light cast confusing shadows and for a moment I didn't see it. But then I did. An 'X', grey like an old tattoo, only about a centimetre in diameter.

'A tattoo?'

'I've always had it. We all have. But you don't.'

'No. I don't,' I agreed. 'Does Nick have one?'

He nodded. 'Your lack of marking may be enough for many.'

'Well that's ridiculous,' I exclaimed. 'My lack of marking makes me just like the other seven billion people on the planet.' The words burst out of me as I swivelled my head from side to side, like a measured pendulum. The only advantage was that it made him return his hand to my arm.

'I wish it could all make sense to you Kate. That we could talk and you could leave feeling safe and secure.'

He looked thoughtful, and I *knew* I still looked sceptical. I wiggled my nose and eyebrows to try and loosen up my features, but stopped when he raised an eyebrow. 'But you're a new variable introduced into the equation,' he continued, 'and that might mean a different answer.'

'What if the variable, doesn't want to be a variable? What if the variable would rather be a constant, like the sun rising in the morning?'

'The variable *is* the sun in the morning, Kate. Sunlight after such a long night.'

I rolled my eyes, wishing he would stop talking in riddles. I sat mute, like a mummy, wrapped and ready for burial. Outside the breeze broke up the lights in the puddles.

'Faith …' I mumbled after a while. 'You're asking me to accept something based purely on what you're saying. Something so far from all I've been taught is possible, real …' I threw my hands at my face and held them there for a moment before dropping them.

They immediately leapt up again like salmon heading upstream and then fell with a slap onto my legs where they began wringing the life out of each other. A wild, perplexing fluttering filled my mind, like a cornered spirit struggling with the darkness, and then vanished as quickly, dragged back into the unfathomable depths.

Outside the breeze died abruptly and the moon came out

in a ghostly glow which failed to hit the abandoned side-walk. 'Of course, it could mean that I just don't have Ed-wards' blood, or genetics, or whatever it is, inside of me. Maybe I was accidentally swapped with another baby at the hospital and that's why I am not *marked* in the same way.' *The eyes. The eyes, Kate.* I was definitely an Edwards.

'Or it could be that you are not marked in the same way, because your spirit is not fallen in the same way,' he replied.

I clasped a hand to my forehead hoping to restrain the im-minent explosion which was threatening there.

'Maybe the end *is* coming,' he said, 'and darkness will reign here and it will all be over.' The sound of his acknowl-edgement sent a shiver down my spine. 'But there are some of us who will fight against the darkness until there are no more opportunities to do so.'

The crack of the door handle was loud in the silence. I pushed it open. Today was not going to bring me any closer to understanding. It was only going to build frustration and confusion. Today needed to end, to make room for tomor-row.

'So will you still be hanging around?' I asked, trying to sound dignified and a little affronted maybe, but in truth conflicted. It was hard to imagine *not* wanting James around.

'We'll be around,' he said. 'Believe it or not, we only want to keep you safe. Because if you *are* The One, and the Watch-ers become aware of that, you will not be safe.'

He leant in towards me and I swallowed hard. I felt his heat, the flicker of my pulse. My breathing moved into the top of my chest. It was impossible to gather myself to think.

'Ummm …' He moved nearer, and my heartbeat built to a crescendo. I closed my eyes and his breath was hot on the nape of my neck. But then he was gone, suddenly, like the moment had never happened, sitting upright in his seat staring straight ahead. My heart pounded heavily, refusing to believe that the moment had passed.

'O-kay,' I managed finally. 'I think I'd better go.' He gazed ahead giving no indication as to whether or not he had even heard me. After a moment I pushed the door open wider and stepped out.

'Take care, Kate,' he murmured quietly as I closed it.

The rain had stopped, but the wind had picked up again. Goosebumps prickled across the base of my neck. Suddenly the shadows seemed infinitely and inescapably black.

I jumped at the sight of Ethan. He was perched on the brick wall in front of me, a smirk on his face, his hair in wild disarray. He hadn't been there a moment before, I was certain of it.

'Look like you've just seen a ghost,' he quipped, jumping off the wall and falling in beside me as I walked back to the house. He raised his eyebrows at my outfit, but said nothing else as he walked with a slight swagger and a carelessness which hid what I sensed was lethal force.

I shivered, but it had nothing to do with the cold, more a sense of what was coming. He regarded me and I noticed *his* eyes, how they were different to James' tonight. They were more cobalt than purple, cloaked in mystery and alive with messages which seemed to be going places I didn't as yet understand.

'Bye Ethan,' I called as he walked away, so much hidden behind the mask of his retreating image, so ordinary, so at odds with his extraordinary life.

The house had returned to silence. A glow came from beneath Mads' door. I snuck stealthily into my room, relieved not to have to explain anything to anyone. I was tired, but my confused brain writhed. For hours I tossed and turned, the silky metal surface of the angel on my chest warm from constantly running my fingers over it.

Eventually I fell in and out of a strange twilight sleep. I thought I saw a glowing ember outside my window, the hard contours of Ethan's face lit for a moment by orange radiance before it died, only to be reborn in gold as another glow burst to life, and then his eyes changed and it was James and then everything vanished in a puff of smoke and I felt a deep aching loss. A well of emptiness. The smoke became mist, and a multitude of winged angels disappeared into it, and then the mist became morning, but by then I had finally drifted into a deep and thankfully dreamless slumber.

32

DEB AND NICK

Daniel's funeral was closed to outsiders, but I went anyway and hid in the shadows of a large crooked tree with wide beams across the road from the church. A magpie regarded me with beady eyes, but otherwise I went unnoticed. The Edwards family arrived in sleek black sedans, a knot of dark clothes and hats. Nick's mother's face was hidden behind a veil but her body had a slump to it which was very different to the proud posture of the photos in her house. Even her gloved fingers seemed limp on her husband's arm. He was a tall distinguished-looking man with a curl in his greying hair who stood soldier-stiff, propping her up and resolutely holding back his own emotion.

Nick arrived at the last minute, just as I thought he wouldn't. He emerged from yet another black car, his face chiselled like a fine wooden carving, his eyes hidden behind dark glasses and his hair cut military short. It took me a moment to realise that this stranger in a formal suit, a white lily in his lapel, was actually him. He stood beside his mother, tall and strong, his head held high in a way that set him apart from the other mourners. She seemed to inhale his strength and stand a little straighter as she reached out to him gratefully, almost desperately, clasping his hand in hers like it could return Daniel to her. They proceeded into the church,

Nick on one side of her and his father on the other, and the others followed.

The priest, his white robes a stark counterpoint to the mourners, stood outside for a while initially engaging in a head-bobbing conversation with Brendan while shaking hands and offering commiserations as those gathered sombrely passed into the church. Beside him an older man with a Santa-Claus beard and mane of white hair plaited down his back stood sagely. His sunglasses were the only thing which seemed modern about him. He too wore white robes but his feet were shod in sandals which looked as though they dated back to biblical times. He leant on an ornately carved staff and I noticed that most deferred to him as they passed.

When everyone had finally entered, he too disappeared into the shady interior. After some minutes, the strains of Amazing Grace drifted out and touched me and I cried quietly, snivelling alone, hidden behind the tree, the magpie my only witness. I remained there with the bird even as the bell tolled and the hearse and families departed and everything grew silent again.

Suddenly Maggie warbled melodiously and flapped her wings. I looked up to where she sat, alone on the branch and she stared back at me with curious eyes. It seemed strange that she had remained so still until now. As I stepped out from my cover of shade, she emitted a short, loud call and then clapped her beak together in alarm, like a machine gun. When I stepped back she fell silent again. We stared at each other for a while.

'What is it?' I asked, a little self-consciously, given that I was now conversing with a bird.

'Are you lost? We can't stay here forever.' I gazed out at the abandoned church. Mist had begun to settle on it, whitening its stone façade and the land surrounding it, although the sky above was clear and bright and the sun was dazzling on the road. I'd never seen mist this late in the day before. It made the church seem like an island in a bubble of its own, like a catatonic being, both there and someplace else, a very, very long way away.

'Look at that,' I marvelled, 'an incredible sight, and no-one but us to see it.'

The breeze picked up and moved tendrils of the damp swirly haze towards us, unsettling Maggie again. Clearly she struggled with any sort of change.

'It's okay,' I soothed, 'just an atmospheric phenomenon.' But she wasn't happy. Her caw was ear-splitting and she flapped her wings unhappily.

'You go,' I said. 'I'll be fine.' She cawed again and then departed, the branch bouncing as she left, leaves fluttering to the ground in her wake. I watched her move away, a strange wistfulness coming over me as she became smaller and smaller and finally vanished. I envied her freedom.

A strange cool sensation settled on the surface of my skin. Tiny beads of moisture from the wisps of mist had collected there in a fine coating. I began to tingle. It was almost pleasant at first, like mentholated balm, but the feeling deepened and suddenly it was agonising.

It was impossible to stand still. Inadvertently I stumbled further into the mist to where the air was densest as I tried to relieve the ache. The murmurs started then and the ground trembled slightly, like I'd stepped into the world of Lilliput and each footfall was enough to cause an earth-quake. Suddenly the discomfort stopped as did the need to move. I halted and the world shivered. A ripple of fear dissipated as my surrounds settled and everything seemed the same again. But my relief was for a moment only, because it was then that I realised that the place in which I was now standing was *quite* different to the place I had been in before.

I was inside the cloud now, within its shade, the line of sunlight at its perimeter as clear a boundary as any I'd ever seen. Around me the vapour was alive with movement and sound. I turned and the world spun, the church and the tree and the whispering mist whipping around me in nauseating coils.

Tottering slightly I placed a hand to my forehead and closed my eyes. Without the visual cues everything stilled.

'Who are you?' I called tremulously.

The answer came from all around me, no single voice discernible, more like a choir of drafts, many different windy tones. *'We are the light which is separate from the darkness.'*

My gut twisted like a ferret in the beak of a hawk, but I could not run. 'I am afraid,' I cried.

'Do not be afraid,' the choir called in lyrical wistful tones. Strangely the words seemed to reassure me. Exhaling at last I dared to crack open my eyes. The air had grown denser still, like it was filling with spirits of the mist who were crowding together. I forced myself to inhale and exhale, although my heart was beating so frantically it hurt and my breath felt jagged rather than smooth.

'This is the place where we lost our darkness. The place where it was taken …'

Foreboding washed over me as the voices faded away. I closed my eyes again. It seemed easier that way. I frowned so deeply, it almost sliced my forehead in two.

'I don't understand.'

'He called out to our light when he stole our darkness, but he could not take it … not like he did with the others. It would not go into him. Sometimes that is the way. There is light that must wait … wait for the vessel which is most pure. Wait for The One.'

The voices lifted like a preacher embracing rhapsody.

'The hope of the future. The vessel inside you ...'

The reassurance I had felt earlier deserted me. There was clearly some misunderstanding here.

'No,' I whimpered.

'The One.'

'No,' I cried out, even as I trembled.

I reached out in desperation towards the tree like a sailor to a sinking boat. It had offered me sanctuary before. It represented salvation, a safe place to retreat to. But as I tried to run in that direction, a breathtakingly beautiful great blue-white light bloomed in the midst of the shadows, breaking them up and altering the fabric of what was there into the continually shifting patterns of a colourful kaleidoscope with the brightest light at the core. It was like looking into the sun and I had to reach up to shield my eyes from the glare. As it moved closer I tried again to run but the air behind me had turned into glass and I was trapped, powerless against it. The light moved closer, burning through my fingers into my eyes like a welder's torch even as I clenched them shut.

'Please,' I entreated. 'Leave me alone.'

It didn't. Maybe it could not comprehend my words, or maybe it knew so much more than I did about anything. It came up against me, hard and penetrating, burying itself in me with such force that I fell to the ground, screaming in agony. It was as though I'd swallowed down a mug full of broken glass, and my insides were being liquidised. The agony was horrific. Pain became my world. And then a sense of horrendous isolation and vulnerability hit me as I twisted on the ground in front of the church.

Quite suddenly it all stopped. I became aware of a different light. The sun which shines in the sky every day. Its warmth bathed me in kind healing which simplified every-thing. I was back where I belonged. The whispers had gone. All around me was warm and silent, just as it had been be-fore. Slowly I straightened myself, the tightly knit ball of ten-sion which had claimed me gradually releasing. And what had been so recently intolerable was replaced with warm an-aesthetic numbness and I felt enormously grateful. Strange as it may seem for a while I think I slipped away.

When I came to I was lying flat on my back in the middle of the road between the church and the tree, the pale blue forever hanging over me. Stumbling to my feet, I scurried from the road and back to the shelter of the tree. What had happened to me?

Branches swayed and leaves murmured in the breeze. The bark was cool and hard and bumpy, with pieces flaking off it, just as it had been before. But even so, the world seemed a little less familiar to me now, a little less solid. I clasped my arms around the broad trunk. It felt firm and reassuring. I stayed that way hoping that no-one would drive past and wonder at the crazy girl with the penchant for trees. Had I fainted? A car could have run over me. But one hadn't. One hadn't even stopped. There hadn't been a single car in all this time. Not one.

Finally as the minutes ticked by and everything remained just so, I ventured cautiously away from my zone of safety and looked around. The scene seemed desolate and surreal, but I knew I was back and not still in that other place. Noth-ing remained of anyone, not a tissue, or a flower. Nothing. And the mist had disappeared. There were no clues as to *an-ything* that had happened here today.

In both directions the road remained empty, the church a silent sentinel. I *must have* fainted, it was the only explana-tion. I had fainted and I'd had some kind of nightmare. I'd been alone. It had been a scary experience.

I touched my stomach, the place where I'd thought the light had entered me. Already my recollection seemed unreliable, in the way of dreams. My stomach felt fine. In fact, it felt better than fine. It was glowing, like a little bit of sunlight was vacationing there. I shook my head.

'God help me please,' I prayed, heading down the hill towards home. 'I need to pull myself together and get on with living my life.'

33

KATE

Monday's master class was a complete disaster. I felt like running from the room screaming or sitting under a sign which said 'flaky moron with big bum,' because that would be less humiliating. Much throat-clearing accompanied the end of my performance and Lara left the room, presumably to use the toilet, although I knew better. She was sweet, couldn't bring herself to say, *'That sucked big time, Kate.'*

'Are you okay, Kate?' Kristina, my piano teacher, asked quietly, taking me aside from the others and inclining her head towards me. 'You don't seem yourself today.'

I dropped my head. I was *definitely* not myself today, but how could I explain? *Err, don't worry about me, Kristina. Nothing more than a little homicidal ideation. Hee ... hee ... I was just wondering whether I would transition today or possibly tomorrow into ... into ... err something really bad, and mow you all down with the machine gun I've just recently stashed away in my boot.* Cue maniacal laugh. *Don't worry, only kidding.*

'I'm fine, just tired … a difficult weekend … personal stuff. I'm sorry!' I swallowed hard, not wanting to cry.

She continued to look at me with pity-filled eyes for a full minute, wondering whether I might disclose anything further. Lucky for her, I didn't. 'I don't want to pry,' she eventually added, 'but you don't look well.' She wasn't joking. I closely resembled Morticia on a bad hair day. 'Maybe go home and get some rest. Take the day off and get back into the swing of things tomorrow.'

'Sounds good,' I nodded with a shallow smile. I had absolutely no intention of following her advice. Rest at the moment, didn't seem like a remotely possible goal, or even a good idea really. Now was the time to refocus and in order to do so I needed the solitude and inspiration only music could offer me. Practising would distract me and help me relax.

I headed to the practice rooms, closeting myself, head down, hammering away at a poor undeserving piano, the keys almost flying from the board in fright. My softer side seemed to have abandoned me, not even Debussy could entice it out, but after three hours I could breathe a little more evenly.

I tried to call Nick that evening, but couldn't reach him. He was probably already on a flight to some faraway destination. Thanks a lot! He'd left me to shoulder this alone, thinking maybe that he'd done his duty by appointing James and Ethan to watch over me, but in truth abdicating responsibility.

'You look like you need a hug, a couple of pills and a *very* long sleep,' Francois said that evening as we sat in his room. He drew me close and rubbed my back soothingly as I slumped against him like a little child, letting everything go for a moment. 'I can help with two of those things.' He stood and returned moments later with a glass half filled with water, and two small white pills.

'No, no, I'm fine. Really.'

He looked dubious, his lips drawn together. 'Take them anyway, they might help you sleep.'

I threw them back with a slug of water. 'I just need a sack

to pull over my head.' Falling back on his bed I pulled the pillow over my face instead.

'Katie Baby,' he said with a small grin, lying down on his side next to me. 'Why so grim?'

Pushing the pillow off my face I opened an eye, realising for the first time that he was dressed in a carefully co-ordinated ensemble. I looked down to his feet.

'You're wearing your Jimmy Choos … in bed.'

'Uh huh,' he nodded, waiting for me.

'You're wearing your Jimmy Choos because?'

His grin turned into a beam so wide it looked like it might hurt. 'Pierre's sister is here for a few weeks. We had lunch.'

'Oh that's lovely,' I replied, knowing how much Pierre missed her.

'*She's* lovely,' he nodded enthusiastically. 'He told her about us. She was fine about it.'

'What?' My own smile grew broad as I forgot my troubles for an instant and hugged him tightly. 'That's fantastic for you guys. Such a relief.' We lay for a moment, squeezed together and then fell apart. 'You look like you've been set free.' He smiled up at the ceiling.

'Oh Kate, it feels that way.' Suddenly his expression changed. 'We've just got to work out how to tell the folks.' He turned to me, but now he looked as though he'd sucked a lemon.

'That's not going to be easy.'

'No. Anyway, we'll get there one day.' We lay in silence for a while both lost in our own thoughts before he spoke again. 'But we're talking about me, when you're the one who looks like you're in training for a role in *The Adams Family*.'

I closed my eyes, felt like they could just stay like that. 'Seriously,' he interrupted and I could hear the concern in his voice. 'What about you? You don't look good.'

'No? That's not the first time I've heard that today.' I just didn't have the energy, couldn't burden him. And I didn't want to be institutionalised.

'Kate!' he insisted, irritated by my lack of response.

'I can't tell you how long this weekend has been, Francois.' My voice was as gruff as the growl of a grizzly bear low on its daily Omega 3.

'Poor Baby,' he replied soothingly, and I realised that he was thinking about the assault on Saturday.

'Like you say, I just need a very long sleep and then I'll be okay again.'

'Come.' He tugged me off the bed and dragged me through to my room.

'You go do your teeth.'

'Okay Mum,' I replied compliantly.

When I returned he had turned my bed down. The warm yellow glow of the lamp made my room cosy.

'Now hop in,' he commanded. I did. His bossiness was comforting.

He lay down next to me stroking my hair and I yawned.

'Tell Pierre I'm happy for you guys.'

'I will Baby.' He kissed me on the cheek and then began to hum. I drifted.

34

DEB AND NICK

I tried to move on, to focus on my schoolwork, but it suffered. I was continually preoccupied with working out ways to see Nick, to see that he was okay, and then doubting whether or not I should even try, whether or not he would want me to. Why hadn't he contacted me yet? Alone in my room in the afternoons, my books a prop only, I became absorbed in one scenario or another, my imagination carrying me over walls and through windows, into his arms. But then futility would hit me and I'd become dejected, gazing endlessly at the white ceiling above my bed.

When I phoned yet again, I was startled by the voice of a woman on the other end. I had become so used to the machine when I called. 'Hello.' Her voice was deep and authoritative. His mother, I realised.

'Hello,' I replied hesitantly. 'Could I speak to Nick please?' There was an extended silence, like she'd been caught off guard and didn't like it.

'Who is this please?' Deep and authoritative had become demanding, although she remembered her manners.

I sighed. There was no point lying. 'It's Deb.' Again she paused, like she was working out how to say what she wanted to say. Finally she decided to go with simple and ditched the manners.

'I know it's hard for *you* to understand, but we don't want *you* calling here.' Her emphasis on the *you* turned me into something despicable. 'That includes Nick,' she added nastily.

Her words hurt, but I forged on regardless. 'But ...' I wanted to tell her that I did understand, a little anyway. I only wanted to make sure that he was okay and if he didn't want to speak to me then let him say so and I would disappear.

'He won't be taking your calls, so don't bother trying again,' she said, cutting me off and replacing the receiver abruptly.

Weeks turned into one whole month or thirty days, that is seven hundred and twenty hours, or forty-three thousand two hundred minutes. I sensed the individual minutes of the days pass without the usual kind blur of time. Slowly, without change, without release. Grief and frustration, intermingled and building. Like a swollen, muddy river swirling and tumbling, writhing, gathering, until it eventually bursts its banks, spewing itself into the turbulent ocean.

But finally I forced myself to make a decision. I couldn't go on like this. I would go to his house again, but this time I *would* gain entry somehow and see how he was. I would not leave until I had. I'd have to take a stand. If I had to then I would face his family, formidable or not, I would not be a coward. I would be brave. The situation warranted it. Anyway his mother had said he wouldn't take my calls, she'd said nothing about visiting.

Any potential rebuke was well worth the chance of seeing Nick. What other options did I have? If my pride needed to suffer then so be it.

My brother accompanied me for moral support and even my mother was supportive of the idea. She was concerned at how my low mood was impacting on my study and my exams were only a month away. They were both sick of seeing me sad and moping around the house. I needed closure.

'Yes?' His mother's voice answered after I'd pressed the intercom at the gate.

'Is Nick err, Nicholas in?' I asked hesitantly.

'Who is it?' *You know exactly who it is, Cow*, I felt like saying, but didn't, just clamped my teeth down hard on my tongue until the urge passed. 'It's Deb, his friend. I just wanted to say hello, see that he's okay.'

'He's not in, but I'll tell him you were here.' Although her voice was clipped and abrupt, the quality of it had changed somewhat. She'd lost the angry edge and something else … Something that was hard to make out over the intercom because of the static. It was like she was just stating the words, without her previous passion, and that she was no longer confident that they were the right ones.

'When will he …' But the intercom had already gone dead and only a dry crackling sound remained. The wall was too straight and high to climb, the tangle of vines too dense. I wasn't Tarzan. The house was a fortress by any definition. It rebuffed intrusion. A sense of hopelessness descended on me as I returned to the car and slumped into my seat.

'So?' George asked.

'Forget it,' I answered, shaking my head slightly and trying not to cry. 'Waste of time. They're not going to let us in.' I swallowed a small sob, but he noticed and squeezed my knee reassuringly.

'Come, come. What happened to your earlier resolve?' I shrugged, and it was hard to get my shoulders back to their normal position afterwards.

'My God, Deb,' he cried despairingly. 'Just as well you're not a heart surgeon or something.' His voice took on a high falsetto as he mimicked. 'Oh, no, a paper cut. I guess he's not going to make it ...'

I couldn't help the smile that crept onto my face. George had that power. It was his gift. I tried to swat him, but he moved out of the way.

'You don't give up *that* easily do you?'

I regarded him evenly. 'I'm open to suggestions, George. I suppose you have one?'

'It's just about trying a little harder.' He sat up and started the car. 'The Edwards family may have money, but we have perseverance, and brains on our side. Plus we have time, lots of it!'

He smiled mischievously and drove, or spluttered and smoked, a short distance down the road where he pulled to the side. Once the fumes from the car exhaust had cleared, we had a reasonable view of the gate from the rear-view mirror. We sat low in our seats and watched. His decrepit car stood out in stark contrast to the manicured surroundings, like an elephant at the opera.

'George, what *actually* is our plan?' I asked curiously, casting my embarrassment aside as bourgeoisie conceit.

'We'll wait and see if he leaves the house. If he does, we'll follow him and then you can talk to him. Otherwise, maybe his folks will leave and then we'll get in somehow!'

'What, breaking in?'

'Maybe we can get a message to him via one of their 'staff'.' His tone was patronising.

'This car is disgusting!' I said, noticing for the first time the empty cans and fast-food wrappings which littered the floor.

'Complaints. You must be cheering up.' His smile was playful.

'We could be parked here for hours.'

'Please send all grievances in writing to PO Box XXX, No-one Cares.' He turned on the radio and started fishing around on the backseat.

'Shut up. I'm just saying.'

'Not like we have anything better to do - work, study.' He dragged an eski onto the front seat.

'Don't you think we're going to look a bit suspicious?'

'Who cares? There's no law that says we can't park here.'

'No?' I looked around to make sure there weren't any parking restrictions and was surprised that I didn't find a sign stating: *'No parking for cars older than six months.'*

'I wouldn't be surprised if the laws *are* a little different around here actually. In fact I wouldn't be surprised if these people have their own private police force!'

He cracked a can and I was relieved to see that it was cola and not a beer. 'What about you Sis?'

We sipped drinks and annoyed each other, but after about an hour his feeble attempts to distract me from my slump were becoming annoying. At last the gates inched open. We scrunched down further in our seats, peeping out over the window ledge as a large silver sedan with tinted windows exited the driveway and purred haughtily past us. It was impossible to see who or how many were inside, but on the plus side, I think we were invisible too.

'I'm just assuming that wasn't him,' George advised disparagingly. 'Hopefully he wouldn't be seen dead in something so ostentatious, otherwise there's no hope for the poor bastard!'

'Maybe *you* should go to the gate now George.'

I watched in the rear view mirror as he approached the gate and spoke into the intercom. After a moment he beckoned frantically to me. Leaping out of the car I rushed towards him, noticing as I neared that the gates were opening again. We ran briskly up the driveway to the house.

'What did you say?' I asked, hoping it wasn't, *'Pharmacy delivery. I've got the condoms Mrs Edwards ordered.'*

'I just asked to see Nick,' he explained over his shoulder. 'Brendan opened.'

As we reached the front door it opened and Brendan stood before us. He looked anxious and preoccupied, like a war was waging inside and he was yet to make up his mind which side he was on. His brow held deep ruts and his jaw muscle was tightly clenched, but he wasn't surprised to see me beside George. He let us in with only the slightest hesitation.

'Thanks, Brendan,' George said, adding, 'This is Deb.'

'I know who she is,' he replied brusquely, cutting George off. George turned and looked at me with one eyebrow raised and I bit my lip. There was a lot I hadn't shared with George, and I felt a little bad about it, given his involvement now.

'We thought that maybe it was best you just get this over with,' Brendan continued haughtily, implying some sort of a family gathering since my earlier conversation with his mother. Suddenly the car leaving and our easy access made sense.

'I just wanted to see how Nick was, that's all,' I said.

'Of course, we're so sorry about Daniel. It's terrible,' George cut in anxiously.

'Thank you,' Brendan said. His voice was stiff, but it seemed that he was at least trying to be a little more gracious. He chewed his lip for a moment. 'It's been difficult.' His eyes, the same mesmerising ones Nick had, but a shade colder, fixed on me for a long second.

'I'll let him know that you're here and see what he wants to do,' he said suddenly, clicking his heels in a sharp turn and leaving us standing awkwardly in the hallway.

Minutes passed and I gazed at what *was* a truly strange assemblage of Edwards' family members on the photo wall. I hadn't fully noticed that before, the extent of the peculiarity, the uncanny similarities, especially the eyes, spanning so many generations. I guess I'd been distracted. Stepping closer I noticed another peculiarity. The frames were thick with dust.

A door opened on the landing and murmuring voices could be heard. I sensed Nick's arrival at the top of the staircase. I *knew* he was there because my spine began to prickle and tingle and everything around me seemed to slow as his presence tugged at me, turning my head and making my eyes move to his as he stood, as still as Buddha, gazing down at me.

He was changed again from the last time I'd seen him outside the church. His eyes were unnaturally bright against the grey pallor which touched his skin and darkened to almost black under his eyes. His usual vitality was lost in his shrunken form. He looked exhausted. Roads I had never noticed journeyed to many places across his forehead, robbing him of his youth.

His appearance shocked me, especially after he'd seemed so strong and vital at the funeral. George stood in frozen astonishment beside me.

'I'm so sorry, Nick,' I whispered, slowly ascending the never-ending flight of stairs leaving George at the bottom. Guilt blanketed my shoulders.

I stopped at the top. This close, he looked even more vulnerable, so fragile. My hand tethered me to the balustrade as though afraid of what awaited me should I be set free to go to him. The space between us was thick with suffering, but the strange sensation I had experienced the last time I was here was gone. The door at the end of the corridor was shut and the room now empty of its former occupant.

Nick's eyes were on me, I could feel them boring into me, like he was reading a book, but when I turned to him he turned quickly away, to the landing windows and out to the restless sea. The weather had changed suddenly. The wind had picked up outside, gathering dark clouds into a forbidding cluster and pummelling the house. The ocean was a mess of wrestling steel and white.

'Nick?' I whispered. He turned reluctantly.

Reaching out I took his deathly cold hand in mine.

'Come,' I said, pulling him towards his bedroom, where it was more private.

'No, not there.' His voice was hoarse as though speaking for the first time in days.

'Oh?' I glanced into his room. The interior was murky, but even from this distance I could see that it was in a state of some disarray. The bed had been dismantled, the mattress was hanging half off the base and the sheets were twisted and strewn.

'What's going on?' I asked shocked. I dropped his hand and walked into his room. There were great gaping holes in the walls.

'What have you been doing?' I was pretty sure that if they were going to remodel, the Edwards would get in professionals.

The door frame was rough and splintered as though it had been forced open at some point and the bottom of it was irreparably damaged. Sturdy brass locks had recently been mounted to the outside.

'Why are these here, Nick?' I remembered Daniel. Was Nick a prisoner?

'You shouldn't have come up here,' he said. 'I was going

to come down. I didn't want you to see me this way.'

I shook my head. He still just didn't get it. Going to him I touched his elbow. 'Come.' Half-heartedly he followed me into his room.

'Help me with this.' I reached down and tried to lift the mattress back onto the bed but he waved me away and shifted it back on himself. His room was dishevelled and gloomy, the curtains still drawn, and the air stale and strangely musty, like a tomb unopened for centuries. Moving to the drapes I pulled them back. Grey light made the room no friendlier. Reaching forward I opened the window. Violent air jerked the latch from my hand whipping the curtains to and fro.

'Oh, dear,' I exclaimed, reaching out and grabbing for it, my hair thrashing across my face as I did so. A rumble of thunder startled me. The storm was approaching rapidly. Finally I managed to grab the latch and tug it closed.

'That's some storm coming,' I said, as I turned back to face him. He stared through the window at the ominous sky.

'I wish I'd come sooner Nick. I can see how you are suffering … how you have suffered, you're wasting away.'

'I am?' He sounded vague, as though he hadn't realised that until now.

'You are,' I answered firmly, my attempt at eye contact failing as he resisted my gaze. I dropped onto the bed. 'It's been really hard to get to see you. Your folks have this place wrapped up tighter than Fort Knox.' I glanced towards the locks on his door. 'To be honest, it's hard to remember your room as it was, it *seems* prisonlike now.'

'You might think that.'

I huffed and threw my hands into the air. 'There are locks on the outside of your door!'

'I guess they think it's best that way.'

I leapt off the bed, frustrated by his lack of reaction, not understanding his submission, the person he had become.

'Why?' I asked, a cold hard sick realisation hitting the pit of my stomach as the words left my mouth. *Because he's suicidal, like Daniel.*

I felt him struggle against the thick catatonia which seemed intent on claiming him and gather himself with supreme effort, drawing on some hidden reserve of strength. I wondered whether he was taking something or whether the force that was holding him down with such power was grief. Suddenly he grabbed my arms hard, startling me. Urgency made his voice raw. 'Get away from here *now*, Deb. Don't turn around to look back. This place will only damage you. *I will only damage you.*'

His words were garbled, tumbling over each other in a sudden gush. 'Have they been holding you captive here?'

He almost laughed. 'What, that lock?' He shook his head, like the lock was some kind of joke, which it clearly wasn't. 'No, and if they ever did, it would be because they needed to ... for my own sake.'

I wasn't so sure about that, but I didn't say anything.

'I want to help you Nick, I just don't know what to do,' I said, a desperate edge to my voice. 'I know you're sad, I know you might even blame yourself. I want to help. Please, let me help. I can see something bad is happening to you. Don't shut me out!' The whine to my voice escalated and I forced myself to stop and exhale. Touching his arm I realised that his body was rigid with tension, unyielding to my touch. My lip wobbled and I bit down on it hard.

He shook his head. 'You don't understand. This is the way it is. Whatever we may have wanted, we have to accept that this is the way it is. There is desire, and then there is life. Life you have to accept. I am changed, and I am sorry, but I can't go back to before now. My life is here, *with them.*'

I shook my head. 'There are always options, always.' But defeat had already begun eating its way into my soul and I recognised it. Why was this person so important to me? Why would I willingly embrace suffering if it meant I could be with him?

'I never wanted to hurt you, Deb.'

I shrugged and walked to the window as the frames rattled in the force of the wind. 'Maybe not, but you have.'

'I know I have.' His voice was so low it could hardly be heard, but he came to me and took my hands in his. For the first time he made eye contact and held it. His pupils were small, overshadowed by green and orange-gold swirls and striations. 'But that hurt is like a blister, compared to what it could potentially be. Leave now and it *will* heal. I promise you that. There will be a mark for a while, but … not for long. Don't wait around here to be mauled, to die from wounds that will *never* heal, because that's what this place is … and the people in it. Misery *lives* here. Misery and darkness … and if you stay, you *will* be infected by it.'

He dropped my hands and moved to the window, opening it again and letting the wind gust into the room. It seemed to force air into his lungs, helping him breathe and he turned to face me, a wild man.

'Daniel was so gentle, so different to the rest of us. But in the end, even he couldn't escape. It got him …'

'What got him, Nick?'

'Life … inevitability …'

'You did what you could, but he couldn't be stopped. You couldn't be everywhere at once.' I moved closer to him and reached out but he pushed me away lightly and turned to lean precariously out of the window into the gusting wind. After a while he drew himself back in and I felt relieved.

'There is evil here and it will taint you. It will claim you. I've seen it happen. Don't let it take you, Deb. Don't let it rob you of your goodness ... your light.'

'Come away from here. Go your own way.'

He shook his head. 'I can't right now. One day maybe.' His voice lifted with sudden determination. 'I'm trying to get my head around so many things. I'm trying to understand the incomprehensible. Everything has come at once - my brother's death and ...'

He stopped abruptly and then spoke again. 'My family is cursed, we are all infected.'

'That's not true, Nick. You can fight it.' He dropped his head sadly and I wished that we'd run away together all those weeks ago.

'No,' he mumbled, his expression unfathomable, but his voice resigned.

'I know about the issues with my father, the relationship with Sofia, their child. We never got to talk about any of that, but I don't understand why it can't be laid to rest after all this time.'

There was a moment of silence before he tried to laugh, but it was a cold, hollow sound. 'Oh Deb ...'

'Where is Sofia anyway, maybe she could speak for herself, put the past to rest?'

'That's not possible. Sofia was lost a long time ago.' Suddenly I understood a lot, the raw emotion on his face the day he had first brought me here, the hatred his family had for mine.

'My father?'

'I don't blame your father for that ...' he sighed, 'but my family – they're not so easily convinced.'

A wretched smile stole his face. 'You're young and so full of life. You've got plans. Live your life. Forget about me.

Please. It will be better that way.'

I squared my shoulders, about to argue, but his words stopped me.

'Please Deb, I want you to.' His voice was quiet, but determined.

This was the end. Of what? I didn't even know. My eyes prickled.

'What happened between the funeral and now?' I asked, suddenly.

'What?' He sounded shocked and I was glad. It was better than the dampened range of emotion which had been our constant companion throughout the conversation.

'I was there.'

'Well you shouldn't have been. It was private.'

'I was there, hiding outside. I just wanted to see you. See that you were okay. And I did see you. You looked good, you looked strong and healthy. You don't look that way now.' My voice had changed, become stronger and more deliberate. I wanted an answer.

'You shouldn't have been there, Deb. I wish you hadn't been. There were ...' His speech which had started off passionately, was becoming increasingly laboured. He ran his hand through his hair and I realised how wasted his arms had become.

'What?' I prompted. Something inched its way up my neck as I remembered my strange experience outside the church that day.

'It was a moment of release, of saying goodbye and letting go.' He shook his head as though trying to clear it. 'But in the instability of those moments there can be danger for outsiders.'

'What sort of danger?' Lightning cracked in two white lines across the windows and thunder growled discordantly.

He forced himself to turn away from it and back to me and I noticed fear again in his face and the rigidity in his arms as he forced them down at his sides.

'I'm not all there at the moment, you must excuse me.' He marched to the door, gesturing stiffly for me to follow. 'It's the medication talking.'

I followed him out of the room. 'I'm being looked after, Deb. You can trust in that.' He wanted me to go, needed me to. The degree of rigidity stealing over his body was scary, the increasing tension like an omen of something approaching. Something wildly unpredictable and explosive. I felt a ripple of terror.

We were on the landing now and I noticed movement below. It was Brendan, his face deadly serious as he looked up at us from his position next to George.

'It's time to go,' he stated firmly. 'Nick needs to rest.' I looked back at Nick, at the stranger who had stolen the man I'd thought I loved. His face was marble-like.

'This was always going to be a dark place for us, Nick, wasn't it?'

'I guess so,' he murmured.

Shadows from the slamming trees outside the windows flicked violently across the floor and then onto his face. 'Don't come here again.'

I hesitated and Brendan's voice boomed out from below. 'Now!'

As I left him, I sensed the change in atmosphere, the sudden drop in temperature and a loss of pressure. Maybe it was simply the storm which was almost overhead, or maybe it was something else. I was too distressed to give it much consideration as I ran towards a worried-looking George. Brendan ushered us out impatiently, but he needn't have. By that point, all I wanted was to escape.

We rushed past him, almost desperate in our bid for freedom from the oppressive environment of the house, embracing the howling gale and biting rain instead. Wind whipped my hair into a wild frenzy and rain seemed to gnaw at my skin, but I didn't care. As we ran down the drive, lightning speared the sky and the roar of thunder made the ground vibrate. Tears of frustration blurred my sight and my throat ached from the swell of supressed emotion.

I could feel his eyes on me through the windows of the upstairs landing. I knew that something wasn't right, but it was something so far out of my field of experience that it was pointless even considering it. Rounding a bend in the drive I realised that we had finally vanished from his sight.

We made a swift retreat to the car as the gate closed and I collapsed there, my chest heaving, snivelling and moaning as I sobbed. George looked alarmed at the extent of my feelings, uncomfortable in the presence of emotion so visibly displayed, but lovingly tolerant. He touched my arm.

'Just go,' I managed. 'Let's get away from here.'

Without hesitation he started the car and drew away from the curb with a screech. Driving was easy.

'We shouldn't have gone,' I blubbered. It was impossible to hold onto fantasy now, or even memories. Everything was tainted.

'Yes, we should have,' he replied resolutely. 'At least you know where you stand now, Deb! You can be miserable and you can get it over with and get on with your life. Move away from *this* place.'

I stared out of the window. The fortresses were obscured by dense rain and thick air. George drove cautiously along the slippery road, leaning forward to try and improve his visibility. Trees thrashed wildly in a ghoulish dance and vegetation was strewn across the road forcing him to detour every now and then.

'You've got so much living to do Deb. You're barely an adult.' I scowled in response, but he ignored me. 'This will be hard for a while, but you'll have fun again, you'll see. Getting caught up with such a strange family, well that would stay with you, damage you.' He chanced a quick look across at me, before returning his eyes to the road. 'He's not well, Deb, anyone can see that.'

He was definitely 'not well', whatever that meant. I felt exhausted. I closed my eyes.

'Must say,' he said as I drifted, 'I thought they'd have staff. I mean, it's such a big place, no wonder it gets so dusty. It would take you a month to get from one end to the other and then I guess you'd have to start all over again.'

He drove for a while and I noticed that outside the weather had settled. 'And the garden. I was expecting more. Something manicured. It was so overgrown Tarzan would get lost. You'd think they'd at least sweep the leaves up from time to time.'

'Must just have been the storm, George,' I mumbled, opening an eye. He glanced across at me and raised an eyebrow.

'I don't know,' I added sitting up a little straighter in the seat. You had to wonder. Where *had* all the staff gone?

35

KATE

Weeks passed and the weather started improving. It was unpredictable at first, tantalising warmth interspersed with colder snaps. Tiny cherry blossoms appeared and the days were brighter for longer. We were all a little more cheerful.

James and Ethan were around although they seemed less obvious than before, a face in a crowd, a car falling in somewhere behind me, a muscular shoulder vanishing around a bend as I neared. They no longer pretended to be philosophy majors in the park near the practice rooms. But sometimes I'd find James leaning against the practice room door as I arrived in the midst of a group of students, like he wanted me to know he was around. He'd disappear almost as soon as I saw him.

'James …' I called, stopping him, since I was alone.

'Don't go.' He returned, looking at me expectantly like I needed to have a good reason to call him back.

'Uh …' I fumbled, thinking how bizarre it was that he knew so much about me, but that I couldn't even ask a simple question without anxiety. 'How are you guys?'

His eyes blazed. I'd almost forgotten how intense they were. I swallowed and a finger found its way to my lip. 'Fine Kate. And you?' Could this be any more surreal, I thought, flashing back to our conversation in the car weeks ago.

'Okay. I just ...' I reached up to brush a strand of hair away, but my hand stayed there like a shield and I looked down, increasingly hesitant. What exactly did I want from this man? It was very confusing. Suddenly he reached out and I felt his fingers on mine as he moved them away so that he could look into my eyes. His brows were drawn together, his lips were parted slightly. Goosebumps prickled along my arms and I felt light-headed.

'You just?' he prompted, as Nishlyn and Lara rounded the corner, distracting me for a moment. When I turned back he was gone.

'Who *is* that?' Lara prompted, nudging me.

I waved my hand dismissively. 'No-one, just a friend.' She winked at me and I blushed. Nishlyn swiped his access card and I followed them into the practice block with a last glance back. Nothing, just light and shadows.

I wasn't even sure what I'd wanted to say to him. I wished I could say that I didn't think about him, that I didn't wish he was an accountancy or actuary student, or that his brother wasn't quite so forbidding. But then I would probably never have met him. My feelings presented potential complications, for me, for them. Still. I couldn't say that I didn't want what I couldn't have.

Nick's ongoing silence was confusing me. Although he was notoriously inconsistent and I never knew what to expect, dumping this on me and vanishing seemed a bit extreme even for him.

His revelations had scarred me, had shaken the ground beneath me and lifted it to reveal the truth. There was no ground. He had cursed me with knowledge. I envied those around me, still waiting, still enjoying the illusion. Maybe they would be lucky enough to hold onto it until the end.

The night was warm and close, unusual for October. Inside, the kitchen was a hive of activity, alive with the sounds of cooking and chatting, with clattering cutlery and crockery. I stole the solitude, inviting no-one as I slipped out on nimble feet to the pool, the rumble of traffic providing a dull background noise, but no intrusion.

Gliding through the water I dived down and then burst through the surface, rolling onto my back. A slippery seal, maybe even a mermaid. Yeah right! Peace. I floated, supported, relaxed. My hair was a fan around me, soft and wet and heavy. Immersing myself in the sensory serenity, I drifted.

And slowly my eyes grew heavier and I closed them as I slipped across the smooth surface, the tiniest of ripples propelling and lulling me. I was an organism, an element maybe, almost one with this mysterious fluid. The weight of self-determination lifted and a great sense of well-being descended. I looked up into the gathering dusk, observing the darkness merging with the light, leaving only the tiny stars glinting far away messages. I sensed red farewells and blue arrivals and in noticing, I realised that we were there too, maybe even more there than here. That the fleeting instant of our consciousness, a tiny flickering flame, is embraced by forever at the end, whatever that means. That we are always, somewhere, somehow, in some way the tiniest part of everything. Backwards and forwards, forever, in the elements, or in the spaces we know nothing about.

The darkness around the pool came to life. Shadows tangoed, sharing passionate embraces, while the silver mist whispered and thickened over the water, spiralling into wild eddies as the breeze tugged at it.

Fused with the water I became a part of the moment. As the disembodied sensation increased, so did the realisation that my perception had changed, that I wasn't simply observing and judging, but being. I was a part of nature, intertwined, enmeshed, inseparable. Fused. Even space was alive, the nothingness, the voids and cavities were alive, the air moving in and out of my body, revealed a billion mysteries. As I became more and more immersed, the gloom seemed to lift and spin into millions of tiny sparkling splashes and spots, spiralling, twirling in every colour imaginable, and I became entranced, hypnotised by the beauty of the spectacle.

And then I became aware of another in the moment with me. Another who was also aware, who was watching me, waiting somewhere behind the mist on the other side. He had the advantage, like looking through a one way mirror, pressing a button which overrode my mind's controls, removing the inhibitions imposed on me and showing me what I could not usually know. Suddenly, without any conscious intention on my part, like it was driven there by another driver because that was where it had to go, my mind zoomed in to focus on the presence, and I saw a face.

My heart pulsated frantically as it hovered somewhere in the middle of the multitude of flickering spots. I wanted to cover my eyes and scream. Such a thing could not be real. But as much as the image was overwhelming, confronting, too strange, terrifying, it was also glorious and amazing and if it was real, I realised on some level, that it should be seen.

Slowly the flickering spots vanished and space seemed to settle and become space again, shadowy voids. He stood at the edge of the pool. Shade enveloped his body, but the moon shone on his sculpted face, making him glow vampire-white. He observed me without discomfort, with the curious scrutiny of one from another realm.

The essence of my being, not the physical body which still felt the water on it, was magnetically drawn through time and space into his slow presence and he examined me. It felt like an eternity, but it was more likely seconds, and then the spell was broken as great wings broke up the night sky. I gasped and spluttered in the pool, sinking beneath the surface and reappearing to a night much colder than I had realised. Shivering, my teeth chattering so hard they hurt my jaw, I stumbled from the pool desperate for warmth and security, the golden glow of the kitchen. The mist was gone. Shaking with cold and shock I tottered into the house to thaw.

Who was that? God? The devil? Or one of those angels? Something else from the other side? Was it that simple? Was I that delusional? It was quite possible.

I rubbed myself so hard with the towel that afterwards I looked as though I had a nasty case of shingles.

'You must be completely insane,' Pierre scolded, flicking on the kettle. 'You'll die of hypothermia.'

'It was such a nice day,' I chattered.

'Yeah, but the water's freezing and the air still gets really cold at night.' He shook his head and I hung mine.

'Get dressed and I'll bring you some hot tea.' Shaking uncontrollably I did my best to pull on another pair of attractive pyjamas, these with bows and bunnies.

'Tea,' he said a few minutes later, passing me a mug. Hot and sweet.

My heart swelled with gratitude. 'That's delicious Pierre.'

'You're as white as a sheet, Kate.'

'It's just the cold.' He covered me with the doona and sat beside me.

'Next time remember. If there's no-one else in the pool it's probably for good reason.'

'Go away,' I said, and he did, but with a gentle kiss to my forehead.

Unsurprisingly, my sleep was disturbed by unsettling dreams. Mist at the window. Dense, a sheet of white, but alive. And then a face in the mist, the face from the pool, disembodied, distorted and exaggerated in the way dreams are, the features gaunt and hollow, the skin grey, the black hair longer, hollow malevolent eyes staring through the glass at me. The beauty was absent, stripped away, only the darkness was left. His lips flared in an angry spitting snarl of incomprehensible words as he spoke. And then I woke. It occurred over and over again. Disappearing as I stirred, reappearing as I slept, unreliable memories that vanished as I sought them, like bubbles popping when you touch them.

36

DEB AND NICK

Burying my head in my books I did my best to put Nick and his family and everything that was weird and screwed-up aside, but two weeks later life threw me a curve-ball. My period was extremely late.

I tore down the road to the pharmacy, kicking myself all the way. Idiot! Who would have sex without protection in this day and age? Everyone knew the risks. My mother had taught me about the birds and the bees when I was young, tried to immunise me. We all knew about HIV. I'd failed, refused to learn, allowing myself to succumb to lust, to throw caution to the wind. Did I value my life that little, or him that much? I shook my head, trying to shake off my foolishness, but it stuck like a lifetime of hurts.

I had exiled my Nick memories to dreamtime and now they were haunting me. Love I realised, that sweet madness, had become bitter fear, regret even.

Cap pulled down low and glowing like a light bulb I purchased a pregnancy test. Rushing home I locked myself in the toilet, and counted down the endless minutes. I prayed. *Please let there be only one line.* Over and over. Two undebatable lines appeared.

I'd never felt so alone, so afraid and uncertain. Ashamed.

'You're looking tired Deb,' Mum said the next morning.

Her hair was still wrapped in a towel, her glasses propped on the end of her nose as she ate breakfast and read the paper which was folded in half on the corner of the counter. 'You're studying too hard, staying up too late.'

I shrugged and fiddled listlessly with my food. 'You okay, Deb?'

'I don't know, Mum.' Her eyes held sudden fear.

'It's Nick, isn't it?' she guessed. Her lips pressed together in a firm line as I nodded.

'Men,' she despaired, shaking her head and taking my hand.

'I'm pregnant, Mum,' I spluttered. My words hit her like a slap. She dropped my hand and clasped hers to her mouth. In that instant she aged ten years and I felt horrible.

'Oh Deb … How far along?' she managed. Her hands now covered most of her face; her eyes were terrified as they peeped over the top of her fingers. I knew what she was thinking. *Laugh Deb. Please laugh so that I can breathe. Let this be a cruel trick, a joke, a sick joke, a lie. I don't care. Anything but the truth.*

But all I could do was stare back at her. Finally her shoulders slumped and she exhaled. The image she had of my future was lost. 'Seven weeks,' I mumbled.

We remained at the table for a long while. The breeze made the drapes billow carelessly. The Lorikeets bickered and squawked outside. The odd fig fell to the ground with a thump.

'You'll be late, Mum,' I said eventually, 'you're not even ready yet.' Usually she took at least twenty minutes to blow dry and style her light brown hair before setting off to work. She didn't leave until it was perfectly flicked, until she'd applied make-up and perfume. She was an attractive woman but right now she looked old and tired. I'd brought back every ordeal she'd ever experienced, sucking the life from her.

'I don't care Deb. I work long enough hours that on the odd occasion I can take a little time if I need it.'

Standing up she took her bowl to the sink and let it clatter to the bottom. 'It's totally up to you whether or not you tell Nick. After everything that's happened you don't owe him anything.'

'Maybe,' I agreed.

She turned back to me. 'Do you know what you want to do, Deb?'

The enormity of making such a decision was terrifying. 'I only know that I can't raise it, Mum.' I felt too young and too impulsive for motherhood, and I had scant means of support. Maybe I was just plain selfish, not ready to make sacrifices.

'If you want to I'll help you, we'll survive.' Her kindness made me tearful and I blinked hard and sniffed.

'No, no I can't Mum.' The idea alarmed me. I wasn't ready to face the harsh reality of life with a baby at eighteen.

I looked up at her, at the strain on her face. 'Others have managed,' she said.

I writhed on my seat. I would not remain intact under those circumstances. My world would become a horrible place, and I horrible in it. My child would suffer.

'I can't Mum.' I shook my head with grim determination. I felt like a failure. She came to me and wrapped me in her arms tightly, creating a twilight world where I was her little girl again, and everything was alright.

After a long while she released me and clasped my shoulders instead, looking into my eyes earnestly. 'You do what you think is right. I'll support you.'

'I don't deserve you Mum,' I cried, sobbing with relief and

gratitude.

She smoothed the hair on my forehead away from my face. Tendrils stuck to the tears on my cheeks. 'We don't measure these things Deb. Look at the things you and George have had to go through, the pain your father and I have caused you! It's nothing to do with deserving or not deserving, it's purely about loving. And the love I feel for my children transcends everything, it always will ... no matter what.'

The next morning I wandered down to the beach early. I sat on a large flat rock, far from prying eyes. Only the aimless gulls witnessed my emotional contemplation, my confused pondering. After everything we had been through. How would I tell Nick?

The water was filing cabinet-grey. Soon it would become blinding, like sheets of steel burning up in the sun. Usually this was my favourite time; the breeze was still cool, the sun warm, but not yet fierce, the sand almost bare. Later it would be cluttered with noise and movement, with so much distraction.

Nick had a right to know, we were both equally responsible, but I didn't want him to feel trapped ... or worse, to try and force me to do something I'd regret. The thought of how his family might react and what they were capable of made me shiver, even in the warm sunshine. They would frame me, the girl who had ensnared him, the one who had plotted to trap him.

As I reached for my bag, I recognised him. Fate had called him here. He rounded a bend on the beach and my heart immediately leapt into my throat, crashing and burning when I noticed that he was not alone. It was only a fortnight since I'd last seen him, but he looked very different, reanimated. Beside him, standing almost as tall as him was a slender girl with long blonde hair. They walked together in the shallow water, her hand held loosely in his.

I clamped my eyes shut. Nausea clutched at my gut. When I opened them the image was just as cruel as before, worse as they merged in a kiss. Self-pity threatened to spill onto my cheeks. I swallowed so hard it hurt, cursing myself for my stupidity, the self-inflicted vulnerability of my situation.

Quickly, I hastened to escape the beach as fast as possible, to bury myself in some murky oblivion, to wallow in misery. My movement drew his attention and he turned to stare in my direction. I ran.

Later I lay on my bed, Bon Jovi's *You Give Love a Bad Name* playing too softly in the background, torturing myself. He was obviously recovered from whatever mental problem had plagued him. So rapidly too. He seemed restored. Physically at least. I felt like punching my belly, but something stopped me. Instead my hands lost velocity and fell limply onto my stomach. For a minute I continued to wish that I could gouge the thing out from inside me and destroy it, knowing that I could if I had an abortion, knowing that I would hate myself for it, forever. Morbid thoughts polluted my mind, sickening me with ideas I would never act on. Only the throb of his motorbike nearing distracted me from that dark place. Why now? Why had he come now? Guilt because I'd seen him on the beach?

I peeked over the window ledge, my heart racing, but not in the way it had all of those months ago. I did not want to see him. I did not want to speak to him. For a long while he remained where he was. Finally he dismounted and walked slowly up the path and out of my sight. I pulled the sheers quietly across the window with trembling fingers and collapsed face down on my bed.

Mum was prepared.

'Nick, hello,' she said, a brilliant actor after years of experience, hiding the hurt that she felt on my behalf so well.

'Is Deb around Mrs Brayshaw?' he asked directly as, unable to contain my curiosity, I crept stealthily into the passage to listen. I was confident that my mother would not betray me.

Her voice was firm, but not unkind. 'I'm sorry Nick, but she's not.'

I sensed his hesitation. Did he want to know where I was? 'Will you tell her that I stopped by, that I wanted to say hi?'

'Sure,' she answered. I heard her start to shut the door. 'You take care now.' He paused on the doorstep and I had a sense that he knew that I was in the house. Eventually his footsteps retreated.

I did not run to the door and wrench it open. I did not yell for him to come back. Instead I slumped down on the passage floor and began to cry, my knees up, my forehead on my arm. Great shaking sobs heaved through my body.

'You'll be okay baby girl,' Mum soothed, rushing over and dropping to comfort me. 'Just let it all out. I won't leave you.'

And that was the one certainty I had. Something I *could* trust. She would not leave me and she never lectured me. What was done was done. My shame and sadness were burden enough.

37

KATE

Time passed and summer proper arrived, driving the experience of that October night away, with barbeques and night-time sunshine, with the increased pressure of final term. The night terrors had returned, despite my efforts at sleep hygiene, slowly worsening in a frustrating cycle which made it hard to pin-point reasons for the escalation. I couldn't be definite, couldn't say that as of today they were bad, that yesterday they were better. It was like a slow trend, waxing and waning. Some nights were peaceful, others were not, and slowly there were more that were not.

James and Ethan continued as a constant blur on the fringe of my life. Sometimes I almost forgot that they were probably lurking in the shadows. At other times I felt resentful, although I remained inexplicably tolerant, maybe out of respect for Nick, or maybe because I had never really learnt to be assertive, I was too fearful of the consequences. Maybe I enjoyed the ridiculousness of the situation, or the twisted flattery it implied.

To some extent I feared them. What did I really know about them? Trust was the biggest thing. I did not fully trust them.

Sometimes we met up, not that I even had a phone number for them, or had asked for one. I wasn't confident that I wouldn't succumb to further difficulties as a result of having it, that in a weak, or lonely moment I wouldn't make a complete fool of myself. I'd done it before. Best forgotten, but never forgotten, thank you Sam. I flushed just thinking of it. *'Scary stalker girl'*, Sam whispered. It had been one pathetic moment, and it had involved a teacher. Luckily he did not have a Lolita-type inclination, but I could never live my foolishness down, in my own mind anyway. Understandably, not wanting to spend his best years incarcerated, he had avoided me. So much oestrogen, so little testosterone. A girl's boarding school was a pretty unnatural place!

Instinctively I knew that if I ever needed James or Ethan they would not be hard to find, they'd rescued me twice already. They appeared at my side while I was walking to a lecture, or down to the practice block, like they could walk through walls, or sprout from trees. On other occasions they waited for me in the dimness alongside my car after work, suddenly apparent as I neared.

'Have you heard from Nick?' I asked them one night.

'He's okay, Kate, just incognito,' James replied, trying unsuccessfully to reassure me as he hefted my leaden music bag into my boot.

'Why?'

They looked at each other and I began to feel irritated.

'Don't do that,' I insisted, 'it's rude.'

James shrugged. 'Sometimes he has to get away.' He leaned against the side of my car. This was about as close as I got to ever imagining him *in* my car. The door opened with a squeal like a pig on slaughter day and I got in.

Raising my eyes I sighed, disappointed. It wasn't something I understood, but Nick seemed completely incapable of staying in one place for long. 'What's he running from?'

'I think you know the answer to that.' James pushed himself off the car and slammed my door shut. I wound the window down.

'Me?' I guessed.

He regarded me evenly.

'I want to talk to him.'

He dropped to his haunches. I thought of a panther. His spellbinding gaze locked with mine. A thousand butterflies took flight in my stomach and then into my throat, filling the car as I exhaled.

'I know you do.' And then he and his brother were gone, leaving me to my contemplation.

I wondered about James, about where he'd come from, what *he* wondered about, whether he thought me pretty or frivolous, what he thought when he saw me having dinner with friends or drinks at the bar. But in quiet twilight-moments of half-sleep, the nature of my preoccupation changed and I became consumed by frightening ideas. Sick, twisted scenarios seemed to rise like living dreams, unbidden, from the depths of my troubled mind. They did not involve James and hot wax. Instead I saw him murdering me. Bent over my body, his muscles tight and sinewy, the veins across his forehead raised in pressured pulsation, as he pulled the cord around my throat taut. I choked as Ethan looked on, unflinching, knives in his icy, violet eyes. The sick, nauseous hurt of unremitting betrayal was like a never-ending kick in the guts.

Just when it was so important to do so, it was becoming harder and harder to concentrate on my studies. My performances were increasingly unpredictable.

'Is she using drugs?' I heard whispered amongst the faculty as they checked off some of the usual suspects. Weight-loss, yes; edgy and unsettled, yes; erratic, God yes; emotional, yes; tired, yes; crazy unfathomable energy when not tired, yes.

But I confused them. Sometimes I delivered inspired performances and moving interpretations, easily eclipsing my peers, leaving them baffled and excited.

'Well if she's on anything it can't be *that* bad.' Heads together, brows furrowed, marvelling at the marvellous, however short-lived.

Then a miserable failure, 'Oh, yes it can.' Hands covering mouths, flabbergasted at the new lows I'd discovered. What the hell is she doing here? *'You definitely suck.'* Sam summarised.

I shared my predicament with no-one, making my friends curious about my mental health, my constant state of distraction. My parents were never a consideration. They would be heavy-handed, stepping in and forcing me home, possibly alerting the police to James and Ethan's over-involvement in my life.

I thought about Deb, remembering the anxiety I'd heard in her voice when she cautioned me about making contact with Nick. *'The last time I spoke to him he wasn't himself. He wasn't well, some sort of breakdown after Daniel. I know he got better after that. I saw him from a distance and he looked okay, and Mum said he was. But that last time I spoke to him. Well, that's my clearest memory. It kind of haunts me. He was a stranger. I didn't know him. Be careful, Kate.'* Her words bothered me, but she lived a simple life now, content with her isolation, her family around her. I would not bring this to her door, again.

Days lengthened and we ate late, sometimes on the veranda at the back of the house. Usually, when I wasn't working, Francois, Pierre and I ate together. Since I'd stopped hanging out with Mads after work I barely saw her for more than an instant, usually in a swirl of perfume and big hair dressed in something from Trash Monkey, maybe grabbing a chip off my plate, or a slug of my tea. Sometimes she'd appear wrapped in a towel and ask whether I had a top she could borrow, her mouth turning down in distaste at the neat row of Target specials.

'Jeez Kate, I've got to take you shopping some time.' But she'd be back the next week asking the same thing, her laundry an untidy mess behind her door.

'Your clothes look beautiful on *you*, Kate,' Francois said kindly, as Mads swished out the door. He shopped at Politix.

Mercifully nights were short and when everyone else had headed to bed I retreated to my room to study until I could procrastinate no longer. When rest became a necessity and not an option, I'd sink into a dark slumber.

And so it was on this night, like so many others, that I met with the void which was the door to my unconscious. Anticipation entered my dream, quickly followed by a sense of menace, of suffocation, and of death, long and agonising. And then, unexpected brightness. A harsh glare. Light from the inside of a cold hard barrel pressed against my eye. Click. Annihilation. No. Not yet.

I leapt out of my bed and ran to the window in a desperate bid to escape, ripping the curtains from the rail as my brain responded in its pre-programmed, primitive way. My survival instinct drowned out all other voices. Fear was my narrow lens.

Rustling. In a split second I had turned to attack, to fight for my survival, every inch of my body alert, tense. My hands were raised, my fingers claw-like as I moved to throw myself in the direction of the sound. Kill or be killed.

Gentle words. I froze.

'Shhhh, it's me,' and again, 'Shhhh, it's okay Katie.' Soft, soothing sounds. A voice. A male voice. The agony of confusion tumbling through my mind.

Then another voice, whispered in my thoughts. *'Don't listen to their lies.'*

Indecision. 'Where am I?' I must have spoken because the voice in the corner answered.

'You're in your room. You're safe.' So slow, so measured, so deep and calm, so soothing, familiar.

No. No. It's not possible. Yes. Maybe … maybe it will be okay. A jumble of thoughts, but the whispering had stopped.

And so I started coming to, the usual confusion melting into a slow wave of mental acceptance, my body following with a shock response. I had been dreaming, again. It was only a dream. I shut my eyes and opened them. The room blinked and settled back into the present.

A human form stood in the corner of my room, cloaked in shadows. I screamed.

'Shhhh, it's me. It's okay.' That familiar voice again, words repeated as he rushed across the room.

'James?' I asked in confusion. His eyes luminesced in the dark.

'Yes.'

'What are you doing here?'

My teeth chattered. I had started the inevitable trembling, hands first, body following. My heart hammered so hard it hurt and I struggled to catch my breath. I worked to control my breathing – deep and slow, deep and slow. The gears in my mind changed down. Fight-flight to vigilance to protective mode to dazed.

'You aren't meant to be here,' I mumbled, as he reached out to comfort me.

'I'm trying to keep you safe,' he said. Nothing made any sense. 'Come back to bed.' A muddle clouded my mind as he took my hand. James was here. On his own.

'How'd you get in?' I asked, as he lay down beside me and took me in his arms. A warm circle of security embraced me.

'I have a key.' He dangled one in front of me and then dropped it back into his pocket.

'Of course you do!' The thought of strange, albeit handsome men wandering around in my room in the dark was somewhat alarming, just not right now.

'We won't let the darkness take you, Kate,' he whispered.

'What if it already has?'

'It hasn't,' he said with such certainty it inspired confidence. 'It's just anxiety messing with you.'

'Where is Ethan?' I imagined him on the wall outside, his face set in a scowl, knowing that James was inside alone with me.

'He had to go back to our home for a while.'

'Where is that exactly?' He pulled me closer and tiny pulses of electricity tingled where we touched. It was intense.

'A long way away from anywhere … out in the desert.'

'Is Nick there?'

He shook his head. 'I don't think so. Sometimes he's hard to find. He gets a bit down … needs to escape.'

'Because of me?'

'He'll come back. When he's ready he'll come back.'

I shifted away a little, to try and reduce the intensity of the feel of him alongside me and to ask how he knew this. But as I opened my mouth to speak, he swiftly closed the gap, clasping my body against his firmly and claiming my mouth with his lips and his tongue. I reached for his unruly hair, at last able to entwine my fingers in the thick lusciousness of it as his hand glided under the waistband of my pyjamas and cupped my bottom, kneading my flesh as he drew me more savagely against his hardness. My insides began to smoulder.

'James ...'

'It's okay Katie,' His voice hitched. 'I've waited so long to kiss you.' His lips found mine more gently.

'James ... I can't ... I'm ...' How to tell him I was a virgin. Suddenly I remembered he knew ... thanks, Mads.

'I won't,' he whispered in my ear. I wanted him to, of course I did, but the past haunted me. My beginnings. And weren't there a thousand other possible complications here ... none of which I understood?

His lips fell onto mine again as his fingers moved to my front, to where I was hot, to where I was waiting for his touch. And in a tender torturous rhythm he used them to build a frenzy of indescribable sensations which flared and swelled until finally they erupted and convulsed, like a volcano spewing fire to heaven before it finds the ground and scalds everything in its path.

As the feeling eased I began to feel embarrassed. I was clinging to him like a limpet monkey to a branch on a windy day. Easing up on my grip and hoping that I hadn't dislocated his shoulder I rolled onto my back.

'You're so beautiful, Kate,' he said. I didn't know where to look, or what to say. My body throbbed gently.

He chuckled. 'It's what makes you so special. A girl like you ...' He shook his head. 'You just don't know it do you?'

'What?'

'It doesn't matter. Sleep now,' he commanded.

'Thank you,' I murmured, and then realised that I had better clarify. 'Thank you for protecting me.'

I think I spoke anyway, but I'm not completely sure. It was so hard to keep my eyes open. I felt him lift the pendant I wore and then he let it go. It felt hot as it touched my skin again. His arms wrapped around me protectively. If he said anything else, I didn't hear it.

38

DEB AND NICK

As my belly began to swell, a strange transformation occurred. I became protective. And I began to connect with the fact that the tiny germinating seed inside me would one day be a baby, skin and blood and bones, a heart that would beat and that would be broken. Although I continued to grapple with the burden of my decision, I started eating differently, making healthier choices. Now when my hands fell to my belly they became a shield, protecting the foetus from the outside world. *Close your ears Baby, you don't need to hear about Mummy's silliness.* And yet I spoke, I talked about my father, my greatest insecurities, and when I could I talked about Nick. It was dangerous. Because as I talked I grew to love the little one who listened silently.

'You need to see a stylist, Deb,' Elizabeth advised, disapproving of my baggy top and pants as we sat cross-legged on the floor in my room one afternoon studying, 'or you'll never get a boyfriend.'

'I can't begin to tell you how little I care.' I flapped the page of my book over noisily not bothering to glance up at her.

'We can tell,' Anna added cheekily, wiggling her eyebrows, 'from the clothes … *and* the way you never go anywhere anymore.'

I lifted my head and took them in, seeing through their

smiles to the concern behind. I couldn't tell them, because they would slip up at some point and then everyone would know. *He* would know and I'd already made that decision. 'I'm just hanging to get out of here, so what's the point,' I lied, slathering a grin across my face. Of course, they suspected that my transformation had something to do with Nick, that I'd been put off men for good. Maybe they were right. Either way it was okay. Suspicion was just suspicion.

'*Fun* is the point,' they cried in unison, laughing.

'You're eighteen, not eighty.' Anna tossed a scrunched-up piece of paper at me.

It hit me on the nose and I chucked it back. 'Well, you go and enjoy yourselves, don't let me cramp your style, girls.'

'You're such a dork, Deb,' Anna chirped as we settled back down to study.

Somehow I managed to claw my way through finals, but I gave the graduation party a miss, much to the horror of my friends.

'Who would I ask, anyway?' I enquired as they droned on about what I was missing and how I'd never have another opportunity like it.

'We can think of at least ten guys.' Elizabeth looked at me over the top of her glasses as we drank colas in the kitchen. Her black hair was scraped into a side pony tied with a luminous green bow. Mum was out. 'You might need to invest in something from this decade though.' She eyed me up and down.

'I'm not going,' I stated plainly. 'It's not long until Mum and I go away and I've got lots to sort out.'

Finally they gave up on me, leaving me to make wisecracks from my spot on the bed as they giggled, indulging in a madness all of their own and finally departing with big crimped hair and colourful make-up, in shiny minis and big belts to go drinking and celebrating. They made me laugh, but I felt relieved when they left. Relieved, and a tug of something bitter. Regret maybe.

With five months of my pregnancy still left to go, Mum and I told George together, physically restraining him as his face turned puce and his eyes bulged as though about to pop out of his skull. 'Mother-fucker!' he yelled, wrenching himself free. 'I'm going to kill the bastard.'

'George!' My mother was shocked. I'd never heard him swear in front of her. His eyes slid guiltily over to her, but her look of condemnation wasn't enough.

'I. AM. GOING. TO. KILL. HIM,' he exploded again, without the expletives this time, but smashing his hand against the wall passionately for added emphasis. He glowered at me as I slunk back, avoiding his fiery gaze.

'Of course you're not George,' Mum said calmly, instantly deflating him. She put the kettle on. 'This is something that happened between Nick and Deb. Deb is eighteen and well … she willingly took part in this and she's not ignorant, she knew what could happen.' Had I really? What I remembered was a moment in time and him and I in it. And now there was this consequence to deal with.

She returned to where he was standing and took his arm in hers, drawing him to the kitchen where he slumped reluctantly onto a stool at the counter. 'We're going to respect her wish, that's what we're going to do. It's the right thing.'

He seethed impotently, knowing that he would do Mum's bidding but the cup of coffee she placed in front of him remained untouched.

'He'll be okay tomorrow, Deb,' she insisted, pouring his cold coffee down the drain when he'd left. 'Just give him a chance to process this.'

But he wasn't and I missed him. His protectiveness and

his idiocy, his teasing. I even missed the dirty mugs and plates he'd leave scattered around my room. He avoided me, possibly because he felt that he'd failed somehow and because it hurt too much to talk about.

I told everyone that I was going on an overseas adventure with Mum, but in the last months of my pregnancy when we could no longer hide my belly, we bid George a subdued farewell and travelled to rural Victoria. We moved into a slightly dilapidated but quaint rental house on an immense wheat farm, set in front of a stand of eucalyptus and surrounded by rolling hills and meadows. Little house on the prairie.

In the mornings we'd wake to a blanket of white over the trees and hills, like a ghostly world had been watching us sleep. I'd stand on the veranda in the cold, thawing fingers wrapped around a steamy mug of coffee, watching it slowly recede, rising in wisps and puffs, the trees magically reappearing in patches of disembodied branches and trunks with darkness behind.

Strange sounds, unheard by other humans, haunted the fields and forest then. Lonely sounds. An owl, like a lighthouse in the fog just before dawn. Whispers like static carried to me by long-fingered phantoms, spiralling and withdrawing, chilling me inside. '*Deb.*' The mystery called to me, drawing me across the field and into the forest, to where the darkness still lingered a little, to where mint and pine filled my nostrils and to where I could touch the rough bark and reassure myself that this was real, that it wasn't a delusion, and it did not disappear each evening.

I saw the boy there. Small and dark-haired, always somewhere in front of me, visible only in quick snatches of tantalising bits I couldn't describe, possibly the bounce of his hair or his laughter.

'Hello?' I called, disquiet making my voice ring out hollowly as his chuckle became the flap of wings above me, the glint in a magpie's eye. Slowly I retreated, creeping backwards cautiously, arms out wide as I picked my way over the uneven ground. I never felt threatened as such, but I did feel watched. I felt like someone or something was watching and waiting in those woods.

But the sun would arrive and I would forget the feeling. I'd trip through the wheat fields in jeans and boots pretending I was in France, maybe Tuscany, although I didn't have a clue what they farmed there. Sometimes in the hours of my solitude on glorious days as I lay on a hay-bale chewing long stalks of grass and watching the sun set I'd imagine that my baby was extraordinary.

'It's just you and I Chicky, and we're a long way from everywhere,' I said, pulling my beanie down low and plucking another piece of grass, which was difficult with mittens on. My stomach quivered as if in answer. 'We've got to hide, but I know you know that.' In my womb she listened. 'It's because you're so special. All of that love inside you wants to burst out in golden rays like sunshine.' Another wriggle and a gentle knock. 'But there are bad people in this world and they are afraid. They are afraid that when you share your love and everyone is happy, there will no longer be a place in the world for them. You scare them Chicky, and they will come after you. I *know* they will.' The photos which hung on the wall at Nick's house flashed into my mind, the many faces … the haunted one in their midst. 'So it's just you and I for now … and Granny,' I added with a sad smile, knowing that my mother's future would be as haunted as mine.

The sun was setting in broad orange swathes vivid against the gathering darkness as the measured chug of a tractor arose. Sitting up I saw farmer Jim nearing, a collie on the back and one running behind.

'All good?' he asked with a wave.

'All good,' I nodded.

He cut the engine and jumped to the ground, rolling a cigarette slowly and carefully from loose tobacco in a bag he tucked back into his pocket when he was finished. He stood with one foot on a hay-bale, leaning forward onto his raised knee as he smoked, exhaling so that the tendrils drifted in sluggish threads away from me. His hands were powerful and enormous; his fingers calloused and stained with tar.

'You were in the woods yesterday,' he remarked, his face unclear through the smoke for a moment before it drifted away.

'I sometimes go there,' I admitted.

'Mysterious places, woods.' I turned to him, waiting for more, wondering what he knew, but he said nothing else. He was kind of still inside, that was his way. Still and self-assured, not interested in making an impression, honest. It kind of appealed. I felt comfortable around him, breathing came easily and I didn't feel the need to explain myself.

'Yes,' I agreed, catching his eye for a moment before he turned away to gaze off into the twilight.

'You want a ride back?' The dirt track passed our home, the grumble of the tractor on its journeys to and fro a regular feature of the landscape.

'Okay.'

He helped me up and I squashed in beside him. The tractor made us shudder gently against each other as we crawled along the bumpy dirt road with the dogs running behind. Every now and then my eyes drifted sideways to him. I noticed just how big he was, how the muscles rippled in his tanned forearm and how square his jawline was. He was rugged, masculine, but there were laughter lines around his mouth and eyes which softened him a little and his flaxen hair curled under his hat into the nape of his neck.

Our gaze met as I appraised him, but it wasn't awkward. 'You ever been to New Zealand?' he asked suddenly.

'No, never.'

'It's a beautiful place,' he said, wistfully, lost in memories.

'Oh?'

'My brother is over there. Sometimes I think I should go.'

'You should, Jim.'

He regarded me for a long moment, his eyes drifting briefly down to my stomach and then back to the road. It seemed as though he might say something, but we continued on in silence. It was another thing I liked about him, he never asked and I never had to explain.

39

DEB AND NICK

As my pregnancy progressed I began to experience vivid recurring dreams. They were triggered by the turmoil of emotion inside me, I think. Dreams of loss. In them I looked down at my baby girl asleep in her crib, perfect and beautiful, her cupid bow mouth making suckling movements, her tiny fingers twitching as she dreamt. I stood in breathless awe of the miracle that was this little creature, the love inside me swelling and almost overwhelming me. But as I leaned over to kiss her warm forehead, I heard the static, the whispers, not 'Deb,' but 'Dead,' over and over again and her skin became increasingly translucent, the peach turning to white and then fading to grey. Fading until she disappeared, like the mist in the morning, going, going, gone. Vanished, like she had never existed, except for the gut wrenching feeling within me. I woke with my hand on my heart, sickened and sweaty, hot tears on my cheeks.

'Dreams are like fun-fare mirrors Deb,' Mum said, and I thought of a house of horrors and my reflection in one of those mirrors. A monster.

My waters broke one bright afternoon as I sat on an old wooden rocking chair on the porch, my feet dusty-bare, pushing back and forth in a gentle creaking rhythm. I had one eye closed and my book was on the floor. Sooty, Jim's cat, was in my lap. It wasn't what I'd expected, not a sudden gush, just a gentle leaking wetness. Mild cramping soon followed.

'Mum,' I yelled. 'It's happening.'

The contractions continued throughout the night, mild at first but more intense and closer together as morning arrived. Mum fetched tea and rubbed my back. She sang to me and let me squeeze her hand, saying nothing when I swore and almost crushed her fingers. I paced. Finally she became too nervous to wait any longer.

'It's time, Deb.' She grabbed my bag and helped me into the car. The mist was thick. I'd never seen it this dense, like a wall we had to drive through.

'Lord help us, Deb,' Mum cried. 'I feel like I'm driving by feel.'

I clung on to the arm rest, my body rigid with tension and pain as another contraction hit me with a vengeance. Breathe and count. Breathe and count.

'I guess we're not usually out this early,' I gasped, as the car inched along the long farm road. If it weren't for the bumping under the tyres, it would have been hard to believe that we were anywhere at all. The whiteness outside the windows was total, like we were driving through nothingness.

Suddenly up ahead, orange lights beckoned through the fog.

'Thank the good Lord.' Mum tooted the horn. In less than a minute Jim was at the driver's side window.

'You okay Mrs Brayshaw?' The sweet smell of tobacco filled the car.

'Well Jim, it's the baby. It's time.' His eyes swept across to me, to where I sat sweating and counting. I caught them for just a moment, kind dependable eyes, calm even now. Backing away he beckoned to my mother.

'Follow me; I'll escort you out of here.' My mother exhaled loudly, her shoulders slumping with relief.

The tractor started up again and we followed close behind its orange beacons. Just before the main road the belt of mist ended and we drove into brilliant sunshine. It was as though we'd been in another universe altogether. *Like the church outside Three Kings*, I thought suddenly. Jim pulled over and waved to us as we passed him. When I looked back I could see him still standing there, gazing after us, the dogs at his feet.

'You're a champion,' the midwife cried, as I nearly bit through my tongue. 'One more push and the head will be out,' she lied. I did as she said, wondering when my body would finally give up, or give out. My hair was plastered to my face, my nighty was wet and sticky in places and my lower half was completely exposed but I just didn't care.

'Almost there, just one last one ...' she coaxed. Violent bloody images of what I might do to her came to mind.

'You said that already ...' I shouted, pushing against my mother as my insides stretched and tore, my body opening impossibly to finally release her out into the world.

Exhausted and bloody, battered and bruised, awash in sweat, so utterly drained, I reached for her. She was placed on my abdomen, still slightly gooey and warm.

'She's perfect.' The midwife's voice was touched with a pang of sadness now. She busied herself wrapping up soiled sheets. 'You've done so well. It went beautifully.' Departing, she left Mum and I together. Mum leant over quietly to examine her.

'She *is* beautiful, Deb.' Tears glistened in her eyes. I swallowed, but I could not swallow down the emotion that went with such empty suffering and I sobbed.

'Julia,' I blubbered the name of my baby. Mum's name.

She opened her eyes and I immediately saw that they were very unusual in a baby. Brilliant and green. The eyes of her father. There could be no mistaking it.

She stared up at me reproachfully, and after a short while she began to wail. The three of us cried for a long time.

I fed her only four times, her soft mewling and snuffling alerting me to her needs. She fed on the rich yellow colostrum my body had already prepared for her. Her skin was impossibly smooth and she was soft and warm with her own indescribable baby smell. Her tiny fingers were fragile, like matchsticks, perfectly formed and delicate next to my thick ones.

Her little body was already plump and pink and thick black hair covered her head. *Hello Chicky.* Her gaze tore my soul apart. I saw myself, unkindly reflected in her pupils. Her mother. Failing her before her life could even begin. She would carry the shadow of my past into her future. I clung to her, terrified of letting her go, petrified of keeping her. What would she face without me, without her protector? What would she know?

You have to go Chicky. You'll be safer without me. They'll come for you otherwise, and I want you to spread your love. I don't want you to live in their shadow-land. I want you to glow and shine and be everything you can be.

A lonely bouquet sat on the window sill of my hospital room. Pink and white orchids from Jim. Unexpected, although he didn't come to visit. The note read: *Deb, the mist has cleared and you can see the stars.* I gazed at the flowers and I gazed at the note. I wondered about life and all that had brought me to this place, and to him.

'Are you ready, Deb?' Mum asked ludicrously the next morning. I'd spent the night awake, drinking in every aspect of my tiny one, my state of mind somewhat close to insanity.

How could you ever be ready for something like this?

'It's all organised. A wonderful family, who are desperate for a child.' The hint of a quiver touched her voice. I looked at my baby one last time. 'Will you take a last photo, Mum?'

'Of course, Darling.' Her hands shook so much the photo was sure to be blurred. I tried to smile, but my mouth quivered.

'Just take one of her, Mum.'

When she had I leant down and kissed her. She was warm and swaddled in pink. *Goodbye Chicky*. Her eyes closed and her mouth pouted as she drowsed.

'Take her, Mum. Just be quick. Don't bring her back no matter what you hear,' I cried desperately. I placed her in Mum's arms. Quiet tears seeped out of my eyes. She took her and turned away.

'Are you sure Deb?'

'Go Mum!' I shrieked, racking sobs consuming me as she rushed from the room.

I gave her up. I'd so conditioned myself to the idea. Become almost superstitious about it. If she stayed with me then she would not be safe. Something bad would happen. I let them take her, because that was what fate intended for my child of light. But my heart was broken. For many nights I woke believing she lay in my arms. My body waited for her, my breasts leaking and tender. I could feel her warmth, her tiny body. I could hear her cry. But it was only a phantom. Each time I realised it I'd grieve her loss again.

Mum returned to Three Kings soon after Julia's birth, but I stayed on in the countryside sharing tractor rides with farmer Jim and stories of the ideal that was New Zealand. It started to sound appealing.

In the early morning he showed me how the mist had disappeared and how you could see the stars and he put his arm around my shoulders and it felt good. He didn't ask questions, but I knew he'd listen if I spoke. I just didn't want to.

'It's weird isn't it?' he asked one day and I nodded. It made no sense at all. The mist and the watchful waiting presence were gone. Gone, like they'd never been there at all. Gone. Why?

Although the world around it seemed to move, Three Kings was no different when I visited six months later. The great stone entities regarded me unsympathetically as the sea tugged at the beach and although it was as warm as always, everything seemed chilly to me. This was goodbye. Goodbye to the place that had never seemed like home anyway.

'He's gone,' Mum said, and I knew she was pleased. I shrugged like I didn't care and that was partly true.

'You're going to do well Deb, I know it,' Mum said, trying to convince herself as well as me. 'You've got your whole life in front of you.'

I left soon after. The memories were not as easy to leave behind as I'd hoped. Although I never saw Nick again, althhough I moved to New Zealand and married Jim, I couldn't help but think of him whenever I thought of Julia, and so the sadness of the past remained a part of my present.

EPILOGUE

KATE

Dreams of warm wet beaches and a perfect turquoise ocean found me as I lay in James' arms. Dreams of a place where lovers embraced and the sun never set ... where time stood still. Where love spread her long golden fingers and pain disappeared like it had never been there at all.

A small boy with black hair and sandy feet ran and played in the ocean shallows. A boy living life, just as he should. And from where she sat nearby, his mother sang as she watched him.

Suddenly he looked up. *'Come home, Kate,'* he called.

The green of his eyes swirled like the coldest, deepest waters, and yet the gold around his pupil was like the sun, like a perfect day. I felt the shade of a cloud and then a breeze as it blew across the sand, whisking the grains into the air and forcing the boy to raise a hand to protect his eyes.

'I can't. I don't know where home is,' I replied.

Nick stood on a small dune at the edge of the beach where the sand met the straggly grass. He seemed frozen, more a part of the scenery than the action. He gazed out ... not at me, because I think I was invisible, but at the young boy who'd called, and who now danced along the beach in the direction of an upended bucket and half-built sandcastle.

In the sky above the hill behind him a great and dark expanse had opened like the funnel of a tornado. Fingers of darkness extended from it.

An army of shadowy figures spewed from the belly of the beast. An army marching forward … towards the boy who played, oblivious, and alone. His mother had disappeared, her song lost to the past.

Too soon the ghouls would arrive. Panic swelled inside me. I had to do something.

'Come, Kate,' the boy called again. *'Come home.'*

I stared at him, deep into the world within his eyes. The reality there had changed. What had first appeared to be the truth was no longer.

A TASTE OF: *ODYSSEY*

1

KATE

The bed jolted and I was rudely awoken. The warm chest which had been my pillow slid out from under me. I sat up, bleary-eyed in the dark. The mattress bounced and I felt him bending down to pull on his shoes.

'James?' A feline flash of gold in the night, the radiance in his eyes as he turned back to me for a moment before turning away.

'I have to go, Kate,' he said intent on his laces as I flicked on the lamp and stared at him.

'Why?'

Finished, he ran his fingers through his messy hair and turned to me.

'Ethan. He needs me.'

'In the middle of the night?'

He shrugged. 'I have to go.'

'He snaps his fingers and you jump,' I snapped bitterly, immediately remorseful and also wondering how it was that he had even heard those fingers snap.

He didn't lower himself to arguing with me, just continued to pull on his jacket. His hair was in disarray. Some of it fell forward and some stood straight up. His clothes were rumpled, but he had been sleeping in them.

'This probably wasn't the best idea anyway,' he said. I swallowed down something sour.

'Well, it wasn't mine. *You* were the one who appeared in my room last night.'

'I know.' There was a moment of silence.

'How do you *know* he needs you?' I asked, wondering whether I really wanted the answer. Maybe it would have been better to turn over with a *'See you later.'* In fact, if only I'd stayed asleep and he'd vanished, leaving a note. I sighed wistfully.

'I can't explain now.' His voice was as mechanical as the quick peck he gave me on the forehead. He moved towards the door briskly and I leapt up, rushing after him.

'But I thought ...' What was it I had thought, exactly? That we were a couple now? That we could pretend that there was nothing at all strange about the way we had been thrown together and that I could take him home to meet my parents? I sighed heavily. 'I thought he was in the middle of nowhere.'

He stopped in the doorway for a long moment and then turned slowly. 'You're safe for now, Kate. I wouldn't leave you otherwise.'

I rolled my eyes ungratefully. Safety hadn't entered my mind, although terror *had* stolen part of my night. Terror which had stemmed from nightmares, forgotten too soon maybe, because sometimes you needed to hold onto the darkness long enough to understand it.

He tried a smile, but it looked more like a grimace, his jaw too tight and the white of his teeth showing. He seemed annoyed and I suddenly realised that this wasn't necessarily all about me. I was being selfish. Suddenly he seemed to gather himself and so did I. I walked towards him.

'Is he okay?'

He hesitated and then came to me and reached for my

hand. 'All will be well soon.' A soothing current flowed through his fingers into my body. 'I know it, so you can relax,' he said, his voice like the murmur of panpipes in the wind. For a moment I was mesmerised before I shook myself out of it.

'Relax?' I blurted. He seemed surprised by my reaction.

'Were you trying to do something to make me less of a nuisance, James?'

He shrugged.

'Of course you were.' It hadn't worked for long. I shook my head.

'I want to come with you.'

'No. It's just not possible. I'm sorry.'

His face softened. 'I'm sorry I have to go, Kate … and that you can't come.'

'Really?' I asked tentatively.

'Of course.' His smile was small, but genuine this time. He lifted my fingers to his mouth and his kiss was like a whisper. Then he moved away again, fast, striding out of my room and into the passage. I ran after him, my hair cascading wildly down my shoulders in curls and snarls.

'When will you be back?' I called, but he was gone, the door banging behind him and the house quickly returning to silence. In the distance his car engine rumbled and then the sound waned. Desolation descended.

I flopped heavily onto the bed. It seemed a much colder and less welcoming place now. The sheets and pillows were still indented from where he had lain but his vitality and warmth were lost. When I held the pillow to my nose I could smell him faintly. My mouth watered.

The clock blinked. Five a.m. It had been a *really* long night. I wondered what hell the morning would bring.

WHAT'S NEXT?

Also by Janet V Forster

Odyssey; Book 2, *The Last Anakim Trilogy*

Ascension; Book 3, *The Last Anakim Trilogy*

ABOUT THE AUTHOR

Janet V Forster is a psychologist and author who has lived in Melbourne, Australia with her husband and two children for the past fourteen years. She was born in South Africa where she spent the first twenty-five years of her life before moving to London for two crazy years and travelling extensively. Throughout her childhood she devoured books like a great white shark does hapless sardines and was frequently accused of being anti-social as a result. Thankfully she didn't really care, often preferring to escape into the magical world of fiction, or music, which is her other passion.

Whether you want to find out more about Janet, her books, watch trailers or clips or start a conversation, she would love you to visit her at www.janetvforster.com or feel free to connect on Facebook or GooglePlus.

If you enjoyed *Awakening,* please look it up on Amazon and post a review. Your feedback is highly valued by the author who reads each and every one.

Made in the USA
Charleston, SC
26 April 2016